Take Her Man

Take Her Man

Grace
Octavia

Kensington Publishing Corp.
http://www.kensingtonbooks.com

DAFINA BOOKS are published by

Kensington Publishing Corp.
119 West 40th Street
New York, NY 10018

All Kensington Titles, Imprints and Distributed Lines are available at special quantity discounts for bulk purchases for sales promotion, premiums, fund-raising, educational, or institutional use. Special book excerpts or customized printings can also be created to fit specific needs. For details, write or phone the office of the Kensington special sales manager: Kensington Publishing Corp., 119 West 40th Street, New York, NY 10018, attn: Special Sales Department, Phone: 1-800-221-2647.

Dafina and the Dafina logo Reg. U.S. Pat. & TM Off.

ISBN-13: 978-0-7582-1848-3
ISBN-10: 0-7582-1848-6

First trade paperback printing: May 2007
First mass market printing: June 2009

10 9 8 7 6 5 4 3 2

Printed in the United States of America

*For my sisterfriends who have
made this journey much sweeter,
this road a little longer,
but certainly worth the road trip.*

Acknowledgments

Following Father God, there are so many people who have helped this book come to fruition. At the top of this list is my grandmother, Julia Elizabeth Reid, who read every page, every day and has always encouraged me to follow my dreams. My agent and former colleague at Simon & Schuster, Tracy Sherrod, for her invaluable support and advice throughout the years. The entire editorial team at Kensington including Selena James, who has remained patient with me throughout this process and Mercedes Fernandez, who listened to my sob stories over the phone. Stacey Barney for first believing in my project and helping resurrect it from my mental grave. My sistergirl readers—Monica Harris, Naima Cochrane, and Daheli Hall for giving me honest feedback.

To the accidental philanthropists who kept money in my pockets and fed me when I needed it—Garry Harris of HTS Enterprises, the English Department at Clark Atlanta University, Yvette Caslin, Munson Steed and the entire *rolling out* team, Raymond Williams, Tamika Maxwell, Duane Nix, Lou Matthews, Omar Imhotep Bowles, Shorter College, Julius Kevinezz, Sadiqa Banks, and countless others. Thanks for the support!

To my family. First, this would not be possible without my parents—Michelle Williams and Calvin Reid. Who I am is who you two were, and I am eternally grateful. May you both rest in peace knowing that your fruit is growing strong. My brothers and sisters—Cindy, Kenyair, Eric, and Jacala. My Aunt Tina, nieces and nephews, uncles, cousins and extended members of my family who have listened to my stories when people just called them lies (remember the story of the pink elephant I saw, Gracie?). I can't name you all, but know that you are always in my heart.

To my instructors and classmates in the writing classes at all of the schools I have attended. Thanks for forcing me to get the work done and encouraging me to continue to grow in the craft. At New York University I developed my creative talent, at the University of Georgia I learned to trust my talent, and at Georgia State University I have learned to control it. I am still getting better. You all are the best. Special thanks to Judith Ortiz Cofer whose kind words will never leave me, and Sheri Joseph, Josh Russell, and Reginald McKnight, who devoted so much time to reading my work and giving feedback, it still surprises me.

To the strong men in my life who laugh at my jokes and make me feel brilliant and beautiful. Jamison, Dwayne W, Erskine, Richard, John S., Jojo, Jerrod, Monty, Lavington, Kamau, Rasheed, Lemuel, Mr. B, Uncle Sam, Uncle Al—you all show me what true men of purpose exemplify, and the positive men in this book are my letter of love to you.

To my church family at First Iconium. Debbie Copeland who always looks for me in the pews and Reverend McDonald for connecting me to the spirit. That Sunday blessing keeps me grounded.

To fellow writers and people within the industry—don't stop the dream. Ronda P, Trae, Isoul, Raqiyah, Ivory, Rodney, and many others. Keep making noise and believing in what you do.

I have saved the sisters for last. As I once heard Dr. Beverly Guy-Sheftall say, the bond of sisterhood has been the tool that made the obstacles of life bearable for women of color. Sisters keep you sane. I happen to have the best sisters in the world and this book is dedicated to all of you—seen and unseen. First, to my sisters of Delta Sigma Theta Sorority, Incorporated, who have remained consistent comforters in my life—especially those of the Epsilon Tau Chapter in

New York City. Thank you all for being an endless supply of fodder for the book—Tanya G., Carinda, Sasha, Danielle, Tanya D., Keya, Frankie, Tyritia, Stephanie L, Aretha, Chastin, Sharee, Ifill, Timyiaka, Tanny, and Krista. The list is endless but I pray you know how much I miss you all. Your emails and kind words always mean so much to me. To my Southern Belle Delta crew—Billie, Felicia, Shamita, Crystal, Renita— you ladies are also a barrel of laughs. The NYU Rubin Hall ladies, Bobby, Tasha, Chika, LaChrista, and Kamal—where do we go next? To my running buddies Tiki and Valeasia— all the talking we do should count for something. Essence T., Kaia Shivers (the other negress), and my other baby sisters of Xi Gamma and Pi Pho—love you much.

Finally, to the sistermothers who make this joy of being a black woman immeasurable. Toni Morrison, bell hooks, Oprah Winfrey, Angela Davis, Alice Walker, Shirley Chisholm, Halle Berry, Sapphire, Nikki Giovanni, Terry McMillan, Dorothy Height, Ruby Dee, Judith Jamison, Aretha Franklin, Maya Angelou, Johnetta Cole, Gloria Wade Gayles, and Pearl Cleage, I too "speak your names" and am so proud to walk in your paved steps and dare to dream a dash beyond them. You amaze me to tears, and do it with the kind of spiritual grace that proves to all why we are still "ego tripping."

Thank you.

*Ain't no woman in her right mind gonna sit back and
let another woman come in and take her man—
if he's really worth having.*
                                        —Millie Jackson

Prologue

Put the Jimmy Choo on the Other Foot

I know what you're thinking: How does a fine, successful, educated sister find herself mixed up in a situation where she actually believes she has to try to take her ex-boyfriend back from another woman? Shoot, I'd be thinking the same thing if the Jimmy Choo was on the other foot, so I can't even blame you for initially judging me. I mean, if I would've heard any other sister even whisper the words "Take her man," I would've immediately asked her what kind of ghetto situation she was involved in. What happened to black sisterhood? We've come too far to be scratching each other's eyes out like there's only one brother left on the plantation. Trust me, there are plenty of fine fish-in-the-sea—especially in the sea known as New York City. In this city I call home, brothers come in all shapes and sizes, colors and hues. They have multiple degrees and talents that range from the boardroom to the bedroom to the kitchen. So why would any sane sister be stuck on one?

Like most sisters caught up in this kind of love triangle, I didn't see it that way at the time. It didn't just come to me all at once. It was slow . . . gradual . . . like the damn fat that starts to grow on top of your perfect abs after you turn twenty. You sisters who broke down and bought the Ab Lounge know what I mean. Yep, in the beginning, everything was going fine between me and Dr. Julian James. I had "a man and a plan" and I was about to get my "ring by spring." Everything was perfect. Nothing could hold me back.

But then something went stupid somewhere along the way and I watched as my perfect world began to fall apart one tiny piece at a time. I'm still not sure exactly when it all began, but if I really focus, I'm pretty sure it was somewhere around the time I heard my future groom utter four very ugly words we all hate to hear: "I need a break."

Is it starting to sound familiar yet? I know I'm not the only sister in the world whose heard that bull crap before. Well, it should've been the end for me. But, again, like most sisters with even the tiniest bit of pride and ego—the other eight million Queens of Sheba, I took those words as an inevitable bump on the road to marriage, a temporary predicament, a moment of confusion, a blip. He'd wake up. His ass had better wake up. And why wouldn't he? Like I said in the beginning: I'm a fine, successful, educated sister. A blind man wearing black shades in a dark room could see that. I didn't believe that I had to "try" to take my man back from anyone. . . . He was mine in the first place. It was quite simply a matter of reclamation. An ego challenge. Like my best friend said, "It might take three days, it might take three weeks or three months." Either way, I would get my man back.

So, there it is, and thus, here's my little story—blow by devilish blow. Read, weep, and rejoice, and never forget what you would do if the old Jimmy Choo just happened to be on the other foot. And in case you find yourself in the very same predicament and lack the knowledge of the Queen of Sheba, I've provided little instructions along the way. Warning: Things are about to get hot. This is definitely not for the faint of ego. *

I'm Not Crying . . . It's the Wasabi in My Eyes

As I said, it all started with . . .

"Troy, I need a break." That's what the love of my life said to me that sad March afternoon as we sipped sake over sushi in midtown Manhattan. For a minute, for one moment in my life as those dreadful words fell from my beloved's lips, I forgot everything—who I was, where I was, and how I'd gotten there in the first place. All I could see was his lips moving and the sad frown he was obviously struggling hard to keep on his face. It was like I was watching one of those sad breakup movies where some gorgeous guy breaks the girl's heart in slow motion . . . over and over and over again.

"A break?" I managed, fighting my way back to reality. "What do you mean, a break?"

"I think we need to not speak to each other for a while." He took a sip of his sake. I could hear him gulp it down in a struggle.

"Not speak?" *What the hell was he talking about? How can you be in a relationship and not speak to the person you're in a relationship with? And did I say that out loud?*

"That's what I mean, Troy," Julian said, confirming my Freudian slip. "We're not in a relationship. We never were. I told you I didn't want that when we first met. Not right now."

The room went spinning. Raw fish was flying everywhere, waiters and customers were holding on to tables for dear life, and the sake in the glass in front of me was spilling over into my lap. I imagined that the world all around me was falling apart; the one I'd tried so hard to create was slipping away from me like the tears slipping down my cheeks.

"Oh, this is a fine time to bring that up. That was over a year ago that you said that crap. You didn't mention anything about not wanting to be *in a relationship* when you introduced me to your parents as your girlfriend. Hell, I don't remember you saying any of that when I was taking care of your ass last month when you had the flu or when I picked up your damn laundry last week or the week before that." I was getting mad. I knew it because I could hear my voice getting louder, feel my cheeks getting hotter, and see the other people sprinkled around the restaurant beginning to turn around to sneak a peek at us. Normally this kind of display wouldn't be accepted in the circles Julian and I traveled in, but I couldn't help myself. I wasn't about to just let my dream man get up and walk away from me. Not over sushi!

"And what about Pookie?" I asked, bringing up the cotton ball colored Chihuahua we'd picked up one day strolling in the Village.

"The dog is yours, Troy. You bought it. I was just there," he said. "Stop making this hard. Neither one of us wants to be embarrassed."

I pushed back from the table and exhaled. I was losing control. I tried to remember a passage, a line, a chapter title, anything from one of those Iyanla Vazant "self-help for sister girls" books to help me from making a complete ass of myself at my favorite sushi bar, but it was too late. Tears were chasing each other like track stars down my cheeks and so many people were looking at us that Julian was covering his forehead to hide his identity. I wanted to disappear my damn self.

"Stop crying," Julian said. "This is not about you. I just can't do you, and the hospital, and myself right now. Why can't you see that?" He reached over and snatched the last piece of dragon roll off of my plate. Eating at a time like this? Just then I realized that there was some kind of invisible wall between us. A wall between me and the man who had filled my apartment with nine bouquets of magnolias on my last birthday—one for each month we'd known each other. And I didn't know where the wall had come from or who'd put it up. I could only be sad that it was so obviously there.

I wanted to pick up a big chunk of wasabi and rub it in his eyes . . . make his ass cry, cry like I'd been doing over the last three months each time he got frustrated with other areas of his life and asked for more and more space to figure things out. I wanted him to feel my pain and realize how much I loved him and that we could work through all of this stuff together if he would stop being so damn selfish. Sitting across from me with the wall between us, Julian seemed like a mean, coldhearted person, but I knew that he had the perfect heart. He treated me better than any man I'd ever dated in the past. During the year that we'd been together, he'd taken care of me when I was sick, helped me through my first year of law school at NYU, and remained a perpetual shoulder for me to lean on when I needed it. He was kind, and strong, and smart, and successful, and fine as all hell. And he listened to me. No matter how difficult I was being—and I could definitely be difficult—he always listened to what I had to say. Sometimes we'd sit up for hours on the roof at my apartment just talking about nothing at all. He was my best friend, my lover, and my confidant.

He was just going through a rough spot. It wasn't easy being a third-year resident at the hospital, and his family offered little more than stress. Sometimes it seemed that since he couldn't do anything about either of those things, I got all of the heat. But I was understanding, and like Julian did for me, I tried to be by his side and simply listen. Couples had ups and downs. It was a fact of life. They just had to see them through. As my pastor always says, as surely as we see good days, we'll see bad days—we just have to be willing to work through the bad ones to see the good ones. I mean, the only truly bad day we ever had, the only time Julian did something that would even potentially ruin our relationship, was when I caught him with that girl, Miata (yes, the trick is named after a damn car). She was some brain from Queens with no class and even less looks who Julian fooled around with a month ago. Julian came clean about the whole thing— the man shed tears—and we worked through it. Our bad day. So surely we had some good days coming. One, big, white-laced, good day.

"But we were doing so good," I said, sounding completely pathetic—I'd regret I said that later as I lay in bed crying to my Mary J. Blige CD. "We got over that girl you were seeing from the hospital. We can get through this, too. I know the hospital expects a lot from you and you need to be there around the clock. We can just see each other less."

I was beginning to feel guilty for all the complaining I'd been doing about not seeing him enough lately. I even felt bad for making him come meet me for sushi. He'd been awake for three days straight. What was I thinking? He was a damn doctor. He didn't have time for my drama. As one of my girls who had been married to a doctor for five years put it, if I wanted a man of that caliber, I had to find a way to live with him and his demanding job.

I needed to calm down. I was pushing him away. Julian was a good man and he was out working hard for a good cause. He was worth waiting for. I just had to be patient and more creative. There's nothing wrong with bringing the sushi and sake to the hospital.

I reached under the table and patted his leg to assure him that I was ready and willing to change.

"I love you, Dr. Julian James," I said with all of my heart inside those words. "And I am not willing to lose you. I mean, just think"—I cracked an uneasy, well-intentioned smile—"we just exchanged keys to each other's places. We're official." I batted my eyes like my grandmother taught me and blew him a kiss.

Julian looked down at his lap and slid a little silver key onto the table. It was apparent that it had already been taken off of his key ring. *Had he planned all of this?*

"What about my keys to your place?" I asked, realizing that I'd put my foot in my mouth as soon as the last word came out.

"Hand them over." He didn't even pause. His voice was so cold and distant that I felt as if I didn't even know him anymore, like he was someone else, a ghost of himself who had caught ebola or the bird flu during his last stint in the emergency room. The wall between us was growing.

"What do you mean, *hand them over?*" I was in complete disbelief. I sat back in my seat and looked around the restaurant. Everyone seemed to be having such a great time. There was the couple in the corner cooing at each other, and the sister with long blond dreadlocks feeding her baby sticky rice. Everyone, even the damn waitress who couldn't speak a word of English, seemed happy, except for me . . . and I was sitting across from the man I loved.

"What did I do to deserve this?" I looked back at Julian, feeling as desperate as I sounded. I could feel my heartbeat change from fury and shock to just plain sadness. I was fighting a losing battle and I knew it. Even the waitress, who was now standing next to Julian with our bill, looked like she was about to bend down and give me one of those big church-mother hugs. "What did I do?"

"See, I knew you would try to make this about you.

Everything revolves around you, doesn't it? No one else can dream or speak unless it fits into your little script of what life is supposed to be about." He paused and handed the waitress his black AmEx card before she walked away. "I just can't take it anymore. You're just too spoiled."

"Why are you being so cold? How could you treat me like this?" I asked, wondering how the waitress got back to the table so fast with the card. Without answering me, Julian signed the check and handed it back to her. He leaned toward me, smiled sweetly, and reached across the table for my hand. *Was he playing with me? Was he about to propose marriage?* I wiped my tears and gave him my left hand. He squeezed it—clenched it like he was Dr. Phil and nodded his head in this therapy-ish way he could have learned only in medical school.

"Look, just put the keys in the mail," he said as coolly as if he was setting up our next date. He kissed me on the forehead and smiled. "I've really got to go, darling."

Just then, as he turned his back on me, the clock struck 3 p.m., his pager went off and my Prince Charming walked out of our favorite sushi bar and into the streets of New York—alone.

So that's how my sad situation started. Walking out of that restaurant that Wednesday afternoon with every eye fixed on me, I was sick and nearly suicidal. It's funny how losing your man, more than any of the other things in your life, can make you like a woman on her deathbed. You feel like you'll never see the sun rise over Manhattan again.

I felt like I was on some silly candid-camera show. While Julian and I definitely went through our share of "I need space" drama, that didn't separate me from any other woman who was dealing with any other man—especially a successful man. I never would've thought that he would really split up with me—not for real, for real. Inside, I couldn't even believe he was serious this time. He was just as feisty and nervous about commitment as all of my other friends' boyfriends-turned-husbands, and everyone had assured me that if I stuck it out, he'd come around and realize that he was supposed to be with me. So what the heck was happening? As I said, Julian was one of the good guys. The man visits his ailing grandmother every Thursday night. He's no heartbreaker. Julian was just heaven-sent—at least that was the way it had seemed when we met just over a year ago at the bookstore at NYU.

It was definitely an unlikely meeting. It was the beginning of my second semester at NYU Law and I was there to pick up a book . . . and maybe even a man if one crossed my path. I spotted Julian as soon as he walked in because he looked like a lost mountain man. His beard was completely overgrown, his shirt was all crooked and crumpled, and his hair was in desperate need of a cut. Before I got a good look at him, I thought that he'd just escaped from the city jail, but the closer he got, the more I knew this wasn't the case. Even a lesbian had to admit that beneath the rough edges, there was a fine-ass black man.

Looking at his calm hazel eyes and roasted-pecan skin, I just wanted to have his babies and play in his thick, jet black hair for the rest of my life. While I was sure he wasn't a good fit for me socially (seeing as how he was an escaped convict), within the two seconds it took for me to squeeze past him in the doorway, I rationalized that we could live off of my salary after I graduated from law school and settle down in one of my father's properties in downtown Brooklyn. I could clean him up a bit, show him the high-society ropes, and help him get back on his feet. Squeezing by only made my interest grow. My hazel-eyed, ex-con/future-husband smelled like a cloud and his stomach was completely solid when I stood on my tippy toes and brushed my bootie up against it—don't be jealous, I said excuse me.

When I turned to put my school bag in one of the free

lockers, I decided to drop my book and prayed he would notice. He'd pick it up, I'd smile and say, "Thank you. Let's go
home now, fine-ass man." I thought it was a pretty solid plan.
I pulled my torts book from my bag and looked toward him
to make sure he would notice the drop and have no choice
but to acquiesce.

That's when I saw the scrubs. The blue freakin' scrubs.
My heart started racing. I felt sweat beads forming on my
forehead. I reached for my compact; I needed to check my
makeup. I reached for my two-way pager; I needed to text
my girls. I reached for my phone; I needed to call my mother.
A doctor, I thought, feeling my Gucci bag fall to the floor.
He's a doctor. Did I say that aloud?

"Yes, I'm a doctor," Hazel Eyes said, looking at me. "Can
I help you?" He reached down and picked up my bag.

Dumb ass, dumb ass, dumb ass. I silently cursed myself
for letting "doctor" slip out. Now I was looking like a gold
digger—thank God I don't fall for that label. Seems like
every time a sister reveals that she's trying to have a successful man by her already successful side, folks start calling her
a gold digger. I say it's bull. I'm not a gold digger. I'm a gold
sharer; I have mine and my man had better have his own.

"Are you okay, sis?" Hazel Eyes asked. I couldn't say
anything. I was stunned. My future son's father was a door-
opening panhandler when I first walked into the store and
now he was a doctor. I needed time to work it all out in my
head. I needed a new plan.

"I'm sorry. I was just trying to remember my professor's
name," I managed to say. *Good catch. Good catch.*

"Oh, I thought you were talking to me," he said. "I was
wondering how you knew I was a doctor." He smiled and I
do believe I witnessed the cutest white teeth I'd ever seen. I
couldn't help but to return the favor. By the time he handed
me my purse, we were exchanging names and numbers. It's
amazing what a smile and a growing concern over the irreg-

ular heart palpitations I only experience in bed will do. Hey, I just needed some advice.

A week later, while walking through Central Park, Julian would tell me that he knew I was lying about not knowing he was a doctor, but he thought it was cute that I was so fast on my feet. He was doing his residency at NYU Medical Center and that day he'd stopped by the bookstore to pick up a book for a new recruit. He was glad he did. He'd noticed me as soon as he entered the bookstore. He said my skin that was just a few shades darker than the sweetest vanilla bean ice cream was striking. Right away he noticed the thin spray of light brown freckles that swept across my nose from cheek to cheek—a genetic gift from my mother I was always trying to hide with makeup—and thought he'd like to kiss each one of them as he made his way to look into my dark brown eyes. Plus, he'd always had a thing for sisters with a little extra shape to their derrières, and mine was looking like a perfect size ten in my fitted black slacks. I was definitely his type and he was trying to find a way to introduce himself when he heard me say "doctor." It was music to his ears. And listening to this description of me as we walked through Central Park with snow falling all around us and kids laughing and playing was certainly music to mine. I do believe I was already falling in love with Julian.

With a romantic beginning like that, who ever would have thought that we'd end up breaking up over sushi? I kept asking myself that question over and over as I drove home from Shimizu. That was just not how love stories went—not in any of the romantic movies, fairy tales, books, songs, poems, or limericks I'd ever laid eyes on. It was supposed to be happily ever after like it was for Cinderella and that green girl in *Shrek*. It was supposed to be a happy ending. For once, it was supposed to be *my* happy ending.

But it wasn't, and after spending the rest of the day and the entire night crying and thinking about where in the world

I'd gone wrong, I was feeling down and I was definitely out. Locked up in my apartment for almost twenty-nine hours straight, I was feeling like the loneliest person in the world as Wednesday had washed away into Thursday. Although I was used to being alone on Thursdays while Julian visited his grandmother in Queens, it didn't feel the same. There was no one waiting to see me, no one I was waiting to see. Just me and Pookie, *the damn dog I picked out,* locked up alone in my apartment. I was now a single dog parent, a neglectful one, and there was only one thing I could do to stop myself from completely losing my mind and swallowing a bottle of Ambien. Call my girls.

Meet the 3Ts: Troy, Tasha, and Tamia

While there are some things I absolutely hate about being a woman (crippling cramps and bad hair days being at the top of the list), the one thing that makes up for all of the drama is having girlfriends. They know your dirt, they keep your dirt a secret, and when called upon they're usually willing to *do* your dirt.

I just happen to have the best dirt-doing girlfriends in the whole world—Tamia Lovebird and Tasha Lovestrong. No, those aren't their real last names; we all chose best friends' last names when we formed our ultimate girlfriend supper club during our sophomore year at Howard University. Swearing off all other girlfriends, we held hands around a bucket of KFC in my dorm room, took on last names that all began with the word "Love" (mine being Troy Lovesong), and named our alliance "The 3Ts." After that faithful, finger-lickin' night, we were stuck together like Krazy Glue and it's been that way for the last six years. Hands down, while they can be a little crazy, my girls are my rocks, and I wouldn't want it any other way.

It had been twenty-nine hours, about twenty-nine thou-

sand tears, and twenty-nine million doubts after my breakup
with Julian when I finally picked up the phone to call on the
other 2Ts. While inside I just wanted to barricade myself in
my bedroom and cry for the rest of my life, I was sure that
little plan wouldn't work, because my father would stop paying my rent at some point. So it was time to face the girls and
talk it out. Wasn't that supposed to make things better?

"Hey, T, I'm about to meet my study group at the library.
Can I call you back?" Tamia asked, answering my call on the
first ring. She always picked up on the first ring, and no matter what time of day I was calling, she'd sound as if she was
wide awake, bright-eyed and bushy tailed, studying, studying, studying. That was just her thing, though. I guess you
could say she was the nerdy friend. Tamia got straight A's all
through Howard U. and she was now in the top 1 percent of
our law school class. Yes, she was the 3Ts resident Einstein,
but Tamia's brains weren't to be mistaken for a lack of beauty.
She definitely wasn't the kind of girl you'd introduce as simply being "nice." While she preferred less social circles than
the ones Tasha and I frequented in undergrad, Tamia was the
envy of the campus. Crowned Ms. Howard University twice
(yes, twice), Tamia complemented her brains with a beauty
most of the women on campus found unattainable and the
men found irresistible. Her flawless deep mocha complexion
played second fiddle only to her near black, brown eyes that
seemed to always be looking at something beautiful. Her lips
were perfectly round and puckered in a perpetual kiss that
needed not a dab of lip gloss.

"Okay," I said, trying not to sound too sad. I guess the
Mary J. playing in the background gave me away.

"What's wrong?" Tamia pried. "Is that Mary you're listening to? You okay? Everyone okay?"

"I'm fine." I burst into tears for what had to have been the
billionth time. Even the idea of saying what went down with
Julian the day before made me break down again. What a

mess. "You can call me back when you get done at the library," I rattled off.

"Well, you don't sound fine," she said, now whispering as if she was in the library. "What is it? Tell me. I have a minute."

"We broke up, T," I managed, blowing my nose on a napkin from the huge box of Kleenex I had stashed next to my bed.

"What happened?"

"He just said he needs . . ." Another breakdown was coming. "space . . ."

Pookie looked up at me sitting on the bed. Even his huge Chihuahua eyes looked sad after hearing my words. I wondered if he understood what was going on: that his human daddy was gone and never ever coming back. Never ever ever.

"Oh, Troy," Tamia said, "I'm sorry to hear that. When did it happen? What did he say?"

"Well, we had lunch at Shimizu yesterday and he just said it there. He said he's too stressed to deal with me right now and that's just it. That's just all he said . . . all he said . . ."

"Slow down; you don't have to go on." She stopped me. "I can't believe this. I never thought he'd do this. Are you sure it's not just one of his things? You know he gets stressed and starts acting crazy. Maybe you just need to give him some space. I mean, you're going to need the same thing when we graduate."

"No, I'm sure this is it this time, Tamia. I could see it in his eyes." I threw the box of Kleenex to the floor. Pookie jumped up and ran out of the room. I could hear Tamia whispering to someone on the other end of the phone. "Tamia?" I called frantically for no apparent reason. I just needed a little attention. Comfort. I mean, my entire world was only literally ablaze. Who gave a damn what was going on in that godforsaken library?

"Yeah, I'm here." Tamia groaned into the phone. "Look,

I'm so sorry, but my study group is here, so I have to get off of the phone."

"Okay," I said.

"But I'll be done soon. Have you told Tasha yet?"

"No." I started crying again at the thought of having to re-peat my sad saga. With all of this crying it would be a won-der if I was able to open my eyes in the morning.

"Well, don't worry about telling her. I'll call her when I get out of my meeting. Do you want to meet tonight? You know, for the party?"

I took a deep breath and looked up at the dust-ridden ceil-ing fan above my bed. I felt the unmistakable air of reluc-tance building in my chest.

"My breakup party?" I asked sadly, half questioning and affirming Tamia's suggestion. This was because the party she'd mentioned, *my breakup party,* was the first thing each 3T did when she broke up with a man. It was a tradition we started back at Howard. Whenever one of us broke up with someone, we'd forgo the usual girl grieving stage of hiding underneath the sheets and avoiding all public appearances, by making an official announcement to the other 2Ts, putting on our most slut-alicious dresses, and stepping out for a night on the town. We called it "the Breakup Party." It sounded crazy to most people, but it worked. At its best, the party gets the man off your mind for a few hours. At the very least, it gets you out of the house.

"Yeah, tonight is fine for the party," I muttered uneasily between tears.

"Good. So I'll call Tasha and we'll meet at Justin's at 8," Tamia said.

"Okay."

"And, Troy, keep your head up," Tamia added. "Remem-ber, the first 3T rule of breaking up is having the 'face of grace.'"

"I know. I know," I answered. My girl was right. We all agreed that the most important thing a girl had to do after a breakup was present herself as if she was together even if she was all apart inside. She had to face the world with grace no matter what. A brighter day would come, although I wasn't so sure I believed that after Julian.

"Good. I love you," Tamia said.

"I love you, too." I sniffled and buried myself back under the covers.

The Goodbye Girl: The 3T Breakup Party Guide

So it's over and Mr. Right turned out to be Mr. All Wrong. Don't sit around all day and cry about it. No, this is a time to celebrate your new "player-ific" lifestyle with your girls. Plan a breakup party and say goodbye to yesterday.

Must Haves: A picture of your new ex, a hot outfit no man can say "no" to, huge shades in case your eyes look droopy from crying (don't be embarrassed; people will think you're a celebrity), and fabulous friends to celebrate with.

Instructions: Make an announcement to your closest friends via e-mail or telephone—this will eliminate any unnecessary gossip. Just put it all out there and invite your girls out to your party. The location must be someplace really cool where you're guaranteed to be seen in all of your glory. Arrive late and hand the picture of your ex to your girls so your bitter memory can be torn to shreds. Then let the games begin.

Do's: Cry if you want to, dance until your feet hurt, wear a dress so skanky you can't wear underwear, have your friends pretend you're a celebrity, smile at every man you see, and let everyone and their mama know you're a free agent.

Don'ts: Party at a place special to you and your ex (bad memories), drink too much and pass out singing "End of the Road" by Boyz II Men, or call your ex . . . ever, ever, ever.

The Babbling Bourgeois Baboon vs. the Democrat Octoroon

In the car on the way to Justin's, I couldn't stop thinking about Julian and trying to figure out where our thing fell apart. How did we even get to the "Troy, I need a break" breaking point? Being honest with myself, I had to admit that the relationship was no cakewalk. Julian and I had shared some hard times and disagreements. Most notable, of course, was the time Julian invited my parents to meet his parents. (Note: Why in the hell would this man want our parents to meet if I wasn't his "girlfriend"? And he says I was the confused one. . . .) Anyway, though I was excited about the parental union (seeing as how it usually led to other *unions*), I should've seen that train wreck coming down the tracks from a mile away.

The highlight of that night came when my mother, a rich girl gone artsy after her divorce from and remarriage to my father, called Julian's mother a "babbling bourgeois baboon" and stormed out of his parents' Harlem brownstone.

That insult occurred after my mother wasted what was left of a perfectly full glass of red wine—something I'd never seen her do before—on his mother's Persian rug. The drama all began when our parents started talking politics during an after-dinner chat. I need to correct that—they started talking *black* politics. Let me explain why this distinction is significant. My dad, a retired international pilot, couldn't give a damn about much else other than his money, me, his money, where he's traveling to next, his money, whether he has to take my mother with him, his money, and his mother (my Nana Rue) and her money, which someday will be his money. Ask him about the war in Iraq and he'll pull out his Black-Berry and measure Iraq's distance from Morocco—his vacation destination of choice; ask him about starvation in Africa and he'll bring up his trips to Dubai and how well he pays the cleaning lady at our vacation home there.

Dad's goal in life is to not get his "pressure up," and the man has never had high blood pressure, so I guess he's doing a good job. Since he retired, Daddy spends his days playing accountant and keeping the two ladies in his life (my mother and his mother) smiling and out of trouble. This disposition fared well on his good looks that had yet to begin to fade even though he was far into his fifties. Standing at 6'2" tall, my father had deep mahogany skin, and even though his eyes were browner than anything I'd ever seen, they shined with hazel flecks that guaranteed he'd catch a few double takes from women in any crowd.

My mother is one of the most outwardly confused people I know. The "drama with mama" was endless, but most of the time we all put up with it because we knew the source—her past. See, my mother was born to one of Manhattan's black female socialites in the 1950s. Only my grandmother wasn't *really* black with a capital *B,* as in "Black and proud." Grandma Lucy was mixed. As was her mother before her, her mother before her, and her mother before her—you get the picture. To make a long story short, this twisted past led to my mother (the child of Grandma Lucy's marriage to a white man who didn't know my grandmother's race until he proposed marriage) having serious issues wherever race was concerned. In contrast to what one would think, she turned out nothing like Grandma Lucy. My mother hated the idea of passing and the privilege it seemed to provide her with as the sole heir of the son of a Texas railroad tycoon. The importance Grandma Lucy placed on color, brooding over my mother's dusky tan skin whenever the sun was high and insisting that my mother was "lucky" to have inherited my grandfather's straight nose, rose-strained cheeks, and straight blond hair, ate away at her. Sometimes I felt as if my mother was always standing in between the lines of her color—the light side and the dark side. She was too afraid or embarrassed to embrace her light skin for all that it meant to Grandma Lucy, so she kept her blond hair dyed black, frowned when someone praised her light hazel eyes, and always seemed to feel a need to shower people with dark skin, including my father, with compliments. She wanted people to know that she was Black (with a capital *B*), she was down for the people and not, as they say, still passing.

With all that in tow, fast-forward about twenty-five years and you have my mother sitting in Julian's parents' brownstone. Two doctors who came from generations and generations of old Harlem doctors, they believed in self-determination and every man for himself achieving the American dream. Julian's parents were staunch Republicans. They had money and they wanted to keep it . . . period. After listening to them share their political philosophies over many dinners in the past, it was clear that they felt that the more poor, ignorant black people there were out there, the less they had to worry about losing what they had.

My mother, who really didn't have to work or go to school, for that matter, hated Republicans and specifically despised *black* Republicans for what she called "their nerve." I know it sounds contradictory, but it was simply the kind of position my mother's affluence and color afforded her. She didn't have to worry about people taking what she had or to complain about higher taxes paying for government programs. There was an endless supply of railroad money in her life. She couldn't spend it all if she tried—*I would give that venture my all if someone would let me.* But with that kind of good old American money comes a certain amount of shame. Somewhere between her lunches at Saks with other wives and days at the spa, my mother peeks out onto the streets of New York and feels bad for folks who have less than she does, folks who didn't benefit from the history of having a passing mother and rich father. This empathy, I mean sympathy, leads my poor, guilty mother into the *barrios*—the ghettos—each weekend to do her part by painting houses with her sorority or the Links. Do good. Give back. It's all a little pathetic, but hey, other people get to benefit from it.

Needless to say, my mother's a Democrat. So on that precious night at Julian's house, the two of us had two Republicans (Julian's parents), a man staring into his glass hoping his wife didn't smack someone (my father), and a Democrat who was really trying to make up for the fact that she's filthy rich (my mother), talking black politics. *Black politics.*

Yes. Disaster.

Between revitalizing St. Nicholas Park and taxes, I knew my mother should've put her drink down. She gets this little white-girl nervous twitch when someone's pissing her off. Her cheeks flush and then she keeps taking deep breaths to show how annoyed she is. Julian kept looking at me. Suddenly, his charming eyes that I always compared to a chipmunk's, looked like a deer's in headlights. He'd heard the stories about my mama drama. I was about to intervene by saying that I had to get to the library to study for my upcoming midterms when my mother had to open her big mouth. After Julian's mother said, "You black Democrats need to see the big picture," my mother's glass hit the floor and she was on her feet. Dad picked up her purse and headed to the door. When my mother stands up, it's like Oprah rolling up in the juke joint in *The Color Purple*: "It's time to go." Mama's white-girl side makes her prone to slapping people at random. One time it landed her and daddy in jail. You just can't go around smacking senators.

"What self-respecting black person calls themselves a Republican?" my mother said, looking up at the ceiling like she couldn't even stand the sight of the rest of the people in the room. The twitch was growing to an all-time high. Damn near seizure level. "You're like George Bush. You don't love black people. You're just a . . . you're a . . ." I waved goodbye to Julian, I gave him the "I'll call you later" look and grabbed my mother's hand, pulling her to the door. We were almost out the door. Almost home free without my mother having said anything that would forever damage any possible relationship between Julian and my parents when the right words came to Mary Elizabeth Smith, a mixed woman from the Upper West Side who stunt-doubles as my mother. "You . . . you babbling bourgeois baboon," she hollered somewhere between the threshold and the car.

Did I mention that Julian's mother told him never to invite me over again? In the car, my mother looked over at my father, who was trying his best to keep his hands on the steering wheel and off her neck, and said, "Tell your daughter, my sweet Troy Helene, that I forbid her to see that man again." She pushed a lock of stray black hair behind her right ear and turned to look at me in the backseat. "Darling husband, tell my baby Troy that idiots only give birth to bigger idiots and she doesn't see it now, but Mama knows best. That Julian will only break my baby's heart. She's only 26. She can find someone else."

Daddy peeked at me in the mirror and offered a look of condolence. Sometimes I felt like he was my only ally between my parents. We had an understanding. I stay in school and he pays my bills, calls me once a week at 8 a.m. on Tuesday just before his preferred tee time at our country club in Westchester, and when I need him, when I really need him, he's there to listen.

Sitting in my car en route to the breakup party, I couldn't get my mother's words out of my head. "You babbling bourgeois baboon. You babbling bourgeois baboon. You babbling bourgeois baboon" was playing in my mother's voice over and over. I was about to scream when my phone rang.

It was Tasha.

"I'm parking the damn car," I hollered into the phone as I pulled into the parking lot down the street from Justin's. It was the third time she'd called to make sure I was coming since I left my apartment.

"Well, get your ass in here, hoe," Tasha said on the other end. I could hear Tamia in the background giggling.

"Time to party," Tamia said.

Though my heart was in pain, I had to laugh at my girls. Ever since I met them they've always been down for a good party, and always down for me. When you mix a good party and me . . . well, there's usually a fight over when to open the champagne.

I met Tamia my sophomore year. I was sitting in my first informational for what would soon become my sorority when Tamia walked in decked out in the cutest crimson cashmere sweater I'd ever seen—hands down. I smiled at her, thinking that any sorority with members who dressed so cute must be the one for me. That was right around when Tamia came and sat down next to me. This action, of course, confused me because the big sisters (who were all wearing crimson) were sitting on the other side of the room. As my mother instructed me to do during our morning telephone chat before I went to the event, I wore tan, so as not to "offend anyone by wearing aggressive colors." Crimson was aggressive; crimson was *their* color. It was definitely a no-no to wear *their* color. I left all of my crimson attire at home in New York when I departed for school.

"I can't wait to pledge Crimson and Cream," Tamia said, snuggling into her seat. "My name is Tamia. Tamia Dinkins," she added, reaching out to shake my hand. I wanted to look away and pretend I didn't see her, but everyone was watching. Though I didn't want to ruin my chances of pledging, I shook her hand anyway. And I'm so glad I did. Tamia turned out to be a sorority shoo-in. Not only was she directly related to the first black mayor of New York, David Dinkins, but she also had a 4.0 and her deceased mother, who died of a rare heart illness when Tamia was three, once was a member of the chapter.

Tamia Dinkins, after a little grooming, ended up pledging with me and following in her mother's footsteps by being the next chapter president.

Soon after we graduated, she moved to New York with me to go to law school at NYU.

Tasha, who will curse out anyone who calls her by her birth name, Natasha, is a different story. Though I met her at Howard, I'm still trying to figure out how she got there, and how in the hell she managed to graduate. Tasha was a West Coast escapee who ran away from home when she was in high school. Okay, that sounds dramatic, but it's Tasha. She did "escape" from L.A., but it was from a Beverly Hills mansion with an American Express card and a BMW in tow. Her mother, Porsche St. Simon, is a black soap opera star who raised what Tamia and I call a "Hollywood brat." Tasha spent most of her childhood getting to know nanny after nanny after nanny. She got to wear cool clothes, drive nice cars before she was of legal age, hang on the beach, and eat fine food, all of which she despised—along with Porsche St. Simon for giving it to her.

"It's all so fake. They're all so fake there," Tasha explained to me in the lobby of our dorm one evening. She revealed that one morning she got in her mother's BMW and drove until she couldn't anymore. Alone and seventeen, she found herself at her grandmother's house in Washington, D.C., which is only a few blocks away from the university. Somehow her grandmother, talked her into using her AmEx card for good and not for evil and she enrolled at Howard the next semester. While it's rumored that some strings were pulled by her grandmother, who had a lot of money wrapped up in the school, I can confirm that Tasha did go to class (at least the ones she had with me) and she did buy the books (even though they never really left the bags from the bookstore). If Tamia was the brains of our little threesome, Tasha was certainly the brick house beauty. Porshe St. Simon's beauty queen/ soap opera starlet genes led to Tasha having a bodacious body that left grown men salivating whenever she passed them by. She had one of those hourglass shapes that demanded attention even when she was wearing a sweat suit and sneakers. Her buttery sand colored skin never revealed the markings of one popped pimple and her smoky brown eyes were mysterious.

Somehow the class diva who refused to pledge with Tamia and me made it through all four years and when we said we were heading to my hometown for law school, Tasha said she was coming too. While Tasha found little work with her Communications degree, she did manage to find a fine catch of a husband. Tasha's eye-catching curves caught the attention of her new groom, New York Knicks starting player Lionel Laroche.

As a friend, I'd say Tasha evens Tamia and me out. She knows how to have a good time and if you need to curse someone out, she's your girl.

Love them or leave them, those were my two best friends. We've been joined at the hip since our days at Howard when everyone on the yard knew of the 3Ts. We were notorious. Together, we raised hell all over Washington, D.C. From frat parties to road trips, we had a ball. Tasha still can't operate a vehicle in Washington, D.C. over some stunt we pulled our senior year.

After taking the ticket from the parking lot attendee, I reached into my purse to pull out Julian's picture for one last look before I said goodbye and delivered it to the ladies for shredding. I decided to offer up my favorite picture of us at Tasha and Lionel's last New Year's Eve party. Julian looked so adorable in the black and gray suit we picked out together to match my sexy black dress that would do Halle Berry proud. He was intoxicated by the time Tasha took the picture of us standing by the bar, so his face was a little red. "Smile for our picture, Mrs. Julian James," he whispered to me. Needless to say, that got my juices flowing and my ass is grinning from ear to ear in the picture, looking like *I'd* just won an Academy Award.

I shook my head and slipped the picture back into my purse. "I can't believe this shit," I said aloud. For one second I thought of turning the car back on and heading over to Julian's place to talk about things. Then my phone rang. It was Tasha *again*.

"Get out of the damn car and walk into the restaurant," she said. "You can't turn back now." The phone went dead. It was a 3T intervention. Tasha was right. I had to get moving. Talking to Julian would only make things worse and I was not about to play myself. Walking toward the restaurant, I took a self assuring deep breath and looked down at the sexy copper colored halter dress I decided to wear. I didn't pick it because it looked more than fantastic on me—although it did. I chose it because the tight, yet forgiving fabric wrapped around me like a second layer of skin—a tougher, thicker layer I needed to make it through the evening. It was the perfect choice for the less than perfect occasion. It certainly didn't look like a breakup party dress. It looked like a birth-day party dress, and the way I saw it, if I was going to cele-brate my new birth as a single woman, I may as well look good doing it.

It's Ladies Night . . . But I'm Not All Right

I could see those two crazy chicks waiting for me toward the back of the restaurant as soon as I walked in. I wanted to walk right over to them before Tamia guzzled down the last of the champagne, but, in perfect "walk of fame" tradition, I had to pretend not to see them. This was all part of the game we used to attract attention from guys standing around by the bar. We believe that men like it when a woman looks lost and alone. It gives the guys a reason to talk to the woman without fear of looking obvious and being obviously rejected. No, they prefer to look concerned and helpful, so they say silly stuff like, "You look lost, sweetie. Can I help you?" or "You came here all alone?" It never fails. So sisters who claim they can't meet a decent brother simply need to stop sitting and socializing with the group and look a little more single.

I looked down to make sure my tatas hadn't somehow found their way to freedom out of the top of the halter dress I'd forced them into, and then I made my way to the bar. I strutted slowly and deliberately, pretending to search for my lost friends. I scanned the faces of each female I saw.

"You looking for someone, sweetheart?" a bald cutie asked

as I struggled not to laugh at how ridiculous this entire tradition was—but, then, I guess that was the point, because I was laughing and, therefore, not crying anymore.

"Yeah, I'm looking for my girls," I said, looking him up and down and silently comparing every inch of his body to Julian's. I hated doing it, but a long time ago I realized that the whole "compare the next to the ex" thing was just a part of the breaking-up process.

"There she is," I heard rowdy-ass Tasha yell from the other side of the room. "There's that fine-ass movie star who's my friend." Tasha and Tamia began to clap. Everyone, and I mean everyone, in the restaurant lifted their heads and looked at me. All I could offer was a weak wave to all of these celebrity gazers who'd obviously flocked to Justin's in hopes of seeing someone of more fame.

"There they go," I said to old Baldy. I walked to the table with all eyes on me. "Y'all are so crazy," I said, quickly squeezing into a seat next to Tamia.

"Don't act, because you were worse when I broke up with Corey before Christmas," Tamia teased, handing me a bouquet of roses—another tradition. Tasha nodded her head in agreement.

"So . . ." Tasha looked down at my hands.

"So?" I said, playing dumb. I knew what that trick wanted, but I wasn't offering it up that easy.

"Hand it over," she said, putting out her hand.

"What?"

"She's right, Troy. Hand it over," Tamia chimed in. I looked away from them. "Was I this bad with Corey?" Tamia asked Tasha.

"No, girl. Ms. Troy Lovesong over here is just wrong. She's breaking all of the rules. But she'd better act right before I have to cut her." Tasha reached for a butter knife that was sitting on the table beside her.

"Whatever," I said. I threw my purse on the table and sat back in my seat. I watched as Tamia pulled the bag open like a lion looking for fresh meat. I thought I saw saliva dripping from the sides of her mouth, her fingernails growing longer, vampire-like teeth hanging down like fangs. She snatched the picture of Julian and me out and grinned ghoulishly.

"Hahahahahaha," she laughed like an evil witch. "You have the tools?"

"You know I came prepared, Ms. Lovebird." Tasha pulled two menacing pairs of scissors from her purse. Tasha took the breakup parties more seriously than any of us—perhaps that was because before she got married, she had the most breakups of any other 3T. Over the years, she'd become the unofficial breakup party organizer. She made sure you got there and had a good time. It made her a pretty annoying person when all you wanted to do was stay at home and cry over the lost lover, but at the end of the day hearing her voice harassing you to get up and out was promising. And she actually made the parties pretty good.

"Ready?" Tamia asked like we were preparing for a race.

"Ready," I replied, afraid of what was coming.

"Ready!" Tasha said, handing Tamia one of the pairs of scissors.

"Rock-a-bye, baby," Tamia said. I rolled my eyes and swallowed the shot of Patrón that was waiting for me on the table. I tried not to watch the massacre, but, well, it was hard with all of the confetti floating in the air in front of me. Tasha, who had more male horror stories tucked away in her skeleton closet than anyone I knew, had a way with scissors. I once saw her cut up an 8x10 of her own ex in 3.2 seconds. She snatched it, saying Tamia and I were moving too slow. That girl was a serial killer in her last life.

"Mazel tov!" Tasha said, slamming the scissors on the table. I looked down to see the damage. All I could make out was a piece of Julian's silver tie. It was over. I could feel tears coming to my eyes.

"It's because we love you, Ms. Lovesong," Tamia said, handing me the cutout of my face.

"Yeah, and we hate that fool!" Tasha added. "Now let's have a round of City Girls and talk about our dearly departed like the dog he is." The waiter handed each of us a City Girl—the over-sweetened version of the *Sex and the City* Cosmopolitan that we drank at most of our get-togethers. The tasty mix had just enough kick to get the tears rolling early on in the night and the feet moving on the dance floor later.

"Take your time, T. We have all night," Tamia said, patting me on the back. "Tonight is about you. It's your party. But you have to talk about it. We can't pretend it didn't happen."

Along with being the smartest person I know, Tamia is the most rational. She was raised by her father, a judge who retired when Tamia's mother died so he could spend time with Tamia. Tamia said he was a good man, but his love for the courtroom never left him. He taught Tamia the basics of his favorite cases when she was just in elementary school and convinced her that she would be the first black female Supreme Court justice. This resulted in Tamia being just that . . . "just." She followed the law to a T—returned library books on time, never parked in handicapped spots, and at most times in my life, she stood as my voice of justice and reason—when she wasn't locked in the library until daylight.

"Thanks," I said, folding what was left of my relationship with Julian into a napkin. Tasha raised her glass.

"A toast to my fly-ass friend and the motherfucker who will never know it," she laughed. "I'm for real. No sense crying over spilled, spoiled milk . . . especially when you're the cream still on the counter."

"Drama queen," Tamia said. She lifted her glass, too. "But she's right. You're fly and soon you will find someone who sees that." She looked at my glass. "Soon both of us will find someone who sees our flyness. We deserve it."

I picked up my glass and joined the toast.

"To my girls," I said. "To my ride-or-die girls." I drank the City Girl almost as quickly as my shot and shook my head as the liquid danced down my throat. Silence fell over the table. It was time for the dish—time for me to tell my girls what had happened.

"I don't know, y'all," I managed to say before picking up my second drink. "I don't know where this one went wrong." I looked down into my glass, searching the pretty liquor for answers. "I don't know why he dumped me." I could hear myself crying. I was already drunk. "I just feel fucking pitiful. You know? Like, why am I not good enough?" I looked down at my lap and sighed. "I know that sounds stupid and ridiculous, but that's how I feel. Like I've been loving this man and he could give a rat's ass about my dumb ass. I feel stupid."

"Girl, fuck that feeling-stupid shit. We all go through that shit," Tasha said, pouring me another shot. "Don't think it's just you. That's just how it feels. It hurts. Just let it out. And let it go."

"Exactly," Tamia said.

"But I just feel like maybe I missed something or should've seen something or done something or maybe even—" I looked up at Tamia. She was looking directly past me toward the front of the restaurant. Her eyes were as wide as they could get and she hadn't moved her drink from her open mouth.

I tried to go on with my sad little speech.

"I thought we'd be together forever. I thought he . . ." I looked at Tasha sitting on the other side of Tamia and she was looking past me, too. Her eyes also were as wide as soup spoons and I could tell that she was hitting Tamia beneath the table. I decided to turn around to the door to see what they were looking at.

"No, that negro didn't," Tasha said.

"Don't turn around," I heard Tamia say in slow motion as I turned to face the door and see what Tasha was talking about.

It was Julian. My baby, my future husband, my *ex-boyfriend* was standing at the maître d' stand. *What the hell?*

"Grab her ass," Tamia said. Tasha swung around to my side of the table like a superhero, sandwiching me between her and Tamia.

"What are y'all doing?" I asked, trying to sound more confident than I really was. My heart was beating so fast I thought I was about to faint. "I saw Julian. It's no big deal. I'll go say hello. Remember, I have to show the Face of Grace." I looked over at Tamia. She was looking toward the door. There was fear in her eyes. "Maybe he's here with his grandmother. He usually hangs with her on Thursday night." Even I didn't believe what I was saying. Who takes their grandmother to Justin's on Thursday night?

"Is it her?" Tasha said to Tamia. "Is it that bitch?"

"I can't remember," Tamia said.

"Remember what?" I asked. I tried to stand up to see what Tasha and Tamia were talking about, but they were both holding me down.

"You can't see the girl behind him." I felt like someone had just gutted me like a fish. Tamia looked intently into my eyes. "We think it's Miata."

I turned from Tamia and looked back toward Julian at the door. He smiled at the maître d' and signaled for a table for two. He put his arm back (the arm that used to hold me at night; the arm that I used to love) and pulled the trick he cheated on me with a month ago from behind him. I couldn't believe it. He was with fucking Miata, at Justin's, the night after our breakup! The night he was supposed to be with his sweet old grandma!

I was about to go postal; rationality was leaving me; prison time was a possibility!

"I'll kill him," I heard myself say just before I stabbed the table with a butter knife and stood up. The people around us looked and Tamia pulled me down so Julian couldn't see me. I pulled away from her and fought to get up from behind the table. I didn't know what I was about to do, but I knew where I was going, and I was still holding that butter knife. Clearly,

I wasn't going to kill anyone—that's just dumb—but someone had to explain to me just what in the hell was going on. I'd almost escaped the table when Tasha and Tamia tackled me back to the chair.

"Don't embarrass yourself," Tamia said, pulling me under the table with her. "Don't embarrass yourself over that clown. Face of Grace. Face of Grace. Have the fucking Face of Grace."

"Fuck the Face of Grace, Tamia. My man is with another woman," I cried.

"No, Tamia's right," Tasha said, easing her legs under the table with a drink in her hand. She looked almost as mad as me. "You know I'm always ready to roll crazy with you, but he isn't worth it. And neither is that hoe standing next to him. I won't let you go out like that." She swallowed everything that was left in the glass. "Now we have to get out of here silently so I'll lead the way."

The City Girl Martini: A Must-Have for Any
Breakup Party

Mama said there would be days like this. The good and the bad. You can expect them, and you must accept them. Invite the ladies to join you for a sip and see who can get to the bottom of the glass first.

<u>Do's:</u>
   1. *Drink out of a fancy glass.*
   2. *Flirt shamelessly as you sip.*
   3. *Have cool company to drink with.*
<u>Don'ts:</u>
   1. *Think about anything other than having a good time.*
   2. *Have just one.*
   3. *Drive drunk, because that's just dumb.*

Warning: Sipping these drinks might cause you to have a good time. Don't serve to lame asses and people you don't like.

<u>The City Girl Martini</u>

<u>Ingredients:</u>
1 part cranberry vodka
1 part orange liqueur
1 part sloe gin
1 splash sour mix
1 splash apple-cranberry juice
1 splash of orange juice

<u>Directions:</u> Mix equal parts of liquors and a splash of each juice.

The Plan

"I can't believe that motherfucker's with that bitch," Tasha said angrily. It was exactly what I was thinking, but at that point I was too upset to say a word. We were all sitting in Tamia's car in front of Justin's. Tasha had convinced the manager to open the kitchen exit so we could get out without walking past Miata and Julian. Though I wanted so badly to approach them, Tamia and Tasha convinced me that it would be a bad idea to confront them in the restaurant. After climbing out from under the table, I moonwalked the entire way to the kitchen, watching their every move. Julian slid his arms around her shoulders and pulled her head into his chest. He kissed her on the cheek and whispered something in her ear. It looked like he said, "Mrs. James."

With every moment that passed, as I maneuvered my way around each table, my heart broke a little bit more. I wanted to scream, jump on top of the bar, and demand that Julian come home with me. Not her. Not the girl named after a car.

"Tasha, calm down. You're only making things worse saying things like that," Tamia said, looking at Tasha behind me in the backseat. "I knew it was a bad idea to come here. Are you okay, Troy?"

"I can't believe this. Why her? Why here?" I looked out of the passenger-side window and shook my head. "I don't understand. One minute everything's perfect, then he just dumps me. Now he's here with her? This shit is crazy."

"I know it doesn't make sense. But you've got to move on. That's what breaking up is all about." Tamia put her hand on my shoulder. I could hear some old Luther Vandross song playing in a car passing by. I wanted to jump out of the car and roll around in the street, screaming Julian's name out loud. It was dramatic and it wouldn't make me feel better, but at least then people could see my pain. I got played by a man I thought was going to marry me. "You have to move on," Tamia went on over Luther. "And I know it's kind of harsh, but clearly Julian has."

"Bullshit," Tasha said from the backseat. I could tell she was a little intoxicated from the excess of sass in her voice.

"What?" Tamia turned to her.

"That's bullshit, what you said, Tamia. Something else is going on." I could see Tasha's hands moving around in my side mirror. She was getting riled up and ready to fight. While Tamia was always trying to see the pot of gold at the end of the rainbow, the good in mankind, Tasha was the drama queen of controversy. If you needed to find out if your man was cheating, if your boss was stealing money from the company, if you were lying to your damn self, Tasha was on the job. She trusted no one and she could smell a dubious dilemma like doo-doo on a shoe. When we first met, Tamia and I wondered where Tasha got all of her street savvy. The girl could curse better than a sailor and I once saw her jimmy a lock faster than anything I'd ever seen on *MacGyver*. Apparently, her *90210* existence wasn't as "totally awesome" as her mother's career choice promised. When Tasha grew tired of sitting in hotel rooms and playing cards with her nanny, she slipped out to the streets to play gangster girl to get even with Porsche.

From stealing clothes she easily could afford, to hanging out with boys that might have been featured on *America's Most Wanted*, Tasha said it felt good to be out in the street doing things that could get her killed or at least force Porsche to have to come to the police precinct to bail her out.

"What do you think's going on?" I begged, desperate to find out what Tasha was talking about.

"Oh, don't listen to her ass, Troy. She's going to turn this into some craziness." Tamia tried to turn on the engine.

"No, girl." I put my hand on Tamia's to stop her from turning the ignition. "I want to know what she thinks."

"Did you love that man?" Tasha pushed her head into the front of the car like a bobblehead. "Like really love him?"

"Yes, of course."

"And did he love you?" she asked.

"Yes."

"Are you *sure?*" Tasha stressed the last word. "I mean, *we* all thought Julian loved you, Troy. We really did and you could not have told us any different."

Tamia nodded her head in agreement.

"But the important thing is," Tasha went on, "do *you* think he *loved you?*"

I turned to face the huge glass window that separated the people inside of Justin's from the rest of the world. I squinted to see if I could see Julian standing by the bar. He wasn't there.

"Yes," I answered Tasha, searching the rest of the restaurant. I remembered the first time I met Julian there for dinner. It was raining outside and he'd just completed some residency requirement. "I need to celebrate, baby," Julian had said to me on the phone. By the time I walked into Justin's, he was already there, sitting in the waiting area. "I did it. I did it," Julian said. He jumped up from the white leather sofa and opened his arms. My baby was looking fine, like a young Billy Dee putting the moves on Diana Ross in *Lady Sings the Blues*. I ran to him and jumped into his arms like I was

Billie Holiday getting out of rehab. He held me close and kissed me on the forehead. "And I have you to thank," he whispered into my ear. "Now everything's going to be perfect for us." I believed him then. I still believe him now.

"Tasha, get to your damn point," Tamia said.

"I will, if you calm down." Tasha put two fingers in front of me. "So that's two points: You love him and he loves you. Now, let's see if we can get to three."

"Yeah, let's see if three makes any sense," Tamia jumped in again. Tasha and I looked at her. "Okay, okay. I'll shut up. Go on."

"One: You love Julian. Two: Julian loves you. Question three: Does he love that bitch?" Tasha pointed toward the restaurant.

"Wait, I'm not having that," Tamia said. "This is not about that girl. We're all black women and she's not a bitch. Her name is Miata." Tasha sucked her teeth and waved her hand at Tamia. "No, I'm sorry, ladies. I will not let you all make this about that girl. *Julian* broke up with Troy. *Julian* brought someone else to the restaurant. Not Miata. She's innocent in this. We have no clue what kind of person she is."

"We don't need to know what kind of person she is. What we know is that she's *the kind of person* who's in the freaking restaurant with our friend's man—"

"*Ex man,*" Tamia said.

"What-the-hell-ever you want to call him," Tasha said. "All I want to know is, is that bitch—I mean Miata/bitch or whoever or whatever you want to call her—really innocent in this, Tamia? Is she innocent or smart?" Tasha sounded like a lawyer cracking a witness. "Now, answer the third question, *Troy.* Does *he* love *her?*"

"You don't have to answer that, Troy." I could feel Tamia's hand on my leg. "I know it's hard for you right now."

"Leave her alone, you corny ass," Tasha said to Tamia.

"I love you anyway," Tamia teased.

I leaned my head on the headrest and closed my eyes.

It was just before we were about to leave for a three-day vacation in Key West that I found out about Miata. It was innocent, really. Julian had left both the two-way pager he used for work and his cell phone on the bed that morning when he'd left for the hospital. I picked the up two-way, trying to find a message from the hospital so I could give him a buzz there to see if he wanted me to drop off his stuff. I checked the messages, figuring he had to have at least one text message from the hospital within the past ten hours. He had been on call the night before.

"Miata" was the first name I read. "What kind of name is that?" I thought, scrolling past the name. But I didn't stop. After realizing that there were no messages from or to the hospital, I took a mental note that the last seven messages were from Miata and tossed the phone and pager back on the bed.

"He'll come back," I thought, slipping off my nightgown and heading to the shower. Along the way, I kept saying to myself: *I'm confident.* I didn't have to worry about my man, whom he was seeing and why in the heck she'd sent him so many text messages.

I wasn't the type to go through a man's pager. That was child's play. That was for insecure little girls who had nothing else to do with their time. Drama queens. Chickenheads. Baby mamas. Those were the kinds of women who went through pagers. Not me. I was different. I had things to do. In fact, I had a class that afternoon and I needed to get to the library to study. No time for little games. But, as I said, that's what I kept *saying to myself.* What I was *thinking* was, *Who in the hell is this woman, paging my man?* I was trying to be mature but something in the atmosphere clearly was working on me. If there's one thing I've learned thus far in my short life, is that when there's something working on you—when your old inner phone is ringing—you'd better answer.

I turned to walk to the shower, going over my busy day in my head, and the two-way started vibrating. "Keep walking,"

I said to myself, recalling the time Tasha's telephone spying on one boyfriend led to her unknowingly calling his mother and accusing the old lady of sleeping with her man. Clearly, they broke up.

"I have no reason not to trust my baby, right Pookie Po?" I said, bending down to pet the dog. That's when it happened . . . The damn two-way went off again. Even Pookie Po looked at the vibrating device that time. "Should I read Daddy's message, Pookie? Do you think it's important?" I asked, looking at the dog's tiny face. Now, I know it sounds like I'm tripping, but I swear the dog shook his head "yes." It was a sign! And I don't ignore signs. I immediately picked up Julian's two-way and read the message . . .

Where are you, handsome?
I'm waiting at the fountain in the park.
I miss you.

—Miata

WTF? I dropped the pager, nearly hitting Pookie Po on his head. Who the hell was this "Miata" and what was she doing meeting my Julian by the damn fountain?

Now, here's the blackout in my story. I don't really remember how I ended up dressed in a sweat suit, sitting beneath a tree by the fountain in the center of Washington Square Park with Tasha and Tamia, but I was there. I was there and my poor dog, my "reason" (per Tasha) for being in the park missing class, was looking up at me like I was crazy.

"When you see them, just walk over with the dog and say hello," Tamia explained, hiding behind a copy of the *New York Times*. "It's a free park. There's no law against walking your dog."

"But how do we even know they're coming here? It could've been Central Park she was talking about," Tasha said. She snatched the newspaper from Tamia.

"We know because Troy said this is Julian's favorite park." Tamia tried to snatch the paper back, but it tore in half.

"Okay, okay." I spotted Julian sitting on the side of the fountain, talking to a girl. They were sharing an ice cream cone.

Pookie suddenly barked (he never barks), jumped from my lap (he never jumps), and headed toward Julian.

"Damn," Tasha said. "Get the dog! Get the dog!"

I stood up and followed behind Pookie.

"What do I say?" I asked.

"Say hello," Tamia answered, pointing to Julian. I turned to find that Pookie had already made his way to his daddy's arms. Julian was standing there holding him up, looking through the crowd like he was seeing things.

"There you go, baby," I said, reaching for him. "Oh, Julian," I added, trying to sound surprised. *I didn't.* "What are you doing here?"

"I was wondering the same thing," Julian replied. He was wearing a white cotton pullover and khakis—not the scrubs he usually wore at the hospital, where he said he would be.

"Oh, I was just taking Pookie for a walk." I took him from Julian and fought not to stare at the girl, who I already had decided was ugly.

"But this is, like, over twenty blocks from your apartment." Julian smiled.

"Pookie needs the exercise, Julian," I said, smiling back at him. "Who's your friend?" I didn't look in her direction.

"I'm Miata. And you are . . . ?" she asked, putting her hand out to shake mine. I pretended to try to maneuver Pookie around so I could shake her hand, but I couldn't. I must've looked so clumsy.

"The dog," I said, looking at Pookie. "The dog." Although I'd completely decided that Miata was kin to Pookie when I was looking at her from across the park, I had to admit that she didn't look that bad in a "God bless the child," "all of

God's children are beautiful" kind of way. Like if I was Mariah Carey, she could definitely be one of my backup singers. Nah, she wasn't that bad looking. In fact, in another life, I might have called her attractive. She had dark brown skin, slender, exotic eyes, and a weave that was so perfectly brushed, I might have thought it was real if it wasn't one inch above her ignorantly round, clearly over-exercised ass.

"This is Troy, Miata," Julian said. "Troy, this is Miata." *Well, I was introduced. What next? Do I get to smack the bitch now or later?* I smiled and nodded my head. "Miata's an intern at the hospital."

"Great," I said. Then there was complete silence. I rubbed Pookie's back, trying to figure out when Julian was going to introduce me. *Me. Hello, it's me. Troy, your girlfriend. Your future wife . . . Mrs. Julian James. That's what you said when we took that picture on New Year's . . . say it now . . . say it now!*

But still there was just silence.

"Oh, I'm sorry," Julian said just as I was about to burst into tears. "This is Troy. Troy's in law school here at NYU."

"Okay," Miata said.

I looked past her and saw Tasha standing on the other side of the fountain. She had her hands on her hips and she was saying something to me. I couldn't hear her, but by the look on her face, it was bad. "Stand your ground" was about all I could make out, trying to read her lips. "Stand your ground."

"I'm Julian's girlfriend," I blurted out before giving my mind enough time to catch up with my mouth.

Miata looked stunned. She nearly dropped the ice cream cone. And while Pookie looked happy his parents finally had tied the knot, Julian looked like I'd just told him his mother died. I knew I was breaking some awful dating rule by declaring the magnitude of our relationship without Julian's approval, but I was losing my cool. I could only imagine the nerdy convo they shared about the latest in syringe technology and cell growth. *Who did this heifer think she was, anyway?* I'm Troy Helene Smith. She can't just come in and take my man. In the eleven months we'd been together, we'd built up a history: movies, dinners, trips, family outings. *We were in love.*

"Oh, this is her?" Miata turned to look at Julian. He nodded and she looked back at me. "The woman he loves?" I wanted to believe that she was saying it in a sweet, "let's celebrate your black love" kind of way, but in reality her voice was an Erica Kane–like mix of snot and smug.

"Well," Julian managed, stuttering. "Well, this *is* Troy."

Miata shifted her hips and grinned slyly. I put the dog down and poked out my chest. I had never had a fight in my life, but if she was looking for one, she'd found it. Plus, my girls were just a few feet away.

"Well, Julian," she said, licking her ice cream cone, "I'll just leave you with *this person.* You know where to find me . . . when you're ready to stop playing Barbie and Ken."

"Excuse me?" I asked.

"Something I said you didn't understand?" she asked coolly. She clearly was trying to make me lose my cool and embarrass myself, because Julian had this dumb look on his face like he had no clue she was insulting me. "I swear, NYU must do something about its open-admissions policy."

This woman was the devil. I had nothing to say to that. No defense. At that moment, I wasn't even sure what I could say to that. I just really wanted to hit her. But then I'd look like the bad, irrational, crazy girl, and that was what she wanted.

I looked back toward Tasha. She was shaking her head. "Say anything," I made out from her lips.

"Well, I think it's a good school," I said. *What? That's all I could think of to say?*

"Okay," Miata said. "Whatever." She tossed the ice cream in the garbage and looked back at Julian. "Call me," she said.

Before I could put the dog down and jump on her, she

turned and walked away, looking as calm and collected as she had when I'd first laid eyes on her.

I wanted to throw something at her: a rock, some scissors, darts, some of Pookie's shit. But I was standing there stunned, flabbergasted, aghast. Hell, I thought women like that only existed on television. I needed backup quick.

Julian didn't speak to me the entire walk back to my place. We stopped at a little grocery store to pick up some dog food, but that was the extent of our conversation. I was beginning to feel like I'd made a huge mistake, walking up on him in the park like that. I mean, I didn't know if they were dating or what. All I had on him was a shared ice cream cone. Miata had made it clear that she knew he had a girlfriend. She didn't look even a little bit surprised when I said I was his girlfriend. Maybe I was wrong; maybe I was being childish and risked losing him altogether.

I slipped my key in the door when we got back to my place and just as I was about to apologize for my little stunt, Julian grabbed my arm.

"Don't go in," he said, pulling my arm away from the door. "I have to talk about this first."

"Okay," I answered, certain he was about to break up with me.

"I'm sorry. I don't know what I was thinking." Julian looked into my eyes and I could tell he was sincere. For the first time since we'd left the park, I looked at his face and noticed that his eyes were red. "I would never hurt you and I'm just mad you had to find out about her like this."

"Who is she, Julian?"

"I did meet her at the hospital, like I said." Julian took a deep breath and put his hands in his pockets. "I only wanted to be friends at first but she wanted more. She made a pass at me and . . . I guess I just went for it."

"But why? What do you see in that girl?" I asked. Other

than the fact that she was going to be a doctor, which, if they got together would make their union the eighth of its kind in the James family—something I always knew Julian wanted— she just didn't seem like his type.

"I don't know. She's just different—not what I'm used to." He paused. "But it doesn't matter. She doesn't mean anything to me. I just hope you can forgive me." Julian took Pookie Po from my arms, put him on the ground, and pulled me close to him. "You forgive me, baby?"

"Yes," I said. I closed my eyes and vowed never to bring up the incident again.

"Earth to Troy . . . Earth to Troy," Tasha said. I opened my eyes to find both her and Tamia looking at me intently.

"No," I answered, remembering that night at my apartment. "No, he doesn't love her. He loves me."

"Exactly. That's just what I wanted to know," Tasha announced.

"And?" Tamia asked.

"And . . . my point is this: Troy loves Julian, Julian loves Troy, and Julian doesn't love Miata." Tasha counted off each of the points on her hand.

"So why is he in there with Miata?" Tamia jumped in again.

"Exactly, and what's Troy going to do about it?" Tasha said, whipping her head around to look at me.

"What's Troy going to do about it?" I asked, referring to myself in the third person—Tasha's rationale does that to you sometimes.

"I'll tell you what you're going to do. . . . Oh, I'll tell you what you're going to do," Tasha said, sitting back in the center of the backseat. She sounded like the Wicked Witch of the West putting together a plot to kill Dorothy. "You're going to take her man."

"Now I know you're crazy." Tamia tried to turn the ignition again. "We're leaving. Where's your car, Troy?"

"No, listen," Tasha said, stopping Tamia from turning the ignition. "Troy gave us all of the facts. This is real love. While Julian is confused right now by that hoe, what they share is real love. I don't know about you, but I believe her. I believe her and I'm going to support her."

"No, you want Troy to be desperate and chase some man around. That's childish. I say, and I do believe I'm the only sane one in this damn car right now," Tamia said, looking at me, "I say, if Julian loves Troy he'll come back to her on his own. She'll have him if she waits."

"See, that's what I'm talking about, Tamia. Why do we always have to wait? I don't know about you ladies, but I'm tired of waiting to exhale. I'm ready to beat down that hoe! She clearly has some kind of voodoo spell over poor Julian." We all laughed. "All I'm saying is, anything worth having is worth fighting for, Tamia. Like how I fought for my husband," Tasha said, waving her wedding ring in the front seat.

"You didn't have to fight for shit with Lionel. He loves you so much he'd drink your bathwater," Tamia said. She had a point. Lionel loved two things: basketball and Tasha. He showered her with all of the love any woman could desire— the one thing I know in my heart she was in search of when she jumped in that car and left L.A. all those years ago. Due to her insecurities, Tasha was used by old boyfriends, but Lionel adored her. And he wasn't a bad catch either. He was Haitian and Peruvian and had the kind of impeccable dark chocolate skin that you had to look at twice to be sure the man wasn't wearing some kind of makeup. He was well over seven feet tall, with a hunky build and had the cutest dimples I'd ever seen on a grown man. He was more than easy to look at. While I was sure a baby was nowhere in the near future for him and Tasha, between the two of them, when it did happen, the baby would be born with the kind of unearthly cuteness that would make all of the other babies born on that day refuse any nursery photos.

"Yeah, how do you think I made that happen? Lionel loves me, but Lionel has a dick. We had some drama along the way, just like everyone else. I'm not stupid. Now, listen to me, 'smart girls.' When you meet a man, you plan your outfit, what to eat so you don't look stupid at the table, when he can kiss you, when you will accept another date, and when you will invite him to your bed. You plan everything," Tasha said.

Tamia and I couldn't help but nod our heads along with her. She sounded like she was giving the "get-a-man gospel."

"So why not plan a way to get and keep your man? That's our damn problem. We get a man and stop damn planning. Stop getting our nails done, complimenting him, dressing nice, talking about interesting things. Pretty soon, we stop planning interesting things to do in the bedroom. You know what happens then?" Tasha pushed her head back into the front seat. "Your man ends up at some damn half-fancy black restaurant with a bitch named after a fucking cheap car. And why?"

"Why?" Tamia asked.

"Because the other woman had a plan," Tasha said. "See, you two don't experience dealing with chicks like Miata, but I do. I know those girls like the back of my hand. She's a hustler. She's a smart hustler who's hustled your doctor away from you."

"That's crazy," Tamia said. "The girl is going to be a doctor herself. She'll have her own money. Why would she need to marry a doctor?"

"Girl, what's better than one doctor? Two! Please, from the moment I laid eyes on that girl I knew she was a ghetto girl on the come up. She's smart. She's smart and she had a plan . . . a plan to take Troy's man. Trust me. I know all this time she's been in that hospital, she's been dragging her thang around Julian, looking all sweet and smart, going over medical stuff out loud like a damn dictionary. Black men love that stuff. Especially the ones who know what in the hell she's talking about. She's probably being everything Troy isn't."

"What are you saying about me?"

"I'm not saying you're dumb, sweetie;" she said with a smile, "but come on. Julian is your man. He knows the fun you; he doesn't see you in the classroom playing super lawyer. He doesn't really get to see on a daily basis how smart you are. Miata knows that and she's probably been trolling her ass around the hospital, giving him advice about you and making you seem like the most vain, superficial person in her world. She's been telling Julian her stories about getting out of the ghetto, making herself look like the best thing since sliced bread to your man. I know it. Trust me."

"Well, what am I supposed to do about it?" I asked.

"No, Troy. This is so unhealthy," Tamia interrupted.

"Listen to her and you'll be alone, with her." Tasha put her hand up in front of Tamia's mouth and Tamia pushed her away.

"What do you want me to do?" I asked again. To be honest, I thought both of them were right. But I wasn't ready to give up my man just yet. Like Millie Jackson said in that old song, "Ain't no woman in her right mind gonna sit back and let another woman come in and take her man—if he's really worth having." Julian was worth having.

"Listen very closely, because I can't repeat these words and you must do them in this exact order," Tasha said in her usual theatrical fashion.

"Why can't you say it again? Is that from *The Book of Hoes* or something?" Tamia giggled.

"Tamia!" I said, annoyed but equally amused. Tasha was pretty much a card-carrying member of the Former Hoe Club of America. She wasn't one of those nasty crackhead skeezer hoes or anything. She just had skills and wasn't afraid to bite and be bitten. It obviously had paid off. She was wearing a six-carat Harry Winston.

"First and foremost, I have to repeat one thing: In order to get him back, you have to be sure he really loves you and not her. Before you begin the plan, you need to really think about that, Troy. Like tonight, I want you to go over the entire situation in your head. You must be sure that he loves you and be sure that he's worth it. If you answer no to either one of those questions, there's no need to try to break her spell over him. All you need to do if you even suspect that he loves her over you is move on with your life. Okay?" I nodded my head at Tasha's request. "Okay," she went on, "once you're sure his heart is with you, you start the 'Take Her Man Plan.' "

"Where does she come up with this stuff?" Tamia laughed.

Tasha growled at Tamia again and then she went right into the plan to help me get Julian back from Miata. She explained that from that point on, I had to think of Julian as "Miata's man" because that was how Miata stole him from me in the first place. She was the new, fresh thing in Julian's life. She was the greener grass when I was the old nagging hay. Now the tables had to be turned. I was now single and I actually had the green-grass allure. I just had to use it to my advantage. Making him "her man" essentially made me the new, fresh thing in his life.

After she explained the whole role-reversal scenario, Tasha went into the actual plan, which she claimed she got from some white girl in her apartment building. Over coffee in the lobby, the white girl said the six-point plan apparently was something many women had been using for years. She told Tasha that there was a rumor that the plan was actually how Diddy's baby mama got him back from that J. Lo and her big booty. Now that's results.

"Step one," Tasha said, jumping into the steps. She ran down the first few quickly, stopping along the way only when Tamia protested for some reason or another.

"You mean be a helpless little girl?" Tamia said, rolling her eyes when Tasha made her way to one of the points— The Damsel in Distress.

"No, not helpless, but worthy of rescue," Tasha said, defending the point.

"Are you kidding me? You want her to be a 'damsel in distress'? That's silly. It's 2007; that's the kind of crap that brings women back like one hundred years as a sex."

"Oh, Tamia, please. Don't act like you don't turn on that girlie stuff when you need something from a man . . . smiling all sweet. You're no damn Angela Davis yourself."

We all started laughing. I couldn't tell if it was because Tasha was completely right about Tamia or that we were surprised that Tasha knew who in the hell Angela Davis was. I guess she did read those books in college.

"No, Tasha's right," I said. "I read in this magazine once that all men have this superman complex or ego thing that makes them feel a need to be needed by people—like a superhero or something. It said when they're not being used, they feel useless and find someone who will use them or make them feel needed."

"And how are you supposed to do that if you really don't need them to do anything? Why should you pretend you can't?" Tamia asked, still annoyed.

"Well, for me and Lionel it's simple," Tasha said. "I let him do all the crap I don't want to do around the house. It's his job to make sure the cars are working and fix stuff when it breaks. I make him take the garbage out and when we get in the car, I make him drive—even though I say where we're going." She smiled. "I'm saying, those are things I don't want to do."

"I just think it's too late in the game to go giving my power away like that," Tamia said. "I have a problem when someone expects me to do something . . . like cook and clean and care for children. Then they have the power."

"It's not about power, Tamia," I said. "It's about sharing your life and admitting that you don't have to do it all alone. The days of the strong black woman carrying it all on her back are way done and over. I say, if you can find a strong man willing to carry his weight, you should let him. Loosen up your own load. I wish I had someone to take my garbage out."

"Exactly, Troy," Tasha said, continuing with the rest of the plan. I sat still in my seat listening as it all came together like a puzzle in my mind—the change, the makeover, the sweet smile I had to give to get my man back from that woman's lure. It was such an elaborate scheme—a wicked plot of reversal of fortune that made so much sense I wondered why the three of us hadn't come up with it on our own a few heartbreaks ago.

"And if it doesn't work—if this whole shim sham doesn't work, what will Troy do?" Tamia asked when Tasha concluded the outline with one long exhale. She turned on the car and drove away from Justin's. "What will Troy have then, other than a broken heart?"

"Then Ms. Lovesong will look better because she's had a makeover, she'll have met a new guy because she's been dating other people, and she will have had a chance to really tell Julian how she felt about him without being angry." Tasha reached over the seat and gave me a hug just as Tamia pulled up in front of the lot where I'd parked my car.

I kissed her on the cheek and took a short sigh of relief. I had felt so powerless shuffling out of the restaurant like I had done something wrong. But now I felt like I had something to do with my pain, the big swelling sea of doubt that was raging in my stomach. I wasn't gonna waste another minute crying and being angry about Miata. I was gonna get my man back and live my happily ever after. The Take Her Man Plan was on.

"Wait, Troy," Tasha called as I turned to walk toward my car. "Just remember one last thing: The plan must be put into action in the exact order it is given. If Julian truly loves you, and not Miata, he'll come back to you. It may take three days . . . it might take three months, but he'll come back. . . . Just be ready and look marvelous, Ms. Lovesong." She poked her head out of the back window. "In the meantime, don't stop living. Move on with your life. Join a gym. Take a knitting class. Do something you've always wanted to do. But be ready to answer the phone when Julian calls . . . just not on the first ring." She blew me a kiss, Tamia tooted the horn, and they were off.

The Take Her Man Plan: I Declare War!

So your man walked out the door and into someone else's arms. He said it's over and you just can't understand why. You're sure he loves you and that he's "the one." Don't spend money calling a psychic to see what the stars have in store for you; change your own stars by taking back what was yours in the first place. Follow these Six Steps to Success and he'll come crawling back in no time.

Six Steps to Success

1. *Light as a Feather (Not Stiff as a Board)—Let go of the past and move forward with an open heart. Hold no grudges against your dearly departed and assure him that you are his friend. Be just as light and easy as you were when the two of you first met. Don't expect anything, stop asking those annoying relationship questions, and stop, Stop planning. Be easy and breezy, because this most likely is how you got him in the first place.*

   Finally, no matter how much you want to, don't bring "her" up. This will only exacerbate the situation and put a damper on things. Just be patient. It's your time with him. Do you, and remember the witch will be gone soon.

2. *Change, Change, Change—Usually when men cheat it's a sign of boredom in their current relationship. Men are simple creatures and the slightest sign of regularity turns them into panting puppies begging to roam free. This is probably why your man began to stray initially. Face it, since you've been spending all of your time on him and too little on yourself, you're stuck in a beauty-less rut you never intended to get into in the first place. Since you two started dating,*

*you've probably put on a few pounds from all of the
free late-night dinners and breakfasts in bed. Your hair
color is grown out and your gray is showing because
you haven't had time to make it to the salon between
your dates·with Prince Charming. Your once perfect
"single girl with lots of time on her hands" manicure
has now turned into a botched home job because
you've run out of time to visit the nail shop. And worst
of all, you probably keep wearing the same outfits because you've already decided that you know what he
likes. This old house is falling apart and in need of
total renovation. Get a new look to keep your old man
guessing. Get a new hairstyle, renew your contract at
the gym, keep those nails fresh, purchase a couple new
pieces for your wardrobe, and buy a new shade of lip-.
stick. It's a new you for you . . . the only bonus is that
he'll surely come sniffing. That's what got his attention
in the first place—what he saw visually. If you can
turn his head once, you can turn it twice more.*

3. *Say You, Say Me—After you've adapted to your new
look and flaunted it before his dancing eyes, it's time
to remember what things about your personality attracted your ex to you in the first place. Were you funny?
Did you read him poetry? Did you laugh at all of his
jokes? Whatever it was, remember it and remind him
of those qualities by being yourself. Remind him of the
cool you and the good times you two used to spend together—the camping trip in the Rocky Mountains, the
fishing trip with his parents, the time you two had sex
in a public restroom. This will make him begin to dwell
on the past and remember that the grass was actually
greener on your side . . . Don't be surprised if you get
a few late-night calls during this stage. He may even
try to come back to you, but remember that every step*

of the plan must be completed to make sure he won't go roaming again. He's got to work to get you back.

4. *Fellas, There's a Jealous Boy in This Town*—Nothing gets a man's blood boiling like plain old jealousy. Fight fire with fire by making sure your old beau sees you with a new one. And it can't just be any new beau—this man must be fine and obvious competition. And if history repeats itself, as it always has with just about every man since the beginning of time, he'll react by attacking the situation head-on. He'll want to know who the guy is and where he came from. Out of anger and confusion, he may try to accuse you of sneaking around when you two were together. Don't reveal anything. Be vague with your answers. If he asks what you two have been up to, say, 'A little bit of this and a little bit of that,' and then rush off of the phone, because your Chinese food is at the door.

   Now, the hardest part of this step is that his jealousy may lead him to try to get you back. And this doesn't mean he'll try to get you back mentally. He'll try to get you back physically. Sorry to say it, but it's kind of like how dogs pee on trees to mark their territory. If one dog even senses that another dog has urinated on his tree, he'll try to spray his special scent all over it. Don't be offended, of course. No one's saying you're a tree and no one's peeing on you. It's just a man law of nature. So, he'll try to get you into the sack. But be strong. Cross your legs . . . um, fingers.

5. *The Damsel in Distress: Oops, I Did it Again*—(This is a tricky one for all those independent sisters.) Though they try to act like they don't, men love to feel needed. You can be the smartest woman alive, but don't touch the damn barbecue grill, mama. He may admire you

for this and initially be attracted to you because of your independence. But the day he realizes you don't need him, he's about as gone as last month's period. Stop trying to take on the world all by yourself, sister. Create a random act of need . . . a kitten in a tree, you fell while bicycling, your apartment is being painted and you need a place to stay. Then ask for his help. And when the moment comes, simply thank him for being there for you during your time of need. Say, 'I don't know what I would've done without you.' But the thing is, don't appear too needy. Men hate needy women. So don't turn on the waterworks, and whatever you do, don't beg him for anything. Just allow his help to be at his suggestion—not yours.

Remember, if you were successful with the first four steps, he's dying to be with you. Think of him as a woman with a credit card (with no limit) and you're a pair of suede Gucci boots . . . it's about to go down. He will acquiesce, and if things go as planned, you will wake up the next morning by his side . . . leading to step . . .

6. *Let Your Feelings Be Known—Now it's time to open up and let him know how you feel about him. Tell him how much you love him and how much it hurt when he left. Tell him how it feels when he holds you, how he makes you smile when you think you've run out of reasons. Don't be pushy or suggest that you get back together. That's his job after he hears you out. Don't worry . . . he will. Remember, by this point, he's panting, begging to be with you. His mind is telling him so many things and when you express your feelings in a noncommittal way, he'll jump right in to claim his prize. That's you.*

Jesus Loves Harlem, Too

I fell in love with the golf course at my parents' country club when I was still too small to realize just how big the world was. I'd traveled to many foreign places and seen many strange things by the time I was ten, but as I sat in my father's golf cart, watching him play round after round on those big rolling greens that seemed to be continuously manicured, everything else seemed sad, dull, flat, and gray in comparison. I never really understood the game Daddy was playing with his friends, but I adored looking at the tall hills that seemed to stretch on and on until forever, the pretty pink flowers that bloomed in the spring, and the trees that hung strategically to provide us with shade.

While there were a few very rotten apples in the mostly white bunch, the people there were friendly. My dad's friends would give me chocolates and their wives doted on me all afternoon. "I'd die for this olive-colored skin. It's so exotic how it tans so beautifully in the sun. You look like Liz Taylor in *Cleopatra,*" one woman said to me, pinching my cheek with her glittery, diamond-clad fingers when I was twelve. My mother was furious when I returned home, bragging about what I took for kind words. She told me that the next time one of the club house women said such a thing, I should tell them that both Cleopatra and I were black. I didn't understand this statement then. It sounded like more of my mother's anger coming out. But later I'd learn that Liz Taylor was a white woman, playing a black woman in what my mother called "black face." The more I learned about my family history of women pretending to be something they weren't, the more I understood why my mother wanted me to have nothing to do with such a comparison. But I let that go. As a young girl, the doting still felt good, and being with my father felt even better. Daddy usually would rush over and beg for more time to play. "It'll only be a little while longer, T.H.," he'd assure me, using my first initials—Troy Helene. He'd pat me on the head and say he knew I was tired of being at the golf course with "old Dad," but he was wrong about me being tired of the golf course and, more important, about being with him.

I loved being on the golf course with my father. I loved it mostly because of how he was when we were there. Daddy smiled, laughed, and told jokes with the other guys when he played golf. He seemed so happy, so in control, and at peace with every terrain we encountered in the little cart. We talked about school, my friends, and even all of the boyfriends he intended to make ex-boyfriends. He asked about my dreams, my goals, and everything I wanted out of life, and he listened as I listed each one as they came to me, never laughing when I changed my mind along the way. Together we'd plan for my future, laugh at old stories he told me about growing up in Harlem, and just relax in the New York heat.

Those comforting memories led me to ask my father to meet me at the country club the morning after the Justin's debacle. After all the drama I'd been through the night before, I just wanted to feel safe and at peace, sit in a tiny golf cart, and daydream the day away as my daddy played another round like nothing had ever happened to change my world. I didn't realize how much seeing Julian with Miata had affected me until I got home and was sitting in my apartment all by myself. Lying in bed, I prayed that Julian would just show up and say everything that had happened was just some big joke. But he never came, and even after one Ambien, I didn't sleep a wink. I just threw on an old Seal CD and stared out of my bedroom window watching the ceaseless downtown Chelsea traffic. When the sun came up and Pookie Po came running to get me for his morning walk, I knew just what I had to do to find a way out of my funk. I called my daddy and told him about Julian after making him promise not to breathe a single word of disaster to my mother—the last thing I needed was her overreacting. He was cool as usual, insisting that I meet him at the country club before I even made a suggestion.

"T.H.!" Daddy said, stepping out of his car in front of the clubhouse where we'd agreed to meet up. He handed the valet his key and grinned at me just enough to make everyone around us imagine how handsome he must have been when he was a young man. "I'm so glad you came out here to meet me," he went on. "I don't get to see you much now with you being a law school big shot and everything."

"Oh stop it, Daddy," I said, laughing. "I'm never too busy for you."

My father had beamed when I mentioned during my sophomore year that I was considering law school. Between my mother, Nana Rue, and Grandma Lucy, I'll admit that I was pretty spoiled by the time I left my parents' house for college. While my mother tried her best to keep me "independent and strong," you can't help but be a bit corrupt growing up in a penthouse on the Upper West Side. Other kids grew up begging their parents to buy them fancy clothes and leather sneakers, but most of my wardrobe came free from the studios of designers trying to get in good with my father's mother, Nana Rue—a New York stage actress. So, from RL to Burberry, I wore it—*and well, might I add.* I seldom had to want or wish for anything other than a break from playing dress up in all the stuff that seemed to magically appear in my bedroom—sometimes despite my mother's best efforts. I was a bona fide budding brat. However, all that changed when I arrived at Howard and was forced—via my mother—to live in the dorms my first two years.

There I met people who had to bust their behinds just to stay in school. My first roommate worked two part-time jobs just to pay her tuition. LaKeisha was from St. Louis, and one night she told me that she would either be dead or on her way to her deathbed if she'd stayed there. She showed me these cuts she had on her arms from joining a gang when she was just ten years old. I couldn't believe it. I mean, I guess in my ignorance I just assumed that stuff didn't really happen to people.

My relationship with LaKeisha wasn't exactly grand after she told me about her past. Because of my disbelief, I kept bringing it up and she must've grown tired of my constant quizzing, because she cursed me out. "You're a silly bitch," she said to me one day in the cafeteria after I asked her to show another girl the cuts on her arms. "My life ain't no damn after-school special. I told you about it because I trusted you. So much for that shit, white girl." She looked completely violated that I'd brought it up and didn't speak to me for weeks. When I came back from Christmas break, my dorm director said LaKeisha had switched dorms.

I felt like a complete asshole, but it was a lesson I needed to learn. My circle was small until I went to Howard. It was composed of a select group of black Jack and Jill kids and white classmates from school. All privileged, all far from harm's way. We were basically cookie-cutter kids who'd had the world promised to us, or so our parents wanted us to believe.

I know it sounds corny but after I tried unsuccessfully to

contact LaKeisha several times to apologize for my insensitivity, I decided that I needed to do something about the information she'd given me. It wasn't enough for me to just be aware; I felt a need to get out and act, really do something. So I decided to try to help children who found themselves in situations like LaKeisha's. After interning at the Children's Defense Fund in D.C., I realized that the best way I could do this was in the courtroom. Going to law school to be a children's advocate was a hard decision—little money and less acclaim—but it was what I was most passionate about, and it made my daddy proud.

"Please, girl, you're just saying you're never too busy because I'm the one picking up that fat law school tab," my father said, reaching out for me in front of the country club. "Come give your dad a big hug."

Walking up to the car to hug him, I looked over his shoulder and noticed a man getting out of the other side of the car. *Tall,* I thought almost immediately. The brother was stretching out to be at least six-four. He was pretty handsome, too, and I could tell that he was younger than most of my dad's other friends by the way his chocolate skin wrapped tightly around his flawless features.

"T.H., this is Reverend Hall from First Baptist," my father said, noticing my short stare.

"Hey, that's Reverend *Dr.* Hall to you, Mr. Money Bags," he joked, taking my hand. "But you can call me Kyle." He grinned at me and opened the door to the clubhouse for me to enter. "I am off the clock."

As I passed by him, I could see that he had good taste. He had on a cream Polo golf shirt with khakis. It was a classic and unpretentious country club look—the direct opposite of my father, who seemed to be going for old man pastels and plaids these days. *Kinda sexy, Rev,* I thought, watching him walk by. *But what the hell was he doing with my father on golf day?* I'd told my father about my breakup with Julian over the phone. I'd told him I was coming to the course to spend time with him . . . alone. I wasn't in the mood to share his attention. I just needed two ears, not four—I'd had enough of that the night before.

"Reverend Hall and I were about to have breakfast. You want to join us?" My father smiled, looking as if he was reading all of my doubts as they bumped around in my mind.

"But, Daddy, I came to watch *you* play golf," I said, trying not to sound upset.

"I know, T.H. But Reverend Hall and I have a venture we're working on down in Harlem and, well, I just can't get this guy out here. This is really the only time. Do you under-stand?" my father asked in front of Kyle.

I always hated it when people asked me questions in front of other people. It was almost as if I was being forced to be the bigger person to save face. I mean, I couldn't exactly say, "Hell, no. Tell his ass to go home so I can cry my eyes out on my daddy's shoulder alone." That would make me sound spoiled and selfish. So I had to settle . . .

"That's fine, Daddy," I said, gritting my teeth. He signaled for a table and off we were. Great, breakfast with a monk. That's just what I needed after my breakup with the love of my life. Maybe *Rev. Dr. Hall* could bless my breakup and talk me into joining some nunnery upstate. I know it sounds bad, but give a girl a break. I go to church every Sunday and I tithe—and I don't have a job! But there's a time and place to spend time with your "sanctified" friends. For example, I wouldn't invite my saved friend Sheena to a strip club, and it would be a bad idea to ask my pastor out for drinks on a Fri-day night. It's wrong. Too much temptation for them; too much censorship for me. Point-blank, it just wasn't a good time for me to sit across the table from *Rev. Dr. Hall.* I could just imagine what he would say when I stabbed my smoked salmon, Julian's favorite, repeatedly with a knife. He wouldn't understand. He'd probably want to pray over me . . . wash the demons away.

"I'm actually glad to meet you, Troy," Kyle said, pulling

out my chair. "Your dad talks about you so much." I gave Dad the evil eye from behind my menu. "I think it's great— the work you're doing with the kids down at the Kids in Motion Settlement."

I lowered my menu and looked across the table at Kyle. Had my father really told him about the volunteer work I do at the artistic community center? I didn't think my father knew much about it. I mean, I talked to him and my mother about the little girls in the ballet class I taught, but I didn't think he thought much of it. It wasn't exactly bringing in any clear profits.

"Thank you," I said. "So how's Mom?" I asked, deliberately pointing a question at my father. I didn't have him to myself, but I at least wanted to talk to him.

"She's fine. Just busying herself with a bunch of stuff." My father rolled his eyes playfully. "You know your mother."

"Did she give you drama this morning about coming out?"

"No, she took Desta to her GED class this morning," my father answered, referring to their maid. Desta was an Ethiopian immigrant my mother hired about two years ago. When she started, she could barely speak English and she'd never been to school. My mother made getting an education a part of Desta's duties. Mom said that she didn't see the sense in having someone clean her house for the rest of her life. She explained that she wasn't helping her if all she gave her was a check and a broom. "That way she'll always be a maid, cleaning people's houses. That's no way to live," she said.

"That's cool," I said.

"Yep, she's been stalking that poor girl," my father said. "And it's good too, because Desta finally got a divorce from that crazy husband of hers and they're sending her kids over soon."

"So what kind of project are you two working on in Harlem?" I asked, watching out of the corner of my eye as Kyle ordered his food.

"Oh, some real estate stuff," Kyle jumped in. "Your dad and I are about to save Harlem."

"Save it?"

"Oh, just buying some real estate, baby. Just a bunch of old forgotten buildings no one wants," my father replied, sipping on a cup of coffee the waitress brought over.

"But they do want the buildings," Kyle said. "The rich white investors want them and so do the black residents of Harlem. The residents just can't afford them and the rich know that. So they buy low, renovate, and sell high to white buyers. Good old gentrification. The new whitewashing of Harlem."

"That's a bad situation," I said.

"It's not just bad, Troy. It's wrong. Most of those people have been living in the very houses we're buying for generations. They've been living there and renting for years—just throwing away money that could belong to their families through homeownership."

"So where do you two come in?"

"Well, we plan to buy the land and start putting some of the money back into the community," Kyle said. "First Baptist can do scholarships, fix up the block, get the people to really care about the community again. The church can get them to take ownership in making and keeping *their* Harlem nice. We'll also keep the rent reasonable for the tenants who already live in the buildings. Many of the landlords over there are charging them exorbitant rates."

"Why?" I asked, watching the passion grow in Kyle's eyes. I could see that he really felt what he was saying.

"To be honest, I think they're trying to drive them out. They're charging them double and triple what the places are worth, trying to get a *different* crowd in there. It's a real bad deal, too, for the people who live there. It not only makes saving money impossible, but it keeps their credit bad because they're pretty much living off of what little credit they have to make ends meet—not to mention being late on almost all of their bills," Kyle went on. "So by keeping the rent low, we're actually helping them, because then they can get into one of the homeownership programs at the church and work toward buying the property from us in the future. The sky's the limit. All we need is this man right here to come on board with the investment money." Kyle pointed to my father.

By the time we finished eating, Daddy and Kyle had shared their entire secret plot to save Harlem from ruin. I was so excited about their plan, I almost forgot about Julian and the reason I'd gone to the country club in the first place. Other than the fact that I kept checking my cell phone every five minutes to see if Julian had called, I was as cool as mint gum.

I also learned a bit more about the good Rev. Dr. Kyle Hall IV. A graduate of both Morehouse and Morehouse's School of Religion—just like his uncle, father, grandfather, and great-grandfather, Kyle was what I like to call Holy Royalty.

Nana once told me that back in the day, the big black moneymakers were teachers, doctors, preachers—the latter making the most money. Folks like Kyle's great-grandfather not only organized and owned churches, but they were also insurance men, real estate investors, and business owners. They were pillars in their communities. They had memberships in the best clubs and all the right connections in town. These connections included white people, who used the black preachers to get the favor of the community during election time.

Preachers and preachers' sons (who were practically groomed to be preachers themselves) were treated like gold. That's where Kyle came into the picture in his family. After talking to him, I learned that he was pretty much destined to be a preacher. He grew up in his daddy's church in Memphis. He was giving his own sermons by the time he was twelve. He skipped the twelfth grade to go to Morehouse a year early.

There, Kyle led an on-campus Christian crusade ministry, pledged my father's fraternity, Omega Psi Phi, and was student body president. He graduated in three—yes, three years—and walked across the street to the School of Religion to "follow the call of the Lord" (those were his exact words). When he graduated from the School of Religion, he went home to Memphis to help out with his father's church. He explained to me that it was way too much pressure on him trying to find his way in his father's church, so he headed north to help his uncle out with his church in Harlem. Two years later, his uncle retired and turned the church over to him. That's where he'd been for the past five years, and he didn't plan on leaving anytime soon. Is that all? No, Kyle has no children, lives alone, and has a Jack Russell named Luke. *Damn, I'm good.*

He was an interesting character. Not only was he handsome, in a Morris Chestnut kind of way, but he was also easy to talk to and passionate about what he did.

All in all, while Kyle had an ongoing date with the Lord, he was a nice guy. I mean, he was cool. I'd never date him; I just wouldn't make a good pastor's wife. I hate church hats and I like drinking and dancing too much. I'm saying, Kyle seemed like a great guy, but great and dateable are two different things. Kyle was a good boy and while I tended to be a bit conservative when it came to taste and style, I was definitely a bad girl. We may as well have been oil and water trying to mix at that table.

"Did you have a good time?" Daddy asked as we stood in front of the country club, waiting for the valet to bring my car around. He'd insisted on walking me out when I said my goodbyes.

"Everything was cool. It was great to get out here to see you," I said. It was after noon. We'd spent over three hours talking and laughing at that table.

"Well, I'm glad you did." He patted me softly on the back. "So how did you like Reverend Hall?"

"He's a nice guy."

"Well, to be honest, I invited him out here on purpose today. I lied earlier. I haven't been trying to get to him, he's been trying to get to me."

"Why'd you lie, Daddy?" I asked, horrified that my father wanted to hook me up. *Was I that pitiful?*

"Because I wanted you two to meet and I figured without Julian in the—"

"Whoa . . . Dad," I broke in. "Who said anything about hooking me up? I *so* don't need a hookup, Dad." I covered my face with my hands in embarrassment. I was so humiliated. *Did he tell Kyle I needed to be hooked up? What did he say? "Hey, Rev, my daughter is so desperate, I need to find her a damn date, even if it's a preacher"?*

"Well, I just thought it would help," my father said, pulling my hands from my face. "I know what you're thinking. But don't worry, I didn't tell him anything about you being here or the breakup. He was just as surprised as you were."

"Good." I noticed the valet pulling up with my car. "And don't you get any more ideas, Dad. I'm not interested in this guy. Not even a little."

"I know. Now give an old man a hug before you go." He pulled me into his arms. "Daddy loves you so much, TH. Don't forget that," he said, touching the remaining puff that was still apparent under my eyes. "You don't need to worry about Julian. Just move on."

I walked over to my car and threw my purse inside.

"Why did you and Mom get back together? I mean, after your first divorce?" I asked, not even realizing that it was on my mind. He stepped up to the other side of the car.

"I sat up a couple of nights, reading old magazines and eating like a pig—all the things I promised I would do after the divorce. I even went on a date—"

"Daddy!"

"I'm telling the truth. Your mother knows." He laughed. "But after all of that . . . I just got sad and I realized that I missed your mother. I *really* missed your mother. She can get to me at times, but the woman is just the kind of person you miss having around. That's when it came to me."

"What?" I asked quickly.

"I love her. Your mother can be crazy sometimes. Hell, she's crazy most of the time. She drives me completely crazy." We both laughed. "But she has a good heart and I love her more for it. That's all that matters—that there's only one Mary Elizabeth and I love her *more* than I could ever love anyone else."

I felt tears coming to my eyes. I'd never heard my father speak of my mother so tenderly. It was nice to know a man could love a woman like that.

"Thanks, Dad," I managed between my tears.

"Don't get all teary on me," he said. "Old Dad can take a lot, but not seeing his little girl cry."

"Okay." I took a tissue from my purse and blew my nose.

"See you later, alligator," he said as I slipped into the car.

"In a while, crocodile." I pulled off, watching him watching me in my rearview window.

I listened to my old Donny Hathaway mix CD in the car. There's something about Donny and breakups that just goes together. This man must've been utterly depressed and miserable to sing the way he does, because anytime I listen to the CD, I cry like a big old baby. And that's exactly what I did the entire way back to my apartment. As the trees rolled over the top of my car, I couldn't help but think about Julian. I wondered where he was, what he was doing, whom he was with, and if he was, for only one second, thinking of me. I wondered if he even missed me and thought about how I was doing. I looked down at the phone peeking out at me from my purse and wanted so badly to call him. But I knew better. Calling him at this point would only push him farther away from me, I convinced myself, wiping tear after tear from my eyes.

I pulled the phone out and scrolled down to his number. I just wanted to hear his voice. I just wanted to hear him say hello. I dialed *67 to block my number and pressed the Call button. An anonymous hangup couldn't hurt anyone.

"Hello," a woman's voice said. "Hello?"

I looked down at the phone to see if I'd dialed the wrong number, but it said "Julian" on the screen.

"Is anyone there?" the voice said, giggling. At first I figured it was Julian's mother, but then I realized that I knew the evil voice well. It was the ghetto-ass voice of the chick from the park. It was Miata! "Stop tickling me, Julian," Miata said into the phone. I almost drove off of the bridge. "Someone's on the phone. It could be someone important. Helloooooo?" It was like she was taunting me, like she knew it was me on the other end and she wanted me to hear her voice. "I guess it's no one . . . no one special or they'd answer." She laughed again and the line went dead.

I threw the phone into the backseat. What the hell was going on? It hadn't even been a week since Julian broke up with me and that bitch was already answering his phone? It took him ten months to give me a key to his place and Miata was taking phone calls? Something was wrong. Tasha was right. The hussy had my man under some kind of spell, some kind of sick Louisiana spell. I didn't know what it was, but what I did know was if Miata wanted a man war, she had one.

When I walked into my apartment I headed straight to the refrigerator for my emergency stash of Rocky Road ice cream. I forgot about the bowl and climbed into my bed with the gallon and a spoon. *Who needs a stupid bowl?* I thought, spreading myself out on the bed. I picked up the phone to see if I had any voice messages. There were two: One was from Nana Rue inviting me to a reception for the new play she was headlining, the other was from Daddy, making sure I'd made it home. *None from Julian. None from Julian. None from Julian. None from Julian.* I shoveled ice cream into my mouth.

After watching people parade down the street, laughing and smiling, going on with their lives, *like Julian,* I lowered the blinds in my bedroom and slipped the saddest CDs I could find into my CD carousel, the kind of music every woman listens to when her heart is broken by a man cheating with another woman. There was Jill Scott, Betty Wright, Mary J., Whitney, and, of course, the *Waiting to Exhale* sound track.

Next I put on an old dingy high school T-shirt, pulled my hair up into a lopsided ponytail, and got back into bed.

I must've plowed through half of the gallon of ice cream before deciding to force myself to sleep. I couldn't cry any more. I couldn't call Julian and I couldn't see him. I just wanted to say goodbye to the world for a little while. Since I was just depressed and not psycho enough to kill myself over some man, sleep was the only option. I didn't care if it was just 2 o'clock in the afternoon. I listened to the sad songs on the CD player and rocked myself to sleep.

The 3T Intervention

"*O*pen up, trick," I heard someone who sounded just like Tasha holler like a mad woman. And it was so weird because I was in a park, sitting on a picnic blanket making wedding plans with Julian.

"Open up the damn door or we're coming through it," I heard the voice call again. I looked to the trees and still couldn't see where it was coming from. Then I heard a banging, a loud banging that woke me up from my lovely picnic dream and put me back in my apartment.

"Come on, Troy. These bags are getting heavy," called a voice that sounded like Tamia.

"Hold on. Hold on," I answered.

I opened the door to find Tasha and Tamia, both of whom I can now call crazy, standing in front of my apartment dressed in matching pink Puma sweat suits.

"What are y'all doing here?" I asked, noticing that both of them were carrying paper bags. They pushed their way past me into the apartment. "Why do y'all have bags and why in the hell are y'all dressed alike?"

"Well, we have Chinese food and wine in the bags," Tamia answered. "And we just came from the gym."

"We dress alike at the gym," Tasha said, unloading an arsenal of food on my countertop. "It draws attention, you know, from the guys."

"They always stop and ask if we're twins and drool over our breasts." Tamia giggled. "They can't help it. It's so funny."

"You know, the whole male fantasy thing, twins," Tasha said, handing me two bottles of wine. "Open these."

"But you two look nothing alike." I unscrewed one of the corks. "And you're married."

"I'm married, not blind. Plus, I get a good workout, because they always want to help us, *and* I get to help Tamia meet men," Tasha said.

"She does," Tamia chimed in. "It really works."

"Oh, my God," Tasha said, dropping a carton of what I could see was shrimp lo mein in one of my big serving bowls. She looked at me with apparent shock.

"What?" Tamia and I said at the same time.

"The transformation has already begun." Tasha sucked her teeth.

"What transformation?" I asked, looking down at my outfit.

"Look at you," she said. "You look awful, baby. Where the hell did you find that old-ass T-shirt?" Tasha pointed at my shirt with disgust and looked at Tamia.

"But it's my favorite T-shirt," I said, defending my fashion choice. It was retro. It had a few small holes in it, but other than the bleach spots, you still could make out my school's emblem. But looking down at it, even though I loved the old shirt, I knew Tasha was right. It had to go.

"She's connecting with the past . . . bad symptom," Tamia jumped in, sounding like some fake-ass heartbreak nurse.

"Tamia, go and get this girl something that'll make her look and feel beautiful, *stat,*" Tasha said to Tamia.

"Make that a T-shirt," I called to Tamia as she walked toward my bedroom. "What the hell am I going to be doing walking around you guys looking all cute?"

"Feeling like silk, that's what, Troy," Tasha said, zeroing in on me. "Did you forget rule number two?"

"Change, Change, Change," I said. "I need to remain completely fabulous and look even better the next time Julian sees me. Right?"

"Exactly," Tasha confirmed. "So how are you going to do that looking like a crazy prep-school stalker? I mean, look at you. Your hair looks a mess, your clothes are all jacked up, and you have some kind of chocolate stuff on your upper lip." I wiped my lip to find traces of Rocky Road. "Now, how are you going to be stunning when you see Julian if you look a mess?"

Tamia came rushing back into the kitchen carrying a slinky black nightgown from Victoria's Secret. It was my favorite and she knew it. We'd picked it up at the mall during one of our monthly shopping trips to Long Island.

"I don't know, guys. I was just having a bad day. I was feeling down," I said, more embarrassed about the evidence of my Rocky Road binge than about my outfit.

"Well, that's why we're here." Tamia slipped the T-shirt off over my head. "We figured you were lying in bed, sad and crying—thinking about that Negro. And hadn't eaten anything. So we picked up some Chinese food for nourishment, and wine to wash away your sorrows. We're here to cheer you up."

"Cheer me up? I just want to be alone, you guys," I said, putting the nightgown on. I sighed as it fell over my body. Julian loved how it looked on me. "I really just want to be alone."

"See, that's the problem with women during breakups." Tasha put the last of the Chinese food on my kitchen table. "Men, they stay busy after a breakup. They get out with the fellas, buy a car, invest, date . . . They stay out and about, refusing to admit that they feel any pain," she said, opening the other bottle of wine I'd left sitting on the counter. "But the female species, we like to wallow in our pain, lie in bed sleeping and eating, gaining weight and feeling bad. It's just all really sad and it just puts us at a breakup disadvantage."

I sat down at the table and took a sip of my wine.

"Do you guys think he misses me?" I asked.

"Of course he does," Tamia said. "He probably misses you just as much as you miss him. But he just won't let himself feel it and you know it."

"Exactly, girl," Tasha said, giving Tamia five. "We on the same page." They laughed. "But, really, it's just like I said, he's handling it differently."

"Well, what's up with you guys? I'm tired of thinking about my drama." I shoveled a big spoonful of lo mein and hot mustard into my mouth.

"Well," Tamia started, "following in your footsteps, I'm going to do a spring cleaning." She sat back in her seat. "I just need to clean off my entire roster and start anew."

She was referring to our male clean up. We made up the term when Tasha, out of complete disgust with all the losers she was dating, decided to cut them all off. Afterward, she told Tamia and me how free she felt that she didn't have to talk to any of those losers again. No more wondering where the relationships would go, if they were going to start acting right, none of that. It was Splitsville . . . three times over. Out with the old, in with the new. A true spring cleaning.

"But I thought you liked that guy . . . what's his name, the marketing guy from the record label," Tasha said.

"Jeremy?" I asked. "Yeah, I thought you liked him, too, Tamia."

"Well, ladies, we finally had sex," Tamia said, skewering a tiny shrimp with her fork.

"And? Was it good?" Tasha asked.

"I don't know, ask his penis, Mr. Shrimp." She waved the shrimp in front of us and we all started laughing hysterically.

"I think he had a disease or something—infantile penis. I don't know."

"It wouldn't have been that bad if brother man knew how to work it, but he was just lame," Tamia said.

"I know that's right," Tasha said. "For some reason men still think that size is the only thing that matters."

"Please, I'll take a little man who's going to *smack it up, flip it, and rub it down* over some ten-inch brother who's just going to sit there thinking he's God's gift to the bedroom, any day!" Tamia said, placing the salt shaker next to a bottle of wine.

"So Jeremy didn't even try?" I asked.

"Please, I was lying there just mad that I had to add his ass to the list of men I've had sex with. What a damn waste of a space."

"Oh, his ass doesn't even count," Tasha said with a wicked laugh. "If it was that small, it was just like making out anyway. Like using a tampon." She held up her chopstick.

"Oh, you're wrong for that." I snatched the chopstick.

"No, he was wrong for getting me all excited about Santa and then sending one of his little elves." Tamia snatched the chopstick and handed it back to Tasha.

"Damn, girl. Well, what about Alex from class?" I asked, referring to Tamia's recent walk on the wild side, dating a white guy.

"You know, I like Alex, but I really can't do the whole white/black thing. I just can't trust it." Tamia took a sip of her wine. "I always worry about him having slave-cabin fantasies or something. You know? I just don't think I could—"

"I'm trying to get pregnant," Tasha interrupted Tamia mid-sentence.

"Huh?" I said, nearly choking on my lo mein.

"Oh, now I know the girl is drunk." Tamia dropped her fork. We were all silent. Did Tasha, the ultimate party girl who'd abandoned her own mother, just say she wanted to be a mother?

"No, I am not drunk, Tamia. I've just decided that I want a baby," Tasha said without looking at us. "I'm ready."

"Ready? When did you get ready to have a baby? How? We were just at the gym," Tamia said, looking just as surprised as I felt.

"Wait a minute, Tasha. I think what Tamia means is what made you want a baby?" I asked Tasha delicately.

Tamia and I were sitting there staring at each other with our mouths hanging wide open. It wasn't that Tasha was a bad person or anything. It wasn't even that she was a bad friend, but somebody's mother? I just wasn't sure if I'd bet on the success of that story. There are certain things you just don't expect in life: seeing an alien, being eaten alive by wolves, and hearing that Tasha wanted to be a mother.

"Come on, guys. Y'all are acting as if this is some big shock," Tasha said, holding her wineglass as if we were just sitting in the park discussing our finds at Saks. "I'm married, for Christ's sake. This is just the natural course of life."

"Well, tell us what happened," I said. "When did you come up with this *natural course of life?*"

"Well, it was about a month ago. Lionel and I were bored, so we decided to go for a drive in the city. We ended up walking around, looking at things on St. Mark's Street," Tasha began to explain between sips of wine. "You know, where they have all that punk rock stuff in the Village? Well, we walked into this piercing shop to see if they had studs, and Lionel suggested I get a navel piercing. Y'all know how I feel about piercings."

"You hate them," Tamia said. Tasha always said body piercings were the ultimate symbol of a "cheap trick." While I was impartial to the idea, I had to admit that most of the tricks I knew had piercings.

"Yeah. So Lionel got down on his knees in the store and kissed my navel. It was so cute. Then he said, 'I guess we better not go messing with stuff down here anyway,' and kissed my navel again. When we left the store, I was on cloud nine.

I felt sparks all over my stomach when Lionel was down there. It just felt so right. You know?"

Tamia and I nodded our heads intently. Tasha and Lionel were a match made in heaven. They were good together. But were they ready for a baby?

"Anyway, just before we got back to the car, in the middle of Lionel talking about how the team was going to build up their defense for next season, I asked him if he loved me. Without even stopping to breathe or ask me why I was asking him, he said 'Yes, I love you.'"

"Oh," Tamia and I cooed.

"And it wasn't just any 'I love you,' y'all. It was like the same kind of 'I love you' I heard the first time he said it. It was so real."

"That's beautiful, Tasha," Tamia said, bending across the table to kiss Tasha on her cheek.

"Yeah, but where does the baby come in?" I asked.

"Just there, just right there on the spot, I decided that I wanted to have his children," Tasha answered. Tamia and I looked at each other. That was a big statement. You could date a man, you could love a man, you could even marry a man . . . but saying out loud to the world that you wanted to have his children was pretty big. It was so final. What Tasha had just done—in her own little way—was announce to us that Lionel was the only man she wanted to be with for the rest of her life. It was like the last call for alcohol was coming at the bar and Tasha was heading out the door. I guess Lionel wasn't just going to be her *first* husband like people had said at the wedding. "I decided I wanted a baby and I stopped taking the pill about a week ago," Tasha said.

"Great, did you tell Lionel?" I asked, realizing how silly the question was when it came out.

"Did you tell him?" I heard Tamia say after a moment of silence passed from Tasha's end of the table.

"No, not yet."

"What?"

"What does she mean she didn't tell Lionel?" Tamia's eyes went back and forth between me and Tasha.

"I just haven't. I figured I'd let him know once I got pregnant. Leave all the worrying to me."

"No," Tamia said. "I think you have to tell him, Tasha. It's really selfish if you don't."

"I agree," I said, backing up Tamia.

"Please, Lionel's busy with finals right now. He really doesn't even have time for this."

"What if he's not ready? What if he needs you to wait until the season is over or something? I don't know, but this is wrong, Tasha," Tamia said. "You have to tell him."

"What are you afraid of?" I asked.

"I'm not afraid of anything. I just want to do this my way. That's all." I could tell we were aggravating Tasha. Her eyes were tearing up. "And it's not open for discussion. That's it," she said, wiping a tear. "I was just telling you guys so you would know. I was thinking about making you two the godparents. But if you don't want the job, just let me know. But I'm having my baby." Tasha jumped up from the table and ran toward the bathroom.

I looked at Tamia from across the table.

"Who was that woman?" I asked just as the bathroom door slammed. "Must be the hormones kicking in already."

"Well, she won't be needing this anymore," Tamia said, picking up Tasha's abandoned wineglass. She tipped it up and took the last sip.

The Spring Cleaning: Out with the Old Men, In with the New

"Because a man is like a tissue in a box . . . if you pull it out, there's another one waiting right behind it."

When your love life is in desperate need of a jump start, it may be time to do some old-fashioned spring cleaning. Get rid of those old duds and start anew with a fresh batch of contenders. Think of it as if you're the coach of an NBA team, a losing NBA team, and the only thing standing between you and the championship ring is five lame starting players. The smartest thing you could do is clean off the bench and draft some new blood.

Now, simultaneously dumping each and every one of the men you date is harder than it sounds. Men don't like being dissed (especially the ones you've slept with) and they may get a little defiant. Therefore, you must be quick with the split. Break out your broom and sweep them all up in one fell swoop.

Instructions:

1. *Make a list of all of your soon to be exes and why they have to go (e.g., Michael=cheater, Kevin=cheap bastard, Frank=bad breath).*

2. *E-mail each of them the same note saying that it's over and you don't want to talk about it. Tell them your feelings are not negotiable and not to call, because you've changed your number.*

3. *Change your number immediately. This step may sound drastic but, remember, you can't get a new future if you're holding on to the old past. Call your closest friends and family to let them know your new digits. Anyone else probably doesn't need to have your number anyway. It also stops you from having to deal with*

those awful defiant phone calls from men who can't take no for an answer.

4. *Overnight any connections (e.g., boxers, casserole dishes, CDs, DVDs) to the men you dumped. Meeting to return items will only make things harder. If you're a true bad girl, there's no way you left anything at his place.*

5. *Get a few of your friends to go out with you to start recruiting, wear that one thing you know always turns heads (that dress that hugs all the right places, the stilettos that make your legs look amazing and inspire you to walk like a supermodel, those jeans that make your behind look like Beyonce's), and let the tryouts begin.*

Top Four Reasons to Do a Spring Cleaning

1. *You don't see yourself marrying any of the men you're dating.*
2. *None of the men you're dating is really good for you.*
3. *None of them has any one stellar quality that you absolutely cannot find in another man: amazing sex, engaging wit, or the ability to make you laugh until you cry.*
4. *It's been two years and none of them . . . not one of them . . . is talking about settling down. Stop wasting your precious time.*

Step One: Light as a Feather (Not Stiff as a Board)

Before I let Tasha and Tamia out, we discussed step one of the plan. Hearing Miata's voice on Julian's cell phone had my blood boiling, and I was ready to put the "Take Her Man Plan" into action. After polishing off the last bottle of wine, the three of us agreed that it would be best to begin with a phone call. I was to call Julian, sound extremely light—yet friendly—and invite him to the reception for my Nana Rue's new play. While Tasha said she didn't exactly like the idea of me inviting Julian out to an event that included my family (we'd all seen that go completely wrong a few times), I talked her into it, explaining that Julian was a huge black theater buff and he'd always wanted to see my father's mother, none other than the one and only Ms. Rue Betsch Smith, perform.

During the '30s and '40s, my Nana Rue was known throughout the world as a stage actress and classically trained opera singer. Like most African-American performers back then, Nana Rue despised the American theater and critics for how they treated African-American entertainers. Even established performers like Nana Rue, who'd been trained at Fisk University and traveled all over the world as a Fisk Jubilee Singer, simply couldn't find good roles in the States. While Nana Rue was a child of Harlem, growing up at Sugar Hill's 409 Edgecomb Avenue alongside the likes of Roy Wilkins and W. E. B. DuBois, she didn't want to settle for the "Negro actress" roles that were offered to her after she returned home from school in 1935. She said she wanted no parts of the new "en vogue" Harlem that she felt put the people she loved so dearly under a self-sacrificing microscope that allowed in any ear with a dollar for a cheap thrill. The daughter of a Harlem insurance man, Nana Rue was very proud of the Harlem she'd grown up in and she never wanted to share it with the voyeuristic white faces she saw tucked here and there when she returned. She was no racist, but it was hard not to hate the segregated crowds, the black roles written by black writers who were being fully supported by white patrons. She once told me that she thought she'd left the Jubilee Singers behind at Fisk and she wanted to be seen as an entertainer, separate from her color. It was nearly impossible to do that at that time.

So Nana Rue spent most of her career touring Europe, finding much of her success in Paris, where she married a fellow black actor and gave birth to my father before being forced to return home to Harlem in 1948 when my father was just two months old. By that time, the Renaissance that had what Nana Rue called "spectators and speculators" roaming the streets of Harlem had all but left. She and my grandfather, who died a few years ago, settled back into the home she'd always loved and took on new roles by new Negro writers with new Negro attitudes. Bringing to life their depictions of Negro culture, in all its defiance and resilience, was an honor even Nana Rue couldn't turn down.

Though she stopped touring decades ago, Nana Rue still took on small parts from time to time to "keep her blood young." Everyone in the business knew her, and most of her shows were completely sold out during the first week. When Julian and I had started dating, he'd begged to meet Nana

Rue and said he had to see her perform before, God forbid, she left this earth and her legacy behind. Laughing, I informed him that there was no way that feisty firecracker of a woman was going anywhere anytime soon.

Before Tasha stepped into the elevator, she gave me a few last-minute pointers about step one. "Block your number when you call," she said. "You want this to be a sneak attack. You don't want him to be prepared or he'll close up. Also, you don't want him to know where you are. He shouldn't think you're sitting at home waiting for him to call. Avoid talking about the breakup, only saying that you're fine and you want to be friends. Say you agree with him about the split and that you've just been too busy to call. Then, after he agrees to come to the reception with you, make sure you make it clear that you're meeting him there. Tell him you're having dinner beforehand and you may get 'tied up.' This will not only make him wonder whom you're dining with, but also reinforce the friends thing—only couples arrive at places together. And last," Tasha went on after reapplying her lip gloss, "the final and most important point is that you must hang up the phone first. Are you listening, Troy?" I nodded my head. "You have to rush him off of the phone. This will keep you in control of things. Don't allow the conversation to get too deep. That'll lead to an emotional disaster. You don't want that." Tasha stepped back and gave me a quick once-over. "You'll be fine, Ms. Lovesong. Go get your man back." She blew me a kiss. "Good luck." She pressed the button for the elevator, and she and Tamia and their pink Puma sweat suits disappeared.

The sun woke me up the next morning. After spending the night stuffing my face with Chinese food and cheap wine, I slept like a baby until the midmorning sun came blazing through my blinds. I ran over the night's events in my head, recalling Tasha's news, and climbed out of bed. My situation with Julian seemed so small compared to the journey Tasha was about to begin as a mother. Within the small amount of time I'd spent with the girls at the community center, I'd learned one thing about children: They're hard work. I couldn't even imagine having one of my own. It was an insane idea, but as Tamia and I explained to Tasha after she finally came out of the bathroom, we would support her decision.

I rolled over and looked at the time. 10:37 a.m. It was time to make the call. I had to be at the settlement to meet with the girls by noon, and I wanted to call Julian before I left. I picked up the phone and pressed speed dial 1—Julian's cell. The phone was just about to ring but I hung up. I threw the phone on the bed. I wasn't ready. I missed Julian, but I wasn't ready. How was I supposed to talk to him without bringing up Miata? I couldn't act like she didn't just answer his phone. What the hell was I going to say?

Okay, courage. You need to have courage, Troy, I reasoned with myself. I picked the phone back up and looked at it. "I have to have courage," I said aloud. I got out of my bed and turned on the radio. I wanted to play music so Julian would think I was someplace having a good time—yeah, right, at 10 in the morning. An old Jay-Z song was playing. Good enough. As long as it wasn't Donny Hathaway. He'd think I was really losing my mind then. I blocked my number and dialed his cell. *Round two.*

"Julian James," he said, answering on the third ring. He sounded kind of tired. Maybe even sad.

"Hey . . . um. Hey. It's Troy."

"Troy, wow. Hi." He actually perked up when he heard my voice. "How are you?"

"I'm fine. I'm on my way to teach my class at the center," I managed.

"Oh, yeah, the ballet class, right?"

He still remembered my schedule! Okay, calm down, Troy. It's only been a few days.

"Yeah," I said.

"I wanted to call you, Troy," Julian whispered into the phone. I could tell by the people talking loudly in the background that he was walking through the hospital. "I wanted to say I was sorry for the other day. About how I acted. There are just some things going on."

I was thinking: *What things? What things? Come clean, fool! Come clean now and we can kill the trick together!*

But I said: "Oh, it's fine, Julian. Really. That's why I'm calling. I wanted to tell you that it's okay." *Light as a feather,* I reminded myself. "I'm actually glad you did what you did. I agree with you."

"You *agree?*"

"Yeah. I mean, I could use some space too, with school and everything. I'm very busy," I said.

"You're busy? It's been, like, three days since the breakup."

"Yeah, well, I'm very busy." I couldn't believe he was making me sound so . . . available.

"Cool, I guess," Julian said awkwardly. I had him right where I wanted him. Tasha was right. It was working.

"In fact," I went on, "I want to be friends."

"Friends?" He sounded like someone had dropped a ton of bricks on his Benz. "What are you talking about, baby?"

Let me just say here: There should be some kind of rule about men calling you "baby" after a breakup. It's kind of like playing the wild card in Uno—if you use it enough, you can't lose. He had no right to call me "baby" . . . but I confess, I liked it.

"What I'm talking about, Julian, is us moving on as friends."

"Are you okay, Troy? This isn't like you," Julian said. "To be honest, and don't take this the wrong way, I expected you to be a bit more upset and less . . . well . . . breezy about all of this. It's kind of scary."

"Ju Ju." I used his childhood nickname, knowing he hated that. "We're cool. There's no reason to panic. In fact, I wanted to invite you to a reception for my Nana Rue's new play this Saturday. It's in Harlem at the Harambee Theatre."

"Oh, I really don't know if that's a good idea. So soon."

A good idea? What in the hell did he mean "a good idea"? But then I reminded myself: *Light as a feather. Light as a feather.*

"Well, that's fine. I'll just speak to you later, then," I said, wanting to toss the phone in the toilet. It was the "lightest" thing I could think of. Then, just as I was about to say good-bye . . .

"Wait. I'll go," Julian cut in. "You're right, Troy. We can be friends, and I've always wanted to meet Rue. So I guess this is my chance. When and what time?"

"Well, it's next Saturday at 7 p.m."

"Cool. I'll pick you up at your place?" he asked.

"No . . ." I remembered Tasha's instructions. I wanted him to come pick me up so badly. Maybe he'd come upstairs for a drink . . . maybe we'd end up in bed and . . . *Oh shit! Who am I fooling?* "No, I need to meet you there," I said. "I have a dinner thing before and I may be a little late, so it's best if I catch up with you at the theater." I struggled not to sound like I was reading a script.

"Well, okay," Julian said, obviously a bit thrown with my suggestion. "I guess we're set, then."

"Yeah, we're set." I smiled, thinking of his hazel eyes. For one moment I thought I'd never see them again.

"I'm really happy we're"—he stopped and there was a short, lingering, utterly painful silence—"doing this thing and I—"

"You know, Julian, I'm late and I have to go." I cut him off. I had to cut him off. I felt the silence Tasha was talking about. We were about to start talking about "us."

"Damn, girl. Can a brother get a second?" He chuckled.

"I'm serious, Julian. I need to go. Chat with you later." I hung up the phone before he could respond and threw it on

the bed. I did it. Step one was in full effect. I just had to keep
my mouth shut. Now it was time for a little bit of change . . .
but I had to get through the rest of the weekend alone first.
As the plan said, I had to go on with my life.

"You called him?" Tamia asked, taking a seat next to me
in class on Monday morning. To my surprise Saturday and
Sunday had flown by without a kink. I had a lot of studying
to do since I'd missed three full days of class, and I was able
to keep Julian out of my mind by burying my nose in my
books. I took Pookie Po to the doggie gym and got to work.

I ignored Tamia's question, continuing to go over the case
notes I'd spent the weekend compiling. I knew the suspense
would kill her.

"Well, did you?" she asked again.

"Tamia, I'm trying to study," I said, trying to sound as
lame as possible. "Class starts in fifteen minutes and I really
need to catch up."

"Heifer, don't play with me." Tamia slammed a pen on
her desk. "Tell me everything, blow by blow." She waved the
pen in front of me as if it was a fork she was about to dig into
a big slice of pie. "I wants the dish . . . I needs the dish."

"Okay, okay." I turned to her. I felt like I was back in high
school, sitting in the back of the classroom gossiping about
my first date with Adam Ramsey, the captain of the basketball team. "I'll tell you everything."

"I'm so happy for you, girl." Tamia smiled at me after I'd
given her the details. "I'm happy this is going how you want
it to, so far."

"I thought you hated the plan, Tamia."

"Well, I still think it's ridiculous and all that. I mean, you
can't make anyone love you, but Tasha was right. If you
really believe this man loves you, which I do believe is true,
then do whatever will make you happy. No one wants to
spend the rest of their lives wondering what would've hap-

pened if they did this, that, or the other. I'm your friend and I'll be here for you." Tamia locked her eyes on mine. "And if things don't work out the way you'd planned and you need a shoulder to cry on, I'll still be here."

"Oh, Tamia. That's so sweet. Thank you." I reached over the space between our desks and hugged her.

Tamia opened her bag and put her notebook and a recorder on the desk.

"And as crazy as the plan is, it's exactly why I admire Tasha," she said.

"How so?"

"I know I can be hard on her, but Tasha's a fighter. She doesn't just accept stuff. You know?" Tamia explained, slipping a tape into her recorder. "She's no one's doormat. She calls her own shots and makes her own reality . . . no matter how crazy it is." We both laughed. "No, I'm serious. I really look up to her for that. For her spirit. I wish I had some of that courage."

"Wow, Tamia. I bet Tasha would really love to hear all that," I said. "That would make her happy—to know that you feel that way."

I looked at the door in the back of the classroom just in time to see Alex, Tamia's pigment-challenged admirer, walk in.

"Alex is here," I whispered to Tamia.

"Oh shit," she said.

Alex, whom I also called "Tamia's Rainbow Connection," nearly broke his neck trying to make it to the front of the classroom where we were sitting.

"Rainbow Connection in three seconds," I said. Tamia slumped down in her seat. I counted, "One, two . . ."

"Hey, Troy," Alex said, walking up. He actually looked kind of fine. He had a tan. He must've spent the weekend in the Hamptons.

"Hey, Alex," I replied, hiding my laugh behind a wide smile.

"That was a great case presentation you did last week. I

was blown away," Alex went on. I could tell he was nervous. "Hey, Tamia." She forged a smile. "I called you yesterday. Did you change your number or something?"

"Um . . . yes," Tamia answered. There was a pause. This was the part where Tamia was supposed to take out a piece of paper and give Alex her new number. I counted to ten in my head . . . nothing. Still silence. Alex stood there looking like a cheap prostitute waiting on a john to pay her. I wondered if he'd checked his e-mail in the past twenty-four hours.

Still silence . . . Okay, I had to say something. Anything. They were killing me. It was like an Old West standoff.

"Well, I need to study before class," I said, breaking the silence. *Good call.*

"Me too," Tamia said. She pulled some flash cards from her bag.

"Well, I'll be in the back," Alex said. "I'm not as brave as you ladies." He gave Tamia, who was staring at her flash cards like we were about to take a final exam, one last look and walked away like a wounded cowboy. He'd lost the draw.

"Damn, girl. I guess you've already done your spring cleaning." I looked at Tamia. "You had his ass wrapped around your finger."

"Oh well. He'll get over it," Tamia said coldly.

"Tamia, why are you acting like that about Alex? I didn't know things were that bad between you two. I thought it was just a color thing," I said. I was really surprised by how blunt Tamia was being. It just wasn't like her.

"You want the truth?" she asked without looking up from her flash cards.

"Hell, yeah."

"I'll tell you, but then you must promise to never tell anyone or bring it up again." She finally looked up at me. I nodded my head. "I had sex with him."

"What? When? Where? Why? How was it?" I asked, recalling all the important questions one asks after they've found out a friend has slept with someone.

"It was on our first date," Tamia said, turning red. First-date sex was really not her style. "I mean there was something between us. Like sparks."

"And?" I interrupted. She wasn't giving me the good stuff.

"Well, we stopped by the library so he could pick up a book for class. We went down into the old book stacks and started kissing. It was playful at first," she said, "but then we started touching each other."

"And?"

"And . . . I put my hand in his pants. And I touched it." My mouth fell open and I could tell I was blushing now too. *Not Tamia! The good girl fucking around in the old library stacks! Why didn't I think of that first?*

"And?" I was begging like Pookie Po did for her treats.

"It was so big! It was, like, perfect. Just hard and . . . perfect," Tamia said. I could see by the look in her eyes that she was reminiscing about how it had felt. Her look was deep and longing, as if he was standing in front of her.

Now, this is a bad place for Tamia to be in. Though she is the "good girl" of the bunch, Tamia loves oral sex. It's just how she gets off. I, along with most of the other sisters I knew, were brainwashed to believe that enjoying oral sex (and a bunch of other myths about sex) made us "nasty girls," but Tamia was the first woman I knew who openly said that was a bunch of bull. Our junior year, she left our Black Feminism professor speechless when she said our sexual desire as women wasn't something we should be ashamed of or allow anyone to prescribe to us. Tamia stood in front of the entire class (men included) and said it was time for sisters to embrace their desires and figure out what they liked most in bed. After that outburst, she was on a one-woman mission to find her sexual passion, one self-fulfilling head job at a time. She didn't have many partners, but when she did, it was definitely all about what Tamia wanted to do in the bedroom. Her 3T secret code name was "Head Mistress"—pun definitely intended.

"I had to taste it." Tamia playfully slapped herself on the forehead.

"You went down on him?" I teased. "In the stacks at the library?"

"Yes," she said coyly. I nearly fell out of my chair laughing.

"And?" I asked, trying to figure out where things had gone wrong. The story sounded great so far.

"Well, after he came—"

"In your mouth?" I stopped her. I had to ask. "Yuck."

"Hell, no," she answered. "You know I don't do that. Anyway, after he came, he pulled a condom from his wallet and whispered in my ear, 'Please let me feel you, please.' It was so hot."

"Damn, girl," I said. "I'm feeling hot my damn self." I started fanning myself.

"I know, it was like he was begging. . . . It was so erotic. I looked around and I didn't see anyone, so I said yes," Tamia went on. "Girl, he put that thing in me and I don't know what came over me. I just went crazy. He had me up against the bookshelf, standing up, but I was riding the shit out of him. All he had to do was stand still. I was all over him, Troy."

The gum I was chewing fell on my desk. Tamia's sexual exploits always sounded like a damn porno movie. I was about to ask her if I could call Alex myself. I was on the market.

"Then he turned me around and we started doing it doggy style. I nearly pushed the damn bookshelf over, so I had to hold my ankles."

"Damn," I said. *Was there really this much fun to be had at the library?*

"That's when he said it," Tamia whispered.

"What. What did he say?"

"He was stroking me—and I mean stroking me good, like better than I'd ever expect from a damn white boy." I let out a little laugh and covered my mouth. "And then he said, 'I knew this black pussy would feel good.'"

"What?" I said a little louder than I should have.

"Exactly, Troy."

"What did he say? Say that shit again."

"His white ass said, 'I knew this black pussy would feel good.'"

I turned to look at Alex, my mouth still hanging wide open. I turned and looked back at Tamia.

"What?"

"I know. I couldn't believe it."

"Hell, I can't believe it now," I said. I really couldn't.

"I mean, I felt like a damn slave girl. Like Halle Berry in *Queen*. Like he was out at the old slave quarters or something."

"Getting some of that black-girl juice."

"Exactly."

"I don't know, Mia," I said, running through the situation in my mind. While Alex's comment was a little out of place, in another place and time . . . and with someone else . . . it would've been a turn-on for me. "To be honest, I used to call Julian all kinds of black shit in bed." I laughed. "He called me names too. I loved it." I grinned slyly. "Nothing wrong with a little Roots bedroom action. I am not afraid to help my man make it to freedom."

"Now that's just wrong and nasty," Tamia said, laughing. "For real, though. I'll admit that I've been called 'caramel' and 'chocolate' in bed before, but always by brothers. It just felt different coming from a white man."

"I'm saying, Tamia, I just think maybe you're being a bit unfair. Alex should be able to appreciate your body, your blackness, just as much as any black man. Hell, he should appreciate it more. Just imagine how that poor white boy felt looking at that big black ass in front of him?" We both laughed. "He must've felt like he was at Disney World. It's a wonder he didn't climax in the middle of the first stroke."

"I know, Troy. I guess I just wanted Alex to want me for my mind is all," Tamia said, still laughing. "Like I didn't want to feel as if he was just seeing me to experience the whole 'sex with a black girl' thing."

"Tamia, who gets the best grades in this class?" I asked.

"Me," Tamia replied.

"And who did Alex choose as a study partner last month because she was 'so brilliant'?"

"Me."

"And you're still wondering if he sees your mind? The two of us have known Alex for almost two years that we've been in the program together. You two are friends." I paused. "I'm just saying, make sure you're not making this about Alex's color complex, when it's really about your own insecurities."

"I know . . . I know." Tamia picked up her bag and put her flash cards back inside. "I just can't seem to put it out of my mind." When she went to put the bag back down it fell to the side and a little red pill bottle with the words "Stay Up" written across the front fell to the floor.

" 'Stay Up'?" I read, bending over to pick up the bottle. "What's this?"

"Give me those." Tamia took the bottle from me and stashed it back in the bag.

"You know that shit is bad for you, Tamia," I said, looking at her. Our senior year I caught Tamia following four No-Dozes with two scoops of freshly ground coffee (no water) to stay awake to study for a midterm. While it certainly was not odd for any of us to take something to stay up, I noticed that it had become a nightly routine for Tamia and it was really bad for her since her mother had died of a heart condition. Tamia never had symptoms of her own, but her doctor told her it was a possibility and that she should avoid stimulants that affected her heart.

That night Tasha and I cornered Tamia in her dorm room for a 3T Intervention. We didn't want things to get worse for her. We certainly had problems of our own, as neither of us were quite as focused during the semester as Tamia, but as her girlfriends we decided that we couldn't sit by and watch her risk her life. We sat up with her for hours, comforting her as she cried and explained that she couldn't take all the pressure her father was putting on her to be number one in the class (she was number two). She'd promised she would talk to him about it and stop taking the pills right after midterms.

"It's no biggie," Tamia said now, putting her bag back down. "I know what you're thinking, and don't worry about it."

"Just promise me you'll stop taking them, Tamia," I said. "Do you promise?" I wanted her to say yes and hand me the bottle, but she wasn't a little girl and we weren't in college anymore, so I had to tread lightly.

"Troy, please. I have it under control. Maybe you should stop worrying about me and worry about yourself."

"What is that supposed to mean?"

"It means that maybe you need to be more focused on school," she snapped. "You're just getting by, as usual."

I sat back in my seat and looked at Tamia. While her words hurt, it was more out of the element of timing than ignorance of her opinion. We'd had the same argument before about my grades. I'd always been a solid B+ student. I excelled just enough to get my professors' attention in most of my classes. Learning came easily to me and I didn't have to put much effort into my studies to excel. I studied enough to get enough A's to keep my G.P.A. above 3.7. I was perfectly okay with that. I liked being social and enjoying life. Tamia was the opposite. While she was no stranger to partying with me and Tasha, she took her studies very seriously. She spent most of her nights locked up in the library learning like it was going out of style. Whenever I pointed out that she needed a break, she usually snarled at me and pointed out my own academic shortcomings. Often I listened to her and promised to spend more nights nestled up to books, but most times I told her I'd be waiting for her by the bar when she would be done. Sometimes I thought she resented me for this. I mean, while I put in a little less effort than her, we did both get degrees from the same school and we were both attending the same top tier law school. She was at the top of the class, but I wasn't far behind. The good old B+ was still paying off.

"That was uncalled for," I said, as the professor walked in. "Don't try to turn this around."

"Look," she whispered, "I have it under control. Just let me handle it."

"Okay, everyone, close those books and put the notes away," Professor Banks said, standing in the front of the room.

"Are you serious?" I asked, still looking at Tamia.

"Just leave it alone, T—"

"Ladies, can I please have your attention?" I looked up to find Professor Banks looking at me and Tamia.

"Sorry," Tamia and I said together.

"Great." Professor Banks turned and walked toward her podium. "Now we can begin, since we're *all* focused." I traded another stressed look with Tamia and put away my notes. I still wanted to talk to Tamia, but Professor Banks wasn't exactly the kind of professor you wanted to mess with. She was the only black female law professor at NYU. She was known throughout the school as one of the hardest professors to have. Tamia and I had specifically signed up for her class. We thought she'd make a great mentor even if we had to struggle to pass her class.

On the first day, she'd said, "Five of you will drop my class by next week and five more will drop out of law school because of me, but those of you who make it will be the top attorneys in this country. You won't lose a case, because you survived me. You decide which group you'll be in, because I really don't care." From that day on, Tamia and I sat in the front of the class and studied our asses off.

"Now, let's see who knows the law and who doesn't. Tamia Dinkins, stand up and brief me on every case you read last night," Professor Banks said. Tamia stood up without flinching and starting discussing each case, near verbatim (her line name when we pledged). Something told me—and every other person in the class (including the woman at the front of the room)—that Tamia would be in the last group Professor Banks had spoken of on the first day of class. She was going to be a good attorney. It was her destiny and Tamia was fighting, even against herself, to claim it.

Super Friends: The 3T Intervention

It's not always easy to tell a friend the truth about a bad habit. From advising her to practice safer sex to snatching her credit card when she's about to buy the third Prada bag she can't afford, it seems that opening an unwelcome can of worms will either lead to your best bud pulling out the old defensive armor or, worse, cutting you off completely. With this in mind, it appears that taking a bullet or turning a deaf ear are better options. But, as the old saying predicts, just as surely as there will be some good times, there will be some bad times. The best gal pals must be prepared for both—to get their hands dirty in the name of good old-fashioned, soul-saving sisterhood. So stand your ground and remember that sometimes girlfriends are the only people willing and able to tell the truth—and provide help along the way. Should you find yourself in a situation where telling the truth may make the difference between prosperity and plague, you may need to put on your "Super-Save-A-Friend" cape and have an intervention.

When and How to Intervene

1. *Target the Problem—It's not enough to simply tell your friend you think she drinks too much when you go out on Friday nights. Be prepared to explain exactly what you mean so she doesn't take your words as a simple well-intentioned warning. If the problem is drinking, back up your declaration with facts and details. Tell her exactly how much she drinks and recall exact instances where her drinking made you feel uncomfortable or afraid.*

2. *Get Support—Most often, women have already discussed a budding situation long before the problem has spiraled out of control. This is okay as long as it*

doesn't stop with gossiping that never reaches the ears of the person who needs to hear it most. Discuss your friend's bad behavior only with friends closest to her and those who are directly affected by her actions. (Remember: Trust is key to any intervention. If your friend thinks you're out blabbing her business all over town, she won't open up and things might get worse.) Should you find a trusted witness, use her to confirm your speculations and provide your intervention with a much-needed third opinion. This will stop your friend from chalking your findings up to one person's opinion. Be careful not to include too many people. This may make your friend feel as if she's being ganged up on and she may resent you for discussing her actions so publicly.

3. *Confront Your Friend—Where and when you perform your intervention is very important. Be sure your friend has lots of time to sit and discuss your concerns, so she doesn't have any excuses to rush off. Never confront your friend in public or in a place that makes her feel uncomfortable. It should be somewhere where all parties can feel free to express themselves and get loud if necessary.*

4. *Be A Rock—Be ready for whatever will come your way. Never assume anything about anyone—not even your best friend. You may think you know her inside and out and that all she'll do when you tell her she needs to dump her cheating man is recoil and kick you out of her house. But the reverse might happen. She may kick and scream, open up to you about what's "really going on," and ask you to help her throw his stuff out on the curb. Be prepared for all of the above. Cry about it. Laugh about it. Hug about it. Fight about it. Be her rock and let her know you're not going anywhere.*

5. *Follow Up—Following your intervention, it's probably a good idea to allow time to pass before you bring the topic up again. If she promised to get her credit together, don't be a nag and insist she show you her credit score the next day. Allow some time to go by and then ask if any progress has been made. If you have already noticed a change in her behavior, mention it. If she admits that she still has done nothing, make some small suggestions if she asks.*

6. *Get Additional Help if Needed—If you have a friend that you believe is truly abusing her body and putting herself at risk, there may come a time when you needed to seek more help. Don't sit by and watch her eat herself toward diabetes. Make an appointment with a nutritionist and drag sister-girl there, kicking and screaming if you have to. She may be angry with you for a while, but if she's a good friend, she'll know that it was all done out of love.*

Step Two: Change, Change, Change

If there was one thing, any thing, you would change about yourself, what would it be?

This is the question I asked myself over and over again during the days leading up to Nana Rue's reception. Between dodging nosy phone calls from my mother, who wanted me to come stay at home while I was "mourning" my breakup (Dad cracked under the pressure), and fighting not to pick up the phone and call Julian, I tried to think of how I might change myself in order to meet step two of the plan.

Somewhere in there, I decided that I didn't like the idea of "changing" myself for any reason. I knew I was in serious need of a new look, as I'd been wearing my hair in the Diana Ross, free brown curls look since birth and I could stand to lose the ten pounds I'd put on since I started law school, but to "change" myself meant something was wrong with me in the first place. I just didn't agree with that.

While I was far from conceited, I'd given up trying to impress other people with how I looked when one of my college sweethearts—a campus revolutionary with long dreadlocks—announced that he could no longer date me because my skin was too light and my hair was too straight. After getting burnt for sitting on a tanning bed for too long, trying to be his African queen, I decided that I was okay with me. Little titties, wide thighs, round tummy, light skin, and "good" hair—it was all me, it was all good and good to me.

So changing myself for a man or otherwise just sounded silly and archaic. But on the other hand, I had to admit that being left for another woman was a serious chip to my ego. I mean, I knew it was pointless, but I couldn't help but compare myself to Miata—my tan skin to her smooth, dark cocoa complexion; my wild, curly Afro to her long, permed, jet-black hair. I'd sized up the chick within the few minutes I stood next to her in the park, and from what I could see, she basically was my opposite as far as beauty was concerned. Her eyes were deep and strong, her body was curvaceous and solid. Me? Nowadays, my eyes looked blank and dull and my body was one Cold Stone Creamery ice cream away *Celebrity Fit Club*. I didn't want to change, but I also didn't want part of the reason I lost my man to be a big bootie and long hair, which probably was not even hers.

So I decided that I, the future Mrs. Troy Helene James, needed an "update." Yes, I'd "update" the things about myself I found to be terribly outdated. From the comfortable jeans with matching baby T-shirts I'd grown to love as I walked the streets of the Village, to the hair that had grown from Mariah Magnificent to Mangy Mess, I would update my old look to something more sexy, sleek, and sensuous. Miata may have been what most brothers considered fine, but I was about to be Fabulous with a capital *F.*

But what? What was my new look going to be? After scouring stacks of fashion magazines and battling it out with Tamia and Tasha over cappuccinos, I was clueless. I didn't want the choppy pixie cut Halle Berry had made famous, and Tasha's punk look—complete with spikes and chains—just wasn't me. I wanted to be classy and sassy, elegant and intelligent. And there was only one person I knew who could achieve all that in a New York minute—my mother's mother, Grandma Lucy.

"Somebody get my grandbaby a glass of champagne. We're celebrating," said Grandma Lucy—who'd told me to stop calling her Grandma when I was three—when I walked in the door of her favorite salon, Bei Capelli, in midtown Manhattan. She was wearing huge Jackie O–style Gucci glasses and a white silk Hermès scarf wrapped around her head. Grandma Lucy, like her kind did in the old days, still avoided the sun for fear of getting "too dark." Grandma Lucy's skin was the color of cultured pearls and her hair was as fine as a porcelain doll's. Though she now accepted her past and had even gone so far as to reconnect with our lost family down in Atlanta, my mother said it was an old habit she'd probably never grow out of. Even ten minutes in the summer sun, which would brush her smooth vanilla skin bronze, was too much for her. "I need to see my veins," she'd say, applying sunblock on a thirty-minute rotation.

"She's just a victim. A victim of what people had to do in order to survive in those days," my mother once said, defending Grandma Lucy on a rare occasion. "She's doing what my great-grandmother taught my grandmother and my grandmother taught her."

"Lucy, you promised not to get out of control with this." I smiled and kissed her on the forehead. She was a quite a rare jewel—the complete opposite of Nana Rue and her pro-black ideas and Talented Tenth ideologies (the two were like fighting cats whenever they were forced to be in a room together), but I learned to love my Grandma Lucy just the same. "I'm just trying to update my look a bit."

"Oh, darling," she purred, holding her immaculately white and perpetually puffy bichon frise, Ms. Pearl, in her arms. Grandma Lucy had had Ms. Pearl for as long as I could remember. She went everywhere with Grandma Lucy—the

French Riviera, the Florida Keys, skiing. In fact, Ms. Pearl had been present at nearly every significant moment in my life. She was like a family member, sitting pleasantly beside me in most of my baby pictures, like a cousin. Really, it was amazing that the old dog was still alive. Ms. Pearl was blind in one eye, had no teeth, and couldn't hear a thing, and Grandma Lucy loved her. She propped that old dog up on her lap like she was the cutest thing in the Big Apple.

Grandma Lucy's beautician, Piero, who'd been doing her hair for the past ten years, appeared from the back of the salon. Piero was known throughout Manhattan as one of the hottest beauticians for the city's rich and famous. His client list included everyone from Diana Ross to Elizabeth Taylor when she was in town. He rarely accepted any new clients who hadn't been referred by someone already on his list. Getting an appointment with Piero was next to impossible—unless you knew my grandmother—which is why I had to call her.

"Oh my goodness, this is the *ragazza?*" Piero said, pinching my cheeks. He was fashionably dressed in all black Armani. "Why you no come see me in so long, my bella?" he asked, using his thick Italian accent, although he'd been in the U.S. for over twenty years.

"Just busy, I guess," I answered, trying not laugh. Watching Piero and Grandma Lucy talk about anything was a comedy sketch in and of itself. They were like best friends—rich old black lady and sassy homosexual Italian beautician—a match made in champagne heaven. It was like *Driving Miss Daisy* but with lots of liquor and hair conditioner.

"Yes, busy!" He looked at my grandmother. "Busy not combing your hair. Not doing nothing, I see." He touched my hair as if it was matted dog hair. "Is this the Afro? The Afro is back? No, no, no. Piero no think so."

"I say we flatten it out and try some color. It's too dark," Grandma Lucy said, stuffing a treat into Ms. Pearl's mouth.

"Um . . ." Piero held my chin up and looked at my face

quizzically. "Yes, I see it. You sit down," he said, pointing to the chair. "That's perfect for this girl."

"What is flattening? And what color?" I asked.

"Are you wearing hose?" Grandma Lucy changed the subject. She was always worried about whether I was wearing panty hose, a brassiere, or sunblock.

"No, Lucy. It's 2007. No one wears panty hose anymore," I replied. "Not with a sundress." I pointed to my sundress and open-toed shoes. She flicked her hand at me dismissively.

"I'm not just talking about 'no one,' Troy Helene. I'm talking about my granddaughter, my favorite granddaughter."

"I'm your *only* granddaughter, Lucy."

"Yes, well, then you win by a long shot." She smiled.

Piero's assistant, Bartolo, a more recent immigrant from Italy, came from the back of the salon pushing a cart full of odd-looking beauty products. Grandma Lucy and Piero were silently watching the dark man with jet-black hair line up the little products for Piero in slow, exaggerated motions like he knew they were watching him. Like all of Piero's assistants before him, Bartolo was a real piece of eye candy. Even though he couldn't speak English, Bartolo was studying acting at some studio downtown, and by looking at his ass and abs, I was sure he'd make it all the way to the top. If he didn't, he'd always have work with Grandma Lucy and Piero.

Grandma Lucy didn't start talking again until Bartolo had disappeared again in the back of the salon. After fanning herself dramatically, she turned back to me as if Bartolo had never appeared.

"I'm not talking about just anyone. You're an heiress," Grandma Lucy went on. "And it's improper and unladylike for you to carry yourself in such a way. Like that Paris Hilton on the television. God forbid you squander away my groom's fortune—God bless his soul—like that!"

"I know. Calm down, Lucy," I said. She was about to get

on her two favorite topics—cash and class. I'd heard all of it before. Grandma Lucy kept watch over Grandpa's railroad fortune better than the accountant and she didn't mind sharing findings with my mother and me. It was just the way of the old guard—keep the young ones in check by predicting impending doom if we didn't keep the *good* family name alive.

But I, like my mother, hated talking about money. Don't get me wrong, it was nice to know it was there, but growing up, I just wanted to be like everybody else. Not rigid and snobby like the Jack and Jill kids my grandmother wanted me to hang out with. I despised all of those ritzy, glitzy cotillions and selective summer camps they forced me to be a part of. By the time I was fifteen, I had been about to go crazy if my mother bought me another ball gown. "Just put the damn thing on," my mother had said, stuffing me into my coming-out dress. "I had to do it and so do you."

"Troy, you must accept who you are and be prepared to take on my role when I'm gone," Grandma Lucy said now, sliding her sunglasses off. "Lord knows that mother of yours can't do it; she'd probably give *all* of my money away to charity." I rolled my eyes, but Grandma Lucy did have a point.

Though my teenage angst developed into an appreciation for the finer things in life the first time I slid on a pair of Manolo Blahniks on West Fifty-fourth Street, my mother grew to hate the high-society "to do" stuff when she was a teenager. She became a total BAP (Black American Princess) rebel when she went to Howard—participating in campus sit-ins, wearing the same clothes in one month, living in the dorms past freshman year! Mary Elizabeth was a rebel without a decent pair of shoes. She was walking on the wild side. However, all that had changed when she got married and had me. My mother knew better than to try to raise me any other way. I was Nana Rue and Grandma Lucy's only granddaughter, and neither of them would hear of it. Stuffing me into expensive dresses and sending me to private school at Fieldston, where Nana Rue had gone, were the only ways my mother could keep them off her own back.

"Oh, Lord, Lucy," I said, looking at myself in the mirror. "Can we not discuss your death *again?* I'm here to think about life . . . my new life." I paused. "With Julian," I said under my breath.

"Yes, signora, and you just close your eyes," Piero said.

"What are you going to do?" I asked.

"I'm going to lighten you up, to bring out this beautiful skin you have and loosen you up a bit," he answered, looking at my reflection in the mirror. "You don't worry, signora. You're in the best hands. I do everything myself. Piero make you look like true diva. Trust me. Trust me. Trust me." He began massaging my scalp softly.

Piero was hypnotizing me with each and every word he said. Listening to his voice, I felt like I was drifting down the Grand Canal in Venice on a gondola, or sunbathing on an Italian beach. Piero was working his magic on me. I sat back in the chair and closed my eyes, praying I'd wake up in heaven.

"Oh my God," I said, looking at myself in the mirror when Piero had finished my hair. "Oh my God, God, God." I couldn't believe it. I didn't believe I could look like that. Piero had colored my hair a deep chestnut blonde and straightened it so flat it hung to the middle of my back. I didn't even know it was that long, I thought, inspecting it in the mirror to make sure it wasn't a weave. I looked gorgeous. It was amazing. I knew Julian wouldn't be able to stop looking at me, because I couldn't stop looking at myself. I hugged Piero and kissed Grandma Lucy, who was now enjoying her third glass of champagne, on the cheek.

"You look like a billion dollars," Grandma Lucy said. "I told you she could be a model, Piero. She could walk the runways of Paris if she wanted to."

"Watch out, Ms. Naomi and Ms. Tyra, meet Ms. Troy Helene!" Piero jumped in.

We all laughed and did a group high five—with Ms. Pearl.

After Grandma Lucy and I left the salon, we both did a manicure and pedicure, where I chose "drop-dead red" nail polish. Sliding into the backseat of her Bentley, careful not to touch anything with our still-damp nails, we giggled like we were best friends sharing delicious secrets.

"Oh, Troy Helene, I so love spending afternoons with you," Grandma Lucy said. "You're so much fun for your old grandmother. You remind me of what it was like to be your age."

"Oh, I love hanging with you too, Lucy." I kissed her on the cheek. She really was a lot of fun.

"I just wish your mother could come with us sometimes, you know? That she was more like you. Not all stuffy and angry. I swear that child has a huge chip on her shoulder."

"Lucy, you know what that's about," I said, checking my nails.

"Yeah, but she can't still be angry about all that old stuff. It's just the way it is. The way things are." Grandma Lucy crossed her hands over her lap and shrugged her shoulders matter-of-factly. By "old stuff," she meant my mother's issues with both her own and Grandma Lucy's blackness. And by "the way it is" and "things are," she meant the way black people like my grandmother, my mother, and I were expected to live. The "bourgeois" tendencies my mother had actually attempted to escape.

"I know, Lucy. But she just has her own issues. That's all," I said, not wanting to speak about anything too specifically that would offend Grandma Lucy. While she knew I knew her past of passing, we never spoke of it. I wouldn't say it was because it was painful, it was simply tradition not to talk about it.

"I did the best I could," Grandma Lucy said, surprising me. "The world was just so different then . . . things were so different. You'll never understand the sacrifices I was made to think I had to make in order to find a way to be happy in the world I lived in. I just couldn't seem to fit in anywhere." She looked off out of the window. "I was too light uptown and too dark downtown. It was a sad, lonely time before I met your grandfather." She exhaled and gave me the same longing look she did when she told about the first time that she met my grandfather. The story went that when he approached her at a cabaret downtown, he just assumed the young, striking beauty with icy blue eyes was white. Granddad fell in love with Lucy's smooth skin and chestnut hair. Grandma Lucy said he never even asked her what color she was—she half thought he didn't want to know and she wasn't going to be the one to tell him. She liked escaping Harlem to hang out with the blond-haired boy who had lots of money to shower her with. He was charming and he loved jazz more than anyone she'd ever met. She said that he'd told her something about his heart, how deep and hard it could love.

Grandma Lucy said she wanted that love; as I sat beside her one day on the bench at her vanity, she said something in her spirit that had been abandoned decades before she was even born needed that love and all that came with it. It sounded crazy to me at the time, but the older I get, the more I understand what Grandma Lucy meant as she stared at her pale face in the vanity mirror. While women with skin like hers found little love in the white world, there was even less in the black one. True love to a woman who wasn't really loved in either world meant everything.

A month after they met, Granddad proposed. That's when Grandma Lucy decided to tell him the truth about her past. This was because while she was sure she'd lose him, she was terrified that he'd somehow find out who she really was and break things off anyway. She'd seen this happen time and time again in her family, including when her mother lost

Grandma Lucy's father. "Better to feel the pain sooner than later," she told me. However, it was too late. Granddad was smitten with Grandma Lucy and the two married anyway, vowing to keep her disclosure between the two of them— while he didn't care, Granddad was from a certain world and way of being, and he knew it would be hard for many of his associates to deal with.

Grandma Lucy said her color wasn't exactly a secret, it was more of a "don't ask, don't tell" thing she kept hidden in the sheets between her and Granddad at night. The only downside was that she was forced to live somewhat of a splintered life. There was the life she had on the Upper West Side with Granddad and his acquaintances and their wives, and her life in Harlem where she socialized with her elite circle of friends. She had to keep the worlds separate: telling her friends uptown that she went to Harlem to visit old friends and do community work, and praying that her friends in Harlem would keep her secret.

"I did what I had to do," Grandma Lucy said, glancing out of the car window.

I reached for her hand. I couldn't think of anything to say. I'd never heard my grandmother sound so sad. She never shared the rest of the story and the bits and pieces I did have were what my mother was willing to offer up when she felt like it. According to her, everything was going as fine as one could expect it to be for a passing socialite in the '50s. Grandma Lucy and Granddad were quite happy until they decided to take a chance and do the one thing any passing person was forbidden to do—have a baby. She said it was forbidden because although she had only a few drops of black blood, there was no telling how the baby would come out. Would it be blanc or brown? Have curly hair or nappy hair? A big nose and round cheeks or a pointy nose and high cheekbones? The worries were enough to send a sane person to the crazy house. But they decided to do it anyway and out came my mother, Mary Elizabeth.

My mother, who, as luck would have it, came out with skin darker than Grandma Lucy's, was a teenager in the Black Power '60s, and she outwardly embraced her "black blood"—with the fist and everything. Against my grandfather's wishes, she spent most of her time in Harlem with my father going to poetry readings, making incense, and doing whatever else people did in those days. Her desire to rebel from her past came to a peak in the early '70s when she insisted upon going to Howard for college. This was a decision that changed my family's history.

Certain their stubborn daughter wouldn't change her mind and that there was no way they'd be able to explain Mary Elizabeth's decision to attend an HBCU in the South over an Ivy League school in the North, my grandparents decided it was time for Grandma Lucy to start "telling." By then the white upper class had begun to accept more African-American influence. It was almost in vogue to have "slaves in the family"—as one book would later call it. So being a true socialite, Grandma Lucy researched her history, "going home" to Atlanta and everything. When she returned, she threw a grand New York party and even made her rich white friends donate money in her name to an arts school in Harlem.

While it sounds like a "they lived happily ever after" story, there's a lot more pain there that could never be told and could never be fully explained. The whole "color" thing grew into a gigantic cancer that virtually devoured their relationship the more my mother fought to deal with her issues with color and push Grandma Lucy into seeing the errors of her ways. I wasn't sure either of them would ever fully confront the issue.

"Well, enough of that old stuff," Grandma Lucy said, turning back to me to show sad red eyes. "Let's talk about this doctor of yours. The one you're trying to snatch." Her voice quickly turned from contemplative to mischievous.

"It's not like that." I laughed.

"Sure, I know a snatch when I see one. Now tell me all about this young man."

"He's a dream," I said, smiling. "He's just everything I ever wanted in a man—kind, funny, warm, smart . . . he's so smart, Lucy. Sometimes I think he's one of the smartest people I've ever known."

"What does he do?" she asked, nearly cutting me off.

"He's a doctor. He's probably one of the best doctors ever, but that's not what's important, Lucy. I love him and I want to get him back."

Grandma Lucy frowned and a little crease folded down the center of her Botoxed forehead.

"Well, is he *for* you?" she asked, looking as if most of what I had just said was some foreign language to her. *I just said I love him, Lucy. Of course he's for me,* I wanted to yell. But it was no use. Suddenly, the deep, introspective woman who had been sitting next to me a few minutes ago had faded into the atmosphere and the completely traditional side I knew well was coming out. Other than *doctor,* the other words— *handsome, nice,* and *love*—meant little to Grandma Lucy's complex traditions. By "for me" she meant something very specific, something she'd taught me about how to find a "proper suitor" a long time ago.

"Yes, Lucy," I said, playing dumb. I knew what she wanted— facts, information, a portrait of Julian's past that would let her know if Julian was "for me," but what she wasn't saying was that "good enough" preceded "for me" in her mind.

"Where did the boy go to school? Who are the parents? Where are they from?" Grandma Lucy jumped right in for the elitist pie. The old woman was growing tired of my playing, but I had to let her know that I really didn't think those things were important.

"Who cares about all that, Lucy?" I asked. "I love him and that's enough."

"Little girl, stop your toying." She frowned again and exhaled in agitation. "Paul," she said, lowering the window to speak to her driver. "We'll do lunch at Felita."

"Yes, Lucy. Quickly," said Paul. He turned the car around and we were off to a silent Italian lunch where Grandma Lucy would press and probe me continuously for the information she needed. I didn't falter, however. It was a hard job—especially after a few glasses of red wine—but I wasn't giving in to the old lady. *Never.*

Following lunch, I split for a mini shopping spree at Saks, with Grandma Lucy's credit card, of course. My father would flip out if he saw any new charges on my card. My parents and Nana Rue always said Grandma Lucy spent way too much money on me, trying to make up for the mess her relationship had been with her own daughter. I agreed, but who was I too deny the old lady of my assistance if she really needed it? To balance her financial fun play out, my father put me on a strict monthly budget as long as I was going to school. I was already over my budget for the month. *Takeout Chinese and premium dog food really adds up.* "Ask for Jennifer," Grandma Lucy said, talking about her personal shopper. "She's expecting you." She slid on her dark shades like the paparazzi were lined up along the sidewalk, slipped into the back of her Bentley, and rolled down Fifth Avenue in style. If only I could be that fly when I grew up—a little less crazy . . . but definitely that fly.

Walking into Saks, I thought about all of the old rules about men Grandma Lucy had taught me when I first started dating—all of the rules I'd thrown out the window when I met Julian. While I'd played dumb in the car to teach her a lesson, I still remembered everything.

In order to ensure that all of my suitors met both her social and financial requirements before I even ordered dinner on a first date, I had to ask them certain questions pertaining to what Grandma Lucy called their "pedigree." "Troy, there is no reason for you to go out into the world and break your behind to pursue your dreams and live with some type of dignity, only to marry some gigolo who wants to spend your money and keep you under his control," Grandma Lucy had said one night when she called my dorm room unexpectedly. I scoffed at her declaration and claimed I was on my way to the library just to get off the phone. Grandma Lucy was telling me nothing new. I wasn't dumb, deaf or blind, so I'd already bared witness to much of the surprising divisions that existed between the black folks around me. As sure as I'd learned to walk (without scuffing my Mary Janes), I'd learned that while people hated talking about it, the caste system in India had nothing on high society black folks and their high society class systems. And for gals like me, it all begins with your mother putting you in the *right* clubs, the *right* prep school, the *right* summer camp, and choosing the *right* vacation spots. I myself was a member of the most elite J&J chapter in the state of New York, meaning I had scheduled play dates with the Cosby children; went to one of the most elite schools in the city, Fieldston; and camped at Atwater, a black camping tradition on my father's side of the family that dates back to the '20s. Further, though I grew up on the Upper West Side, where everyone tends to vacation in the Bluffs or Martha's Vineyard, Nana Rue often insisted that we go down South to Hilton Head, South Carolina, for sunshine and Southern charm. She always said that the sun seemed to shine a bit brighter in the South, but I thought the rich blacks down there were completely different than they were in the North. They had way too many rules, and fitting into their many traditions was an annual fight I had to endure. No one knew my family name, so I may as well have been poor and invisible.

These degrees of social separation became particularly defined when it came to finding a suitor. Point blank, he or she had to have what you had or more. There was no marrying down. The perfect pedigree was the only plausible option here.

All of that went flying fast out the window when I bumped into Julian that day at the bookstore.

I didn't care about anything but getting with him. . . . Okay, I confess, maybe I was a bit excited about his little medical title, but other than that, I just wanted to know him, to see what the moonlight looked like in his eyes, to hear his voice before he fell asleep at night.

Julian far outshined any expectations. Instead of carrying his history on his sleeve, he carried it inside like a rare jewel. Like me, he respected and cherished his position in high black society, but he never abused it or used it to separate himself from other people. It was special, it made us special, but not more special than anyone else.

Step Three: Say You, Say Me

When I pulled up in front of the Harambee Theater—approximately fifteen minutes after I was supposed to meet Julian in the lobby (and right on time for my special arrival)—I felt electric. I'd spent the afternoon sunbathing at Central Park with Tasha and my tan skin had turned a light brown, matching my new hair. Tasha loved the look. When I met her at our usual spot on the Great Lawn, she said she would've thought I was Beyoncé if she didn't know any better. I think she was just trying to make me feel good about myself, and it worked.

"No, girl, you'll be the hot thing tonight at the reception," Tasha had reassured me. "You already have half of the men here going crazy," she said, pointing to the steady stream of eyes that floated in my direction. "Imagine what it'll be like tonight."

After finding a parking spot down the block from the theater, I stepped out of the car as an updated woman. My toe tapped the curb and I swear I lit up the entire sidewalk. Grandma Lucy was right about the girl at Saks. Jennifer had a great eye. Without asking my size, she'd pulled a silk DVF dress from the rack. "You'll love the way this makes your skin feel," she'd said, opening the dressing room door for me. And she was right; I did. The dress fell over my curves perfectly—tight in some places, loose and then looser in others. And the color was amazing. It looked like my skin was painted with red wine.

We'd topped off the dress with matching Prada stilettos, a golden egg clutch, and sexy golden chandelier earrings. The last stop had been at the M.A.C. counter, where I'd purchased my favorite mascara and red lipstick. Then I was off to get ready for my Prince Charming.

I looked at my reflection on the car door and smiled at the sight of myself all dolled up like I was on my way to a first date. I didn't look like a woman whose heart had been hurt, whose dreams had been usurped by someone else. I looked more alive than I had in months, felt more sensual than I had in weeks. I laughed and blew my-sexy-self a kiss.

It was funny how the update was supposed to be about Julian, his love and attention, but for that moment, standing there alone, it was all about me. Walking up the steps to the theater, I felt like a true diva on a mission.

There were hundreds of beautifully dressed people crowded into the small lobby; however, my eyes took me almost instinctively to the one person in the room who mattered. Julian was standing in the middle of the sea of familiar faces we both knew, smiling graciously as people walked up to introduce this person or that person to the newest doctor in the prestigious James family. He didn't seem to be paying them any real attention. His eyes kept scanning the room quickly in between conversational pauses. When his eyes almost caught mine, I smiled and waved, but he looked right past me. I headed in his direction with a sophisticated step as I tried to be smooth and calm. "Smooth and calm . . . smooth and calm," I kept saying to myself, trying to maintain my balance in the new stilettos. "Just don't trip!"

When Julian finally looked at me, he squinted his eyes and then smiled so hard I could almost see his wisdom teeth.

"Troy?" he said, moving toward me with his eyes still tight. "Is that you, baby?"

"Stop playing. Of course it's me," I said, smiling to show my freshly bleached teeth. He looked amazed—exactly the response I was going for.

"What the hell happened to you?"

"What?"

"You look great," he said, pulling me into his arms. He hugged me so tightly, I was worried my dress would split in the back.

"Are you ready to go inside?" Julian pointed to the trail of people who were heading into the theater's ballroom, where the reception was to be held. "I think things are about to start."

I led Julian into the ballroom, saying hello to old friends and a few of my nana's former castmates along the way. The place was teeming with Harlem's old guard. The women, mostly members of my grandmother's childhood church, St. Mark's, or the Links, an elite organization Nana Rue was a member of, waved their freshly manicured hands at each other as they strolled along arm in arm with their handpicked significant others. The men flashed French-cuffed shirts with matching cuff links as they handed out verbal business cards and planned golf outings and tennis matches. While I liked to think the event was all about the premiere of Nana Rue's newest play, the truth was that it was only a small part of the spectacle. This was the place where connections were made, news was dished, and people were introduced or excommunicated for some reason or another.

When we entered the ballroom, I saw my parents sitting at a table toward the front, so naturally I headed in the other direction, toward the bar. I just wasn't in the mood to deal with them just yet. Things were going great with Julian thus far and I didn't want anyone to mess it up. My mother was worse than me when it came to my breakups. She took them way too personally. It was as if she thought the men were leaving her, rejecting her, by breaking up with me. She often refused to speak to my exes, ignored them to their faces, and called them all kinds of names behind their backs. I was afraid of what she might do to Julian.

"You don't want to sit down?" Julian asked. I noticed he was wearing a navy blue suit we'd picked out together. He looked great in it.

"Nah, I figured we'd hang out by the bar. You know, avoid the whole family thing," I said, trying to sound breezy. "Let's get a round of drinks to celebrate our newfound friendship."

"Yeah, sure," Julian said. I saw uncertainty in his eyes. "Look, Troy. I'm not really sure about this whole friendship thing just yet," he added frankly. "I'm happy you're doing okay with the breakup, but I really want to take things slow and make sure we're making the right decision—"

"About us breaking up?" I asked, cutting him off. *Warning: I'm about to get my feelings hurt in 1, 2, 3 seconds . . .*

"No," he said swiftly. "I'm talking about the friends thing. I want to take my time with that."

"I agree," I said, signaling for the bartender. *I needed a drink pronto.* I turned my face away from Julian. I couldn't believe what he was saying and I didn't want him to see any signs of weakness on my face. I felt a twinge of uncertainty about my whole plan. The thing was going all wrong. If Julian was so sure about us breaking up, how was it ever going to work? Maybe he didn't love me after all.

"You smell great," Julian said, coming up close behind me at the bar. I felt his chin on my shoulder, his breath at the nape of my neck.

"Thanks." I smiled and ordered a glass of chardonnay for myself and a Maker's Mark and Coke for Julian.

"So what's the deal with the new look?" Julian picked up his glass off of the bar.

"What new look?"

"I'm saying, you've got the hair all straight and sexy, which you know I love," Julian said. *For the record: I didn't.* "You're dressed sexy . . . you just look different."

"Do you like it?" I crossed my fingers behind my back. He had three seconds to answer or it was a lie (3T Guy Lie List #8).

"Yes," Julian said in 1.3 seconds. "I love it, but I'm wondering where it's coming from. Don't get me wrong. I *loved* the old Troy." He put an emphasis on the word *loved.*

"Well, I just needed a change. A new look to give the boys something to look at," I said.

"Boys?" Julian recoiled. "You're dating already?"

"Come on, Ju Ju. I wouldn't kiss and tell. That's not lady-like," I flirted, flipping my hair over my shoulder.

"Troy, we just broke up. How could you be out there dating already?" Julian looked a little perplexed. I wondered if it was the drink taking effect too soon or if he was really jealous—either way, it was a great sign.

"I didn't say I was dating, Julian. I simply implied that I was working to meet someone new. A girl can't wait on you forever," I said, playing with my wineglass on the bar. "So are you saying you're not seeing anyone?"

"Well, to be honest, baby," Julian started. Then, before he could get the words out, Christian Kyle from the country club pushed his way between the two of us. My chin nearly hit the bar. I couldn't believe it. What in the hell was he doing there? *I needed backup.*

"Hey there, TH!" Kyle said, smiling at me as if we hadn't just met for the first time the other day. "What's up?"

I looked at him, trying to figure out what in the hell he was doing in my damn face just when Julian was about to come clean about Miata! He was ruining everything . . . again. Christian Kyle sure had a knack for bad timing.

"Hey," I answered dryly. Holy or unholy, I wanted his ass to go away. He was looking fine in his obviously Italian imported suit (I was mad, not blind), but not fine enough to take down the plan.

"TH?" Julian said. He looked completely dumbfounded. That was the name only my father dared call me. Julian knew that.

"Oh, Julian, this is Reverend Kyle Hall, one of my *father's* business associates. Kyle, this is Julian, my friend."

"Nice to meet you, Julian," Kyle said, shaking Julian's hand.

"Dr. Julian James." Julian put on his business face.

"A doctor?" Kyle stepped back, looking surprised. I searched the room for my father. This was his work. "That's something. Where do you practice, brother?"

"I'm at NYU Medical Center."

"Oh, a smart brother. I love it." Kyle grinned. *What did he have up his sleeve?* "Well, I don't know if TH told you or not, but I'm the pastor over at First Baptist here in Harlem," he said, all chummy.

"No, she hasn't mentioned *you* at all," Julian said. Now Julian was playing the game. *Wait, was he sizing Kyle up?* It was like watching a ping-pong match—only my head was the ball. Julian looked at me and winked. "I know where that church is."

"Yeah, we're looking for some new blood, brother." Kyle pulled one of his cards from his pocket. "You should come to service on Sunday. Check us out. A brother like you could be a great role model in our youth program."

"Yeah, man. That sounds great," Julian lied. He wouldn't be going anywhere near Kyle's church. While First Baptist was getting attention in Harlem, Julian's family had been Episcopalian since they had arrived in the city in the 1800s. The Jameses always attended one of the biggest churches in Harlem, St. Philips Protestant Episcopal Church. And it wasn't going to change anytime soon.

"And I expect to see you in there sometimes, TH."

I struggled not to toss my drink at him—for fear I might never make it to heaven.

"Yeah, well, you know I have my own church," I said.

"Well, I think you'll like us." Kyle pinched me on the cheek and grinned. "We tend to be a little louder than you Methodists, but the spirit is good all the time." He smiled. "Well, I must be getting to my seat," he said, shaking Julian's hand. "It was great meeting you."

"Who was that?" Julian said when Kyle finally made his way halfway across the room.

"I told you already. A friend of my father's." I signaled for another glass of wine.

"He didn't look like a friend." Julian looked at me accusingly. His eyes seemed a bit *greenish*; I could see images of Kyle's solid chest still burning in his corneas. "He looks like he wants to be way more than your friend."

"Let's not ruin our special evening talking about someone so insignificant," I whispered into his ear. "Tonight is about us." I put my wineglass up and we toasted. "And if I can recall, we were in the middle of a little conversation about you seeing some—"

The lights on the stage in the front of the ballroom came up just as I was about to finish my sentence. Rupert Wright, a big off-Broadway director who did most of Nana Rue's plays, walked up to the stage.

"Good evening, ladies and gentlemen," he said into the microphone, smiling as the white on his classic tuxedo gleamed beneath the stage lights. "Welcome to the Harambee Theater." Everyone in the audience began clap. "And welcome to Harlem," Rupert went on. The audience, which represented every politician, clergy member, business head, and organizer in New York City, began to clap even louder, and a few whistles rang out around the floor.

The Harambee Theater had opened in Harlem over a year ago. It marked the beginning of what Nana Rue and her friends hoped was a new age of theater in Harlem. They, along with a few Broadway sponsors, wanted to bring classics like Lorraine Hansberry's *A Raisin in the Sun* and August Wilson's

The Piano Lesson (plays Nana Rue took me to see when I was young), back to the center of African-American culture, providing a way for residents to not only celebrate their heritage but also have the opportunity to pursue careers in the arts.

"This is great, Troy," Julian said. He stood beside me and put his arm around my waist. "Thanks for bringing me."

"It's no problem. I know how much you love this stuff," I said, wondering when I'd get the chance to bring up the special topic again.

"I think you will all be extremely excited with the preview of what we have in store for you with our next production," Rupert added, dazzling the audience. The company hadn't yet revealed what the next production would be, in order to build up industry hype around it. As they had successfully with the last three plays, they only let insiders know who would be starring in the play and provided an "invitation-only" crowd with a sneak peek of the production at the opening reception. While it was a risky move, fans loved it, and even though they had no clue what they were going to see, the opening nights were always sold out. So far, it was working this evening, too. You could see the anticipation rising in the air.

"This season's production features none other than Harlem's own Rue B. Smith in the starring role," Rupert said, introducing my nana under the stage name she'd used since she started performing. The audience clapped louder, and a few people, including my father, got out of their seats. "So, without any further ado, I present to you a preview of the Harambee Theater's summer production of . . ." Rupert stopped in midsentence. "I don't think you folks are ready. I can't even hear you!" he said, defiantly putting his hand on his hip. The clapping turned to a thunderous roar as people screamed and whistled in protest of Rupert's playful delay.

Julian and I laughed, clapping our hands as loud as we could. "Come on, you all can do better than that," Rupert said dryly. "See how bourgeois black folks act when they get all dressed up for the theater!" Everyone laughed enthusiastically. "Now get on your feet, forget about those nice clothes, and get ready as I present to you the Harambee Theater's summer production of *Ma' Rainey's Black Bottom!*"

After running through a preview of about three scenes from the play, the curtain went down on what I was sure was going to be the theater treat of the summer. Nana nailed it along with the supporting cast, which included two prime-time drama actors, a rapper who was trying to break into acting, and Nana Rue's assistant, Abby, who was playing her niece in the play. The audience sang along with most of the tunes, and when it was all over, they begged for more.

"Encore! Encore!" they yelled from around the ballroom. "Encore!"

I can't lie, I was with them. I just wanted to support my nana and the magic she was able to make happen through her talent. For a second, with my hands clasped over my mouth, I imagined what it must be like to have such an amazing talent and not be able to share it with the world. I wondered what it must have been like for my nana back in the old days when people refused to let her do what she does best just because of her skin color. While she and Grandma Lucy had very different realities in life, I'd bet neither of them were easy. Grandma Lucy had to constantly try to be what society wanted her to be, and Nana Rue had to fight just to be herself. Simply said, diva-dom was no simple task.

"Oh, Troy, I'm so happy you're here, baby," Nana Rue said, smiling at my reflection behind her in her vanity mirror. I'd sneaked Julian backstage to meet her before she went into the ballroom to greet her guests. I also wanted to avoid seeing my parents.

"Nana Rue, you know I never miss your performances." I smiled back at her. While Nana Rue's driver's license proved she'd been a senior citizen for a few years, her beauty told another tale. Her enviable, even brown skin looked as if she'd just been dipped into a vat of fresh brewed black coffee. It was taut and still managed to remain soft enough to make other women her age wonder if she'd made some kind of anti-aging deal with the devil. Her wide brown eyes still danced with the enthusiasm of a teenager. She'd clearly seen many things through the years, but let them all roll off her back and managed to keep a smile sparkling in her soul that was evident to everyone who met her.

"Never one, baby." Nana Rue pulled at the curls on her wig. "And who is your friend?" She turned around in her seat and signaled for the two of us to sit down. "Who is this piece of pie I see in my eye?" Nana Rue asked, flirting with a quick rhyme.

"This is Dr. Julian James, Nana Rue," I replied, taking a seat on the red chaise lounge she had put in all of her dressing rooms. "Remember the friend I wanted you to meet?"

"Yes, you did mention a friend." She looked at me and then back at Julian.

"It's my pleasure to meet such a luminary figure in African-American history," Julian said, kissing Nana Rue's hand.

"African-American *history*?" She pursed her lips together. "I know I'm old, but *history*?"

"I apologize, Ms. Smith. I just find it hard not to admire a rose when I see a rose." Julian genuflected in a way I'd never ever seen him do for me.

"Manners and charm . . . I like this one, Troy." Nana Rue allowed him to kiss her hand. "Especially if he's the reason you look so marvelous!" Nana Rue snapped her fingers and winked at me. "Turn around—let me look at you."

"It's just a new look," I said, turning around. "The preview was great."

"Yes, it was Ms. Smith," Julian chimed in.

"Well, I guess I'll have to make sure Troy brings you out to see the entire thing."

"I'd love that. And my parents are members of the theater, so I'm sure they'll see it, too," Julian said just as his pager went off. He slipped it from his hip with both of our eyes on him.

"Everything okay, son?" Nana Rue asked.

"Yes, it's work," he said. He looked at me. "I have to call in. Just one second." He quickly excused himself, stepping out of the dressing room to make the call in the hallway.

Nana Rue turned back to her mirror, begging me to ask for her thoughts with a huge grin splashed across her face.

"Stop it," I said.

"What?" She smiled at me in the mirror and went to dapping off her makeup.

"You know you have something to say. You always do."

"Dr. Feeeeeelgood," she sang. "Looks good . . . sounds good . . . wonder if he tastes good!"

"Stop it!" I scoffed, praying Julian couldn't hear her.

"You asked my opinion, baby." She turned to me and reached for my hands. "Just calm down. I was just playing with you. I know you young folks don't like to think about us grown people making love—"

"Nana Rue!" I protested. We both laughed.

"Look, he seems like a nice young man. Just make sure Dr. Feelgood actually makes you feel good." She stood up and kissed me on the forehead. "And if he doesn't," she said, looking into my eyes, "you may need to go someplace else to get that good feeling." She took a quick dramatic step, snapped her fingers and laughed.

"Nana Rue!"

When Julian and I walked out of the theater, he was smiling at me, leading me down the steps with a confident hand placed protectively in the small of my back. We were laughing and going over the parts of the preview we liked most. It felt like old times. We'd always been active together, enjoying each other's company as we watched plays and went to the opera, roller skating, even strawberry-picking in the Spring when he had a few days off. We joked and jived in a way that made people walking by look at us if we'd been together for years. Older women nodded their heads at me with a look of approval as they seemed to be reminiscing about some great love in their past.

"I might've gone for her back in the day," Julian said as we joked about how Nana Rue still managed to be a beautiful leading lady.

"Don't talk about getting with my Nana!" I laughed, standing beside Julian in front of the theater.

"She's fine, though. She has that cool old lady strut." He took a few steps to show off his rendition of Nana Rue's hip-pounding walk. It was kind of fly.

"Stop it," I grabbed his arm. "She might see you." I let go and turned to look at the building to be sure neither Nana Rue nor my parents were walking out. My mother would show out even more if she realized I'd been there and hadn't said hello.

"You didn't have to let go," Julian whispered in my ear.

"What?" I asked startled.

"Of my arm." He kissed me on the lips slowly and softly. It was mesmerizing, like pouring hot chocolate on a cube of ice. I was melting fast.

"Please, I'm sure the physical isn't a good idea right now," I said flustered. "Besides, I was just joking."

"I wasn't."

"Julian, let's not go there. We're just supposed to be hanging out." I couldn't believe what I was saying, but once again, I had to stick to the plan.

"I know. I know." He stepped back and shook his head. "Look, where's your car? I'll just walk you to your car and say goodnight."

"It's down the street, but I can get there by myself." I wasn't comfortable with Julian walking me to the car. That would surely lead to an odd moment where we'd have to find a way to say goodbye. That would make me weak and I wasn't about to let myself break down.

"You sure?" he asked. "I don't want you walking down the street alone."

"Please, there are still people out here, silly." I pointed to the last few stragglers heading out of the theater.

"Fine," he said reluctantly. "I guess this is it then." He paused. "But before you go, I just have to say one thing, then that's it. Okay?"

"What?"

"You're one amazing woman. All any man could want."

"Thank you," I said, half praying he would keep going and stop at the same time. My weak side wanted to—needed to—hear what he was saying, but my strong side knew it was a bad idea to listen to the pantry-charming play.

"No, I'm serious. You know, as we walked around in there, I was watching everyone and thinking about you and how you were the most beautiful woman in the room."

I couldn't say anything. I was speechless. Well, not exactly. I was happy to hear his words, but at the moment all I could think of were a few choice questions. The first one was, "Well, if you feel that way, why did you break up with me?" But time and experience taught me that asking that would only amount to me pushing him and the last thing I needed to do to a vulnerable man that was expressing himself was push. He'd just run. Julian would have to figure out the answer to that question on his own.

"It's hard being around you right now," he continued, "I just want to hold you and take you home with me."

"Well, we have to do what's right. As friends."

"Yeah . . . I know. So, when do we *friends* get to hang out again?"

"I don't know," I teased. "I guess I'll have to let your peo-

ple get with my people and then maybe we can work something out. I'm a busy lady, you know?"

"I know," he said. "I'll have to have my people get with
your people then . . . sooner rather than later." He hugged
me and gave me a quick kiss on the tip of my nose. "Goodnight beautiful."

I felt like I'd lost ten pounds, walking back to my car. I
was light as a feather, floating on air like an angel. The perfect result of step one was all I could've wished for. Miata's
wicked spell was already breaking and I was so happy, so
very happy that I didn't notice the gaping hole in the space
where my car was supposed to be. I looked up and down
Adam Clayton Powell Boulevard, trying to remember where
I'd parked, when I realized I was standing there. *Right there.*
The first thing that came to my mind was that someone had
stolen the car. I pulled my cell phone from my purse.

As I dialed 9-1-1, I looked up at a sign that was posted on
the curb beside the spot where the car had been. It was one
of those red and white parking signs that people tend to miss
when they're in a rush. I was afraid to read the sign. Afraid
to discover the fate of my vehicle.

NO PARKING 6 p.m.–6 a.m., Fruitlessly—since it was 10
o'clock at night—I tried to remember when I'd parked the
car. It was at least 7:30 p.m. I remembered because I'd been
late meeting Julian. I closed the phone just as the operator
picked up. My car hadn't been stolen by a damn fool. It was
towed because my fool ass had parked it illegally! I wanted
to fall out right there in the empty space, but then I'd ruin my
new DVF dress.

Just as I contemplated walking back inside to explain
everything to my parents, who'd never let me live it down, a
black BMW pulled up beside me.

"Need some help?" the driver asked. I peeked in the window to see who it was. Rev. Dr. Hall had shown up in the

nick of time again. "Car get towed?" he asked, looking up at the sign behind me.

"Looks like it," I answered reluctantly, turning to face the theater to make sure my parents hadn't sneaked up behind me. Kyle smiled and turned on the light in his car.

"It's pretty late. You need a lift? I can take you to the garage to claim it or home if you just don't feel like dealing with it tonight," Kyle said, sounding a bit too hospitable. I imagined that he was behind this entire drama. He'd set up the entire thing: He'd scheduled Julian at the hospital so he would have to leave early; he'd made me park in the stupid spot so my car would get towed; and he'd called the tow company. Yeah, I know, it was a stretch, but he was *tight* with the man upstairs.

"Okay, Kyle," I said, walking up to the window. "I'll let you take me home as long as you promise not to tell my father this ever happened . . . like, *ever.*"

"Well, I can't tell a lie if he asks me directly, but I can try to avoid the topic." *How smug.* It was gonna be a long ride back to Chelsea.

I exhaled and looked up and down the street. Not a cab in sight.

"Okay," I said and got in.

Kyle and I laughed the entire way downtown to my apartment. He did an impression of the look on my face when he'd pulled up beside me on the street, and I couldn't stop giggling. Maybe it was the wine I'd had at the bar earlier. Maybe it was just because I really needed to laugh. But he was hilarious. He said I'd looked like I was about to key every car on the block because mine had gotten towed. "I had to stop you from getting arrested," he said jokingly.

I found Kyle's humor comforting. He seemed to know just what to say to make me smile, and while I couldn't get over the fact that he was somebody's pastor, I was beginning to like him. *Maybe I could hook him up with Tamia,* I joked with myself as Kyle pulled into a space in front of my building.

"Oh, you don't need to walk me up. I'm fine from here," I said, watching him turn off the ignition. *What was he trying to come upstairs for? Evening worship in my bedroom?*

"I'm a gentleman, Troy." Kyle got out of the car and came over to open my door. "I wouldn't have it any other way."

As Kyle helped me out of the car, I realized again how tall he was. Though he was a little stocky for my taste, he could pass for a basketball player.

"Don't worry. Nothing's going to happen," he said, walking into the building with me.

"Nothing?" I asked, assuming the *nothing* he was referring to was sex.

"Not a thing."

"Well, how much *nothing* has there been?" I toyed with him, stepping into the elevator.

"Funny. But that's not the *nothing* I meant." He gave me a look that had *you're a nasty girl* written all over it. "What floor?" he asked.

"Ten."

"But if you're asking about *something.*" This time he was talking my talk. He reached over me to press the button. "Then you can know, there's never been *something.*"

"*Never?*" I was stunned. Surely we were talking about two different things. Suddenly I hated allusive conversations. But how skanky would I look if I asked the pastor straight out: *Boy, are you a damn virgin?*

"So, *never . . .* never?" I repeated for the only kind of clarity one can get in these conversations filled with innuendo.

"*Never,*" he said with no shame.

I had a million questions for Kyle about his *never* when the elevator doors finally opened on my floor. A grown-ass thirty-year-old virgin? All those years in Hot-lanta and *nothing?* All those women at the church and *nothing?* Everyone knew that pastors dipped into both the collection plate and the parishioners.

When I stepped out of the elevator, pushing the envelope a step further with each question I asked Kyle, I saw Tasha sitting on the floor in front of my apartment. I could tell she was crying by the pile of tissues in front of her. I rushed over to her, with Kyle following close behind me. He bent down to help her up.

"Tash, what happened? Are you okay?" I asked. "Why are you crying?"

"It's nothing," Tasha managed. Her mascara was everywhere and I could barely see her eyes. I checked her face for bruises. You never know. "I just needed to talk." She began to sob loudly.

"I can leave if this isn't a good time," Kyle said, holding Tasha up.

"Yeah, I think I need to be with her." I picked up Tasha's purse from the floor.

"No, I'll leave if you have company," Tasha said. She looked at Kyle and then back at me. "I just didn't know where else to go." She blew her nose in a napkin that looked like it had already been used.

"Don't be ridiculous." Kyle massaged her shoulder. "I was just leaving anyway. Troy, I'll see you later."

I opened the door to my apartment and Tasha walked in. I looked back at Kyle, who had already made his way to the elevator and then waved.

"Thanks, Kyle," I said.

"No problem. I couldn't leave you standing out there."

"No, not just the ride. Thanks for everything. You really helped me in ways I can't explain." I had to say it.

The elevator doors opened up.

"Well, you can make it up to me if you like," Kyle said, holding the doors open with his foot. "Dinner . . . 8 p.m. tomorrow at Paola's?"

I exhaled and grinned. Sneaky Christian Kyle.

"Okay," I said.

Dinner wouldn't hurt. No, it wouldn't.

"Don't stand me up now!"

"I got it." I laughed at his insistence. "8 p.m. Paolo's."

"What happened, baby?" I said, rushing over to the couch where Tasha was sitting. Pookie Po was sitting at her feet and she was still crying.

"Well, you know what I told you the other day?" Tasha asked. She looked a mess, wearing old ripped jeans and a T-shirt.

"You mean the baby? What about it?"

"Well, it's not going to happen. I'm not having a baby." Tasha punched the arm of the couch and Pookie Po jumped up.

"Lionel doesn't want it?"

"No, I still haven't told him."

"So what is it?" I asked. It was the first time I'd seen her so worked up.

"I can't have a baby," Tasha blurted out. She pulled a piece of pink paper from her purse and handed it to me.

"What is this?" I said, unraveling the crumpled-up piece of paper.

"Remember when I said I stopped taking the pill?"

"Yes."

"Well, that was about two months ago," Tasha went on. "After the first month, I was a bit worried when nothing happened. So I decided to wait another month. But then there was nothing."

"Okay," I said, reading the paper: PATIENT LAB REPORT— Natasha Adrianna St. Simon.

"Well, last week I couldn't take it anymore, so I went to my gyn to see what was wrong. And today I got the results." Tasha pointed to the paper. "Read it." Tasha grabbed the paper from me and held it up in my face.

"It says I can't have a baby," Tasha cried. Her words hit my heart like a sack of quarters. I took the paper from her hands and pulled her into my arms.

"I'm so sorry to hear that, Tasha," I said. "I'm so sorry." I rocked her back and forth slowly. "Are you sure they have the right diagnosis? What exactly did they say?"

"It's my fallopian tubes. The doctor said they're blocked, so my eggs can't get fertilized," Tasha cried into my chest. "Not without surgery, but even then it may not happen."

I stroked Tasha's back and fought to hold back my own tears.

"Well, you said it yourself, Tasha. You can't get pregnant the regular way, but there are other options," I said. "Like in-vitro or something. Have you discussed that with the doctors?"

"Yes. They're going to let me know on Monday if it's even possible."

"See, there's hope," I said. "Don't worry, Tasha. Just pray that this will happen for you and it will." Tasha sat up and looked at me.

"I want you to come with me," she said.

"Me? Don't you think that's a job for Lionel? It just wouldn't feel right."

"I'm not ready for all that yet. How am I going to explain that I even went to the doctor?"

"Tasha, you have to tell the man everything," I said. "He's your husband. You have to trust him."

"I know and I do trust him. I love my husband."

"Then tell him what you want."

"I know. I know this is my bullshit, but I just have to work through this and then I'll tell him. But right now . . . right now I need you in my corner." Tasha started to cry again.

"Fine," I said. "I'll come with you to the appointment, but then we really have to talk about some things, Tasha.

"When is it?"

"Monday," Tasha said. "Monday at 3 p.m."

"I'll definitely come and support you, Tasha," I said, spinning my schedule around in my head. I got out of class at 2 p.m. on Mondays, so I would be able to make it. "You're my girl. I have your back."

"Oh, and, Troy"—Tasha suddenly perked up a bit and smiled—"who was the cute man you were with?"

Though I'd planned on getting in a quick thirty minutes on my StairMaster, I went to bed right after Tasha left. It was after 1 a.m. and my body just needed to rest. Between Julian and Tasha, I felt mentally and physically drained. I didn't bother to explain who exactly Kyle was to Tasha. I just told her he was a friend of the family. From the look on her face, I could tell my old friend was ready to cook things up between the two of us, and the last thing I needed was more drama, drama, drama.

After closing the blinds and checking my voice mail, I prayed for Tasha. I prayed that she would find peace in whatever God's will was for her. Whether or not he saw fit for Tasha to have the baby, I wanted my friend to be happy and realize that even if she didn't have a baby, she had a man at home who loved her. And all of us couldn't say that—*amen*.

I snuggled under the covers and closed my eyes, praying that sleep would come quickly. I felt my body unravel between the Egyptian satin sheets I'd given myself for my twenty-first birthday. The kinks in my back relaxed and my limbs felt heavy by my sides. Before I knew it, I'd fallen into a peaceful sleep.

I could hear my cell phone ringing. It sounded louder than ever before, sitting on the night stand beside me. I groaned. Why did my phone have to ruin such a perfect dream? If I could get back to that place, I'd stay there forever.

"Hello?" I growled, angrily picking up the phone. It was a blocked number, so I was wondering who it could've been calling me so late at night.

"Don't you 'hello' me, girl," said the voice on the other end of the phone. I instantly knew who it was—my mother. "You should've said hello to me last night. Don't think I didn't find out about you sneaking that . . . that scoundrel in!"

"He's not a scoundrel and I didn't sneak him in, Mom. He was invited," I said, climbing out of bed. Pookie Po looked at me and ran out of the room. She didn't want to talk to my mother either. "And why are you calling me so late at night from a blocked number?" I asked.

"I got a new block on the phone and it's early, Troy. It's almost 7 a.m." My mother was one of those people who liked calling folks first thing in the morning. The ultimate diva of the world was up, so everyone else in the world should be up too. I looked at my clock—6:52 a.m. Damn.

"What are you still doing in bed, anyway? Shouldn't you be studying for school tomorrow? Aren't you going to church with your nana? Was that *boy* over there last night, so you're too tired to wake up?" My mother had a way of stringing question after question together so tightly that you wondered which one she wanted answered first. Or if she wanted you to answer any of them at all. Maybe she thought she already knew all the answers. She paused resolutely, pulling in air for the next series, I supposed. Sometimes I swore the woman was reading from some kind of list—*Questions Mothers Should Ask*.

"I guess you've taken him back after the breakup . . ." she said. I couldn't tell if she was asking me if I'd done it or telling me.

"No, Mom. Nothing happened between me and Julian. In fact, I caught a ride . . . Oh shit, my car!" I mistakenly said into the phone. I'd forgotten all about my car. I had to get to a garage in the middle of the Bronx to pick up my car and then get back downtown for church with Nana Rue. I'd never make it. Even if I did, I'd be too tired from the journey to consider going to church.

"Are you cursing at me now? And what happened to your

car?" my mother asked. I rolled my eyes, trying to figure out how she could've picked up on the thing about the car. *Damn! I only said it once.* She was like a private investigator.

"No. Nothing is wrong with my car." I tried to calm her down. "I just realized that I have something really important to do, so I need to get going."

"No time for your old mother now?" she said. I could tell she was having one of her dramatic days. "You know, one day you're going to wish you were nicer to me. Then maybe you'll spend days shopping with me like you do with your grandmother. How do you think that makes me feel to hear her brag about your little trip? You know she likes to throw stuff like that in my face."

"Mom!"

"I'm serious, Troy. You're my only child."

"I know, Mom." I started the shower. "Maybe you should spend more time with Grandma Lucy, too. She's really not that bad."

"Please, I've been down the 'let's be friends' road with my mother already. It didn't work."

"Look, Mom," I said, looking at the time again, "I'll come by the house this week and we can talk about it." I tried to comfort her. She wasn't going to back down until I came home.

"Tomorrow for an early dinner. Say 6 p.m.?"

"Fine." I was sure I'd be done with Tasha and the doctor by then.

"Troy, I miss you. Don't cancel."

"I won't." I pulled off my T-shirt and threw it on the floor.

"Great. Well, I'll have Desta cook something fantastic."

My mother and Grandma Lucy had little in common, but one thing my mom had gotten from Grandma Lucy was a love of entertaining. Although she definitely hung with a different crowd, Mom was the type of person who could turn one person coming over for dinner into a fiesta. She'd pull out all the stops and make the visitor feel like royalty. "I want everyone to feel special in this place," she'd say, preparing for her girlfriends to come over for their weekly Bloody Mary lunch break on our terrace. They'd sip on the red stuff until the sun went down.

My mother's desire to entertain didn't escape me and my friends either. In fact, her habit came in handy when I was growing up. While other parents tried to force their children out of the house when their friends came over, my mother welcomed everyone with open arms. I'd have friends over and she would make us special treats and let us play dress-up in her closet for hours.

"I'll be there," I said, remembering my mother running around the apartment to get everything perfect before she would accept visitors.

"Yes," she answered. "And one last thing, Troy."

"Yes, Mom."

"Be nice to Kyle at dinner tonight." She hung up quickly and I sat frowning, looking at my cell phone. How had she found out about Kyle? *See what I mean . . . private investigator.*

Divalicious

It's next to impossible to become anything if you don't have a role model. If you're an aspiring diva, there's a green room full of divalicious role models to choose from. Salute the savvy sisters of yesteryear. From Patti's "Lady Marmalade" to Aretha's fierce furs, those sisters keep it interesting and oh-so divalicious. They paved the way so you too could wear chinchilla in the winter and Manolo Blahniks in the spring. Don't forget to add the divas in your life to the list. A toast, please!

Name and Divalicious Destiny

Aretha Franklin: Soul singer who demands R-E-S-P-E-C-T. Most folks know not to mess with "The Queen."

Diahann Carroll: The one sister on *Dynasty* who showed the world what it's like to be brave, beautiful, and brown.

Diana Ross: Bold eyes and big dreams. The diva supreme proved that *Mahogany* is where it's at.

Leontyne Price: The original diva who was the first black international classical singer.

Madame C.J. Walker: Became one of the richest black women in history by giving sisters a new 'do.

Oprah Winfrey: Media mogul who makes her own rules and breaks every one of theirs.

Patti LaBelle: Made every black girl dream of flying after hearing her sing "Somewhere Over the Rainbow."

How to Kill Two Birds with One Lip Liner

If it wasn't for my desire to curse out Kyle's ass for telling my parents about our date—no, *meeting*—I would've gone straight home after church. I was dead tired from all the hustling to get the car from the Bronx and then down to Harlem to pick up Nana Rue for church, but I had a bone to pick and it was with Kyle. Where did he get off telling my mother about our *meeting*? I was in the middle of trying to get Julian back and I wasn't interested in Kyle—no matter whom he had on his side. Period.

When I arrived at Paola's for dinner, thirty minutes late, I peeked inside to see if Kyle was still there. I found him sitting at a table in the back of the restaurant. There was a vase filled with magnolias sitting on the table in front of him.

Determined to get my point across about him calling my mother, I stormed toward him, ready to use even my lip liner as a weapon.

"Kyle," I said angrily. Just as I was about to speak again, he looked toward me and smiled wide enough to make me stop dead in my tracks. He stood up with a bouquet of flowers in his hands.

"These are for you, Troy." Kyle handed me the bouquet and pulled out my chair. I sat down, holding the flowers in my arms, and I do believe I literally felt myself melt. My anger got lost somewhere between his smile and the calming scent of the magnolias. In the spring, Nana Rue decorated her entire brownstone with fresh-cut magnolias. The scent was so strong you could smell them in the street when you walked by. They were my favorite. But how did he know?

"These are lovely," I said, looking at the flowers. "My favorite."

"Well, I wanted to surprise you, so I called your mother this morning to ask her what your favorite flowers were. I hope you'll forgive me."

"Kyle, this is really wonderful." I paused. "It's amazing." Sitting there with one bouquet of my favorite flowers in my arms and another on the table in front of me, my little complaint about Kyle calling my mother felt tiny and insignificant.

"I just wanted to cheer you up after last night. I know you were stressed about the whole thing with your car and then your friend. How is she?" Kyle smiled, and for the first time I noticed a tiny dimple in the middle of his chin. It was just small enough for me to stick my pinky finger in. It was adorable. I had to admit, Kyle was truly a good-looking man. He had a kind of classic, young Sidney Poitier fineness to him.

"Tasha's better," I said, forcing myself to look at the menu and not at the dimple.

"Well, that's good to hear. She seemed pretty shaken up."

The waitress came over and Kyle ordered for both of us.

"I must say, it was nice to see you last night," he said as she walked away. "It was nice to get to know the *real* Troy."

"The real Troy? What does that mean?"

"Well, in the car, I realized that you're really down-to-earth. You're funny, Troy." He grinned. "You're not just a . . . what do they call them . . . Black American Princess."

"Oh, so now you think I'm a BAP?" I laughed. I was used

to the "BAP" classification. It always amazed me how quickly people wanted to put me into some category as soon as they found out my family had a little money and I had decent taste. Hell, for the most part it was true. I was a BAP poster child.

"Well, let's be honest, at the country club you seemed a little snobby," Kyle said. "I wasn't exactly fond of you." He held up his napkin like a shield.

"Snobby?" I said, grabbing the napkin. While I could handle being called a BAP, I was not snobby. Shoot, I could drink and cuss with the best of them! "Please, you know you were trying to get with *this*," I joked.

"Troy, you were acting like a spoiled little rich girl that day. Not my type." We both laughed. I couldn't help it. He was right. Kyle wasn't even on my friend list.

"But that's the past. And what I know now, after talking to you in the car and seeing how carefully you took care of your friend, is that there's more to you. There's a lot more," Kyle said. "And I'm happy you came out today, too," he went on. "I was afraid you'd stand me up."

"Stand you up?"

"Yeah. I know how you ladies can be about going out with, you know, religious men who have dedicated their lives to God. And you didn't seem too thrilled about me being a virgin." Kyle started laughing again and I realized that I'd almost forgotten about his occupation.

"It was nothing, Kyle. Really," I said. "I mean, it's a choice."

"I'm glad you feel that way, because I didn't want to spend all of my money on these flowers trying to impress you and then get dissed."

I sighed and looked down at the flowers. They were great. Kyle was great. But I had to tell him the truth.

"No, the flowers are lovely, Kyle. But I have to be honest with you." I paused, giving the waitress time to put the food on the table. "I'm not really looking for anything right now. I'm kind of in between places."

Kyle said a short prayer over our food and looked at me.

" 'In between'? Oh, that's a new one." He dug into his steak forcefully. I could tell he was annoyed with me. It was obvious that he had gone through a lot of trouble trying to impress me. Hell, the man had called my mama! It was the right gesture—just the wrong man. Why couldn't Julian have done something like that for me? Suddenly, the spring salad I'd ordered tasted incredibly dull in my mouth. I wanted to eat my words.

"It's not a line, Kyle," I said, sliding my fork onto the plate. "You just caught me at the wrong time, that's all."

"So my obligations don't bother you?"

"Well, I'll admit, I'm not exactly thrilled with it, but it doesn't make me not want to be your friend." I reached across the table and grabbed his hand. "And I do want to be your friend."

"Hmm . . ." He gasped. "Friend?" He looked me over. "I guess that'll work. Besides, then I'll get to see you again. And that would be a blessing."

"Great!" I said. He smiled, and judging from the appearance of the chin dimple, it was a truce.

"Troy," Kyle said, looking at me, "whoever *he* is, he's a lucky man."

"Thanks, Kyle."

"I really mean that or I wouldn't even be here. I don't exactly have a shortage of women trying to get to me at the church."

I had to laugh. Those church sisters were a trip. They loved trying to get with a single man of God—or even a married man of God. I saw the way they flocked to the pastor at my own church. They carried cakes to church, asked for special "prayer" meetings—some of them even tried to have their mamas hook them up. It was some stiff competition going on in the Lord's house.

"So are you throwing the church ladies up in my face?" I frowned playfully.

"No, I'm just saying, I don't want you to allow people to take you for granted." He stared deeply into my eyes. "No one should ever take a woman like you for granted. You're smart, loving, witty, and more beautiful than any one man could ever deserve."

"That might be one of the nicest things anyone's ever said to me, Kyle," I said, after turning to look behind me to see if he was talking to someone else or reading from a script. The man was unreal. His words were so sweet, I didn't know if I wanted to cry or jump over the table to hug him.

"It's true."

"Enough about little old me," I said, blushing. "What about you? Tell me about you."

"What about me?" Kyle asked. "I'm an open book. No secrets."

"I mean, you mentioned the whole 'obligations' thing. What made you become a pastor? How did you finally decide to just do it?"

"Hmm . . ." He looked up at the ceiling like he was searching for the right thing to say.

"I'm sure plenty of people ask you that. I'm sorry if it's a stupid question."

"No, it's not stupid," he said. "In fact, I like to answer the question. It reminds me of why I'm doing this. Keeps me focused." He paused. "You know, my family history was one thing. I was born and raised in the church. It was all I knew for a long time. But then when I turned twelve and I thought I could go against my father and my grandfather, I decided that I didn't want to be a preacher. I was like, 'To heck with them and this whole church thing. It's corny. I want to be a rapper.'"

"What happened?" I laughed. I couldn't imagine Kyle the Rapper! Christian Kyle was funnier. "I know they didn't like that."

"No, my father always had this way of letting people see the truth for themselves. So he didn't fight me." Kyle smiled.

"He went and got me a notebook and told me to write my rhymes in it."

"Really?"

"Yeah. So I changed my name to MC K-Lover and I was writing rhymes, and my cousins started writing too, and we made up dances and stuff. It was crazy. We thought we were some kind of Tennessee rap group, about to take the world by storm," Kyle said, laughing. "But then my father started asking me about the things I was saying in the songs. He asked me what I wanted to do with my music, how I wanted to change the world and touch people. I guess it had never dawned on me, because I couldn't answer. I could think about the girls and the cars, but I didn't know what in the heck I wanted to say in my rhymes."

"You wanted to be like the rappers in the music videos. Like Slick Rick," I joked.

"Exactly. So when I ran out of things to write about—there wasn't exactly a lot of murdering and drug dealing going on in our small town in Tennessee—I just started putting little things about God in the songs. It was really all I knew. So then we turned into Christian rappers."

"No, no, no." I was laughing so hard I almost spit out my food.

"I swear. We performed in the church pageant and everything. Now, this was a big deal in Tennessee in the late '80s. Then one day my father said he wanted me to do one of my rhymes for the church. In the church."

"Really?" Even I knew folks wouldn't like that. Rapping in the church?

"I thought, this man has lost his mind. I couldn't rhyme from the pulpit—people would hate it. We'd lose the whole church after that for sure. So anyway, I told my father it was a bad idea and he pretended he didn't know folks would have that bad take on it. I say he *pretended* because I now know the old man was just setting me up. So he said, 'Well, boy, I

think you have some powerful things to say and I really want
the church to hear them.'"

"So what did he suggest?"

"He was acting like he was thinking about how we could
pull it off and then he was like, 'I got it. You can read one of
the rhymes. Just read one of them to the church so they don't
know it's a rhyme.' "

"That's a sermon," I said.

"Exactly, but I didn't see that back then. All I knew was
that MC K-Lover had a gig."

"Sneaky man." I laughed.

"Yeah, so that was my first sermon. Well, it was a rap, but
it was a sermon. I read it up there and I was just over-
whelmed when the crowd responded. I felt the energy moving through the room. I could see the Holy Ghost touching
people as I spoke. It was an amazing feeling. I wasn't even
reading the words anymore after a while; it was just coming
from inside me. Like fire. Soon, I stepped away from the
pulpit; I was in the aisles, walking around, touching people.
I couldn't stop. I just wanted to preach the word." He paused
reflectively. "I was just twelve."

"Wow. So what happened to the rap thing?"

"Please, I was young but not dumb. The women and the
cars and fly stuff didn't have nothing on what I felt in the
church. It was a young love between me and the church, but
it was a beginning. I never turned away again. Not once."

"Wow" was the only thing I could say. I'd never heard
anyone speak of what they did with such conviction.

While we ate, we discovered that we both loved the free
summer jazz concerts at Bryant Park, and though he stayed
away from R&B for obvious reasons, he loved listening to
jazz. As the waitress cleared our table, Kyle and I decided to
check out the opening concert coming up in two weeks. I
didn't exactly have a packed schedule, and he was good company.

I felt such a sense of relief, listening to Kyle talk. I grew to like him even more, and I was looking forward to being his friend. Plus, he was a good distraction from all the stuff with Julian. And every girl knows that a good dude distraction is the best thing a girl could have when she's trying to heal a broken heart.

"I have another confession to make," I said, standing beside my car in front of the restaurant.

"Oh no, don't drop another bomb on me like last time." Kyle playfully threw his hands up in the air. "I can't take it anymore."

"It's nothing like that, silly." I laughed. "I was just going to say I was mad at you before I came here."

"And why was that?" He placed the magnolias on my passenger seat.

"I found out that you told my mother about our dinner and it made me really upset."

"I'm sorry, but I had no other way to find out your favorite flowers, and I wanted to do something—"

I placed my index finger over his lips. "But it's okay now. I understand." I got into the car and turned it on. Kyle turned to walk to his own car, which was parked behind mine, but he kept looking over his shoulder.

"Bye, Kyle," I said, waving at him.

"Bye, Troy," he replied. "Get home safely and don't go getting towed."

"Kyle," I called. He turned back around. "Thank you."

How to Get a Dude Distractor: I Do . . . Just Not You

When you know the main course will take more than a little while to come steaming out of the kitchen, the best thing you can do is feast on a tasty side salad. Why should your love life be any different? Stop sitting at home watching *Living Single* reruns, waiting for the man of your dreams to come knocking at the door. There are many men out there willing to be your tasty Caesar salad . . . you just have to place your order. A Dude Distractor (DD) is someone you hang out with (not date) temporarily to distract yourself from whatever's ailing you. Say you're dating a guy you really like, but you're afraid you may be crowding him—get a DD to occupy your time. The same applies if you're waiting for the love of your life to show up, your lover is acting up, or you're just hungry and broke as hell.

<u>DD Do's:</u>
1. *Contact the sexiest DD possible.*
2. *Make it clear that you don't want a relationship.*
3. *Keep him in rotation with other DDs—spread the love.*
4. *Use a condom . . . if you have sex.*

<u>DD Don'ts:</u>
1. *Use a friend as a DD.*
2. *Ever tell your main guy about your DD.*
3. *Lie to a DD about your feelings.*
4. *Do anything that may cause your DD to catch feelings. Examples: answer late-night calls, take long walks, travel, meet his friends, go on family outings, let him stay at your place—or vice versa, cook for him, buy or take gifts, etc.*

Girl Fight

I opened my CD box to find my old Lauryn Hill CD so I could put it in and listen to it on the drive back downtown. By the time I looked up, Kyle had pulled away. I slipped the CD in, and just as I was about to pull away from the curb, a familiar face walked out of the restaurant beside Paola's.

"Miata?" I said to myself. "No, it can't be." It was her. My heart started beating fast. I didn't know why, but I wanted to do something, say something. From what I could tell, she was alone. I had to say something. Maybe I could connect with her and find out, once and for all, what was really happening between her and Julian.

I stepped out of my car when she turned toward me. I didn't know what I was gonna say or do, but I was all heart, all emotion. Suddenly my initial rationale left me and I kept thinking, *That bitch took my man.* And though I wasn't born in the ghetto, I knew the rules of the ghetto. She needed her ass whooped for that.

"Miata," I said, stepping onto the sidewalk behind her. It stung to hear her name said aloud.

"Yes," she turned and smiled. She looked uglier than I remembered. I didn't know what to say after her name. I mean, I expected her response to be something I could work with. She was supposed to call me a bitch and then I'd pull out my lip liner and start stabbing. *Yeah, that was how fights went.*

"What are you doing with Julian?" *Oh, my God. I sound like an ass. Those aren't fighting words; Troy,* I said to myself. "I mean, I'm just asking." I was punking out and the fight hadn't even begun.

"Excuse me?" She stepped toward me with that stupid grin on her face again. "Do I know you?"

"You know you know me. Don't even try it. What are you doing with Julian?"

Miata stepped close and batted her eyes seductively.

"Everything."

That one word, that one single word, was enough to make me want to jump on Miata and beat her until the cops dragged me off of her lifeless body. But I knew better. I was raised better than that. Obviously, she wasn't.

"And he's loving every moment of it," she added. Suddenly I felt stupid for even getting out of my car. I wasn't a confrontational person. My fights with my mother didn't count. What was I trying to prove?

"Look at you," she said, "you can't even say anything." She stepped back. "Poor precious little rich Barbie doll. I guess you're about to cry."

"What is your damn problem?" I asked.

"My problem is you, Troy. I want Julian. I'm the kind of real woman he needs by his side. Not some little girl who hasn't worked for *anything* in her life. I've worked hard for everything I have. And I'm willing to work even harder for Julian."

"You sound crazy. You must be crazy." I shook my head. "You can't make him love you. You can't make a man love you."

Miata laughed and stepped back, tossing her purse over her shoulder.

"Once again you've proved me right," she said. "Rich and obviously not very smart. If you want Julian, you try to take him from me and then you'll see what I can and can't make someone do."

I wanted to say something cool like, "Well, it's on, trick," but all that came out was, "Whatever."

Defeated, I turned to walk back to my car, but then I heard Tasha's voice in my head saying, "Stand up for yourself."

I turned back around toward Miata and I tapped her on the shoulder.

"On second thought," I said, "just who in the fuck do you think you are?"

"What?" she said, stepping back.

"You don't know shit about me other than what Julian has told you, so I'd appreciate it if you kept my name out of your nasty-ass mouth. You may have been through a lot of shit, but if you don't stay away from my man, you're gonna have to go through a lot more. And that, my dear, is a promise."

Miata's mouth was hanging wide open. I looked her up and down, sucked my teeth, and stepped back toward my car. I knew better than to turn my back on her.

On the way back home I got myself further riled up after slipping in one of Tasha's old West Coast gangsta rap CDs. I was pissed and ready to fight, and I actually liked the feeling of adrenaline rushing through my veins.

Miata's little silly scene that proved she was completely insane was just the fire I needed on my backside to push me on to the next part of the plan. She asked for World War III and she was about to get it.

Female Defense/Offense: Playing for Your Man

Make no mistake about it—no matter who your man is, how he looks, or what he has, some other woman has her eyes on him. It's simple mathematics. Women outnumber men three to one, and the numbers get even worse the higher you climb in social status. The number of good, well-bred men out there is low. This mathematical fact has led to a sometimes cruel world where a woman is left with no choice but to fight to keep her man . . . if he's really worth having.

It may sound a bit catty, but ignoring the possibility of another woman trying to ruin your happy home could leave you with scratches on your back. You must be prepared for when women attack.

<u>Signs Your Man Is Under Attack:</u> The other woman laughs too hard at his corny jokes, she volunteers to spend time with him, she calls a little too late, she's always saying how much she admires your relationship, and she's always asking him to come by to fix something or help her out—she needs to find her own "Mr. Fix-It."

<u>Women to Look Out For:</u> The assistant, the ex, women at church, his "girlfriends" who can't seem to respect you, and, sadly, sometimes your friends attack, too.

<u>Do's:</u>
1. *Be cool. Paranoia is a bad sign.*
2. *Know your man and his limits—a dog will be a dog. Turn him loose if he is.*
3. *Stop talking to people about how good he is in bed.*
4. *Stay away from the drama.*
5. *Support your man.*

<u>Don'ts:</u>
1. *Fight fire with fire—this will only make the attacker think you're on her level. Remember, you're in control here.*

2. *Allow her to cause you and your man to fight.*
3. *Accuse your man of anything you can't prove. And if you do, be prepared to act on it.*
4. *Leave your man alone with her for any reason.*
5. *Confuse high self-esteem with blindness. Thinking "my man loves me and he won't cheat" won't stop this hussy from taking off her clothes in his office.*

Note: Trust your man and talk to him openly about your feelings. But don't nag.

Bloody Mary and the Soap Opera Baby

Sitting in the waiting room at Tasha's doctor's office, I couldn't stop fidgeting. She'd been behind the sliding glass doors for over thirty minutes and I was beginning to worry. Did she get really bad news and break down in the doctor's arms? Was she too embarrassed to come out to face me and the rest of the cruel world? *Positive thinking. Positive thinking,* I kept saying to myself, rocking back and forth. The obviously pregnant woman sitting beside me was looking at me like I was crazy. With my new gangsta-girl attitude in tow, I would've said something to her for staring, but I couldn't blame the sister. I felt just as crazy as I must've looked.

I stared up at the ceiling, counting the dusty white panels like sheep jumping over my bed to lull me to sleep. I'd spent the past thirty minutes trying to count each square. So far, I was up to seventy-three.

While I didn't mind hanging around hospitals, thanks to spending many lunch hours sitting in the cafeteria at the NYU Medical Center having lunch with Julian, I hated doctors' offices. There was something creepy about them. They were so quiet and spotless. Everyone was always smiling and trying to be so damn pleasant, but beneath all of it, I always felt that something evil was looming behind the big, scary doors that separated the offices from the waiting room. Something waiting to reach out and get me. This was because while everyone was smiling outside, thumbing through old-ass copies of *Redbook* and *Mademoiselle* in the waiting area, inside you knew some woman was getting the worst news of her life: She was dying, she couldn't have kids, she had to get her toe removed, the doctor she was in love with was seeing the new intern . . . It was a pretty scary place if you thought about it.

With all these bad thoughts swirling around in my head, I was about to hyperventilate and pass out in the pregnant lady's arms when Tasha finally came easing through the door. She was smiling.

"What happened?" I asked, meeting her halfway down the hallway. "What did he say?"

"He said . . ." She paused. "He said I'm a good candidate for in vitro! I just need to get Lionel in here." I nearly picked Tasha up off the floor. We held each other as we danced around the hallway, crying our eyes out. I was so relieved for her. It's one thing to get pregnant by accident, but to try to get pregnant and then find out you couldn't—that had to hurt. But now, all was good.

"I can't believe it. This is really happening to you," I said, walking out of the doctor's office arm-in-arm with Tasha.

"Well, at least I know I can be a mother," Tasha said. "It's on Lionel now."

Tasha looked much better than she had the other night at my apartment. The sun seemed to be sitting in the sky and smiling down on her. She had on a cute pink sundress and sling-back Mary Janes. Her hair was pulled back in a tight bun and she was wearing the diamond earrings Tamia and I gave her for Christmas. She seemed to have the pregnant glow already.

"I'm so excited. I never thought all of this would feel this good," Tasha went on. "Just imagine"—she looked down at her stomach and rubbed it—"someone's gonna be living in there in a little while. My baby. Hey, we should celebrate. Let's go out for cocktails. You know I need to get my last drinks in before I get knocked up. It's gonna be a loooooong time before I can drink again."

"Oh, I can't." I searched my purse for my keys. We'd driven to the doctor's office together. Tasha had parked her car at my apartment in case she got bad news at the doctor's office and couldn't drive. "I have to go to my parents' for this dinner thing after I drop you off downtown," I said.

"Oh, too bad." Tasha got into the car.

"Actually, you could just come with me." Tasha would provide a great distraction for my mother. With someone else there, she wouldn't be able to get all in my business about Julian. Plus, she loved Tasha.

"That sounds like fun. You know I love kicking it with your mama. Is she making her slamming Bloody Marys?" Tasha asked, laughing. The last time I took her and Tamia to my parents' house, the three of us had to stay over. We got so drunk sipping on my mother's Bloody Marys that Tamia and I fell asleep outside on the terrace and Tasha somehow ended up in the penthouse cabana. We still joke about her going missing, saying she had an affair with the pool boy—no, my parents don't have one.

"You know she'll make them if we ask her to. Mary Elizabeth loves to entertain," I said. I pulled into traffic and Tasha called Lionel to tell him she was going with me to my parents', so she'd probably be a little late getting home.

My phone rang just as Tasha was ending her call with a parade of "I love yous" between her and Lionel. It was a welcome interruption, because I was about to vomit if I had to hear her say "I love you, poopie," again. I opened the phone, sure it was my mother calling to see if I was still coming. My heart fluttered when I looked at the name on the caller ID: Julian. I turned the phone to Tasha so she could see.

"Answer it," she said, putting her phone in her purse. "Remember step three. Answer it and just *be yourself*. Don't bring up the incident with that girl and if he does, just play it down. Make her look crazy."

I'd told Tasha all about the Miata run-in as we sat in the waiting room waiting for the doctor to call her in. She'd cursed Miata's name so many times as I told the story that the nurse got up and personally handed us magazines as if to say, "Shut up."

"Hello," I said, turning on my earpiece. There was silence. I looked at the phone again, afraid I'd missed the call.

"Hey, baby," Julian said.

"Hi, Julian," I replied, sounding even more awkward than he did.

"I was just having lunch in the cafeteria and I was thinking about you. You know, old times."

"Really?" I grinned and gave a thumbs-up to Tasha. Step three: "Say You, Say Me" was in full effect. He was reminiscing just as the plan predicted. "We did have some great times there," I said.

"Yeah, I don't think I would've made it through my residency without you." I could feel Julian smiling on the other end of the line. "You really stuck by my side . . . bringing me lunch every day."

"Well, I was just being myself. I know you hate cafeteria food." I winked at Tasha. "Any good *friend* would've tried to help you."

"Friends . . . that's actually why I'm calling." *Oh no, he was about to bring up the thing with Miata.*

"Okay," I said, ready to explain myself.

"I need to talk to you about something."

"What?"

"Well, it's really important, but I need to see you in person to talk about it," Julian said. I heard the hospital page him over the loudspeaker in the background.

"When and where?" I asked. Tasha rolled her eyes. I was

being too easy. "*I mean,* let me know as soon as possible when you'd like to meet because I'm very, very busy right now," I added. Tasha smiled, giving her sign of approval.

"Troy, I just got paged to the ER," Julian said quickly. "I'll call you later to set things up."

"Okay, bye," I said and hung up the phone.

What the hell was going on? Had Miata told Julian or not? I wanted to turn the car around and head to the NYU Medical Center. I had a damn emergency! I wanted to know what he had to say. I threw the phone into the backseat.

"What?" From the corner of my eye, I saw Tasha looking at me. "He said he has something to say," I said. I was confused. A million things were running through my mind. Did he want me back? Did he want to be friends? Was he marrying Miata? Did he need a damn kidney? What was it, dammit?

"Hmm . . ." Tasha let out in a knowing way.

"*'Hmm'?* What does that mean?" I asked. "Is that a bad sign? Tell me, Tasha." I made a sharp right and nearly ran over the curb.

"Damn, don't kill me, girl," Tasha said, putting her seat belt on. "It doesn't mean anything. I'm just surprised."

"Surprised?"

"Yeah, that he's come to a conclusion so fast." She pulled down the passenger mirror and smoothed her hair.

"What kind of conclusion?" I asked, slamming her mirror shut.

"It's like this: Women think too much. We're always worried about what men want or how they feel when they're really quite simple. Men are just like black or white—one or the other."

"So what's your point?"

"Well, what I mean is this: Either Julian wants to be with you or he doesn't. Case closed." She opened the mirror again.

"But what about the thing with Miata?" I asked. "You think it's about that? Damn, I made a fool out of myself."

"Please, ain't nobody tell you to roll up on a ghetto girl if you wasn't ready to fight." Tasha laughed at me. "But, to be honest, I don't think she told him anything about what happened. If she did, he would've said something right away or not even have called you again. Men don't like female drama. Tasha paused. "This bitch is slicker than I thought. She didn't tell Julian." Tasha laughed. "Whew . . . her ass is slick. Miata is a smart girl. She has her own little plan in effect with Julian. And if she knows men don't like drama, she's not going to bring any to him. She wants you to tell him about the fight so you sound dramatic and crazy to him. That's why she said all that crazy shit to get you all riled up. She was playing you, Ms. Lovesong. She probably wanted you to hit her and get your dumb ass arrested."

"So I could look like the crazy one," I agreed.

"And then Julian would see it and then—"

"Dump me."

"Exactly." Tasha laughed. "I told you this bitch is smart. We have to really get on our game. Your next move has to be tighter than a virgin's cootie cat."

"You're so nasty," I said, laughing.

"I know, but you're my friend, so that makes you nastier because you should know better."

When I handed my keys to the valet at my parents' apartment building, I realized that I had to talk to Tasha about how I felt she was handling her infertility before we went upstairs. I decided I wasn't being a true friend if I didn't tell her how I really felt about her actions. Though I was her friend and I would stand by her side no matter what, I couldn't support her lying to her husband.

I led her to one of the Victorian-style couches that no one ever sat on in the lobby of the building. "I need to ask you something and I don't want you to be mad," I said, trying to go slow on her. Tasha could get really defensive at times and

I didn't want her to simply dismiss my thoughts and walk away. She would.

"Okay." She sat down next to me.

"When are you going to tell Lionel about wanting to have a baby?"

"I don't know," Tasha said. "I guess I have to now. Unless I plan on using someone else's sperm."

I chuckled at the thought. She'd make headlines with that one. KNICKS PLAYER'S WIFE KNOCKED UP BY NEXT MAN. She'd be all up in "Sister2Sister."

"Seriously, Tash. He has a right to know about all of this," I said. "I know I said I'd stick by you but you have to know I don't approve. I know Lionel. I've seen the two of you together and I know he will stand by your side."

"I know that." Tasha looked at me.

"So what are you afraid of? Why do you think he'll say no?"

"It's not about him saying no. It's about me. I know that already." She paused. "I've never had to answer to anyone. I left home when I was just a teenager and since then I've made up all my own rules. I've done it on my own. Even marrying Lionel was my decision." Tasha looked down at the marble tile and played with her wedding ring as she spoke. "So when I decided to have a baby, I just wanted it to be my decision."

"But having a baby isn't about one person's decision. It's about two people coming together and agreeing that they have enough love to give that baby." I grabbed her hand. "You have to make sure Lionel is ready for all this."

"I'm just afraid, I guess. I'm afraid to give all that away . . . the control, you know? To let someone else make that decision for me."

"Tasha, marriage doesn't work like that and we both know it. You said it yourself the other night to Tamia," I said. "My parents have the oddest relationship, but I did learn one thing from watching them." I paused and reached over to turn

Tasha's face back toward me. "And it's that you have to make decisions together. You have to give up some of your power in order to be more powerful with your husband. And you've got to do that with Lionel. You have to tell him, Tasha. And not just about in vitro—about everything. About wanting and trying to get pregnant behind his back. You have to tell him so you two can try to understand why you felt a need to do what you did. You can't keep secrets like that in a marriage. He deserves to know. And if he's a good man, like I know he is," I said, staring into her eyes, "he'll stand by your side and forgive you."

Tasha put her head on my shoulder.

"You're right," Tasha said. "He doesn't deserve this." She paused and a tear rolled down her cheek. "I can't promise anything tonight, but I am going to tell him. I just have to find the right time."

"That's enough of a promise, Ms. Lovestrong," I said, patting her knee. "That's enough."

"Mommy?" I called, walking into my parents' living room. "I'm here." As usual, everything had been changed since my last visit. My mother was a compulsive decorator and this time the decor was Indian, reflecting my parents' recent trip to India.

"Hello, Troy," Desta said, rushing out of the kitchen. Only a few years older than me, Desta was stunningly beautiful. Her skin, dark as Pepsi-Cola, was smooth and clear. She had enticing brown eyes, and though my mother said she plowed through the fridge like a racehorse, she never went a pound over 120.

"Hi, Desta." I smiled. "This is my friend Tasha," I said, turning to Tasha, who had made herself cozy on the new sofa my mother had had shipped from Bangalore.

"We've met already," Tasha said, waving. Desta smiled pleasantly and nodded her head again.

When Desta was just seven, both of her parents died of AIDS and she was sent to live with distant relatives in Kenya. The people were really nice to her, but she said they couldn't afford to have her, so they sold her to be married when Desta was twelve. The man was much older than her and he beat her so severely, Desta's first child died in her womb. When she was twenty-four, she secretly applied to a program that allowed women to come to America to work, and luckily she got in. So on her twenty-fifth birthday, she left her home in the middle of the night, leaving behind her three children. She told my mother it broke her heart but that she knew it was the only way she would ever be able to do anything for them.

"Your mother outside," Desta said. She pointed to the terrace. "She wait for you." I pulled a reluctant Tasha up from the couch and headed outside to the terrace.

My mother was sitting at the table yapping away on the phone. She was saying something about needing more bricks to finish the porch on the new Habitat for Humanity house she was building with her sorority sisters.

"Well, would you want to live in a house with no porch?" she said, holding the phone beneath her chin and balancing a cigarette in one hand and a glass of wine in the other—it was a skill she'd picked up a long time ago. She smiled when she saw me and Tasha and nodded for us to walk over to the table. "I know they're poor, Mr. Councilman, but they deserve options, too." She skillfully took a pull from her cigarette and stood up to kiss me on the cheek. "Look, if you can't give me what I want, I'll just call Judge Shivers up and see what he's willing to donate. Maybe you'll match his offering." She paused. "He is running for your office next year, right? Let me remind you of the black Greek's voting stronghold in the community." My mother had him right where she wanted him. Votes. I loved watching her play hardball. Lord knows she could raise some damn money. Get donations from a poor man. "Well, thank you. I knew we could come to a compromise. I'll look for that check in the mail," she said, smiling. She was wearing her favorite orange and black sari, another Indian import. "Yes, and it's great doing business with you, Mr. Councilman." She hung up the phone and grinned mischievously. "Darling, I can't believe you're here," she said, kissing me on the forehead again.

"You invited me, Mom." I sat down at the table. She had it set up for a formal dinner.

"Don't get smart with me, girl. You're still on my bad side, after that stunt you pulled last week at the theater—not speaking to me."

"Hi, Mrs. Smith," said Tasha, my ineffective distraction.

"Hi, baby," my mother replied, kissing Tasha on both her cheeks. "Troy didn't say you were coming over. Are you staying for our dinner?"

"Dinner and some of your famous Bloody Marys, I was hoping," Tasha said.

"Oh, flattery will get you young ladies everywhere in life." My mother smiled. "Desta," she shouted, "I'll need another setting." I counted two settings on the table. "And a pitcher of my Bloody Marys."

"Daddy's not here?" I asked.

"No, he had a thing at the country club. You know your father." She stubbed out her cigarette in the ashtray. "Besides, I wanted to spend time with my little girl. Seems like everybody gets to look at you these days except for me. I see you're finally losing some weight. And what happened to your hair? Please don't tell me that's a perm! What did Lucy do to you?"

To this, I preferred to say nothing. I sat and looked away from my mother, imagining that I was someplace else. I called it my Vow of Silence. When I was just a small girl, I realized that the best way to get my mother to leave me alone was to ignore her. If I said something, she'd keep going, but if I said nothing, she'd shut the hell up. It was nothing personal. It was just the only way I could ensure that we'd both survive the whole mother-daughter thing.

"Fine then . . ." she said finally. "This is the thanks I get for trying to comfort you during your time of need? You can't even talk to me?"

"Mom, it's not like that," I said as Desta set the pitcher on the table. "I just know how you can get about my breakups—"

"How do I get?" she said, cutting me off. Even Tasha had to smile at that one. Everyone knew how she *got*.

"Well, 'crazy' comes to mind. You kind of take it too personally when I break up with someone . . . heck, you take it too personally when I have an argument with someone. That's why I can't tell you everything."

"Lies. All lies," she cried in her dramatic Scarlett O'Hara voice. "Troy, I'm your mother and I just want to protect you. I don't want you to get your feelings hurt. No real mother does."

"But it's a part of life," I said, pouring the red concoction of Bloody Mary into my glass.

"I know, darling, but I have to be there when things go bad for you. It's my job." She pinched my cheek. "I've been on this earth for a long time. I've been hurt many times. And I think the only reason I was able to get back up after folks knocked me down is that I knew I would have you someday, and I'd be able to use my experience to help you get through."

"Oh, Mom. That's so sweet," I said. I got up and gave her a hug. She was a piece of work, but as my father always said, she meant well. My mother had a huge heart. And while I was always trying to push her away, she never let me go. Plus, she gave me good advice . . . sometimes.

For example, my first boyfriend, Champ (I know it's a stupid name but it was sexy back then), was an Alpha I met my sophomore year after pledging. Champ was the spoiled son of a politician. He was at the top of his class, on his way to law school at Harvard, and he drove a gold CLK—big-time

during those days, even for Howard. I'd set up a chance
meeting between my mother and Champ at my sorority's
spring tea. She hated him. Her exact words were: "He's a
smug bastard. He'll ruin your life." I held on to Champ for
dear life after that—out of sheer defiance. But the very next
semester, a new crop of freshmen showed up on the lawn,
one being Lori St. Croix, a Creole from New Orleans who
took a liking to Champ. Anyway, he started disappearing off
and on, and pretty soon he disappeared altogether. We split
up before the Christmas break.

"So are you going to tell me about Julian now?" She smiled.

"Nope," I said, remembering Champ. I didn't want her to
speak her prediction about Julian into the atmosphere. I
couldn't let her doom my plan like she had before.

"Tasha," my mother said, cutting her eyes at me.

"Hmm?" Tasha managed, sipping on her Bloody Mary.

"Do you keep things from your mother?"

"Well, since I haven't spoken to Porsche in two years, I
suppose I do keep things from her," Tasha said matter-of-
factly. Though my mother, an avid soap watcher, knew who
Tasha's mother was, I'd never told her about their relationship. I figured it was for Tasha to tell.

"Two years?" my mother frowned. "It must be hard for
you." She put her hand on top of Tasha's.

"Not for nothing, Mrs. Smith," Tasha said coolly after finishing her second Bloody Mary, "but I'd memorized the entire menu at the Beverly Hills Hotel by the time I was twelve."
She watched Desta put the food on the table. "And I had a
nanny. Her name was Consuela. I spent so much time with her
when I was a little girl that I called her Mommy. My mother
fired her right in front of me when I was fourteen. I was
heartbroken when Consuela left. I felt like a member of my
family had died. Right there I decided that I hated Porsche."
Tasha looked at me. She'd never told me that part of the
story. I figured it was the Bloody Mary working her magic. I
just hoped she didn't end up in the cabana again. "So, no,

not speaking to my mother is not hard for me. It's pretty damn easy."

Everyone was silent around the table. Even Desta was standing by the door, looking as if she was about to burst into tears.

"Time for a refill," I said, grabbing the pitcher.

Desta disappeared inside and came back with her own glass.

Proud Mary: A Bloody Toast to the Queen

Mix up this Bloody Mary in your blender the next time you're expecting some girlie guests. Full of alcohol, this sipper will make all your visitors feel right at home. Mary will weep and Martha will moan. Just be prepared to collect some keys and turn drinks into an impromptu sleepover.

The Bad Ass Bloody Mary
(Makes a Pitcher for All to Enjoy)

Ingredients:

  23 oz. tomato juice
  23 oz. V8 juice
  1 tbsp. horseradish
  1½ ounces of vodka
  ¾ oz. Tabasco sauce
  1 tbsp. Worcestershire sauce
  1 oz. lemon juice
  1 tsp. freshly ground pepper
  ¼ tsp. celery salt

Garnish:
  1 sliced lime
  celery sticks
  celery salt

Directions:
  Combine ingredients in a blender and mix. Pour over ice into a tall glass rimmed with celery salt. Garnish with a celery stick and twist a lime slice over the glass edge.
  *If you like it very spicy, add ⅛ tsp. of ground red pepper.

One Confused Man and One Confused Womb-Man

The ride home from dinner was eerily quiet. What my mother said to Tasha must've really affected her. So far, she'd successfully avoided all conversations about Porsche. Though people in the industry knew exactly whose daughter Tasha was when she stood in the stands at Lionel's games and photographers often put snapshots of Lionel and Tasha next to Porsche's in magazines, no one ever confronted her about her estrangement from the soap star. Even the producers of *MTV Cribs,* who'd done a special on Lionel and Tasha's New Jersey home, didn't mention it when they aired the show. Everyone gave Tasha her space, but Mary Elizabeth just wasn't that kind of person.

She'd let Tasha off easy, but she hadn't stopped before saying, "You can't bring another life into this world until you've made amends with the life you already have." Tasha immediately shot a look across the table at me as if I'd revealed her secret, but I hadn't told my mother anything about the baby. Mary Elizabeth was just talking. But that was the amazing thing about mothers. They always knew just what to say to either piss you off or put you right back on track.

"I had a great time tonight," Tasha said solemnly as she got out of the car at my apartment.

"You don't have to lie. She gets on my damn nerves, too."

"No, really. I did. Your mother is something." Tasha kissed me on the cheek. "I'm going to head home now," she said. "I have to talk to my husband."

I smiled at my friend as she walked away. She seemed to have grown in some way since she'd arrived at my apartment that morning all nervous about her appointment. Earlier her pink dress had made her seem like a little girl, but with the sun setting behind us, the fabric appeared a soft crimson and Tasha seemed to be walking stronger and taller.

The elevator was broken, so I had to trudge up ten flights of stairs to reach my floor—a common tragedy in New York apartment buildings. I was about to faint when I reached the top step. Sweat was pouring all over me and I could feel my hair frizzing up. It was time to call Piero again. "Guess I won't need to do my thirty on the StairMaster tonight," I said, opening the door to my floor.

I looked down the hallway toward my apartment and saw Julian standing in front of the door. I had to catch my breath. *What the hell is he doing here?* I looked a complete stir-fry mess after climbing the stairs. I wanted to turn around and go back downstairs.

"Troy," he called down the hall just as I was about to pull out my compact to get a quick look at myself. "What are you doing, taking the stairs?"

"Broken," I said, out of breath. "You didn't see that the elevator's broken?"

"I guess it broke while I was up here. I've been standing here for, like, thirty minutes."

"Yeah, I'm thinking about getting a chair out here for all of my unexpected company," I said sarcastically. "Been having a lot of surprise guests lately."

"Well, I've come with treats." He dangled a brown shopping bag in front of me.

"Treats?"

"Yeah, I was at the store and I saw these organic doggie treats Pookie likes, so I picked them up."

"You came all the way over here to give me dog treats?"

"He really likes them." He smiled and handed me the bag.

"Whatever," I said, walking into the apartment with him behind me.

"So what's really going on?" I asked. I dropped the bag on the kitchen counter and led him into the living room.

"Like I said on the phone, we need to talk," Julian said, picking up Pookie Po.

"About what?"

"Remember when I asked you if you were seeing someone else?"

"Yes," I replied uneasily, sitting on the couch beside him. Tasha was right. Men are either black or white. He was about to come clean about Miata. Julian was about to tell me he loved her. *I was about to catch a case!* I could already see the headline on the morning paper: WOMAN KILLS MAN IN APARTMENT FOR LOVE. I wondered if they'd let me keep Pookie Po in prison. I could buy her one of those striped doggy outfits.

"Well, it was because I'm seeing someone else," Julian said. *Oh, Lord, help me now. Help me not to choke this man.*

"Really?" I asked, trying to keep my cool. I couldn't remember what the next step of the Take Her Man Plan was, but I was sure it wasn't murder. *Was it?* "Who?" I asked.

Julian put Pookie down.

"That's not important," he mumbled. He paused and looked back up at me. "I wasn't going to tell you, but things have been happening lately. I didn't like lying to you. That's why I had to break things off."

I felt tears creeping down my cheeks. It was breaking— my heart was breaking again. Though I'd already seen Julian in the restaurant with Miata, it was like watching a movie or something. Now, looking at Julian sitting next to me on the couch, I knew it was real life. It was *my* real-life love and it was getting sadder by the second.

"Don't cry, baby."

"Don't fucking call me baby," I hollered. "I'm not your fucking baby. Just tell me now. Why? Why Miata?"

"Miata? How do you know it's Miata?"

"I just know, Julian. Stop playing games with me. Just tell me why you had to cheat on me with her. Why?"

"I don't know, Troy." Julian looked at me. "She's just different. She doesn't need me like you do. She's a fighter— like my mother, you know?"

"Need you? News flash, Negro! I don't need you for shit," I cried. "And you don't think I'm a fighter?" I jumped up from the couch, leaving him there alone. "You want to find out now?"

"Troy, stop it. It's not about who's a fighter and who's not. I think I just got confused. That's all."

"Confused?"

"See, that's just it, Troy. Before, I thought my mind was made up. I mean, Miata's not like any woman I've ever known. All of the crap we live with—the 'who's this' and 'who's that'—it just doesn't mean anything to her. She's not from that. She just does everything for herself. And she's not afraid to take what she wants. That just caught me off-guard."

"Julian, I really don't want to hear about that bitch right now, so you can just stop."

"Listen to me," he said. "But after seeing you the other night, I realized that I still have feelings for you," Julian said, wrapping his arms around my waist. He pressed his head against my stomach. "I just wanted to see if you still loved me."

"How could you ask me some bullshit like that right now, Julian?"

Julian looked up at me. His eyes turned red and he closed them. A tear rolled down his cheek. It was the first time I'd ever seen him cry.

"Julian, stop crying." I took a deep breath and put my hand on his head. "Julian, stop it."

"I fucked this up. I really fucked it up. I'm sorry."

Julian stood up in front of me, with tears still rolling down his cheeks. He kissed my lips so softly, my body felt paralyzed. I could feel the blood pulsating through my heart.

"I love you," he said, pulling me into his arms. "I love you."

By the time the waitress brought our food to the table, Tamia, Tasha, and I were already feeling all right. It was our favorite weekend brunch at the Shark Bar and we had already enjoyed one round of mimosas.

Tamia had called me and Tasha that morning begging us to meet her for brunch because she had good news. I was tired, after staying up all night studying for finals, but I was glad to meet my girls for some straight talk. A week had passed and I still hadn't told anyone about the run-in with Julian at my apartment. So I guess I had a little news of my own, too. Plus, I needed to get out of the apartment. My marathon study sessions, where I locked myself in the apartment with nothing but textbooks and enough food to eat for a week, were driving me crazy. I think Pookie was about to run away if I didn't give her some time alone.

"Okay, okay, I have news, ladies," I said anxiously when the waitress put my food down in front of me.

"What is it?" Tasha asked.

"No, me first," Tamia interrupted me. "I want to go first," she whined, practically oozing out of her seat.

"Damn, girl." Tasha rolled her eyes playfully. "If it's that serious, you need to go on and let it out. You look like you're about to lose your water."

"Okay, okay. So, remember how I was working on the *Olympia v. the State of California* verdict?" Tamia asked, watching me plow through a serving of macaroni and cheese I had no business eating. *The StairMaster hadn't seen me in days.*

"Yes," I murmured through bites. There's something about pasta and sharp cheddar cheese that's magical. I have yet to meet anyone who didn't like the match in a dish—unless it wasn't made the old-school way.

"Just to fill you in a bit, Tasha," Tamia said, taking my attention back from my plate. "One of our professors, Professor Banks, was a defense attorney in Los Angeles before moving to New York to teach. Her last case in L.A. was defending a white man who was accused of killing his black wife. Somehow, because of some questionable witnesses who didn't even see the murder, Professor Banks lost the case. It was the only case she ever lost."

"Okay. So where do you come in?" Tasha asked, sipping on her mimosa.

"Well, when I heard about the case, I decided to do some research to see if there were any loopholes—some things that didn't match up," Tamia said. She was beaming. I remembered when she'd found a few articles on the case online. She couldn't believe Professor Banks had actually lost a case.

"I'm surprised your professor would let you do that," Tasha said.

"It was ambitious, but Professor Banks gave her approval. She allowed me to look over all of her case files and do an interview with Mr. Olympia over the phone. Anyway, to make a long story short, last week I found two concrete fallacies in two of the witnesses' statements against the husband . . . " Tamia paused like she was about to pull a rabbit from underneath her skirt.

"And . . . " I said, chewing myself into another dress size.

"*And* on account of all of that," Tamia went on, "Professor Banks is trying to reopen the case."

"Oh my God," I said. "That's great."

"That's not it." Tamia grinned happily. "If everything works out, she wants me to go to Los Angeles with her for the rest of the summer to assist her."

"Yes!" I said a bit too loudly for the Shark Bar brunch crowd. I stood up and hugged Tamia. This was a great opportunity for her—to work right beside Professor Banks. I'd never heard of Professor Banks working with any of the students, let alone allowing them to assist her.

"Go 'head, girl," Tasha said, winking at Tamia.

"Go, Tamia. It's your birthday. Go, Tamia. It's your birthday," Tasha and I sang as Tamia did the whomp in her seat.

"Okay, I'm next," I said, giggling. "Julian and I spoke last week."

"And . . ." Tamia said, mocking my retort earlier.

"Black or white?" Tasha asked.

"I don't know." I shrugged my shoulders.

"What?" Tamia looked at me quizzically.

"What happened?" Tasha asked dryly.

"He showed up at my apartment and told me all about Miata and said he loved me and then he just left."

"He admitted that stuff about Miata?" Tamia asked. "Hell, no. This is some craziness." She gulped down the last of her mimosa.

"No, Tamia," Tasha cut in. "At least he's telling the truth right now. That's what you want, Troy. He's not lying to you— which is worse. Give him some credit for that." She sat up in her seat. "It means Miata's wicked, geechie spell over him is breaking like a fever."

"Whatever," Tamia said. "The real question is, do you believe his black ass? Because you know a brother is prone to telling big lies in situations like this. Especially if he got wind of the run-in you and Miata had."

"True," Tasha said. "Did you run the lie test on him? Check for the twenty-one signs of shammery?"

"Yes," I said, laughing. It was a list we'd put together of the signs that meant a man was lying. "And the only one he fell short on was number nineteen."

"Too much information being given for no reason," Tamia said.

"If I had a dollar for every time a man gave his lie away with that one," Tasha added, "I'd be Ivana Trump." She gave Tamia five and we all started laughing. Tasha was correct. Most men fell into at least three of the points on our guy lie list: If he wasn't stuttering, he was trying to divert the blame or cry.

"Damn, y'all, he cried." I remembered number twenty-seven.

Tamia laughed. "That's a good one. It usually makes you cry too—"

"And forget the problem," Tasha said, cutting her off. "Well, we're clear that there may be some untruths in the mix, but the important question is . . . did you two have sex?"

"No. He just left."

"Damn! This one is harder than I thought." Tasha fell back in her seat like a mob boss. "Well, I guess it's time to move on to step four: Make Him Jealous. Your Julian needs a little booster shot to remind him of what he's missing. Yep, it's time to pull out the big guns." She cut her eyes mischievously. "And I have just the right man in mind."

"What? A man?" I nearly choked on my food. I'd completely forgotten that I was supposed to be finding a man to make Julian jealous. I already had Kyle as my mini-distraction—since he was a "friend"—but Julian had already met him and he knew Kyle was a preacher and a friend of my dad's.

"Yes. I have the perfect man." Tasha bit into her croissant.

"Who?" I asked. I never let Tasha set me up. Whenever she hooked me up, it was with one of Lionel's teammates. And though Lionel was a jewel, they were all jerks. I remember one I went out with actually had five children by five different women! I was disgusted by the time the date was over. He kept trying to defend his situation, saying he had enough money to support all of his children. But when I asked him their ages at dinner, he could recall only three. It was all over for him by dessert.

"Darious J," Tasha said. Tamia and I looked at each other from across the table. *Was she talking about "the" Darious J? The R&B singer who'd snagged two Grammys last year and looked like Ginuwine—without the S-curl?* He was fine as hell. Hell, I'd be jealous of Julian if I saw *them* out together.

"'Put It Down on Me'?" Tamia asked, naming Darious's latest song, which was playing twenty-four hours a day on the radio.

"Yes. He's going to be your date," Tasha said, smiling at me.

"How are you going to hook that up?" I felt like a little girl at a New Edition concert. I was almost giddy.

"Darious and Lionel go way back. We had him over for dinner last night and I told him I had someone I wanted him to meet. He's game." Tasha continued to eat her food as if we were discussing movie plans.

"Wait, let me get this straight: Darious J was at your house for dinner?" Tamia asked, grabbing Tasha's fork before she could stuff another forkful of food into her mouth. "And you didn't call me? I'm single, too. You know?"

"You told him about me?" I asked.

"Calm down, y'all. Darious is fine, but he ain't all that."

Tasha played with her fork. "In person, he's kind of average. A little short."

"I knew it," Tamia said, shaking her head. "There's no way one man could be that divine. It's impossible."

"Anyway, he's perfect for this plan," Tasha went on. "When Julian sees Darious with you, he'll drop to his knees and beg for you to come back to him. No man can handle the thought of Mr. 'Put It Down on Me' being all up in the bed with his lady." Tasha and I toasted our mimosas. "When the time is right, I'll set you guys up, and you'll be on your way to the next step."

"Wow," I said, going over my wardrobe in my head. What was I going to wear on my date with Darious J? I'm saying, I'm no groupie, and I'd never seriously date any singer, but there was something about how Darious danced in those videos that just wouldn't quit. I wondered if he could move around like that in bed.

"Okay, so everyone told their secrets," Tasha said. "Now it's time for my news." She paused. "I really wanted to wait until things were final and all, but with all of this good news going around, I can't hold it in anymore—"

"Girl, spit it out," I demanded.

"I told Lionel everything last week, like you said, Troy. And we're going to do it. We went to the doctor together last week and we're going to try. We're going to have a baby."

"Ohhhh," Tamia and I cooed. We gave Tasha kisses on both cheeks.

"We have an appointment with the doctor next week," Tasha added, clapping.

"I'm not gonna cry. I'm not gonna cry," Tamia cried, waving her hands. But it was too late. Happy tears were spilling out of our eyes.

"I have a toast," I said, raising my half-full mimosa. "To my girl and the flyest baby NYC will ever see! To Baby Prada!"

"Baby Prada."

"Baby Prada."

We toasted, and Tasha finished her drink.

"I guess that was my last one for a while," she joked.

"Hey, why don't y'all come to L.A. with me next month so we can really celebrate all of this?" Tamia said.

"L.A.?" I asked.

"Yeah. We could use a trip together. And since I'll be in L.A. working on my case, you guys can just come visit."

"I don't know," Tasha said. She rarely traveled to L.A. or anywhere on the West Coast unless Lionel had a game. "I'll have to think about it."

"Come on, guys. Hot beaches, fine men, great clubs, and shopping—what's not to love about L.A.?" Tamia said. "And don't act like both of you couldn't use a vacation."

I frowned. I hadn't been away since my trip to Jamaica with Julian after New Year's.

"I'm down," I said. I really didn't have much planned for the summer. So far, I was interning at Manhattan Juvenile Court and helping the girls in my dance class at the settlement prepare for their fall pageant.

"Hmm . . ." Tasha exhaled, pushing the last bit of food around on her plate. "I guess so. I guess I'll go if you guys are down."

"Yeah!" Tamia gushed. "So it's set. I'll arrange everything and let y'all know. This is great." Tamia could be so geeky at times. She looked like we were about to go to Disneyland. She'd probably try to fit that into the trip.

"Well, I have to get going," Tasha said abruptly. She put three twenties on the table. "That should cover my portion."

"What's wrong?" Tamia asked, looking at me oddly.

"Nothing," Tasha said, sounding even more distant. Her eyes looked like she was about to cry. "I just have a meeting." She got up quickly and kissed both of us on the cheek. "Congrats again, girls," she said and walked out.

"What the hell was that?" Tamia said, taking the check from our waitress.

"I don't know," I replied. "You know this baby stuff has her a bit sensitive."

"But she isn't even pregnant yet."

"I know, but I think it's something else. Something about her own mother. It must be hard to think about having a baby and your mother not being there to see it," I said. "And when you brought up Los Angeles, she probably got a little upset thinking about Porsche being there."

"But she hates her mother. She says it herself." Tamia shrugged her shoulders.

"Mia, something tells me Porsche affects Tasha a bit more than she lets on," I said, remembering the look on Tasha's face when my mother had brought up Porsche.

"So what are we going to do about it?"

"What do you mean?"

"We have to do something. We can't let our friend be unhappy and do nothing about it. She's about to get pregnant. She can't carry a baby and have all of this anger built up inside of her. Then she'll have an ugly baby. You don't want an ugly niece, do you?"

"I don't know," I said, laughing. "We can't exactly make Tasha forgive her mother."

"Well, maybe if they spoke to each other, they could begin to sort things out."

Tamia had a point. Tasha refused to even speak to the woman. Porsche had called Tasha on her wedding day and Tasha just hung up the phone.

"You're right. But how are we supposed to do that?" I asked. "How are we supposed to get Tasha to agree to speak to her mother for more than one second? If she even hears the woman's voice on the phone, she'll hang up. It's impossible."

Tamia played with her fingers on the table like she did in class when she was trying to figure something out.

"L.A.!" she said with her eyes widening. "We can set it up for them to meet in L.A."

"Tasha would never agree to that," I said. Tamia narrowed her eyes and eased toward the table.

"Who said she had to?"

3T Guy Lie List: Twenty-one Slick Signs of Shammery

Just as sure as the sun will rise in the east and cheap shoes will give you corns on your pinky toes (be careful, ladies), men will lie when caught in a tight situation—and often even if there's no situation at all. The sad part is that grown men feel that they have to lie in the first place, and the sadder part is that women are put in the precarious predicament of trying to spot a lie. However, there is some good news. Not only are women smarter than men, but they're also better liars than their masculine counterparts and, thus, more astute at recognizing a bald-faced lie when it rears its ugly head. Sharpen your skills by looking over the following twenty-one signs that your guy may be cooking up a lie.

(Note: Trust your instinct—your factual evidence of behavior mixed with internal suspicion. If you have sincere reason to believe that your guy is telling a lie, he probably is. But don't spend the rest of your life collecting evidence that seldom leads to truthful confessions. Be prepared to make a change based on the new reality.)

1. *If he begins the conversation with statements like "I could lie but . . ." "The truth is that . . . ," or the infamous "What happened was . . ."*
2. *Silence.*
3. *A sudden desire to go to the bathroom or leave abruptly.*
4. *A slight chuckle.*
5. *Unexplainable sweat on his forehead, underarms, or chest.*
6. *His story is too elaborate—includes lots of friends, twists, and ridiculous situations.*
7. *He gets defensive and tries to turn things around on you.*
8. *It takes him longer than three seconds to answer you.*
9. *He asks you to repeat your question—he's really trying to buy time to work on his lie.*
10. *He keeps asking you what you know—he's trying to figure out what all he actually needs to confess to.*
11. *He volunteers a phone number for you to call to confirm his innocence—he expects you to either back down from making the call if it is another woman or he has his lie straight with the woman or his boys.*
12. *Strong defensiveness and anger followed by statements like, "I don't know what you're talking about" or "You need to trust me more and stop listening to your friends."*
13. *Walking away or pacing the floor.*
14. *Constant obliviousness to what is going on in the conversation.*
15. *He keeps making you repeat yourself in order to convince you that you're crazy.*
16. *He can't look you in the eye.*
17. *Stuttering.*
18. *He wants to talk about something else.*

19. *Giving up answers when you haven't asked any—he's come up with such a good/believable lie that he just couldn't let it go to waste.*
20. *Crying.*
21. *He's lied many times in the past—once a liar, always a liar.*

Step Four: Fella's There's a Jealous Boy in This Town

"And one, and two, and three, and four, turn, turn, seven, and eight," I counted, going over a dance routine with Shanika, one of the girls at Kids In Motion. An adorable eleven-year-old with big brown eyes, Shanika was what I would have to call a "challenged" dancer. I swear the girl didn't know right from left, and that was probably because she had two left feet. Basically, Ms. Shanika had the grace of a chimpanzee in water. I'd had to move her to the back of the studio the first week of class for fear she'd harm someone or herself. Most days she had to stay after class to catch up to the other girls. And that was no problem for me, because while the other students made fun of Shanika, I really enjoyed having her in the class. She worked harder than anyone else did and she took two buses to get to the center from the housing project in the Bronx where she lived.

"No, it's up with the right and down with the left on the next count," I said, correcting Shanika's flailing arms. "Up and down with your right arm on four and then turn." Bewildered and praying Ms. Shanika would get the move sometime during this lifetime, I looked up at the clock to see that it was twenty minutes after class time.

"Like this, Ms. Smith?" Shanika asked, doing everything I'd said in reverse. She smiled sweetly and did it wrong again. Sometimes the child surprised me with how she could change and rearrange every single dance step I taught her within seconds of me teaching it. But she had determination—I couldn't deny that.

"Relax, Shanika," I said, stopping her. "You know it. I know you do. Just think about every step and then let it all out."

"I just can't get it. I'm stupid." She looked at herself in the mirror.

"You're not stupid and you can get it."

"That's easy for you to say. You already got it," she said, looking toward my reflection in the mirror behind her. "And you're pretty. Not me."

"What do you mean, Shanika? You don't think you're pretty? I think you're pretty."

"You ain't gotta lie, Ms. Smith. I know I'm ugly. Everybody says it. I'm too dark, I got big lips, and I'm ugly. Even my mother says it."

"What did she say?" I asked, surprised and angry with what I was hearing. It was hard for me to imagine any mother telling her child she was ugly. But really, it was closer to home than I wanted to admit, and I was sure Shanika's mother was no match for the color whipping Grandma Lucy had put on my mother. "What did she say?" I asked again. Shanika was silent. She just shook her head. "Well, you don't have to answer that, then," I said, stooping next to her. She was wearing a pink leotard and matching jazz shoes she'd had to sell God knows how many chocolate bars to buy last year at our fund-raiser. "But tell me, do you think moms can be wrong sometimes?"

"Yes," she said softly.

"Then maybe your mommy is wrong this time. You know why I believe that?" Shanika shook her head no and looked at me with her eyes wide. "Because I think you're beautiful and I don't think you're too dark either." I turned her back toward the mirror so she could see herself. "I think you're just right." It was one of those moments at the settlement that made me understand why I was there and doing exactly what I was doing. I had to hold back my tears because I wanted Shanika to know that I was serious about what I was saying. I wanted her to know that and I wanted my mother to know it, too.

"Now, I need you to believe in yourself, Shanika. Not what anyone else says about you, but what you know you're capable of. Right?"

"Yes," she said.

"Exactly. Just relax and let it flow. Breathe. I told you that's what dance is all about—breathe and let it flow from within your center." I pulled her to the middle of the floor. "Now take a deep breath and take it from one." I turned on the music and stood behind Shanika in the mirror. "Watch yourself." The music started and Shanika froze at first, but she caught on at the second count and did the rest of the dance as if she'd choreographed it herself. "Wonderful, Shanika," I said, turning off the CD when she was done. I bent down and gave her one of the big old bear hugs my father always gave me when he picked me up from dance class. "You looked beautiful," I whispered in her ear, just as he would have. "Beautiful."

I heard clapping coming from the back of the room and turned to see Christian Kyle standing in the doorway.

"Wonderful," Kyle said, still clapping. He stepped into the studio.

"Thank you." Shanika smiled nervously.

"Shanika, this is my friend, Reverend Hall," I said, trying to hide my confusion and wondering what in the heck he was doing at the studio. I was supposed to meet him in front of the park at 6 P.M. for the jazz concert. It was only 5:15 P.M. and the last time I checked, the park was over ten blocks away from settlement.

"Hi, Reverend Hall," Shanika said, flirting with Kyle in her innocent eleven-year-old way. It wasn't every day that handsome black men could be found walking around the settlement.

"And Reverend Hall, this is Shanika Lewis, one of my *best* dancers," I said. Shanika looked at me like I was crazy as Kyle bowed to her. She was smiling from ear to ear and to my surprise, she crossed her legs and did a perfect curtsy for him. Now, I sure don't remember seeing her do that before.

"God bless you." Kyle smiled. "You're indeed a great dancer."

"Thank you," Shanika said, running to the back of the room to get her things.

"Don't run," I called to her. She grabbed her things and raced back to the door. "I'll see you next week."

"Bye," she said, waving past me at Kyle as she headed out the door.

"Cute," Kyle said when she was gone.

" 'Cute'? What are you doing here? I thought you were meeting me at the park at six."

"I wanted to see you." Kyle looked almost as bad as Shanika with a grade-school crush. His face was sporting a permanent smile and he kept winking at me. The man's nose was wide open and anyone passing by could see it. I was quite embarrassed for him, but it just the ego boost I needed. But I couldn't just let it go on.

"Look, Kyle, we said we're just going to be friends." I stuffed my radio into a locker at the back of the studio. "I told you I was trying to work things out with someone."

"Calm down, Troy," Kyle said, taking my bag from me. "I know about Mr. Tight Suit from the play reception. I just had some extra time before the concert and I wanted to *see* you teach. So I came down here to try to catch your class." He looked at me innocently. "That's it. No strings. I just wanted to see your class."

I looked Kyle up and down. He had on sneakers and a navy blue sweat suit. He looked so cute and *so* not like a pastor. I had to confess, if he was mine, I might've had to pull a Tamia Library Move in the basement of the settlement. But . . . then again, I guessed I wouldn't be doing any of that with the pastor.

"You sure?" I asked, squinting my eyes jokingly.

"I'm sure, Detective Troy."

"You're good with her," Kyle said, walking with me down the street toward the park. I'd told him to meet me at the park after I had a shower at the center, but he'd insisted on waiting for me in the lobby. I swear, it was like my father created this man with his own hands or something. He was every father's dream. Now, whether he was the daughter's dream was still up for grabs.

"You think I'm good?" I asked. I loved working with the children, but sometimes I wondered if I was making a difference. Many of the girls were living close to poverty. I knew for a fact that some of my students were in foster homes because their parents were drug addicts, and one girl said her mother used to make her steal food from the grocery store. The oldest girl in my class, Nala, was fifteen and she already had a two-year-old of her own. Some of the girls said they thought her father had gotten her pregnant. Knowing all this, I worried if my little dance class was doing anything for them. Even I knew learning a pirouette wasn't going to save them from the crap that was waiting for them outside their doors.

"Yeah, you were really patient with her. You seemed to

really be listening to what she had to say. That's worth a million bucks to a kid."

"Thanks." I smiled, walking into the park beside Kyle. "I really just try to get them to work hard in the class so they can see what it's like to work hard at something and finish it." I pointed to a small canvas bag Kyle had on his other shoulder. "So what's in the bag?"

"Just a small blanket, fruit and a bottle of grape juice," he said. "I figured we could sit on the blanket during the concert. Is that okay with you, big head?"

"My head is not big," I said, laughing although I'd heard that before from different people.

"Please, it's bigger than all outside. I'm just trying not to get hit." He ducked playfully.

"Whatever." I grinned. I mean, my head was a bit larger than others but I liked to call it *shapely*—that's how my mother put it when she used to get mad when I couldn't fit any of the hats she'd bought for me as a kid.

"No, but really," Kyle continued, "how did you get into the whole service thing? I mean, how does a lady as privileged as yourself get into working in the community?"

"I'm not privileged," I said. Kyle looked at me like I was speaking French. "Okay, maybe I am a bit more privileged than your average girl in New York." I laughed. "I can't say when I started doing service work. I was always involved in little projects when I was in Jack and Jill growing up. In fact, one park clean-up initiative we did was even in *Up the Hill*."

"Oh, that stupid newsletter Jack & Jill does?" Kyle grimaced.

"Yeah," I said. "How do you know about that?"

"Oh, my parents made me do all that J&J stuff, too," Kyle replied. "I hated it."

"Well, I started doing service with them when I was young, but I didn't really start working with kids until I went to Howard and pledged."

"Oh, no," he said. "Don't even tell me,"—he backed up and looked me up and down—"Pink and Green all the way."

"Stop playing, buster. You know I'm a Delta," I laughed.

"Okay, yeah, I figured that much," Kyle said, laughing. "I pledged Omega at Morehouse."

"Really?" I was surprised. Kyle just didn't strike me as the Greek type. He was just too solitary. "I should've known there was a reason you were hanging with my father . . . one of his fraternity brothers."

"Yeah, it's a tradition in my family. Three generations of Omega preachers."

"It's funny how that happens," I said.

"So go on with the teaching. How did that start?"

"Anyway, my Delta chapter volunteered at a community center in D.C. and one day the director said they needed someone to teach a dance class. I took up the reins since I had been in ballet classes for most of my life, and I've been volunteer teaching in different places ever since."

"That's great," Kyle said. "I've always said it's a true measure of a person's heart when they give even when they do not have to . . . when no one expects it. That's like Christ's love."

"You're right," I agreed with Kyle. It felt odd to have someone bring that up in a conversation on the way to a jazz concert, but he was right. That was one of the things I loved about the church. Free love. Unconditional love. All of us could use that sometimes. Even the fly girls.

Kyle led me toward the area in the park where they usually held the concerts. Even though we were thirty minutes early, people were already crowding around everywhere. Folks had blankets and lawn chairs set up like we were at the beach. There were almost no spaces left.

"So tell me, are you a spiritual person?" Kyle asked, padding through the crowd. "I mean, I know you go to church and that you were raised in the church, but would you consider yourself spiritual?"

"Hmm . . ." I took a deep breath. That was another odd topic for a jazz concert. No one had ever asked me that, not that I could remember. "You know, sometimes I wonder about that. Like, I do believe. I believe in God, but I don't think I'm as holy as some of the people I know. I don't carry my faith on my sleeve, so to speak. I pray every night before I fall asleep and I try my best to see the good in the world . . . to see the good in people. I truly believe that if more people did the same thing, if more people believed in God, and lived faith-filled lives, the world would be a better place."

Kyle stopped walking and stepped back to look at me.

"Wow, that was really well put," he said. "We're going to have to get you a pulpit . . . Reverend Smith."

"Whatever, silly." I nudged him. "Since you're such a smarty-pants, where do you propose we sit, Moses?" We'd been walking for a few minutes and I couldn't see a clear space anywhere.

Kyle walked straight into the maze of people. After stepping over about ten blankets and saying "excuse me" at least a dozen times, Kyle stopped. "Here," he said. He put the canvas bag down and handed over my gym bag. "This is a great spot," he said, pulling out his blanket. I looked around and it was the only spot . . .

"I guess we got lucky," I said.

"Well, you know, I don't need luck." Kyle pointed up to the sky. "I have my friend. If he can part the Red Sea, surely he can get us seats in the park."

"Oh, no . . . no pastor jokes. Please." I laughed.

"Okay, but don't ask me to help you out if it starts raining out here." Kyle opened the bottle of juice. "Then you're going to want to be my friend." Kyle and I laughed so hard, I almost dropped the glass he handed me.

"You're so crazy," I said. Kyle poured juice into my glass and held his up.

"A toast," he said. "A toast to good times and great friends."

"Cheers."

"Looks like they're getting started." Kyle looked up at the stage. The members of the band walked onstage and took their places. The bassist walked up to the microphone and looked out at the audience.

"Greetings, good people," the bass player said in a thick English accent. "Greetings," he repeated, attempting to catch the attention of a few people who were still talking. "I hope you guys don't mind if we warm up a bit onstage before we get things started."

People in the crowd began to cheer. A man sitting next to me and Kyle whistled so loud, I thought my ears were about to pop.

"Great," said the man on the stage. "I'm glad to see everyone's in a good mood this fine evening in the Big Apple." Loud whistling came from around the audience. Kyle bent over and covered my ears.

"I'm especially glad to announce that we have a special couple in the audience here tonight," he added. "And I'd like to invite that special couple up onstage, because I hear that one of them has something very special they'd like to say." The band began to play music softly in the background. Everyone looked around the crowd to find the special couple.

"Oh, this is so sweet," I whispered in Kyle's ear. "I wonder who it is."

"Okay, where are you? Don't be shy," the bass player said, shielding the last bit of sunlight from his eyes. "Audience, maybe the couple will come up here if you all give them a big round of applause," he added. Everyone began to clap.

"It sure is taking them a long time," I said. I looked at Kyle and noticed he'd been dead silent since the man had walked onto the stage. He hadn't even looked at me. In fact, he looked kind of nervous. Suddenly, it dawned on me. *Were we the couple they were waiting on?* "Kyle? Are they talking about us?" I asked, almost afraid to hear his answer.

"What?" Kyle replied, turning toward me. "What are you talking about? We're not a couple. Why would you think that?"

Just then a black man and an Asian woman walked on-stage.

"Kim, I have something I need to ask you," the black man said, taking the microphone from the bass player. The girl's face was as red as a radish and I could see her hands shaking. The man got down on his knees and the crowd started cheering. Even Kyle and I stood up and began to clap. The man pulled a little blue box (good taste!) from his pocket. "Kim, I wanted to ask you if you would do me the honor of being my wife?" he said, holding the ring up to her. The band stopped playing; the crowd fell silent. It felt as if time had stopped ticking. I could see tears on the woman's face. And before she even said it, I knew her answer . . .

"Yes," she said, pulling the man's head to her chest. "Yes." He slid the ring onto her finger, got up on his feet, and kissed her passionately.

"Go ahead, girl," I heard myself say. I wrapped my arms around my waist and gave myself a big hug. It was nice to see two people in love, even if my own love life was turning out to be so tragic.

"What about me? I need a hug too," Kyle said, holding out his arms. I giggled and gave him a hug. When I was about to let him go, the band began to play "Ribbon in the Sky" as the couple walked off the stage. "One dance?" Kyle asked, looking at me harmlessly.

"Okay." I looked up at him. "I'm only doing this because I know you're a man of the cloth and you can't try anything freaky," I said. "Plus, I don't want you to make it rain on my head."

As Kyle and I danced, I noticed how perfectly our bodies moved together. I mean, it's not easy to find a good slow-dancing partner. Usually the guy is either too tall and bony or too short and fat. But I fit perfectly in Kyle's arms and his chest seemed to curve in all the right places for my body to feel comfort. I closed my eyes and pretended he was some-body I loved, someone who had just proposed to me on the stage at a jazz concert.

"Troy?" Kyle said, interrupting my thoughts.

"Yes?"

"Do you love that guy . . . the one from the reception?" he whispered in my ear.

"Yes. Yes, I do, Kyle," I said, wondering why he was ask-ing about Julian.

"Okay." He stopped moving and his arms fell to his side.

"Why are you asking about Julian, Kyle?" I asked, look-ing at him.

"Because he's standing behind you."

"What?"

"Hi, man," Kyle said. I turned around so fast I almost knocked Kyle over.

"What? Hey. Oh, my God," I blurted out. I stuck my hand out to shake Julian's like I was just meeting him. I couldn't believe it. There he was standing right there in front of me . . . me and Kyle . . . watching us dance. *Had he seen that?* "Ju-lian . . . you know Kyle," I said, trying to calm myself down.

"Yeah, we met before." Julian looked right through me. His face was tight. I'd never seen him look like that. It was right there smack-dab in between disbelief and rage.

"Yeah, well, funny, we just came out here to hear some music." I gave a giggle. I wasn't handling the situation very well. *What would Tasha do?* I kept thinking, but all I could see was the green dancing in Julian's eyes. That was it. He was jealous. Julian was jealous because I was with Kyle. But it was . . . Kyle.

"You want something to drink, brother?" Kyle asked, pulling another glass from his bag.

"No, man. I was just coming over here to say hello to

Troy." Julian looked at me. "I'm here with some people from the hospital," he said, pointing to a group of people behind us. "I saw you stand up when the couple was onstage, so I figured I'd come over. I didn't realize you were with someone."

"Well, I'm not with someone," I said. I heard the glass Kyle was holding drop. "Well, I am but, like, you know, not really *with* someone. Just here with Kyle."

"Yeah. Well, I hope you remember the conversation we had the other night at your apartment," Julian said just loud enough for Kyle to hear him. "I was hoping we could speak again soon."

"Really?"

"Yeah." He glanced over my shoulder at Kyle, who had already sat back down on the blanket. "Well, I better be getting back to my people. It looks like the show's about to finally get started," Julian said, looking up at the musicians on the stage.

"Okay," I said. Julian kissed me on my nose and walked away without saying goodbye to Kyle. Watching his back, all I could think of was all the times it was his blanket I had been sitting on under the Manhattan sky. We'd attended most of the shows together. Julian would bring the blanket and a Scrabble set we never seemed to open. I brought the wine and the food—Riesling, brie, and bread. Julian would sit me down between his legs in the middle of the blanket and feed me like I was a queen, kissing me on my neck between bites of dinner. By the time the show had begun we'd be so wrapped up into each other's arms, we'd wish the blanket could suddenly grow walls and morph into a little outdoor hut. It's a good thing that never happened, because then we'd been bumping and grinding in the bark.

Yes, I said to myself, watching him disappear into the crowd. *Yes, yes, yes.* I sat back down on the blanket and turned to Kyle. His face was long and he looked completely disgusted.

"Oh, Kyle. I hope I didn't make you upset with what I

said about being alone," I said. I grabbed his hand and shook it playfully.

"No, it's fine. Really, it's fine," Kyle replied. He slid his hand away and poured himself another glass of juice.

Smart Girls Rule

Everything was flying by so fast. By the time I finished my final exams and finally came up for air, the summer was in full swing. Nana's play opened to a standing room–only audience in Harlem. Kyle and Daddy had just purchased two buildings on the block behind the church, and though Kyle pretended to be okay, I could tell my words at the park with Julian still bothered him. Tasha and Lionel's process went perfectly with the first try and Tasha was three weeks pregnant. There was good news for Tamia, too. Professor Banks was able to reopen the case in Los Angeles and the proceedings were beginning in just three weeks. Tasha and I agreed to meet Tamia in L.A. one week after everything started to give her time to feel her way around.

"Let me get a quarter," I said, holding my hand out to Tamia at the soda machine in front of the law library. She'd asked me to meet her there so I could help her organize some of her paperwork. Professor Banks was giving her a lot of responsibility and Tamia wanted to make sure everything was perfect before she met with the professor to go over everything the next day.

"No," Tamia replied, smiling. "Aren't you supposed to be on the Take Her Man diet or something?"

"It's a damn soda, Mia." I snatched her purse and pulled out her wallet.

"Feisty, are we?" Tamia stepped back. "I guess things aren't going so well in 'man-stealing land.'"

I rolled my eyes at her and pulled a Coke from the machine.

"How's that going, anyway?" she asked.

I cracked open the soda. I had really been hoping to avoid the topic with Tamia. The truth was, Julian and I had hung out once during finals, but we'd just met up for a cup of coffee by the hospital. It was great seeing him. He walked into the restaurant carrying a huge bouquet of roses, saying it was for me, for all of the mess he was putting me through. I smiled graciously and accepted the flowers, but the truth was, I hated roses and I'd told Julian that on several occasions. In addition to being a complete cliché, they just seemed to die too quickly, no matter how much you tried to take care of them. But it was a start.

"Hello . . ." Tamia said, pinching my shoulder.

"Ouch," I yelped.

"Well, I was trying to get your attention. I asked about Julian and the plan. How is it going?"

"Oh yeah," I managed. "I don't know, Tamia. I really don't know. Everything is just so messed up right now. I mean, it seemed so fun at first, but now I just really miss my man. And I wish this was all over."

"Oh, poor thing." Tamia rubbed my shoulder. "Well, what about the next step, Darious J? I actually thought that would work."

"Well, after all of the drama with Kyle in the park, Tasha and I agreed Darious J would just be overkill. If Julian saw me out with two different men, I'd run the risk of—"

"Hoe Status," Tamia said, finishing my sentence. It was the dreaded category no woman ever wanted a man she even remotely liked to put her into. The idea was, there were three categories men put women in: 1. Wifey Status—someone he could take home to Mama. 2. Friend Status—someone fun he could kick it with. 3. Hoe Status—the sex freak who may have sexed half the people in the city.

"Damn, Troy. That's a tough break. So no Mr. 'Put It Down on Me'?" Tamia said, gyrating down to the ground.

"No Mr. 'Put It Down on Me.' " I shook my head.

"I bought a new memory card for my digital camera for that one. Well, maybe I can get Tasha to hook me up with him now."

"Tamia!"

"Well, there's no need for all of us to suffer. I need some loving, too!" Tamia took a sip of my soda. "So what are you going to do?"

"I don't know. Everything is changing right now and I can't explain it, you know?" I said. "And sometimes I wonder if all this is worth it. Since I broke up with Julian, things have been different for me. Everything is changing and now I see all the things that were wrong with me. With how I was acting—Julian was right about some of that stuff he said about me. I put everything on our relationship—the vacations, my parents, wanting to get married, all of it. I was so stuck on being Mrs. Julian James, I couldn't see straight. And now all of that crap that was important to me before just isn't anymore. Now I just want him back."

"Why don't you just tell Julian how you feel then, Troy? Like what's been going on with you."

"Yeah, I know. I want to, but then there's Kyle."

"Kyle?" Tamia said. "Your friend Kyle?"

"Yeah, we've been really close these past couple of weeks." I tossed my empty soda can into the garbage and smiled, thinking of the look on Kyle's face when he was standing in the doorway of the studio.

"That's cool. So what's the problem? Are you catching feelings for him or something?"

"No, I'm not catching feelings. I just don't want to hurt him."

"Look, Troy. If you and Kyle are friends and you want to be with Julian, Kyle needs to understand that," Tamia said, walking ahead of me into the library. "That's it. There ain't no ifs, ands, or buts about it. You can't be worried about hurting his feelings. If he's a real friend, he'll stick around whether you're with Julian or not."

"I know. I just hope he doesn't take all of this too personally," I mumbled.

"Troy, just be honest with Kyle about your feelings for him," Tamia said sincerely. "And be honest with yourself." When we were halfway across the lobby on our way into the library, Tamia just stopped walking dead in her tracks.

I turned to her, thinking she was playing, but her face was turning red and she was heaving.

"Tamia, you okay?" I asked.

"Just . . . just a pain," she struggled.

"Excuse me," I shouted toward the help desk.

"No, don't get anyone," she said. She wiped her forehead. "I'm fine." She took a deep breath and smiled.

"What?" I was confused.

"That was nothing. I'm fine. I just had a little chest pain." She walked over to the elevator and pressed the button.

"Don't play with me," I said, stepping in front of her. "That was not nothing. Something is wrong with you. Are you still taking those fucking pills?"

"No, I stopped," Tamia said. I looked at her. "I swear I stopped, T." I looked harder. "I swear, T. It was nothing. I just had a pain. I was short of breath. Maybe I was working out too hard at the gym this morning. I have been doing chest exercises."

The elevator came and we stepped inside with a small group of people. I looked at Tamia. I couldn't not believe what she was saying. If she said she'd stopped taking the pills, she wasn't lying. But she did scare me.

We got off of the elevator in the basement of the library and headed toward the section where Tamia usually studied. She opened her bag and pulled out pile after pile of papers. I watched her, trying to judge if she was really okay.

"Okay, let's get started," she said, taking a seat next to the chair where I was standing. She looked up at me still standing. "Well, sit down, Troy," she said.

"I will . . ." I looked around the stacks. "But before I sit in this seat, I need you to promise me one thing."

"I stopped taking the pills, T," she said, annoyed.

"No, that's not it. I just want you to tell me this is not where you had sex with that white boy."

"Oh, sit down, silly." Tamia pulled out the chair.

After Tamia and I finished up at the library, we headed out to eat dinner at a cute Indian restaurant on St. Mark's we'd discovered one day after school. Walking into the East Village tuckaway, we were hypnotized by the scent of Indian curry and jasmine incense. We sat at the bar sipping on Indian wine and chatting about our plans for Los Angeles. I was so happy I'd agreed to go away with my girls. I really needed a break from the city and myself.

After eating enough food to feed an entire family on Thanksgiving, Tamia and I went over our plan to reconnect Tasha with her mother in L.A. Tamia had contacted Porsche through the television network two weeks before our trip. Tamia said Porsche was really excited about the new baby and couldn't wait to see Tasha. She kept Tamia on the phone for over an hour, telling her how much she missed Tasha and wanted to be in her life.

Before they got off the phone, Tamia and Porsche agreed to meet at the hotel where we were staying in West Hollywood. Porsche explained that she'd just won her third daytime Emmy and the media was dying to get anything on her.

The idea was to keep it as low-key as possible so Tasha wouldn't feel any pressure and bolt.

"Sounds great," I said to Tamia after hearing her plan. I did feel a twinge of guilt for deceiving Tasha, but in the end, as Tamia said, it was for her own good. Tasha had to face her past. But even if I did disagree with the plan, slumped over in my chair, so full I was about to burst, I didn't have the strength to argue.

Get In Where You Fit In: Female Categories

From the caste system in India to the political parties in the United States, groups make the world go 'round. Whether you're in or out, up or down, hot or not, one thing's for sure—you belong to a group. Black or white, Christian or atheist, fat or skinny, you're surrounded by groups. Perhaps the guiltiest culprits in the grouping game, especially when it comes to the women they date, are men. Like it or not, it's true. Every man you've ever dated put you in a category of some kind. And the worst thing you could do is not know which category you belong to. Read these categories closely and decide which one your guy has you in. It might be a life-changing realization.

1. Wifey Status: The belle of the ball, the grand finale, the queen bee. This is the woman he could see himself settling down with. He treats her like gold and shares his dreams with her.

   Signs It Might Be You: He can't stand the idea of you being with other men, always tries to impress you and take you to nice places, takes you to meet his mama, has a picture of you on display at his place, asks your future plans, wants to take you on vacation, wants to take you to church, always wants to know where you're going, buys you jewelry on holidays, and . . . he asks you to marry him.

2. Friend Status: R. Kelly called her the "Homie Lover Friend." This gal pal hangs with him so much people think they're brother and sister. She's the girl next door who's so cool he simply adores her. He'll do pretty much anything for her.

   Signs It Might Be You: He always says how "cool" you are, takes you places with groups of his friends, never dresses up or wears cologne when you two hang out, tells you all of his problems—including those with other women, and asks about your dates.

3. *Hoe Status:* *The sex is great, but the company may not be. She's not his dream girl, but he spends a lot of time sleeping with her. This is his secret friend no one seems to know about. What you do at your hoe's house stays at your hoe's house.*

Signs It Might Be You: *He seldom takes you out places people really frequent, never wants to see you during the day, won't introduce you to any of his friends, disappears on holidays, always breaks promises, seldom answers your calls, and turns his cell phone ringer off when he's at your place.*

Warning: Men are creatures of habit; therefore, though you can easily change your category from good (Wifey Status) to bad (Hoe Status) by, say, sleeping with his cousin, changing your category from bad (Hoe Status) to good (Wifey Status) is next to impossible.

---

*Friends often advance to Wifey Status.

Amen, That Man Is Mine

"It's right over there," said the old man standing next to my car.

"That's First Baptist?" I looked out of the window at the church. It was so huge it looked as if it was tearing into the sky above the car. Daddy was right, the church was an amazing old building that reminded people of how great Harlem once was. I couldn't believe how many times I must've passed it running through the city going here and there, never stopping to take notice.

"I wouldn't lie to you, lady. You stopped me to ask for directions," the man said, grinning at me in a way that was entirely inappropriate for Sunday morning—not to mention the fact that he was obviously old enough to be my father. I smiled back and quickly rolled up the window before parking my car. I couldn't believe I'd agreed to see Kyle preach the weekend before my trip to L.A. But he'd sounded so cute on the phone, saying I needed to "hear the word" before I left.

"There's not much space left on the floor," a little girl said when I walked into the church. The inside was even more lovely than the outside. I could tell from the beautiful wood paneling and stained glass windows that the church had been there for a long time. "But if you wait, one of the ushers can walk you in and help you find a seat." I looked at my watch. I was thirty minutes late.

"No, that's okay," I said, smiling at her. She looked adorable, dressed in a white lace dress and black patent leather shoes. You can say a lot of things about black people, but you can't say we aren't dressed to the nines on Sunday morning.

The church I attended sometimes in Manhattan when I couldn't make it to Harlem with Nana Rue was predominantly white. They looked like they were going to the mall when they came to church. The little girls had on pants (a no-no in the black church) and the men had on T-shirts and jeans. Nana Rue said they were being disrespectful in God's house. But I didn't mind it so much. Knowing I didn't have to get all dressed up to compete with anyone made it easier for me to get my behind up to go to church.

I knew better than to dress down when I got up to get ready to go to Kyle's church. I'd heard about First Baptist and its sanctified fashion show. From the specially made hats to the matching shoes and purses, the sisters there were church-dressing professionals and I wasn't about to look stupid. Being a guest of the pastor and all, I knew all eyes would be on me. I slipped on my tailored navy blue Chanel suit with matching Jimmy Choo stilettos. Tasha told me I looked like a movie star in that scene stealer.

"There's a balcony upstairs," the little girl said, pointing to a charming wooden staircase to my right. "I like to sit up there. You can see everything."

"Sounds like me." I smiled again and headed up the stairs.

I heard Kyle's voice vibrating through the church as soon as I reached the middle of the staircase. His confident whisper was building to a shout in the microphone.

"I need y'all to listen to me in this church here this morning," I heard Kyle say as I took a seat in the first pew on the balcony. "You must be still in order to receive the blessing the Lord God Almighty wants to give you. You must listen to his call and be prepared to answer when the time comes."

I looked out over the ledge to see Kyle standing in front of a packed congregation. You would've thought it was Easter Sunday the way people were crowded into the church like sardines. Even the choir pews were filled to capacity. From old to young, each row was overflowing with smiling people. Hands were waving in the air, Bibles were being held high, and everyone looked so blessed, so happy to be there, so happy to hear Kyle.

"And he wants to give it to you, saints. I know it's hard to believe for some of you. You're going through what you're going through and sometimes it seems like there's no end in sight. No one who cares. No one to give you a hand. But I need to remind you that, alleluia, our God is the Alpha and Omega. He's an awesome God. A way-out-of-no-way maker. He can pull you through. He's the one who cares. He's the hand you need. He wants to give you everlasting life in his kingdom and it doesn't matter who you are," Kyle said, pounding on the pulpit. "You just have to believe and give your life to him."

Kyle was a tall man, but he looked even taller from where I was sitting. Maybe it was the loud voice booming through the speakers, maybe it was the long cream-colored robe he was wearing, maybe it was the first row that was packed with women eyeing him just a little too hard—either way, Kyle looked better than ever from the balcony.

"I said, he wants to give it to you," he went on. Two women in the front row jumped to their feet and cheered "alleluia" like high school cheerleaders. Another woman, dressed in a red suit (that was just a little too tight) jumped out of her seat and started dancing like she had the Holy Ghost . . . only she didn't. It looked more like a striptease, and a bad one. One of the ushers ran up the aisle and pulled her to the back of the church. I couldn't believe what I was watching. These women were practically purring like cats at Kyle—while he was preaching.

"Don't worry about where you've been or what you've been through—God knows. And guess what? He still loves you. He still wants to give you his hand. You just have to open your heart to receive it," Kyle said. Everyone in the church stood up and began to shout a chorus of "amens" and "alleluias." Kyle took his seat at the altar and the choir began to sing my favorite song, "Order My Steps."

Kyle sang along and looked through the church with all of the admiration and love of a father. He looked so at peace, it was clear that he was exactly where he was supposed to be in life. He was doing exactly what he was supposed to do, what he was made to do. My heart smiled for him. I hoped he would always be that happy.

The women in the front row smiled whenever he looked in their direction and went on to primp their hair or fix their makeup when he looked away. The little girl was right, you could see *everything* from the balcony. I guess that's why God lives in the sky.

About a half hour after Kyle said it would be, the service was finally over. My hair was sweating out from praising and my feet were swelling in the Jimmy Choos. But I didn't mind. Kyle was a master of the word. He ignited each word that came out of his mouth with so much passion and light that you couldn't help but be moved. You had to shout "alleluia" and thank God for everything he'd done for you. And while I was sure my pinky toes would fall off when I took the shoes off, I felt rejuvenated leaving the church. And I knew I'd be back.

"You came!" Kyle said when I finally made my way down the church steps after the service.

"Yeah, I came to see you preach, as promised." I smiled.

"Well, that's really something, Ms. Troy," Kyle said.

The striptease woman in the red suit walked over waving her hands like she hadn't just seen Kyle in the church. "Pastor Hall, that was a moving service," she said, looking like she was asking Kyle if he wanted a lap dance.

"Well, thank you, Sister Glover, but you say that every week," Kyle replied innocently.

"Well, you move me every week," the woman said, and the double meaning was obvious. I wanted to turn around and give her a hug—she was clearly on her last leg, trying to get Kyle's attention, but he wouldn't budge.

"Oh, where are my manners?" Kyle said. "Sister Glover, this is Troy Smith. Ms. Smith is a friend of mine visiting our church." The woman shot her eyes at me like he'd introduced me as Lucifer himself. Then a phony smile washed over her face.

"Hi," she said. "Nice you came."

"Hello," I managed, smiling just enough to let her know I was on to her.

"I was just about to invite Troy over to the hall to eat with us," Kyle said.

"Oh, no, I couldn't," I replied. "I have to get back home, Kyle—I mean, Pastor."

"We understand if you can't come," the woman said with a frown. "Maybe next time."

"Oh, come on, Troy." Kyle bumped me. "Just for one moment." The woman stepped back and looked at me. She smiled, but *Bitch, go home and never come back. Kyle is mine* was written all over her face.

"I guess I could for just a minute." I looked at her. I was up for the competition. "If you insist, Pastor," I said, grinning.

"You've made my day," Kyle said as if the Holy Ghost ship had just landed in front of the church.

"Mine too," Sister Glover muttered under her breath, turning and heading toward the back of the church.

"Kyle, these women are a trip," I whispered when she'd disappeared around the corner. "They're throwing themselves at you."

"It does get crazy, Troy, but I have one calling here." Kyle smiled at a woman walking by. "And that's spreading the message of the Lord God. I don't get involved with women who are confused about that." He smiled. "No late-night Bible study for me. I serve one master and he isn't in my pants." We both laughed. "Really. You have to separate the two."

"I guess so."

"Well, I guess I'll see you in the hall for dinner?" Kyle went on, "I have to speak to a few more people out here before I head over." He pointed to the long line of people behind me who were waiting to talk to him.

"Yeah, I'll see you over there."

"Just walk toward the back. The hall is located behind the church," he said, taking the hand of a man standing beside me.

By the time I stepped through the doors of the hall, I knew my plan to stay was a mistake. I sensed that the woman in red had told everyone that I was Kyle's "friend." Why? Because everyone was looking at me. And as soon as I walked in the room, the girlfriend game of defense/offense was in full swing. By offense I mean they were pretty much lining up to get their shot at the good pastor. And by defense, I mean they were keeping my ass away from the good pastor.

Tasha and I had planned many plays like that to get the attention of men we liked, but these church women set a new precedent for defense/offense. I felt like I was going up against the damn Los Angeles Lakers when I stepped up to the dinner line. By then I'd totally given up on speaking to Kyle. Every time I came within arm's length of him, some old woman jumped in his face before I could get a word in. One woman had the nerve to ask Kyle if he'd seen the dress her daughter had on in church. They were like vultures. Anyway, I figured

I'd be better off getting something to eat and speaking to Kyle later—once I was back downtown and safe from full-on tackle.

"So where's your church home?" asked a woman who had to be ninety, putting string beans on my plate.

"Oh, I go to St. Mark's," I replied, smiling. Surely this sweet little old lady wasn't part of the defensive line.

"Oh, that's wonderful. Nice to see young ladies going to church." She put what had to be half a teaspoon of beans on my plate.

"Yeah, thanks. Can I have some more beans?"

"Sure, baby." She put about half a teaspoon more on my plate. "You know, with you being here for Pastor Hall, I was hoping you were at least a Christian woman."

"Excuse me?" I asked, almost certain I hadn't heard her correctly. "I'm not here *for* anyone."

"Don't be sly with me, girl," the old woman said, giving me the evil eye over her glasses. "Now, you just need to know that the pastor is going to marry a woman of this church." She pushed my plate back toward me with the spoon from the string beans. "I have three granddaughters in this church and I'm not going to see him bring someone in here when there are well-raised Christian women right here in the church. And not a Methodist either."

"Okay," I said. It was all I could do to keep myself from jumping over the table and choking the last bit of life out of her. This woman was playing hardball. And her ninety-year-old ass was winning. I mean, you can't argue with an old woman.

"And the next time you sit in the front row of the bal-cony"—she leaned in toward me—"don't wear such a short skirt." She stepped back and rolled her eyes. "Okay, baby?" She smiled pleasantly. "Now, go on and get more to eat. We have much to be thankful for today. Yes, we do. Praise God."

I took my teaspoon of string beans and a dry-ass biscuit and spent the rest of the afternoon sitting at the table with the children.

I'd gone up against the Lakers and, like most teams, I'd lost.

"They're not that bad," Kyle said, standing by my car door as I got in. After an hour and a half at the children's table, I'd decided it was time to raise my white flag and leave.

"Yes, they are. They had it in for me from the moment I walked in. I was about to call in reinforcements. The woman with the string beans was a mad woman."

"Sister Wildren? Oh, she runs the day school and our out-reach program for the army troop we adopted in Iraq. She's one of my most dedicated members. I can depend on her for anything."

"What about the one in the red suit?"

"Hmm." He laughed. "You may have a point there, but for all of her antics, Sister Glover is a good fund-raiser. She led the fund-raiser we did for the Hurricane Katrina victims. With her help we were able to house eight families and pay for day care. That woman is very dedicated to serving the people of God."

"It sounds like you're dedicated to having her back," I joked.

"Well, at least someone wants to get with me." Kyle laughed but I could tell he was dead serious.

"I'll just say, when the time comes, you won't have any problems finding a wife."

"Maybe I don't want someone in there." His smile faded and he bent to my level in the car. "Maybe I want what's out here."

Now, why did this man always have to find a way to say things like that? Things that seeped into my heart and made me blush from the inside out. Kyle always seemed to have the perfect words for the perfect moment. It just wasn't the perfect situation.

"Kyle, I told you we can't—"

"Don't flatter yourself." He cut me off, putting his index finger over my lips. "I was talking about this lady who lives down the street. She's more my type. She's Catholic and she's seventy-two . . . and Italian, but she's a hottie."

I laughed so hard I honked my horn by mistake with my forehead.

"Stop being silly," I said.

"I'm serious. She really is a hottie."

"Anyway," I said, "on a real serious note, Kyle, you were amazing in there this afternoon. Just obviously made for this thing. I see why First Baptist has grown so much under you."

"Thank you." He looked surprised.

"Yeah, I was just really taken aback. I can only imagine the fire your father has."

"Oh, Daddy's a bad man," he said. "He won't turn you loose 'til you have the spirit."

"Well, the apple didn't fall too far from the tree."

"Apparently not, but I wasn't that good. I didn't see Ms. Troy coming up to the altar when I opened the doors of the church." He grinned and tapped me on the nose playfully.

"I was on my way, shoot, with all the crying I was doing up there. I was definitely on my way." I wasn't lying; there hadn't been a dry eye in the place during Kyle's calling. Even the children had seemed to be touched by his words.

"We'll see next time."

"Sure."

"Well, have a nice time in Los Angeles," Kyle said as I turned on the car. "Don't have too much fun."

"I won't," I said. Kyle stepped away from the car so I could see the smirk he had on his face. "I swear I won't." I laughed. We both knew it was a lie.

"Now, I may be a man of God, but I'm also an Omega man, so I know what happens on those vacations."

"Oh, Lord. I'm not like that. Me and my girls don't get all crazy," I lied again to a man of God in front of a church on Sunday.

"Well, we'll pray over you next Sunday anyway . . . just in case the demons got to you."

"Fine." I laughed. If the trip went as planed, I would need it. Kyle stepped away from the car and waved goodbye. I watched him grow smaller and smaller in my rearview mirror as I jetted into traffic. I wondered when he was going back inside the church, but something told me he wasn't going anywhere until I was safely on my way.

Four short days later, it was Thursday, the night before I was to get on to the plane en route to Los Angeles for a weekend with my girls. I'd dropped Pookie off at her usual weekend kennel earlier that afternoon, so I didn't have to worry about getting her situated the day of my flight. I was alone in my apartment trying to figure out just what I was going to put into the one suitcase I'd committed to carrying with me. I usually packed about three cases full of things I knew I would never wear during my trip, but I thought better than that this time.

The phone rang just when I'd finally managed to stash an extra pair of shoes in my suitcase and mash it closed.

"Don't worry, I'll make my flight tomorrow, Tamia," I said, answering the phone. I saw her name on the caller ID and I was sure she was calling again to make sure I was prepared for my flight. I had a bad history of missing flights. She'd already called me three times that day.

There was silence on the other end of the phone.

"Mia?" I called again. "You there?" I was about to hang up, thinking she'd mistakenly hit the Call button on the phone. It was already after 2 A.M. in New York, so I knew it was long past what should have been her bedtime in Los Angeles.

"Yeah, I'm here," a whisper said on the other end. It was Tamia's voice but it was soft and low like a child's.

"I can hardly hear you," I said.

"I'm scared, Troy. I'm really scared."

"What? Did you say you're scared?" I sat down next to my suitcase. "Are you crying, Tamia?"

"Yes . . ." She paused. "I just don't know what to do. I'm so scared." Her voice was shaking.

"Scared of what?"

"I can't sleep," Tamia said.

"You're still taking those pills?" I couldn't believe what she was saying. "Please say you're not."

"No, I stopped. That's not it. I'm just scared. I don't know what to do here. I don't know why I'm here. I just don't know if I can do this." She sounded erratic.

"Don't be silly." I tried to sound light to calm her down. "You know why you're there. You broke the case. Right? You're there because you had the wit to do it and Professor Banks wants you by her side."

"But what if I can't do it? What if I can't do what they're asking me to do?" She sounded restless, like she was walking around in circles as she spoke to me.

"What do you mean *they*?"

"Everyone," she cried. "Everyone. I'm falling apart and everyone sees it."

"Hold up," I said. "Why do you think you have to please everyone, Tamia? I told you that you don't have to do that. Forget about everyone else; just live for yourself. Just do what you want to do. You have to let some of this weight off your shoulders."

"No, no, no. I *can't*," she screamed. "I can't let it all fall apart."

"Yes, you can, baby. You just have to let it go and breathe. Take a breather." I kept trying to think of something to say to calm her. She sounded so upset, I was afraid she was going to do something to herself. I wanted to get off the phone to try to get her some kind of help, but I couldn't think of the name of the hotel she was staying at and I was afraid if I let her go I might regret it forever.

"There are so many things in my head. They won't let me

sleep. I can't sleep. I can't sleep. I feel like if I sleep, I'll just fall behind and then everyone will know."

"Know what?"

"That I'm a phony. I'm a fake. A failure." She started crying again.

"Tamia, none of that is true," I said. "You're not a phony. You're the smartest person I know."

"But what if I'm not anymore? What if I'm not smart? If I can't keep up?"

"No one will love you any less. Come on, look at Tasha. She's crazy and we both love her." I tried a joke. I was happy when I heard Tamia laugh a little.

"I'm serious, Troy," Tamia said, sounding a bit lighter.

"Girl, I'm serious too. Tasha is crazy. And so am I. We're both crazy women. Sometimes I wonder why you put up with us. I know you're embarrassed by us."

Tamia laughed again, this time longer and with the little snort she usually made.

"Stop making me laugh," she said. "But what if I'm not the smart one anymore? If I stop being the smartest girl in the class Tamia Dinkins, I don't know who else to be."

"So then you can be one of us . . . the crazy Tamia Dinkins. The craziest woman in the courtroom," I said, laughing at myself this time. "I'm serious. We'll love you either way. Everyone will love you either way."

Tamia took a deep breath into the phone.

"I know," she said. "It's just hard. It just gets so hard."

"We all feel like that sometimes, Tamia. Like we're so behind and that we'll never catch up, but you know what, one time I heard Oprah say this quote on her show."

"What was it?" Tamia asked. She loved Oprah.

"She said that wherever you are in life is exactly where you should be. You just have to accept it, find some beauty in it, and prepare for your future."

Tamia was quiet, obviously letting the wise words settle into her mind.

"That makes sense," she finally said. "I don't know how I missed that show."

I shrugged my shoulders. The truth was, I wasn't even sure if it was Oprah who said it. Maybe it was Jennifer Aniston after she broke up with Brad Pitt. Or was it Sharon Stone?

"Thank you, Ms. Lovesong," Tamia went on.

"Okay, I think I can lay my head down now."

"You sure, baby?" I asked. " 'Cause I have plenty more Oprah quotes."

"I'm sure," she said. I listened to her for a while to see if I could hear any more pain in her voice but she sounded as good as anyone could expect from someone who had just been crying her eyes out. We said a prayer together and then we got off the phone.

When I hung up and finally got ready for bed, I said another prayer. This time I prayed for everyone—for Tamia, and Tasha, and Mommy, and Daddy, and Nana Rue, and Grandma Lucy, and Piero and Bartolo, and Lionel and Baby Prada, and Kyle, and Julian, and the girls in my class, and even Pookie Po and Ms. Pearl and their doggie cousin Miata. The world was a hard place. Things happened to all of us that sometimes we couldn't understand or take. We all needed a little bit of sunshine in our lives.

Mother *Still* Knows Best (The Remix)

"Hurry up and get in, Troy. I'm blocking traffic," my mother said, watching me in the rearview mirror as I stuffed luggage into her trunk.

"Mom, no one's behind you. You're fine." I put my last bag in and closed the trunk.

I'd called my father early in the morning to ask him to give me a ride to the airport and he wasn't home. "Off at the golf course with Dr. Williams," my mother said. I could tell she was still in bed. "I'll come and take you, Troy."

Bad news.

My mother was good at a lot of things, but driving just wasn't one of them. Having been chauffeured around by Grandma Lucy's drivers all her life, my mother hadn't learned to drive until she was well into her twenties and she drove like it. She darted in and out of traffic like a madwoman, cutting people off and cursing through the window. What was worse was that to add to her reckless driving skills, she still wanted to carry on regular conversations with people in the car. My mother was famous for doing 90 down the FDR while on her cell phone. And she had the tickets to prove it.

"Oh, I thought I saw someone behind me," she said non-chalantly, eyeing herself in the mirror as I got in. "Hey, baby." She smiled and leaned over to kiss me. "I'm so happy you called me."

"Hi, Mom," I said, returning the kiss. As usual my mother looked stunning, sitting across from me in the car. Even though she didn't have on a dab of makeup and her hair was pulled back in a bun, she looked flawless. She was fifty-six, but you'd never know. There wasn't a wrinkle on her face. She once had told me it was "a blessing from the melanin gods." I prayed they'd bless me, too.

"I think it's just great that you're getting away from the city with your girlfriends." She pulled into traffic without looking in her side mirror. "It's always a good idea to get a break, you know? To say goodbye to the city for a while."

"Yeah, I know." I looked in my bag to make sure I had my e-ticket. Tasha and I weren't able to get the same flight going into L.A.; she had an early appointment at her doctor's office. They wanted to make sure everything was okay with her pregnancy before she got on the plane.

"And I know you could use a break from that Julian, too," she murmured in a motherly way.

"Mom, I really don't want to talk about it."

"I'm serious. The best thing you can do is just forget about that boy."

"Jesus, Mom. I'm not going to talk about Julian all the way to the airport." I looked out of the window.

"Oh my, she's calling on Jesus and cursing her mother. What's wrong with the world?"

"I didn't curse you, Mom," I said, rolling my eyes.

"Well, the point is, you could've, and I don't appreci-ate it."

"How are you going to say you don't appreciate me doing something I didn't do?" I looked at her. We weren't even out of Manhattan yet. There was no way I'd survive all the way to JFK. "Okay, you know what, I'm not even playing into this. I'm just going to be quiet," I said.

"Fine, don't talk to me. You can ignore the problem, but it won't just go away. I know I taught you that."

"Fine," I agreed.

"Fine."

We were both silent. I looked at the cars disappearing behind us. She was weaving in and out of traffic like I was about to miss my flight.

"So how's Kyle doing?" my mother asked, breaching our agreement of silence. I knew it wouldn't last long.

"Mom!"

"Okay, okay. I'm sorry, Troy. Don't get so touchy." She reached over and rubbed my knee. "I know this is a stressful time for you, but I just want to know what's going on."

"Kyle is just my friend. That's it. But I'm not saying anything else about him. I don't want to talk about men right now. This weekend is about me and my girls."

"That's fine, baby. Just let me say one more thing and then we can drop it." She looked at me. I nodded my head just to make her stop. "Okay, let me say this—"

Someone jumped into our lane, cutting her off. "Watch it, speedy," my mother said, sliding her window down. "Can't you see this is a damn Mercedes?" She closed the window, beeped her horn, and swerved around another car.

"Mom, you're going to get us killed," I said, holding on to the glove compartment. Thank God for seat belts.

"Well, like I was saying"—she readjusted herself in her seat—"I know you get mad at me, but there's a reason why I'm so hard on you with these men."

"Why, Mom?"

"It's because I know what you're worth," she said. She looked over at me again. "And I don't mean money. I know what your heart is worth. And I don't want you to accept any man who doesn't know your worth. Do you understand me?"

She paused. "I know it's hard for you, Troy. You see these men out here and they seem like they're everything you want—in more ways than one . . ."

"Mom!" I put my hand over my forehead. This was almost as painful as our sex talk when I was fifteen.

"I'm serious, Troy." She laughed. "My point is, there are a lot of men out there, but you have to be selective."

"I know."

"Yeah, I know how you and your friends rate men." We both laughed. "But that's not what I mean. See, you can find a man with a good upbringing, a great career, and lots of money, but if he doesn't know what you're worth, then he's not worth your time. You understand?"

"Yes."

"Now, that's why I don't like this Julian," she went on. I exhaled and looked away. She was cursing him just like she had Champ. "No, hear me out, Troy. Julian doesn't know your worth. What kind of man just walks away from a beautiful, intelligent, warm woman like you? Saying he needs time?" I couldn't believe my father had told her everything I said about the breakup! "I'll tell you, Troy: a foolish one who's so worried about his own worth and everything else going on in the world that he can't see what's right in front of him."

"I know. You're right, Mom," I said, fighting to hold back tears. I didn't want to hear it, but she was right.

"And your grandmother told me all about your little plan to get him back," she added. I almost had a heart attack. Grandma Lucy—a traitor, too? "And that's okay. You're young, and your ego makes you do crazy things when you're young sometimes. I was there too myself when I was your age. But listen to me good, Troy." She slowed the car down and locked her eyes on me. "You can't ever make a man do something he didn't want to do in the first place. No woman has ever made a man do something he didn't already want to do. Now, when and if your plan goes as you want it to and Julian comes back to you, I want you to ask yourself one question."

"What, Mom?"

"Ask yourself if you really want him back," she said, "and if he was worth all of the energy it took to get him. And, Troy, what it will take to keep him. Because the energy you put out to get him, it will take double that to keep him. And you can quote your mother on that."

"Thanks, Mom," I said, noticing that her eyes were growing teary too as she watched the other cars around us on the road.

"No problem, baby. That's just what mothers do—we tell our little girls the truth." She pat me on the leg warmly as tears began to fall from her eyes.

"Mom? What's wrong? I was listening. I heard what you said about Julian." I turned to her.

"It's not that . . . I'm just going through something."

"What is it? Is it Dad?" I was growing concerned. My mother had always been emotional, but something in her eyes was broken, heavy.

"No," she said. "It's something I've been dealing with on my own. I didn't want to tell anyone . . . I couldn't." She began crying and wiping her tears as she fought to control the wheel.

"Pull over," I said, looking to see that there was no one in the lane to our right. I had over an hour before I had to be at the airport, and she was in no condition to drive. She pulled the car over to the side of the road and rested her forehead on the center of the wheel. "What's going on? Just tell me."

"I promised myself I wouldn't tell anyone. Only your father knows."

"Mom, you're scaring me." I kept thinking she was about to tell me about some awful disease she was dying from. I couldn't take that kind of news, but I had to know.

"Before my father died, I . . . I . . ."

"What?" I asked. My grandfather had died of kidney cancer, just hours after his old kidney had been removed and a new one had been inserted. Before the doctor walked out with the bad news, we were all outside the hospital room, crying happily as Grandma Lucy thanked God that he had been spared. While my mother had been quiet, seemingly meditating in her own space, I'd assumed it was because it had been such a long time that my grandfather had been struggling with his illness. For two years, as the cancer progressed, the doctors had searched all over for a kidney that would save him but he had a semi-rare blood type, so even with his money, it was a difficult process. Even my mother tested out, as she'd inherited Grandma Lucy's blood type and wasn't a suitable donor. By the time the B-type kidney came in, we were rejoicing and looked forward to Grandpa beating the cancer. But then the doctor came out of the room with the bad news. He wasn't strong enough; his body had been weakened by two rounds of chemotherapy and he'd passed. "What happened before Grandpa died?" I asked.

"I wasn't a match. I couldn't be a donor. I . . . I wasn't his child," she cried banging on the wheel. "There was so much going on and I just had to watch my own father die. All those years and there was nothing I could do. Just watch."

"What are you talking about? Not his daughter? He was your father . . . right?"

"Not according to the blood test." She looked over at me.

"But you have Lucy's blood type. Mom, this is crazy."

"Troy," she reached over and grabbed my arm, "your grandfather was a B-type."

"Yes."

"Lucy is an A."

"Yes."

"And I'm an A."

"What? What are you saying?" I was no scientist, but my years of watching soaps in between classes in college made it clear where this was going. Then, just then, I looked out at the street in front of me and began to realize how slow the world moves. While they beg to look fast, people slip by slowly, cars meander in sluggish motion, and even the air sits still if you really pay attention. Maybe it wasn't the entire world that was slowing down. Maybe it was just my world, the one I knew that was coming apart in slow seconds.

"If two people with A and B blood types conceive, the child is always an AB." She looked out of the window. "My father had to have been an A."

"What did Lucy say?"

"What could she say? She lied. The man she claimed was my father was dying and there was nothing any of us could do."

"Did he know?"

She turned to me and wiped a tear from my cheek. She shook her head no and turned to the look out of the side window, placing her hand over her mouth.

"Why did she lie? To you? To him? To me? All these years, Lucy's been lying?"

"My father was a black man. She'd been having an affair with him for years, even before she met my father. He lived in Harlem." She gave a short, sad laugh. "His name was Oscar. He was mixed. Had short blond hair, hazel eyes, freckles like mine across his nose . . . ."

"But Lucy loved Grandpa." I ran my hand along the freckles above my cheeks.

"He was a horn player who played at the club where Lucy and my father met," she went on. "He lived just a few blocks away from the brownstone your father grew up in."

"Did you ever meet him?"

"He died a few months after I was born. Overdosed on heroine."

"This is so sad. I just don't know what to say."

"Don't feel bad, baby. There's nothing you did wrong.

This is our stuff and that's why I've been dealing with it on my own. I didn't want to pull you into it. You're dealing with your own life."

"But this is my life," I said. "You're my family and this is my life." I felt so helpless. Everything, anything I knew growing up just seemed like a lie. I was Troy Helene Smith—that was who I was. My family had its issues, but that was who I was. I'd learned to deal with it. "It's all a lie," I continued, shaking with fear. "My life."

"No, baby. That's exactly what I don't want you to do. You can't believe for one second that anything you have lived was a lie. You are still my daughter and until they put my father's body into the ground you were his granddaughter. That man loved you dearly. And he'd roll over in his grave if he thought for one minute you denied being his granddaughter. Some things go beyond blood and we can't make him pay for Lucy's mistake."

I took a deep breath and sat back in my seat, trying to take it all in.

"So, that's why you and Lucy haven't been speaking lately?" I asked. My mother and grandmother's relationship had always been strained, but since my grandfather had gotten ill, it seemed like they were on opposite sides of the ocean. I always thought it was because since my grandfather died, they'd had no one to play referee and keep the peace.

"I can't deal with her right now. That woman put me through so much with her shit," she screamed. "I just need a break. I just need to get myself together and realize that my mother is never going to change. She's just fucked up. She's been fucked up and that's it."

"Mom, Lucy's not all bad. She has some good sides."

"All of the stuff she put me though, making me believe I wasn't good enough because my skin was darker than hers, making me feel bad about marrying your father, all of it was to protect her lie, to keep that bullshit going long enough so she could cash in on my father's money."

"Do you think that was all it was? Really, Mom? She loved Grandpa," I said, "You know that. I don't care if she lied. She made a mistake. We both know how things were back then. Right or wrong, she did what she had to do."

"Well, she did what she had to do and I'm doing what I have to do," my mother said, wiping away the last of her tears. "I can't live in the past. I may not have a relationship with my mother, but I'm going to make sure *we* have one." She looked at me and forced a smile. "If I get anything from this whole thing, it has to be that I want to have a strong relationship with you."

"Yes," I said, feeling bad for all the times I'd turned my back on her. All this time my mother has been going through something horrible and I haven't been there for her. I felt selfish and mean. I had to help her though this.

As we drove to the airport, I thought of my grandfather, how he loved my mother so much he often told people she was the only thing that made life worth living. While raising her risked everything he'd had, he once told me he would rather have been a poor man if being rich meant he'd never had my mother and then had me for a grandchild. He was a beautiful man who loved us all with everything he'd had. My mother was right; he'd always be my grandfather.

My mother pulled the car to the curb outside the airport. She got out of the car, still silent with sadness, and helped me get my bags out of the trunk.

"I think we all need to go for counseling," I said. "When I get back to town." I looked into her eyes. "We have to talk about this. Sweeping it under the rug will only allow it to get worse."

"We'll see, baby," she said, kissing me on the cheek. "We'll see about that." She cupped my face in her hands. "But now, I want you to walk into this airport and forget about all of this drama. Go and have a good time with your girlfriends. Can you promise me that?" She began to cry again.

"Mom—"

"Just promise me that. I can't let you have this bring you down like it's done to me. I can't let another generation deal with this."

"OK," I lied. "I'll try."

After I made it through the security maze, I managed to make it to my gate just a few minutes before boarding. My mother's news was flipping around in my mind and I was struggling hard not to cry or call Lucy. I couldn't tell if I was mad or just in shock about the whole thing, but all I had were questions that hadn't been answered. I kept trying to stop thinking about the whole thing. If I let it take control of me, my trip would be ruined, and I'd promised my mother I wouldn't let that happen. I'd have to wait and deal with everything when I got back home.

When I sat down and waited for the airline to begin boarding, I decided to call Julian. I wasn't going to tell him what was going on. It just didn't seem like the right time. I didn't even know all of the facts yet. I just wanted to hear his voice for comfort, to remind myself that the rest of my world still existed.

"Hey, baby," I said when he picked up the phone. He sounded like he was still in bed. "Are you sleeping?" I asked.

"Yeah, I'm in bed," he replied. "Shouldn't you be in L.A. with your friends by now?"

"No, silly. I'm at the airport. My flight doesn't leave until 4 P.M. I told you all of this yesterday," I said.

"Oh yeah. I must've forgot. Things are just crazy right now at the hospital," Julian mumbled. "I'm covering for someone. Been doing 72s."

"Well, I didn't mean to wake you up. I was just calling to say goodbye before I left."

"No problem. When will you be back?" Julian asked. He sounded anxious.

"Oh, it's just for the weekend. So I'll be back on Monday."

"What hotel will you be staying at?"

"The Mondrain."

"Great," Julian said. "Well, have fun. And call me as soon as you get in."

"I will." I heard them call my flight for boarding.

"Have a nice trip, baby," Julian said. "Goodbye."

I hung up the phone and looked at Julian's name before it disappeared off the screen.

Though I knew my mother was right about some of the things she'd said about Julian, I didn't know what I was supposed to do with it. I mean, she didn't really know Julian like I did. Yes, Julian messed up with the Miata thing. But was I supposed to make him pay for it for the rest of his life? For the rest of *my* life? Was I supposed to miss out on the one man I loved because he made one mistake? He'd come clean to me about her. I wasn't ready to walk away from him yet. All I knew was that I loved that man and he still loved me.

I handed my ticket to the flight attendant and boarded the plane. Next stop, L.A.

Where My Girls At?

I know why they call Los Angeles "La-la land." The place is so unreal. The people are unbelievably beautiful, the homes are amazing, the cars are immaculate, hell, even the dogs look like superstars. Everything "appears" as if it just came off of a movie set or a dream you wished you had every night. I don't know why or how Tasha ever left L.A. That girl had so much drama, this place was made for her.

Checking out the city from the back of my limousine, I could already tell we were going to have a ball. Tamia had put together a list of things for us to do, and Tasha had had Lionel's assistant put us on every VIP list in the city.

"Your first time in L.A.?" the driver asked, pulling up to the hotel.

"No, I used to come here a lot as a child," I replied. "I guess you could say it's my first time here as an adult."

"You'll have a nice time," he said, handing me a receipt. "The Mondrain is a nice hotel. Go see Beverly Hills."

"Yes."

I saw Tamia standing in the lobby as soon as I stepped out of the limo.

"Troy! Troy!" she yelled, running through the lobby of the Mondrain like it was the Days Inn.

"Hey, Mia." I hugged her. She looked fabulous. She had a great tan and she'd let her hair down for once. "You look great," I said, stepping back to look at her. "I see someone's been doing more than just sitting in a courtroom all day."

"Well, I had to make some time for the boys on the beach." Tamia grabbed my bag. I was happy to hear that. I had been worried about her putting a lot of stress on herself and then falling back into those pills, but she seemed okay. And she sounded much better than she had the night before, like a different person altogether.

"Let the bellhop bring the rest of your things," she said. "Penthouse," she told the bellhop.

"Great," I said, admiring the Mondrain's sleek, cream-colored lobby as we walked through. It was already climbing to the top of my favorite hotels list—and it was a long list. I felt so peaceful standing at the elevator, I couldn't wait to see the spa. In fact, the entire place looked like one big old spa. After the stuff with my mother and Grandma Lucy, I was sure there would be a dark cloud over my L.A. trip, but so far, the hotel was sure lightening things up. In the limousine I'd decided to put my best face forward and wait to tell Tasha and Tamia about my grandfather when we all got back to New York. They were my girls and I knew if I'd told them then, we'd have spent the entire trip hashing the thing out. This was supposed to be our good-time summer trip. I didn't want to ruin it for them. Tasha was pregnant and Tamia was whooping ass in court. Neither of them needed any unnecessary drama. It would all be waiting for us when we got back. "I love this place," I said.

"You know Tasha wouldn't have it any other way. She told Lionel she needed to be *comfortable*." We both laughed. Tasha was milking the pregnancy thing for everything it was worth.

"Wait, Tasha's already here?" I asked, puzzled.

"Yeah, she's upstairs in the room taking a nap."

"But I thought she was coming later than me. That's why we took separate flights."

"Well, apparently she decided she wasn't going to her doctor's appointment and caught the first flight out this morning. I think her and Lionel had an argument. He didn't want her to come," Tamia whispered. "You know how he gets when *his* Tasha is away for too long. And now that she's pregnant—forget about it."

"Oh, that's so sweet," I said softly.

"Yeah, you try telling Tasha that."

"So how's 'Operation Mommy Dearest' going?" I asked.

"Well, Porshe will be here for breakfast early tomorrow morning," Tamia replied. "She has a photo shoot or something at noon, so we had to make it early."

"Does Tasha suspect anything?"

"No."

After I'd put my things down and spent thirty minutes "oohing" and "ahhing" with Tamia about how much Tasha's tummy had grown in the month she'd been pregnant, although it really hadn't, I jumped in the shower to freshen up for dinner. Tamia got reservations at Shonda's, one of L.A.'s hottest restaurants where anyone who was someone on Friday night.

Before we got dressed, Tamia, Tasha, and I laid out our outfits together on one bed. It was a purely superficial ritual but it stopped many a fashion faux pas before we ever walked out the door. Whenever we were going somewhere—a frat party, nightclub, football game afterparty—we'd put all three of our outfits out together and look them over. From the earrings to the shoes, each part of the outfit was judged by the other two girls before a "hell yeah" or "hell no" was given. And if one piece resembled something from another girl's outfit, both girls had to find a replacement. We called it the "Runway Run-through." Tasha, obviously, was usually the most unforgiving of the judges. She'd toss our clothes across the room, yelling like she was putting together a photo shoot for *Vogue*.

Her stylistic fits were usually focused on Tamia, who thought anytime was a fine time to wear a turtleneck. And while I often felt sorry for Tamia as she searched her closet for something "less churchy" to wear, Tasha was usually right. "No lace, no plaid, no corduroy," Tasha would say, standing behind Tamia in the closet.

We were years away from the low riders and hot-pink tube tops we'd worn in college, but things hadn't changed much between the three of us. Tamia pulled a turtleneck from her bag and Tasha immediately sent it darting across the room. We all laughed.

I settled on wearing my white Gucci wrap dress. It was simple and sexy, and it made me look like a movie star—a black Marilyn Monroe. Not bad! I wasn't exactly on the market, but I still wanted to show the L.A. boys what a New York honey was working with. I topped off the dress with matching white single-strap heels and gold hoop earrings. Sexy, sophisticated, and simple. Grandma Lucy and Piero would be proud.

Tasha's outfit, on the other hand, wasn't that easy. She complained that she looked fat in everything she put on. Tamia and I sat on the bed, fully dressed, as she tried on what had to have been seven outfits, before settling on the first one.

"You haven't gained any weight yet," Tamia said, trying to relieve Tasha. It was no use. Tasha didn't even respond. She just kept walking back and forth between the bathroom and the closet, saying how she needed new clothes.

"Mood swings," Tamia and I agreed, watching her. "Mood swings."

Runway Run-through: Because It Girls Care

Remember the saying "You are the company you keep." If you allow your girl to go out with you looking like your third-grade teacher, then you may as well throw on a plaid jumpsuit too. If you run into a situation where one of your girls needs a runway run-through before you go out, be nice, be gentle, and remember, bad fashion happens to everyone.

Instructions:

Set up a getting-ready party at your house. Invite your friend who is in need of attention. Tell her to bring her outfit so you can get dressed together. Have some extra clothes handy in case her clothes are completely awful. Get dressed and turn on some music so you can model your clothes in the mirror together. When your friend is ready, look her up and down and tell her the truth—and nothing but the truth. She may hate you then . . . but she'll love you later when she has her new look.

Do's:
1. *Be completely honest.*
2. *Compliment her whenever she looks good.*
3. *Loan her something that will complete her outfit.*
4. *Tell her if it's too small or tight.*

Don'ts:
1. *Hate on her outfit because it's better than yours.*
2. *Be close-minded.*
3. *Lie because you don't want to hurt her feelings.*
4. *Ever suggest you two wear matching outfits.*

Out with the Girls, L.A. Style

Things got a little crazy after we left the hotel. Well, about as crazy as they could get for a pregnant woman and two law students.

"So who has the first round?" Tasha asked when we finally made our way to a table at Shonda's. Tamia was right—the place was jumping. The crowd outside was spilling out into the street and if it wasn't for Tasha seeing one of the Lakers she knew standing outside, we would've never gotten in.

"What do you mean, *round?*" Tamia said, patting Tasha's stomach.

"I was going to order cranberry juice, Tamia."

"And vodka," I added, laughing. "I can't believe this place is so packed," I said, looking over the crowd. So far I'd spotted two actors, a washed-up rapper, and a group of huge men I suspected were football players. The L.A. scene was strikingly different from the scene I was used to in New York. People were pretty laid-back in New York, but the L.A. dream girls who looked like they were all on starvation diets and the guys who clearly had paid too much for their clothes because they were sipping on water seemed so superficial. Folks were posted up all over the restaurant trying so hard to look important and struggling to look like they were having the time of their lives.

"Yeah, I could've saved the time I spent calling to make a reservation. That woman at the door was evil." Tamia groaned, eyeing the gaunt Asian girl standing by the door. "She doesn't even have a list in her hand."

"L.A. is a very selective place," Tasha said. "Either you're in or you're out."

"Like that outfit Old Girl has on," Tamia said, pointing to a girl walking by wearing a mini-mini skirt that stopped right below her ass cheeks—well, almost below her ass cheeks.

"Exactly." Tasha chuckled. "Who let the hoes up in here?" The girl, who had to be at least a size 22, turned and looked at our table. "Nice skirt, girl," Tasha said, grinning. The girl smiled and kept walking.

"You're crazy, Tasha." I looked for my compact in my purse. I spotted a cutie standing by the door. He was absolutely gorgeous. I would've thought he was Larenz Tate if it wasn't for the dreads hanging down his back.

"What are you getting all cute for?" Tamia asked. I could see her looking at me in the side of my compact.

"Four o'clock," I replied, putting on extra lip gloss. I had only been in L.A. a few hours but the glowing L.A. sun was already affecting my skin. Just riding down La Cienega in the backseat of the drop-top Tamia had rented had turned my skin a deep caramel. It looked radiant, like I had been out sitting on the beach all day.

"Oh, he's fine," Tamia said, spotting the Larenz look-alike.

"The one with the dreads?" Tasha turned to get a look at him. "Yeah, he's cute, but I could do without the dreads. Those things are nasty. You never know what he has hiding up in there."

"I'm willing to find out what he's hiding!" Tamia gave me a high five over the table. "I think dreads are sexy."

He looked toward us and Tamia waved at him.

"He's mine, heifer." I grabbed her hand.

"No, he's *his*." Tasha pointed to Larenz. Another man with dreads walked up to him and gave him a hug that lasted a little too long for friends. They locked arms and walked out of the restaurant together.

"Well, I guess my dreams of finding a husband out here are shot down," Tamia said, looking at the menu.

"No, not if you want to marry a fake actor or a wannabe Spike Lee," Tasha joked. Tamia and I looked at each other and sighed. "I'm saying, it's not that bad, y'all. L.A. is just a place to have fun. That's all."

The waitress finally came to the table after twenty minutes and took our orders. I usually would've complained about how long it took for her to mosey on over to our table, but it took me a while to decide what I was going to order. I'm a fan of eclectic eating, but the menu was out of control. Tamia told us Shonda's was a soul food restaurant, but looking at the menu, I couldn't tell what "soul" she was speaking of. They had fried chicken, but it was pineapple-infused fried chicken on top of a bed of wild rice. What a match. I settled on the pork chops in wine sauce. I was accustomed to high dining and even fusion, but some things should just be left alone.

By the time the waitress brought our food to the table, Tamia was completely intoxicated. She'd had three Midori sours and a glass of white wine a secret admirer had sent her from the bar. She was waving at every man who walked by, and she even got up and talked to a man who looked like Steve Urkel.

"Why y'all looking at me like that?" Tamia slurred, getting back in her seat.

"Because you were talking to Webster's older brother," Tasha said.

"He was fine, Tasha. Don't hate the player; hate the game." Tamia put her hand up in the air so I would give her five . . .

but I didn't. "What? You're hating too, Troy?" Tamia asked, looking at me accusingly.

"He was kind of scary, Mia. I'm just saying." I took a sip of my brandy Alexander.

"Really?" Tamia looked at the guy. He made his way to the bar. He was standing there waving at Tamia with his pants so high it looked as if his belt was wrapped around his neck. "He's ugly? Oh no. Do y'all think I'm drunk?" Tasha kicked me under the table and we started laughing.

"Yes, baby. You're intoxicated," Tasha said, prying the fourth Midori sour from Tamia's hand. "But it's okay. Go ahead and get drunk. Both of you. I'm the designated driver for the next eight months."

"I'm just a little stressed—you know, with the trial and everything," Tamia said. "I just want to unwind. That's why I'm glad y'all are here." She did a little drunken cry. "Y'all my girls."

"Oh, baby." I rubbed her back reassuringly. "It's okay. You know we get down like four flat tires." I looked up to see a chocolate brother walking toward our table. He was handsome, but the blood-red, Suge Knight suit he was wearing made me feel like I was in a rap video.

"Oh shit, let the games begin," Tasha said, spotting him. "Mr. Wonderful is on his way."

"Who's Mr. Wonderful?" Tamia asked way too loud. I eased down in my seat, hoping he hadn't heard her.

"Diamond," the man said. He sat down next to Tamia. "That's my name, honey. And who are you?"

"Who told his ass to sit down?" Tasha whispered in my ear.

"Her name is Egypt and I'm Star," I said, volunteering our club names—the names we used when we weren't interested in men we met at the club and didn't want them to know our real names.

"And who is the lovely flower sitting next to you?" Diamond asked, looking at Tasha.

"Her name is Beyoncé," Tamia giggled. "Beyoncé Knowles." I had to look away to keep from laughing.

"Mm, I love that name. It suits you." The man took Tasha's hand and kissed it. "Beyoncé . . . Beyoncé . . . Beyoncé . . ."

"Yeah, my husband does, too," Tasha said, flashing the *real* diamond Lionel had bought her in the fake Diamond's face.

"Oh, I'm sorry, Beyoncé," Diamond said. "I just had to compliment such a lovely lady. I've been watching you since you came in here."

"Sounds like a stalker to me," Tasha said, hiding her words with her hand.

"Tell your man I'm jealous," he added. "I'm saying, I'd do anything." He paused. "And I'd give anything to be with a woman like you." He slid six hundreds on the table.

"What?" Tasha said, looking annoyed. She grabbed her butter knife. "Are you trying to say I'm a damn hooker?" She was about to get up. I put my hand on her knee.

"Not in here, Tash," I said to her. Just then mini-mini skirt woman walked up to the table and smiled at Tasha. Mini-mini Skirt whispered something into Diamond's ear and kissed him on the cheek. Diamond shook his head and she walked away. Tasha and I looked at each other, confused.

"No, baby," Diamond said, looking back at Tasha. "I just wanted to show you ladies where a brother's coming from. I know y'all are from out of town because everyone up in here knows Diamond and Diamond knows everyone. Let me guess you ladies are from the East Coast . . . New York. Right?"

"Yeah, how did you know?" Tamia begged. I kicked Tasha under the table and tried to get Tamia's attention, but she was too busy grinning at Diamond.

"Oh, baby girl, that's because Diamond is flawless. I can't go wrong, like my jewels." He held up his hand so we could see his rings—all eight of them on one hand. It looked like he'd been playing in Grandma Lucy's jewelry box. "Anyway," he went on, "I figured that money would cover your meals and the bottles of Cristal the waitress is about to bring over."

"Cristal?" Tamia jumped in.

"Yeah, one for each of you." Diamond snapped his fingers like he was Tony Montana in *Scarface*. "The prettiest ladies in the restaurant."

"Diamond, we don't really need any more drinks, and we can pay for our own food," I said, just as two waitresses came to the table carrying bottles of Cristal.

"Don't trip, sweetheart. Let Diamond treat you like a diamond," he said, smiling at one of the waitresses as she bent over to pour him a glass. He grabbed her butt and groped it like he was searching for spare change. I was sure she was about to turn around and slap the crap out of him, but she just laughed and playfully said, "Stop, Diamond."

"Heeeeeeeeeeeey," Tamia said, sounding like she didn't have an ounce of sense in her drunken body.

"Drink up, ladies." Diamond raised his glass. "You don't drink, Beyoncé?" Diamond asked Tasha, who was simultaneously sipping on her cranberry juice and giving Diamond the evil eye.

"No, I do drink, but my baby doesn't," she said dryly. "I'm pregnant."

"Oh, you're breaking my heart, redbone. How are we supposed to be friends if you're pregnant?"

"Well, I figured that was cleared up when I said I was married," Tasha replied slyly.

"Fly and feisty." Diamond sat back in his seat. "I like you already."

"You know this motherfucker is a pimp, right?" Tasha whispered, pretending to nibble on a piece of bread.

"A pimp?" I looked over at Diamond sitting across from me—his gold teeth, red suit, and cane with diamonds encrusted in the top . . . Then there was how the women who came to the table reacted to him and how everyone in the restaurant was staring at us . . . Yeah, Diamond was a pimp.

"Since when did pimps start hanging out in restaurants?" I whispered back to Tasha. She shrugged her shoulders. "Why is he talking to us?" Tasha sat back and gave me the "you know" face. "What?" I said, trying to figure out if I wanted to laugh or call the police.

"You better get your girl," Tasha said, pointing at Tamia feeding Diamond one of her shrimp.

"So what are we getting into after dinner?" Diamond asked, pouring Tamia another glass of champagne she didn't need.

"We're going home," I said quickly.

"No, we're going to the Rapture," Tamia jumped in. "I heard that's the hottest spot in L.A. tonight."

"Hell, no." Diamond laughed. "That club is wack. Look, I'm going to let you ladies in on a little secret. The only way to party in L.A. is private parties. There are too many people at the clubs."

"So where's the party?" Tamia asked.

"Troy, we have to get the hell out of here before this Negro spends any more money on us. He isn't going to go away," Tasha whispered to me.

"You ladies need to come to a little party me and my associates are having at my house later," Diamond said. "You girls ever been to a mansion overlooking the Hollywood Hills?"

"No, and we won't be going tonight," Tasha said.

The girl with the mini-mini skirt came back over to the table. Diamond didn't look so happy to see her again. She tried to whisper in his ear, but I could hear her and was able to make out: "That bitch is fucking your money up." Diamond got up from his seat with heat in his eyes.

"Ladies, I have some business to attend to," he said. "Sit tight and Diamond will be right back." He turned and walked out with Mini-mini Skirt following behind him.

Tasha got up and grabbed her purse.

"Let's go, before he comes back," she said, pulling Tamia's arm.

"Why do we have to leave? I'm having a good time with Diamond," Tamia whined. I got up and took Tamia's other arm.

"What about our bill?" I asked, following Tasha out.

"He said he had it," she said, pulling the car keys from her purse. "Let him get it."

Tamia talked us into going to the Rapture after she promised not to have another drink or talk to any more men. It took us thirty minutes to convince her that Diamond was not marriage material.

By the time we finally made our way around the maze that's called L.A., with Tamia singing every song that came on the radio full blast from the backseat of the drop-top, the Rapture was packed. We decided to go to the club across the street. The line outside the club was what Tasha and I call "diverse," sprinkled with white girls here, black boys there, and everything else in between.

"I hope it's not one of *those* places," Tasha said as we walked in. By "those places" she meant the kind of diverse clubs we'd discovered in New York after college—the so-called mixed clubs where black men went to chase white women. One night we had gone to a club in the Village that had turned into the black man–white woman connection. While the line outside had been full of black men, not one of them would dance with us. They didn't even look in our direction. They had other things in mind.

"I don't care at this point," I said now to Tasha as we made our way to the dance floor. "I just want to dance and forget about Diamond." I laughed.

Biggie Smalls's "Going Back to Cali" came on and Tamia ran to the center of the dance floor, screaming, "That's my song, girl." Tasha and I followed right behind her. Everything was her song at that point.

We danced so hard I felt like we were back at Howard. I

forgot about the people around me and just moved my body back and forth to the music, acting a fool right along with Tamia. I forgot about Julian and school and all of the other drama going on back in New York. I was in Cali with my girls.

After Biggie went off, another one of Tamia's "songs" came on and the one after that and the one after that. A handsome white man slid up behind Tasha. Tamia and I laughed as he struggled to keep up with her. Tasha took it down to the ground in front of him and the man looked like he was holding on for dear life.

His friends, who I later learned at the bar were Stephen and George, came over to dance with me and Tamia. They were investment bankers in L.A. for some convention. They treated Tamia and me to a beer—which I insisted we split—and begged us to dance with them. Now, if there was one thing I knew about white boys from watching my grandfather with Grandma Lucy and hanging out with the ones I met in law school, it was that they knew how to have a good time. White boys loved to party and drink beer, and Stephen and George were no different. They got Tamia and me out on the floor and we had a ball—I guess we had a *connection* of our own going on.

Before I knew it, we'd been on the dance floor for two hours. At around 1 A.M., Tasha's feet gave out and we decided it was time to call it a night. Tasha and I had the guys carry Tamia to the car and we headed back to the hotel. We had gotten the party started and now it was time to get the sleeping under way.

Going Undercover: Club Names

It's bound to happen to every fine woman in her lifetime—you meet a man at "da club" you have no intention of getting to know. Because you're a gracious queen who would never be completely rude to someone—unless you had something to gain from it—you decide to be nice to the poor guy and not pretend you don't see him standing right in front of you. Then he does it—he asks your name. Now you have two options: You can give this Tito Jackson look-alike your real name and listen to him call it all through the club all night, and run the risk of seeing him out somewhere else and calling you by your name, or you could simply give him your "club name." Don't settle on something simple like Ann or Kim. Nah! This is a great time for you to get creative. Try these hot club "standards" if you haven't chosen a name yet. Remember: Simple is good. The last thing you need is Mr. Dragon Breath standing too close and asking, "What did you say?"

Cars	Places	Foods	Earthy	Celebrities
Porsche	China	Sugar	Star	Janet
Mercedes	Egypt	Chocolate	Sunshine	Beyoncé
Jaguar	Dakota	Coffee	Rain	Britney
Lexus	Mecca	Peaches	Summer	Mary
Escalade	Georgia	Pumpkin	Cloud	Alicia

Hangover

Rrrrrring. Rrrrrring. Rrrrrring.

I could hear the hotel phone ringing from beneath the two pillows I had piled on top of my head.

"Get the phone." I groaned, rolling over. I peeked out from underneath the pillows to see the sun blazing through the balcony window. I looked at the clock. It was 8 A.M.

Rrrrrring. Rrrrrring. Rrrrrring.

"Fuck." I looked across the suite into the second bedroom to see Tamia spread out on her bed with Tasha lying in the bed next to hers.

"Hello?" I mumbled, wondering who could possibly be calling the hotel at eight in the morning.

"Good morning. This is the front desk. I have someone down here for Tamia Dinkins, please," said the person on the other end.

"Tamia?" I looked across the room again. "She's asleep. Who is it?" I asked just as I remembered that Tamia had arranged for Tasha's mother to come to the hotel for breakfast.

"It's Porsche St. Simon," the woman said anxiously.

"Mia," I tried to whisper. "Mia!" Tamia didn't move.

"Um . . . yes, please tell Ms. St. Simon we'll be right down. We'll meet her in the restaurant." I hung up the phone and headed to Tamia's room.

"Tamia, wake up." I nudged her. "Wake up; she's here."

"Noooooo," Tamia cried. "My head hurts." She jumped out of the bed and ran to the bathroom. "Urrrrp," I heard coming from the bathroom. She was throwing up."Oh, hell no, Tamia," I said, heading toward the bathroom. "Not today. Not a hangover."

"I can't do it, Troy," Tamia garbled, emerging from the bathroom. "You have to take her down there. You have to do it," she whispered so Tasha couldn't hear her.

"But I can't. I don't even know the lady."

"Neither do I." Tamia climbed back in the bed. "But I can't help. I'm sick."

"Tamia, how am I supposed to get her down there? Have you even thought about that? How am I supposed to get Tasha downstairs?"

"For breakfast? I'm cool with that," I heard Tasha say. I turned around to find her standing in the doorway brushing her hair. "I'm starving."

"Great, so you two can go to breakfast together," Tamia said, rolling over.

"Just let me put something on and I'll be ready." Tasha turned and walked toward the bathroom.

"There you go," Tamia whispered. "Just take her down there and let her mother handle it from there. It'll be cool."

I frowned at Tamia. Somehow I was sure that wouldn't be the case.

Maybe I was suffering from the effects of a hangover, but I felt like Tasha was talking a mile a minute as we headed down to the restaurant. First she went on and on about how much she missed Lionel, then she talked about the baby, and on the way downstairs in the elevator, she contemplated whether she'd have eggs and bacon or fruit for breakfast. All the while, I nodded my head, trying to figure out what I was going to say when she saw Porsche.

"Do you think I should do a fruit and vegetable diet for the rest of my pregnancy?" Tasha asked me, walking into the restaurant. "I read in *Cosmo* that a lot of celebrity mothers do a vegan diet when they're pregnant. It helps the baby or something."

"Yeah, girl," I said. My head was pounding terribly. I felt like I was going to faint. Tasha could've said she was trying a pork and beef diet for the rest of the pregnancy and I would've agreed just to make her stop talking. I looked around the restaurant. I couldn't see Porsche anywhere. Maybe she'd left, I thought. Maybe she'd left. *Great.*

"You're here," the host said, picking up two menus. It was clear she was expecting us.

"Yes, we're here," Tasha replied, still oblivious. "See, these folks expect you when you walk in. That's what I'm talking about. Good service." She turned and took my hand. "Come on, Troy. You're dragging your feet. Are you hung over, too?" she asked, looking at me over her shoulder. I could see Porsche sitting at the table the host was leading us to. I closed my eyes and said a short prayer everything would work out and that Tasha wouldn't slap anyone.

"What the hell is she doing here?" Tasha said when she turned around and Porsche caught her eye.

"Just sit down," I urged Tasha. "Just sit down and talk to her."

"Talk to her?" She looked at the host putting our menus on the table. "What is this? Did you do this, Troy?"

"Um, yes, Tasha," I mumbled, hoping she wouldn't hear me. I looked at Porsche. I'd never seen the woman in person and I rarely caught the show, but there was no way I could mistake her for anyone other than Porsche St. Simon. Tasha looked just like her—from the smooth jet-black hair to the dimple in the middle of her chin, there was no denying this mother-daughter pair. Porsche was stunning, but by looking in her eyes, I could tell she was hurting and afraid of how Tasha might react.

"Natasha," Porsche said, standing up.

I grabbed Tasha's arm and turned her around to face me.

"I'm telling you this because I'm your friend and I love you," I said quickly. "You have to make amends with your mother before you become one. Remember what my mother said." I pointed to her stomach. "I'm not asking you for much. I just want you to talk to her. That's all, Tasha. Just talk to her."

Tasha pulled away from me.

"Talk? Oh, that's what this bull is about? You just want me to talk to the woman? Let's see how this goes." She sighed and turned back around. "Hello, Porsche." She sat down at the table, leaving Porsche and me standing.

"Hello, Ms. St. Simon," I said, shaking Porsche's hand. I sat down next to Tasha. "I love your work."

"Well, thank you, darling." Her voice sounded so smooth and wispy that I imagined that she was an old movie actress like Dorothy Dandridge. "Forgive me. I've taken the liberty of ordering you ladies fruit platters. Nothing does the body better than fresh fruit in the morning, I always say." She sat down nervously.

"Thank you," I managed.

"So, Tamia, how do you know my daughter?" Porsche asked.

"She's not Tamia," Tasha said. "She's Troy and we met at Howard. You know, in D.C., where I ran away to after you left me sitting in that damn hotel alone for two weeks?"

"Natasha, you weren't alone. You had the finest of care, and it wasn't two weeks, either," Porsche said. It was uncanny how much Tasha sounded like her.

"Whatever." Tasha picked up an apple slice. "So why are you here, Porsche? Publicity stunt? Trying to get on *Oprah*? Dying? Or did that twenty-two-year-old boyfriend of yours take all of your money? What kind of stunt are you pulling now for attention? For your career?" Tasha looked out of the window.

Suddenly, I wished I could be invisible. I felt like I was on the set of a soap opera.

"Well, if you must know, Natasha"—Porsche reached across the table and took Tasha's hand—"your friends called me and told me about the baby." Tasha immediately threw darts at me with her eyes. "And I wanted to talk to you."

"About?" Tasha said, pulling her hand away.

"Look, I'm the first to say I wasn't the best mother, Natasha." Porsche tossed her hair over her shoulder. "I had you when I was young and I made a lot of foolish choices trying to chase my dreams. I was a fool." She looked into Tasha's eyes. "But even fools have to grow up. I want to be a part of my grandchild's life."

"Why should I let you do that?" Tasha asked.

"Because I want to give that baby all of the love it deserves, Natasha—all of the love I didn't give to you. I want to give that baby a family."

"I don't know, Porsche," Tasha said. I saw tears welling in her eyes. "It may be too late for all that."

"Baby, it's never too late. It's never too late to make right what you've done wrong in the past. Just let me make it up to you. That's all I'm asking. Just let me be a part of this. I'll do anything you want."

Tasha looked down and started to cry. I began rubbing her shoulders softly. I looked out of the window to see a small crowd of photographers gathering in front of the restaurant. A camera flashed and Tasha looked up at the window.

A man carrying a camera bag came up to our table in the restaurant with a tape recorder in his hand.

"Porsche, is it true that you're reuniting with your daughter, the wife of star basketball player Lionel Laroche?" he asked.

"What?" Porsche looked stunned. "This is a personal matter."

"Get the fuck out of here!" Tasha said, getting up. She looked at Porsche. "What the hell is going on? Did you do this?" She pointed to the cameras that were flashing constantly outside the window. "Did you set this up for publicity? I knew it."

"No, baby," Porsche said frantically. "I wouldn't do that." She looked at me. "Maybe it was someone at the hotel. A leak or something."

"Whatever. Don't flatter yourself." Tasha began to walk away. "This has your bullshit written all over it. You used me when I was young to get close to my father . . . and your tired ass is trying to use me now." She ran out of the restaurant.

"I'm sorry, Ms. St. Simon," I said, getting up to follow Tasha. "She's really upset."

"She walked outside," said the woman at the front desk when I walked into the lobby of the hotel.

I ran outside and down the street behind Tasha.

"Wait up, Tasha," I screamed.

"You don't know that woman," Tasha cried. "You don't know her like I do."

"I'm sorry. I didn't know."

"Yeah, you didn't know, so you should've minded your fucking business."

"I'm sorry, really. I thought it was a good idea," I said, trying to make Tasha stop walking away from the hotel.

"You know why she had me, Troy?"

"No."

"My mother got pregnant by one of the producers of the show. That's how she got on that damn soap opera," Tasha cried. "She got knocked up with me. And when he got tired of playing Daddy behind his real wife's back, she tossed me to the side. She locked me up in a hotel to be someone else's problem."

"Okay. I hear you," I said calmly. "But Porsche was right.

That's the past. You're all grown up now and you have to let that go."

"Don't you fucking tell me about letting go. Your life is perfect," Tasha said, pointing at me. "It's fucking perfect. Your parents are together and you don't have to worry about this kind of shit. If I didn't have Lionel, I wouldn't have anything. So don't you dare tell me about what I need to let go of."

"I didn't mean it like that and you know it. And if anyone knows that my life isn't perfect, it's you."

"You know"—Tasha turned to face me—"I think it's time you turned around and went back to the hotel. I really don't want to talk to you any more."

"What? Where are you going?"

"Where I'm going is my business. Just like my life. So stay the fuck out of it." Tasha turned and walked away.

I was shaking and crying uncontrollably by the time I made it back up to the suite. Tasha had run away and I couldn't find Porsche anywhere. I didn't know anything about Los Angeles and I had no clue where Tasha might have gone. I felt so helpless, and my head was flooded with questions about why Tamia and I had done what we did. We might've ruined our friendship with Tasha forever. She was a good friend and she didn't deserve to be hurt or embarrassed. What were we thinking? Now this was added to all the stuff with my family and Julian. My entire world was spinning and I was finding it hard to hold my ground.

"Tamia, Tasha left," I called, walking into the suite. There was total silence. I went into her room and she wasn't there, so I instinctively headed toward the bathroom. "Tamia," I called, knocking on the closed door. Again there was silence. I knocked again and then I turned the doorknob. As soon as the door opened a little bit, I could see Tamia's body on the floor in front of the basin. "Tamia!" I screamed. I pushed my way in and fell to the floor beside her. She was laying there, completely cold in a little pool of what looked like blood and vomit. I kept shaking her, but her body was so heavy and stiff, I couldn't lift her up.

"Oh my God, oh my God, oh my God," I cried forcing myself to get up off of the floor and get to the telephone. "I'm in the penthouse. I need help. I need an ambulance," I screamed into the phone at the woman at the front desk. "Her name is Tamia Dinkins. I don't know what's wrong with her. She's just lying on the floor. I think . . . I think she's dead."

I hung up the phone and tried to wake Tamia again, but she still wasn't moving. The bathroom was beginning to feel smaller and smaller. I was fighting just to take in air so I wouldn't pass out.

"Please, Tamia," I cried. I tried checking for a pulse and to see if she was breathing, but I was shaking so badly, I couldn't feel anything. "Please don't be dead. I need you here with me. I'm sorry I left you alone. I'm so, so, so, so sorry, Tamia. Please." I started shaking her. "Oh my God, what is happening to my friend? Please help her. She doesn't deserve to die. She just needs your help," I prayed, holding Tamia in my arms.

I sat there in the bathroom with Tamia's lifeless body, waiting for what seemed like hours for someone to come upstairs. I said every prayer I ever knew, even some I didn't, asking God that he might see me through and save my friend if it wasn't too late. I'd already lost one in some small way, and I couldn't lose another—not like that.

The room was soon filled with people from the hotel, cops, paramedics, and people asking me questions about who we were, what we were doing in Los Angeles, and what we had done the night before. They asked if we used crystal meth, cocaine, heroin, crack, marijuana. *No, no, no,* I answered all of their questions. It was just alcohol. Just some drinks.

After they informed me that Tamia was not in fact dead, they began asking me questions about her and what I thought might have happened. I didn't know if I should tell them about the over- the-counter pills Tamia had been taking. I was sure she'd stopped using them like she'd promised me she was going to. But after one of the cops asked me to get her purse, I found something that made my heart heavy for my friend and myself. Tamia had an empty bottle of Stay Up in her purse.

"It's not conclusive yet, but we think she had a minor heart attack and then she went into cardiac arrest. We pumped her stomach and it was clear that she'd just taken the pills. They were found throughout her system," a strange doctor said to me in a strange hospital. He went on to ask if I knew she had been using the drugs and how long it had been. I kept telling him over and over that Tamia was not the kind of person he thought she was. She wasn't some junkie. She was an A student, she was going to be a lawyer, she was the smartest person I knew.

"Ms. Smith, this is very common," he said after telling me that Tamia was in what they were calling a mild coma. "No one's judging your friend. I actually see this kind of drug abuse a lot in young professionals. You get so caught up in being perfect that you get afraid when you realize that you're not. And then you try harder and harder, often abusing these over-the-counter drugs to help you stay up longer and focus harder, but then you keep hitting that brick wall when the drugs aren't enough. And one pill becomes two, then three—then you're drinking cups and cups of black coffee, then not eating, using starvation to stall sleep, then drinking, then you finally come crashing down. Your friend is crashing down right now, Ms. Smith. I can't give you the specifics of her illness, but she shut down her whole system with those drugs. We're just lucky nothing happened to her central nervous system, so we're expecting a full recovery when she wakes up. It's a good thing you got back to the room when you did. She could not have survived much longer with no oxygen getting to her brain."

I fell into the doctor's arms, crying as he held me. His words went exactly as the story did with Tamia. I knew because I had been there for the whole thing and I'd allowed it happen. I didn't do enough to make her stop. I didn't do anything.

"When will her father be here?" the doctor asked.

I'd used Tamia's phone to call her father in the ambulance on the way to the hospital. Through solos, he said he would be on the next flight and not to leave his baby until he got there. "Don't leave her. Don't leave her," he cried like a child as he ran out of his office en route to his car.

"I don't know what flight he was able to catch out of D.C., but I gave him all of the information about the hospital and he was on his way, so he should be here in the next few hours," I said, looking at my watch.

"Good. I think she'll be up by then. I hope she'll be up by then. It's usually really hard for the parents," the doctor said, looking in from the hallway at Tamia's body hooked up to all the machines. "They don't understand how their children could end up here."

I didn't understand it either. It felt like a nightmare that wouldn't stop. Just twenty-four hours ago we had been laughing and picking out clothes for a night on the town. It was girls' night and things were as they always had been. The 3Ts were together. But everything was fading away from me and I felt as if I was all alone in the world. I was miles and miles away from my home, my family, and now my friends.

I needed someone to talk to. Someone to assure me that everything would be okay, that Tamia would pull through as the doctor said she would, and soon we'd be back in New York living out our lives as we had before. I sat down in the hallway in front of Tamia's room in case she woke up, and I called Tasha, but she didn't answer the phone. I supposed she was still upset and had no clue what had happened to Tamia.

I called my mother and father but they weren't home. I figured they off doing their usual Saturday afternoon routine, so I didn't leave a message with Desta. I didn't want them to get it and be alarmed.

Then I found myself dialing Julian's number.

"Hello?" Julian said.

"Oh, it's Troy. Did I wake you up again?" I asked. I could hear sleep in his voice.

"Nah, I'm fine. Just getting some shut-eye before I go in for my next shift. How's L.A.? You're still there, right?"

"Yeah, I'm in a bit of a jam." I started crying.

"What's wrong, Troy?" Julian asked. "You sound upset."

"Tamia just, Tamia just . . . we're at the hospital," I managed. "She passed out, they pumped her stomach, and she went into cardiac arrest—"

"Wait, slow down, Troy," Julian said. "How did this happen? Was she sick before?"

"No, I just found her on the floor in the hotel. And that was it. She was just lying there." I started crying harder. I couldn't tell him about the pills.

"Oh, baby, she's going to be okay. Stop crying like this. I heard everything you've said and it sounds like your friend will be okay. Just listen to the doctors. Are you alone? Where is Tasha?"

"I had a big fight with Tasha and she left the hotel before I even found Tamia. She doesn't know what happened," I cried hysterically into the phone. "And now I'm just here alone at the hospital waiting for her father to get here. I feel so alone. I just feel so alone."

"You're not alone, Troy. There are professionals at the hospital who can help you."

"That's not what I mean, Julian," I cried. "I just feel alone.

That's why I called you. I don't have anyone else. I don't know these people." All of the pressure from the past two days was crashing down on me and I just wanted support. I just wanted him to support me.

"Troy, your friend will be okay. You just have to be strong and know that. You have to stop letting things get you so upset."

"My friend is in a fucking coma," I cried. Everyone in the hallway looked at me.

Julian exhaled.

"You're getting irrational," he said. "I was just trying to comfort you. That's all."

"Well, you're certainly doing a fine fucking job at that," I said weakly. Suddenly I felt wrong for even calling Julian.

"Look, Troy," Julian said distantly. He sounded the same way he had at the restaurant when we broke up. "I'm going to get off the phone now before I say something I don't want to say. Just call me if you need me." He hung up.

I hung up the phone and shook my head. *I needed him now. Now. I needed him now. I needed . . .* Just then Kyle's face came to me and I went to find his number in my phone. I dialed his number and it seemed that almost immediately, he picked up.

"Helen of Troy." Kyle laughed into the phone. "To what do I owe this splendid honor?"

I was quiet. He sounded so happy, I didn't even want him to hear my voice. I didn't want him to hear me crying.

"Troy?" he said again. "Now I know you are not trying to prank call a brother. I can see your number." He started laughing again. "Is that you? Are you crying?"

"No," I replied, trying to straighten out my voice. "I mean, yes, it's me, but I'm okay." My voice cracked and I started crying again. I turned around to see Tamia still asleep in the bed.

"You don't sound okay, Troy. Tell me what's wrong. Why are you crying?" His voice had the same kind of urgency as Tamia's father.

"I'm at the hospital. My best friend had a heart attack. She was taking some pills and my other friend ran away from me. I just embarrassed her and made a fool of myself." The words came from me like a prayer. They escaped my heart before I thought of keeping secrets. I had to put them on someone. Kyle listened patiently like he already knew everything I was saying.

"Angel, stop crying," Kyle said when I finally finished rambling through the story. "It's not your fault. You were just trying to be a good friend. Stop crying. There's work to do."

"I know, but that doesn't change what's happening. I don't know, Kyle. I'm just worried."

"The good Lord didn't take your friend from you, and the other is simply lost. She will find her way back to you. You just have to believe it, Angel. And rest assured in that gift of grace."

"I know, I know."

"I know it's not easy. And sometimes when we want to be strong and not cry, we feel like crying and not being strong, but just know that everything is going to be all right. Everything is going to be all right." Kyle was speaking to me in a way I'd never heard before. He was more than a friend, he was a man of God comforting me. "Our God is a waymaker," he went on. "He is a God of change, of lifting up and bringing to excellence. You need to see that right now, Troy. And you have to know that even if this thing finds itself not as you wished, God is still God."

"God is still God," I repeated, looking at Tamia in the bed. She looked so peaceful, I imagined she was somewhere inside of herself smiling at me, telling me to calm down. *Be strong,* she was saying. *Be strong.* I wanted to be strong. I had to be strong for my girls. The 3Ts were strong. We'd survived everything else in our lives and we would survive even ourselves.

"Look, Troy," Kyle said, "I can't let you be alone like this. You sound awful." Kyle paused. "What time is it there?" he asked.

"I don't know, like 10 or something." I looked up at the clock next to Tamia's bed. "10:06."

"Yeah, it's just after 1 P.M. here," Kyle said. "I think there's a 3 P.M. daily out of LaGuardia."

"LaGuardia?" I sat down in a chair. "The airport?"

"Yeah, I think I'm going to come out there. If I can get that flight, I'll be there by 5 P.M. your time," Kyle said.

"Oh, you don't have to do that, Kyle. Really, it's okay." I lied. Inside I was thinking it would be great if Kyle came to L.A. Tamia's father would be there shortly, but I needed to see another familiar face. But I couldn't say that.

"Look, Troy," Kyle said, interrupting my thoughts. "We're friends, right?"

"Yes."

"And friends are there for each other. I'm just going to come out there and make sure things are okay. If your friend isn't awake by the time I get there, then I'll have fun keeping you company until she does wake up. And if she is awake when I get there, then I'll have two fine women to talk to. That's it. It's really selfish if you think about it. Either way, I get to see you."

"You're silly." I laughed through my tears.

"So I'll be at the hospital at around 6:00 p.m.," he said, after taking down all the information.

"Okay, that's cool," I said. I couldn't believe what was happening. Was Kyle coming all the way to L.A. just for me?

There were no changes in Tamia's condition by the time her father came rushing into the hospital. His eyes were bloodshot and his clothing was in complete disarray. He was a big man, over seven feet tall with a solid frame, but he fell to the floor beside her bed and prayed so loud I was sure everyone on the floor could hear him. He kept saying, "I'm not a praying man, but I can't lose her, God. I can't lose her. I can't lose her."

I stood in the door frame behind him, begging Tamia to

move, twitch her fingers, give us anything to know that she was in there somewhere like the doctors said she was. If not for me, for her father.

The hospital chaplain came into the room with two other doctors and they were able to get Judge Dinkins together. He prayed again over Tamia with the chaplain and then, at the chaplain's instruction, he came out of the room for air. I felt so small sitting next to him in the silent hallway. His tall body was bent and crooked in a way that made my pain, my problems, seem so insignificant. There were no words to describe what he was feeling, how he was feeling. He just kept smiling at me, saying how great it was to see me again and that he was happy I was with Tamia. I smiled and got him coffee and assured him, although I wasn't sure myself, that everything would be all right.

Step Five: The Damsel in Distress

By the time I saw a familiar shadow turn into Kyle's body walking toward me, I was exhausted, hungry, and confused. Tamia was still not waking up and there had been no changes. I'd tried to get Tasha and my parents on the phone but there was still no answer. I was able to get her father to calm down and after sharing just about every story about Tamia he could remember, nothing but silence sat between us.

I couldn't help but stand and smile when Kyle came rushing toward me. He was smiling enough to remind me that the sun was still shining outside the hospital.

"I came straight here," he said, dropping his suitcase and pulling me into his arms.

"Thank you," I said. I turned to Judge Dinkins. "This is my friend Kyle." I pointed to Kyle. "Kyle, this is Tamia's father, Judge Dinkins."

They shook hands and Kyle sat down to talk to him, offering comfort. I watched as Judge Dinkins smiled and breathed a bit easier in Kyle's presence. He walked into the room with Kyle and said a delicate prayer over Tamia's body. I couldn't have been more proud, more touched by how personally

Kyle was taking things. He wasn't there for me. He was there for my friend, for her father, doing what he loved.

"You two need to get out of here," Judge Dinkins said as we walked out of the room to talk. "Troy, you've done more than I could have asked you. You've been here all day and you should go get something to eat. Get some rest. I'm here now."

"But I want to help," I replied.

"There's nothing we can do right now but wait," Kyle said. "The doctors are doing all they can. We just have to wait and be here . . . and healthy when Tamia wakes up." He pinched my cheek.

"Exactly," Judge Dinkins said. "I'll call you if there's a change. You'll be the first person I call. I promise."

I peeked into the room at Tamia and then looked back at Kyle and her father. They were right. My mind needed to be revived. I didn't want to leave but if I was going to help my friend recover, I needed to recover too.

"Okay," I said, hugging Judge Dinkins. "I'll be right at the hotel. Please call me if anything happens, if she moves her toe . . . anything." After he promised me three more times, I said goodbye to Tamia and left the hospital with Kyle by my side. I wasn't sure what would happen, but I knew I had someone by my side.

Kyle and I went to the hotel so I could freshen up and get some of Tamia's things together to bring to the hospital. I asked if there were any messages from Tasha at the front desk, but there was still nothing. I hoped that she was so mad that she'd hopped on a plane and went home to Lionel. I couldn't stand the idea of her walking around in the streets alone.

After showering and changing my clothes so we could go get something to eat, I stood in front of the bathroom sink alone, thinking about Kyle. While my mind was certainly with Tamia in the hospital, in some way my heart was happy I was with Kyle.

"Are you beginning to like Kyle?" I asked my reflection aloud. Could I like Kyle? He was a good guy. A great guy. He was handsome, smart, and funny. Plus, he had principles—more principles than anyone I'd ever known. He was what Grandma Lucy called a pearl deep in an ocean waiting to be discovered.

Just then I felt *that* funny feeling deep in my stomach . . . the same feeling I felt in grade school when my all-time biggest crush, Eric Roberson, kissed me underneath the slide on the playground. It was warm and tickly, almost like butterflies were being released in my stomach, but I wasn't nervous about a thing. I was happy.

Yeah, I could like Kyle, I thought, putting on my lip gloss. Even with the church thing, I could like Kyle. Even with the no-sex thing, I could like Kyle. I stashed the gloss back in my purse and looked at myself again.

What the hell are you thinking about, Troy? I couldn't like Kyle—I was still in love with Julian. "No, no," I said, pointing at myself. There was no way I was going to allow Kyle to get mixed up in the thing with me and Julian. I didn't want to hurt Kyle. That was the last thing I wanted to do.

"You ready in there?" Kyle called from the living room. "I'm getting hungry."

"Yes," I said, walking out of the bathroom. "I just want to call Tamia's father again to see if anything has happened. Then we can go."

"Great," Kyle said. He stood up when I walked into the room and kissed me on the cheek. "How are you, Troy? I know this is a lot for you."

"I'm fine. I just can't believe all this." I folded my arms across my chest. "I never imagined any of this would happen . . . in L.A. of all places. Tamia's in the hospital, Tasha's gone . . . I'm just glad you came."

"Your eyes are puffy," Kyle said, gently touching my cheeks with his hand.

"You know, for one moment sitting in that bathroom with Tamia, I thought she was dead. I really thought she had died. I felt so empty inside. I couldn't do anything about it but just pray."

"It's moments like this that show us just how connected to our faith we are," Kyle said.

"I guess you're right. I just felt so alone, like I'd never make it through."

"Well, that's why I'm here, Angel—to make sure you get through this." He playfully tapped me on the nose.

"Ha, ha. So how are we supposed to do that?" I asked, sounding a bit more flirtatious than I wanted to.

"I don't know, Troy," Kyle answered me, grinning. "I just had the idea. I was hoping you'd have the plan."

"I don't care what you say, this shirt looks completely ridiculous on me." Kyle looked at himself in the dressing room at a store we'd stopped at. After I checked in on Tamia, we'd gotten something to eat and ended up walking around aimlessly in Los Angeles. While I felt a little guilty about shopping during such an odd time, Tamia's father said the doctors told him her vitals were getting better and that she'd be coming around very, very soon.

"Kyle, you look amazing." I stood behind Kyle in the mirror. "Your body was made for Versace."

"Troy, I look like a mob boss or something," Kyle said, pulling at the silk shirt. "I look like a fake thug." He popped up his collar.

"Um, no. That's even worse," I said, laughing. "Just look cool and collected. Just relax. Versace is for strong men—men who know who they are and what they want."

"Oh, that's me." Kyle flexed his muscles.

"Yeah, so wear the shirt. Don't let it wear you." I closed the last button on the shirt and looked back at his reflection. "Perfect. Now this shirt is all you. You have to buy it."

"Are they paying you, Troy?" Kyle joked. "Because you sound like you have stock invested in this place."

"Stop playing, Kyle."

"Okay, how much is it?" he asked. I looked at the tag and didn't bother to say aloud what I read. I just held up two fingers. "Twenty?" Kyle asked. *Versace at $20? In my dreams.* I rolled my eyes. "What? What is it? Two hundred?" I shook my head from side to side. "Two thousand?" I nodded my head. "You know I'm not paying two thousand dollars for this shirt, right?"

"Kind of steep?" I frowned.

"Steep? That's off the charts. That's insane. I know you don't pay that much for those clothes you wear. I know you don't." He paused. I nodded.

"Almost," I murmured. "I have to look good."

"Oh, no. Oh, no." He started taking the shirt off. "Please put this thing far away from me. I don't even want anyone to think I'm paying that kind of money for a shirt." Kyle pulled the shirt over his head like there was a bug in it. He threw it on a rack and pulled my hand. "Let's go," he said, dragging me out of the store.

"It wasn't that bad." I stepped out of the store behind Kyle, laughing. Everyone was watching us. A security guard came out of the store. "He thinks we stole something," I whispered in Kyle's ear.

"Well, that's the only way I'm getting anything out of there." We both started laughing and Kyle grabbed my arm.

"First trying on Versace, now you're talking about stealing," I said teasingly. "I'm going to have to report you to the Pastors Commission or something."

"Make sure you add this, too." Kyle stopped walking suddenly.

"What?"

"This." He bent down and kissed me on my lips.

"Kyle," I said softly. I felt heat growing in my heart and my knees felt weak beneath me. I wanted him to do it again.

"I'm sorry." Kyle massaged both of my arms with his hands. "It's just that . . ."

"What?" I said, trying not to jump on Kyle.

"This is a beautiful city, it's such a beautiful day, and I'm with a beautiful woman." He let me go. He looked into my eyes. "I hope it's okay."

"Yeah, it's fine," I managed. We stood there for a second looking into each other's eyes. "Ice cream?" I said, looking at an ice cream parlor on the other side of the street.

"Yeah. What do you have in mind?" he asked.

"Rocky Road." I pointed across the street.

"My favorite."

"That's mine too." I crossed the street in front of him. "Not many people like it like I do. I have been known to eat it for dinner."

"Dinner?" He laughed.

"Yep."

"Oh no, in the South, Rocky Road is not a meal option. You need some hog mog, collard greens, pig feet, macaroni and cheese, sweet potatoes—"

"Dang, you eat all of that?" I broke in.

"You know I do. And I can cook it, too."

"Oh, a man that can cook," I said, winking.

"Oh, Kyle Hall is no stranger to the kitchen. My nana made sure of that." Kyle opened the door to the ice cream parlor for me. "Can you burn?"

"Depends on what you mean by *burn*." I stepped inside. "I can burn food. In fact, I think I've burned just about everything I've cooked." I smiled.

"Well, I guess we're just going to have to change that. I can teach you a few things. But it'll cost you."

"Cost me?" I asked.

"Yeah, you'll have to buy the groceries—especially if you're going to burn them. Church money don't grow on trees."

Halfway through ice cream, Judge Dinkins called and said that Tamia had finally woken up. She was still a little out of it, but she was doing just fine. He said the visiting hours were over and that we should come to the hospital first thing in the morning. I thanked him for calling and told him to kiss her for me and tell her that Ms. Lovesong was waiting to see her. My body settled a little and somehow the ice cream tasted that much sweeter as I licked my cone. Things, as Kyle had promised me, were getting better.

"One down, one to go," Kyle said, happy to hear Tamia was okay. "We just had to be patient."

After hearing the good news we decided to take a short walk before we headed back to the hotel. I was even beginning to feel better about what had happened earlier between Tasha and me. Strolling from window to window, Kyle told me a story his grandfather used to tell him when he was child. It was about an old man who was losing his sight.

Kyle said one day the man went to see the town's healer to see if she could heal him. The old woman gave him some dried herbs and told him to rub them on his eyes each night before bed for five nights in a row. She told him on the first day when he woke up, he'd have some slight burning, and on the second day he'd be able to see everything, then he'd lose his vision totally on the third day and it would return as clear as it was when he was a boy of five on the fourth day. Then she warned the old man to continue using the herbs on the fifth night even though he could see fine on the fourth. She told him that after the fifth day, he'd lose his sight for ten days and then regain it for good on the eleventh.

The man said thank you and left the healer's house. Then, Kyle said, twenty days later the man returned to the healer.

He was walking with a cane and he was totally blind. "What did you do to me, old woman? Your herbs didn't help me. I could still see when I came here, and now I'm totally blind. Your herbs made me blind." Without moving from her chair, the old woman asked him if he'd used the herbs each night for five days straight. The man said he'd used it the first night and it burned so bad he hadn't used it the second night. Then he told her he'd used it the third night and gained his sight by morning. As she'd promised, by the fourth morning he was using it, and his vision was as clear as it was when he was five. Then he said he decided he didn't want to use it the fifth day, because he didn't want to lose his vision for ten days. He had to work in the fields. "I could see for nineteen days, and this morning I woke up and I couldn't see. What can I do?" he asked. "Nothing," the old woman said. "Nothing can be done. You didn't respect the herbs. They will heal you, but only on their time. Not yours."

After Kyle finished telling the story, he explained that he'd memorized it when he was a little boy and thought of it whenever he was wrestling with something in his mind.

"The point is seeing things through, Troy," Kyle said. "Whenever you start a journey, you have to see things through. The good and the bad. There will be days when you can't see, days when your eyes burn, and days when things appear so bright you feel like you're five years old. But you have to see it through and remember why you started your journey in the first place—why you took the first step," he added. "The reason I'm telling you this story is that you have to remember why you wanted your friend to see her mother and start from there. Forget about what happened today. You're not a bad person because your friend had a fight with her mother. You had no way of seeing that coming. Your intentions were good and that's all that matters. Now all you have to do is figure out how you can make things better. Don't just give up and walk away because you had a bad day"—he smiled at me and pinched my cheek—"or the herbs will get you."

* * *

Kyle and I returned to the hotel and even though I insisted he stay with me and sleep in the extra room, he got a room of his own for the night. He came up to my room with me to talk and sat in the living room to pray as I went to change into something comfortable.

I peeked through the doors to watch him as I slipped on an old sweat suit I'd packed. Kyle looked so peaceful sitting in the living room on the floor, with the Bible resting in his hands. Watching his lips move as he focused on each word, I imagined he'd read every one of those words before, but he read them with so much love, it looked like they were still new to him.

I still couldn't believe he'd come all the way here from New York just to see me. Just to help me. I tried to explain to myself that he was just worried, but there had to be more. I would've been lying to myself if I didn't at least admit that. The truth was that I knew Kyle really liked me and I also knew I'd have to find some way to deal with that, but at the moment I was busy enjoying the view.

Kyle actually managed to make prayer look sexy. I probably shouldn't have been watching him—that had to be some kind of sin . . . coveting thy preacher or something. But, damn, he looked good in that kind of Denzel meditating in *Mo' Better Blues* kind of way. Denzel's fine ass was sitting there meditating as the sun came up. He looked like an African king. Made me just want to tame him.

"You done watching me?" Kyle asked. He looked up from his Bible and smiled at me behind him in the room. I didn't realize how obvious I was.

"Sure," I said, embarrassed. Suddenly I wished the fire alarm in the building would go off or something.

"So are you feeling better?" he asked, changing the subject.

"Yeah, I'm fine."

"Well, that's good," Kyle said, sitting on the couch. "So tell me about your friends. What are they like?"

"Well, Tamia is the smart and silly one." I sat down next to him. "She's just full of life. Always wants to get something more. Always working hard. And I guess you could say Tasha is the fiery one. She's the one who will burn you up if you don't act right. She's really strong, but sometimes I don't think she knows it."

"They sound like fun," he said.

"Oh, they're both a bag of fun. My friends specialize in nonstop excitement."

"I think that's good," Kyle said, "you know, to have such well-rounded friends. Who wants to hang around a bunch of stiff people all day?"

"That's what I say." I sat back on the couch. "I mean, Tamia is one of the smartest, most sensible people I know, but she knows how to party." We both laughed. "You know, it's really cool, Kyle," I said, "that you can just hang with me and not be all sanctified and stuff . . . that you don't pass judgment on me. I was honestly worried about that when I met you—that you'd judge everything I did."

"Oh, don't get confused. I pray for you sinners all the time," Kyle said jokingly. "No seriously, I respect the fact that you're a real person. You're human and so am I. I can't judge anything you do. I can only pray you make the right decisions. Judgment is something I dislike about a lot of saved people. We get saved and act like we forgot about what it was like beforehand, like we never sinned at all. And that's just a lie. I would be lying if I said I haven't had my times. I went to a black college just like you." I laughed. "Besides, I couldn't judge you, Troy. You're not like Mary of Magdalene or anything."

"How do you know that?" I asked just as there was a knock on the door. I got up assuming it was Tasha.

"I just know. You're a lot more innocent than you let on."

"Tasha?" I said, walking toward the door.

I looked through the peephole just as I was about to open the door, and it wasn't Tasha. Julian and a dozen red roses were staring back at me. "Oh shit," I said.

"Troy?" Julian and Kyle said at the same time. I looked back at Kyle. What was I going to do?

"Kyle," I said, "I'll be right back. I just need a minute." I cracked the door open and slid out, closing it behind me.

"Hey, baby," Julian said, opening his arms. "Surprise."

"Heeeeey," I said with forced enthusiasm.

"These are for you." Julian handed me the roses. "I felt so bad after we got off the phone that I decided to make it up to you . . . and here I am."

"Yeah . . . yeah," I managed. "Here you are. You, you, you." I playfully nudged him on the shoulder. Suddenly I thought of asking him if we could sit in the hallway—be rustic and spend the night in the hallway . . . like a really chic camping trip. Then everything would be okay and he wouldn't have to find out Kyle was in my hotel suite.

"First, I figured I'd wait for you to come back to New York, but then I thought, where's your sense of romance? This is the woman you love. She needs your support. Show her you love her," Julian said, taking me into his arms again. "You see, I love you and I want to be with you!" he hollered very loudly.

"Now? Like right now?" I asked. "Like here?"

"Of course, T. I'm here to prove my love to you and ask you to be with—"

The door to the suite opened and Kyle poked his head out.

"You okay?" he asked, looking at Julian and me.

"Kyle?" Julian looked at him, confused, and then looked at me. "Kyle? Your father's friend?"

"Hey, man," Kyle said, shaking Julian's hand.

"Yeah. Kyle, can you go inside while I talk to Julian?" I

added, sounding like a customer service representative. "I'll be right in." Kyle's head disappeared and the door closed again.

"What the hell is he doing here?" Julian asked, pointing at the door. "I thought your friend was in the hospital."

"She is."

"I come all the way here to see you and you have another man in your hotel? When your friend is supposedly in the fucking hospital? I can't believe this shit." I could see a little vein popping out on Julian's forehead.

"Are you with that man?" Julian asked. "Just tell me now and I'll leave, Troy. I'll go away and not come back if you're with him."

"No, baby."

"Well, if you're not with him, tell him to leave. Tell him to go." Julian stepped away and took back his flowers. "Tell him to go and I'll stay."

I pressed my palm against the door and looked at Julian. Everything I ever wanted was in front of me. The man I loved was standing in front of my hotel room holding a bouquet of flowers. I couldn't turn him down, no matter what was waiting behind that door. I couldn't lose Julian again.

"Wait out here," I said, turning the doorknob. "I'll be right back."

Kyle was sitting in the suite exactly where I'd left him. His hands were folded on his lap and he had his eyes closed.

"Mr. Wonderful is back to fix everything," he said without opening his eyes. I sat down on the couch beside him and placed my hand on top of his. "You want me to leave?" He opened his eyes and looked at me.

I nodded my head yes.

"I'm sorry, Kyle. But he came a long way to see me," I said gently.

"Yeah, *he* did. *He* came a long way." Kyle got up from the couch. "You know what? This is exactly—" He stopped and picked up his Bible. "Never mind," he went on. "I won't let you do that to me. I won't." He slipped the Bible into his travel bag. "Goodbye, Troy," he said, walking out. "Goodbye."

Step Six: Let Your Feelings Be Known

That night, in my hotel room, just miles away from the Hollywood sign, Julian made love to me like I was a movie star. He made a line down my spine with his tongue and ran his fingers up and down my thighs. He must've whispered "I love you" in my ear a thousand times. As we moved together beneath the sheets, I could feel his heart beating against mine and I knew he meant every word he said. I struggled to hold my breath to experience every sensation that ran through my body as his chest rubbed up against my back. I had to feel him all around me, inside of me, in order to believe that he was really there and that it wasn't just one of my dreams. I forgot about Tamia, I forgot about Tasha. It was just about me and my man.

I closed my eyes and imagined that we were making love in our own home just days after our wedding. Julian's wedding band was smiling on his finger between us and everything, everything was perfect. Finally, he was mine . . . again.

By the time morning came at 6, I was lying peacefully in his arms, trying to figure out if I should jump out of bed and run through the streets of L.A. screaming, "He's mine," or lie still in Julian's arms and pray the moment would never end. Somewhere between trying to decide what outfit I would wear to run down the street and coming up with something to say to the police when they arrested my ass, I remembered something—the Take Her Man Plan.

I ran down the "Six Steps to Success" in my head and realized that while I wasn't even thinking about it, after the disaster with Kyle in the park, I had completed just about every step. My reaction to Tamia's brush with death and Tasha's disappearance, while awful and totally unplanned by me, was step five, "Damsel in Distress." Just as Tasha had said he would, Julian responded by coming to my rescue and I, as the step says to, "fell into his arms."

I turned to face Julian in the bed. Watching him sleep, his mouth open just wide enough for me to slip a nickel inside, I couldn't believe Tasha's little plan had worked. That day, sitting across from Julian at the sushi bar as he'd broken my heart and given back the key to my apartment, I'd thought all hope was gone. I'd thought it was over, just as Julian said, and I had been ready to give up. But the Take Her Man Plan had worked and here he was, the man of my dreams, sleeping soundly in front of me, just hours after he'd confessed his love.

There was only one thing left to do: step six, "Let Your Feelings Be Known."

"Julian," I whispered tenderly. "Are you asleep?"

"Not now," he mumbled, shaking his head sleepily. "I just woke up when you called my name." He opened his eyes, squinting from the sunlight behind me and smiled. "You okay?" he asked.

"Yeah, I'm fine," I said. "I was just up thinking. That's all."

"Okay. About what?"

"Julian, what's going to happen when we get back to New York?"

"What do you mean?" Julian slid his arms around me beneath the sheets.

"I mean, what are we going to do . . . about us . . . about everything you said last night? Do you remember everything you said?" I asked.

"Of course, baby," Julian said, scratching his scalp—he always did that to wake himself up. "I told you I love you and I want to be with you."

"Yeah."

"Oh, is that it, Troy?" Julian looked at me. "Are you worried about us being together?" He sat up in the bed. "Because there's no reason for you to be nervous about anything. I know what I want and that's you. Okay?"

"Yes, that's fine," I said. "I just wanted to let you know how I feel, too—how I feel about you."

"That's great, Troy," Julian said, getting out of the bed. "And I really want to hear it, but first I need to go to the bathroom." He tiptoed out of the room.

"Fine," I said. "I'll tell you when you get back."

I turned back around to face the window. The sun looked like somebody had tied it to the side of the building—like I could reach out of the window and touch it. It was so big and beautiful. I began to think of Kyle and wondered how he was doing. I knew I'd hurt him really bad, but I had to put Julian first. While my feelings for Kyle were growing stronger, Kyle was my friend, just as I'd told him time and time again, and I had to separate the two.

Just as I was about to close my eyes and say a little prayer that Kyle would forgive me for what I'd done, Julian's pager went off. The vibration rattled so hard, it fell off the nightstand and cracked open. I bent down from the bed to pick it up and put it back. I held it to make sure it wasn't broken and put it on the nightstand.

What the hell is he doing in there? I thought, laying back down in the bed. *Please don't let him stink up the whole suite,* I said to myself and closed my eyes. I yawned and opened my eyes again to find the pager staring at me from the nightstand. Before I could even think about closing the screen, the word *Miata* found my eyes and the pager ended up in my hands.

Reading the page wasn't an option, I thought, listening to hear if Julian was still in the bathroom. I had everything on the line with Julian and before I poured my heart out to him, I had to find out what reason on God's good earth Miata would have for sending Julian a text message. Therefore, without hesitation, I read:

> Got your message about going out to L.A. to see your old classmate in the hospital. I hope he's ok and that the accident wasn't too bad. Call me when you get settled.
> Love, Miata

My eyes closed tight with horror. It didn't make sense. Why would Julian lie to Miata about coming to L.A. to see me, if everything he was telling me was the truth? I opened my eyes and read the message again, for one second, praying I'd read it wrong or that it had been sent from someone else. Any plausible reason for what I was seeing escaped me. First, I thought to run into the bathroom to confront Julian, but if he had already been lying to me, there was nothing to stop him from doing it again. I needed to hear the truth from the horse's mouth and come to my own conclusion.

I picked up Julian's phone and scrolled down to her name.

"Baby," Miata said, answering the phone. "I just sent you a message."

"This isn't baby," I said.

"Troy?"

"Yes." I looked over my shoulder to see that Julian was still locked up in the bathroom. I didn't want him to see me, but really I didn't care anymore. I had nothing else to lose.

"Why do you have Julian's phone?" Miata sounded as upset and confused as I was.

"Miata," I said, "I'm beyond all that stuff with you now. Julian's here in L.A. with me and I saw your message, so I just wanted to call and see what was up."

"What's up?" Miata's voice went weak. "Julian and I are supposed to be together now. He told me he wasn't seeing you anymore."

"Miata, please. Why should I believe anything you say?"

"Well, if you don't want to believe me now, perhaps you'll believe me in nine months."

"What?" I asked with the phone slipping from my ear.

"I'm pregnant and Julian's the father," I heard as the phone fell to the floor.

I'm not a psychologist. And short of struggling to understand my crazy family, I have little experience with the human mind. But I bet there's some kind of psychological term for what happens when something really bad happens to you and your mind just separates itself from your body out of total rage and disgust for the situation you've found yourself in.

My hand flew across Julian's face like greased lightning when I found him sitting on the toilet in the bathroom. I hadn't hit anyone in my entire life, but I knew the slap had to hurt because I could see the red imprint of my hand on his face. His reading glasses went flying across the bathroom into the tub and the magazine he was reading fell to the floor.

"What the fuck is that bitch talking about?" I asked, hollering so loud I nearly startled myself.

"What did you slap me for?" Julian jumped up from the toilet and bent down to pull up his pants.

"No, fuck that," I said, jerking his arm so he couldn't get the pants up. "You're going to answer my question."

"What question? I don't even know what you're talking about."

"I spoke to Miata, Julian." I mashed him in the forehead.

"Apparently, I'm your old schoolmate and that's why you're in Los Angeles."

"Oh, that's it." Julian smiled. "I can explain that."

"Well, I guess you better start, motherfucker." I put my hands on my hips. "Yeah, I guess you better start explaining right where you got your black ass on the plane."

"Look, Troy, the bitch is crazy. That's all I'm going to say." Julian pulled up his pants and shrugged his shoulders. "I'm not going to explain my actions," he added. "I broke up with Miata because she's crazy. I didn't want to tell her I was coming here to be with you because it's none of her business. Just like what I do with her is none of your business."

"Julian, don't make me slap your ass again." I could feel myself beginning to cry. I fought so hard to hold back the tears, but when Julian turned to walk out of the bathroom, I couldn't stop them. I'd played his fool for so long and I couldn't believe he couldn't even look me in the face. "None of my business?" I said, watching him walk down the hallway. "Like the baby is none of my business?" Julian stopped walking and turned back around.

"What? How do you know that?" he said, rushing toward me.

"You got her pregnant," I screamed. Hearing the words come from my mouth suddenly made them real. When I'd heard them on the phone I had been angry and I'd wanted Julian to explain. I'd wanted to yell at him, fight, scream, and cry. But when I'd realized exactly what was going on by hearing myself say that Julian had gotten another woman pregnant, I was done. I wanted him to leave and never, ever come back into my life.

Not only did this man I loved and had taken care of while he was going through one of the hardest times in his career leave me for another woman, but then he had the audacity to think I was fool enough to take him back. And worse—he got the bitch pregnant! *I wanted his ass out.* Who did he think I was? Shit, who did I think I was that I actually thought I had to fight to get and keep this *piece* of a man?

"Get the fuck out, Julian," I said, walking past him into the bedroom. "Get all of your shit and get the fuck out of my life." I started throwing his things at him and slung the Louis Vuitton overnight bag I had bought him at his face.

"Troy, what are you doing?" Julian asked, standing behind me in the doorway.

"I'm moving on."

"Come on, baby. I can explain," Julian said. "She's crazy."

"It's funny how we're always the crazy ones. It's always us, right? Oh, now you want to explain? You just said you weren't going to explain anything and now you want to explain? Make up your mind, Julian." I threw his shoes at him. "You know, I don't know why I'm so surprised that you can't make up your mind. You can't seem to decide what woman you want to be with and can't decide why you're in L.A.," I handed him his wallet. "I guess you should've worn a fucking condom."

"Troy, you're acting completely irrational. You're not being yourself," Julian said, following me down the hallway with his bag in one hand and his shoes in the other. "I think we need to sit down and discuss this so you can calm down. I don't want you to regret what you're doing."

"Regret?" I said, laughing wildly. I opened the door and pushed Julian into the hallway. "The only thing I regret is being with your dumb ass when there's another man out there who really loves me." I wiped of tears from my eyes—they would be the last. "Goodbye, Julian," I said.

It took every bold bone I had in my body to knock on Kyle's door. While I was afraid of making a complete ass of myself, I was more afraid of what would happen if I didn't let Kyle know how I felt and apologize to him again. After I kicked Julian out, I'd sat down in the living room of the suite and thought about all the things that happened had between me and Kyle. I realized that ever since the day I'd met him, he'd been a blessing in my life. Kyle was very good to me— better than Julian had ever been. And while I knew I had feelings for him, I was afraid to let them be known because my mind was cloudy with my desire to be with Julian. I'd been a fool for so long, but I wasn't going to be anymore.

After standing in the hallway for about three minutes, contemplating what I was going to say to Kyle, I finally knocked on the door. There was silence, and just as I was about to turn to walk away, thinking he'd left to go back to New York, the door opened and there he was.

"Hello," Kyle said flatly.

"Hey." I pushed my hands into my pockets. He was fully dressed and I could see his bag sitting on the table behind him. "Shipping out?"

"Yeah. I'm on my way to the airport."

"Okay," I said. "I was wondering if I could come in and chat for a minute."

"Okay." Kyle turned and left me standing at the door. Following behind him, I realized that it was the first time I'd ever seen his back. He was usually standing next to me, smiling and laughing at some silly joke, or walking behind me, making sure I was okay.

"I just wanted to say I'm sorry about last night, Kyle," I said, feeling like I should turn around and leave.

"You already said that." Kyle slipped his Bible into the bag.

"Well, I feel like I need to say it again."

"No need to repeat yourself; I can hear pretty well," he said coldly.

"Okay," I managed. I sat down on the couch and Kyle turned to look at me for the first time. It was one of those *Who the hell told you to sit down?* looks. "And I also wanted to thank you for coming here to help me. I don't know what

I would've done if you weren't here." I played nervously with my hands.

"Yeah, you said that, too."

"I know but—"

"Look, Troy, why are you here?" Kyle asked, interrupting me. "Just tell me that so I don't have to play any more of your games."

"Julian left." I looked toward the window.

"Oh, that's it? He left you again and now you want to play friends with me. I see. Well, you're a little too late, Troy. My plane leaves in two hours."

"No, that's not it," I said. "I meant to say I kicked him out. It's over between the two of us. I broke it off."

"Good for you."

"Well, that's not all. After I kicked him out, I started thinking about you, about us." I looked at Kyle.

"A little too late for that, too. Don't you think?" He shook his head at me.

"No," I said. "I don't think it's too late."

"Well, I do. I'm not your consolation prize." Kyle turned his back to me again. I could hear him zipping his bag. "Troy, I'm not a violent man," he said, keeping his back to me. "I don't swear and I never have ill feelings toward anyone." He turned to face me and I could see his eyes were red. "But after that thing in your room, I was so angry, so mad at myself for allowing you to treat me like that . . . For the first time in many years I was so mad that I felt that I was capable of hitting someone. Do you know what that's like for a man like me? Do you have any idea what that means?"

"No."

"Exactly." Kyle exhaled. "See, that seems to be the thing about you, Troy, never able to see how other people feel, always thinking about yourself. Well, just so you know, it means a lot. I spent all last night in prayer. I sat up here trying to block out all of the pain I felt when I realized that the only woman I've ever loved wasn't able to love me back. Do you know what that's like?" Kyle's words stung me. I wanted to kiss him, hold him, and make him feel better, but with every word that came out of his mouth, I felt him drifting farther and farther away from me.

"I'm sorry, Kyle." I began to cry. Kyle sat down on the couch beside me.

"What's today, Troy?" he asked softly. He looked straight ahead at the wall in front of us.

"Sunday?"

"Where am I supposed to be on Sunday?"

"The church," I answered, wishing I hadn't said anything. I hadn't even realized that Kyle was missing his service.

"Never once have I missed one of my services." Kyle paused. "I wondered for a long time what it would feel like to be in love—how it felt on the inside. How it felt to have that puppy love that makes you do crazy things—in spite of yourself. I'd preached about it, even counseled on it, but I'd never felt it. I'd spent so long focusing on my obligations that I felt that it would never come, that I'd never know what it was like to love someone . . . in that way. Then I heard your voice on the phone the other day. I heard how sad you were and in that very second, I knew I had to be with you. I wanted to protect you. I wanted to hear you laugh and see you smile and I was willing to do whatever it took to do that. After I called my deacon to fill in for me, I realized that that's what love is. It's about wanting the ultimate happiness for someone else—how you make me feel in here," he said, pointing to his heart. "I love you in here, Troy. And that's different than anything I've ever felt." He paused. "But I can't allow you to hurt me. I flew all the way out here just to impress you, to show you how much I loved you. I spent a lot of money I didn't have. Last night you made me feel like a fool." Kyle got up from the couch. "But do you know what I realized this morning? The funny thing is I'd do it all again." Kyle opened the room door. "But only for a woman who could appreciate it."

"Kyle, I do appreciate you. You're the kindest man I've ever known and I don't want to lose you. I want to be with you," I cried. Kyle held his hand over his mouth and closed his eyes.

"I can't do this, Troy," he said with his voice cracking. "I can't make the same mistake twice." Kyle looked at me. I could see tears gathering in his eyes. "I need you to leave," he said, stepping away from the door. "Goodbye."

Tasha was walking out of Tamia's room when I got off of the elevator at the hospital.

"Tasha," I said, rushing toward her. "I'm so sorry—"

"I don't want to talk about it here." She stopped me. "I'm fine right now. I just want to make sure Tamia's okay."

"How did you know?" I asked.

"The people at the hotel told me she was here."

"I tried to call you but—"

"Troy," Tamia called weakly from the room.

"Hey, baby," I said, walking in with Tasha behind me. "I see you're awake now. You had us all so worried about you."

"I know. I'm sorry."

"Girl, please, I think we're all just happy you're okay," I said, looking across the bed at Tasha. We both took Tamia's hands.

"I just want to say one thing about yesterday," Tasha said. "I thought a lot about it and I understand what you guys were trying to do, but I will have to deal with it in my own time."

"That's fine," Tamia said.

"We understand," I added.

"We really have to stick together now, y'all," Tasha said. "A lot of things are happening and I just realized . . ." She started crying. "I just realized that I need y'all now more than ever. We all need each other."

I reached over Tamia to hug Tasha.

"What about me?" Tamia said. "I need love too. I'm the one who's sick here." We laughed and bent down to hug Tamia too.

"Well, I don't know about y'all but I am so ready to get back home," Tasha said, turning to open the blinds in Tamia's room. "L.A. is full of drama, and y'all know I hate drama."

Tamia and I looked at each other.

"Yeah, right," we said together.

"I'm just saying, it seems like this city tried to tear the 3Ts apart—one by one—but we're still standing."

"Exactly," I said. "As soon as Ms. Thang here gets better, we'll be back on track." I looked at Tamia.

"You know, Troy, it seems like you're the only one Los Angeles didn't get to," Tamia said, laughing. "I almost died, Tasha went wandering the streets like a crazy woman, but nothing happened to you."

"You have no clue," I said sadly.

"What?" they said together. "What happened?"

"Kyle was here, Julian was here . . . It was a mess. And then they both left."

"Really? How did all of that happen in one day?" Tamia squealed, easing up in the bed.

"I wish I knew," I replied.

"Oh Lord," Tasha said, pulling a chair over to the bed. "I can tell this is going to be a long story."

It's a New Day

Fall is the calmest season in the city that never sleeps. Everything in New York, from the air around you to the leaves fighting to stay above you seems to slow down. Things willfully adjust from the unpredictable heat of the summer to the peaceful, reflective times of the fall. And while it appears that everything has died by winter, when spring arrives you realize that they were just moving from one stage of life to the next. During the fall they were transforming into something stronger that could last through the winter and preparing to be reborn in the new year.

Looking at the trees along Fifth Avenue, as I headed to the fall pageant at Kids in Motion, I thought about how my life was changing like the city in fall. It had been three months since my now-famous trip to Los Angeles, and I'd learned so much about myself and everyone around me.

After Kyle left, I felt so bad about how I'd treated him that I began to really look at myself in a whole new way. I reflected on everything I had been through, both in my relationship and with my family and friends. I thought long and hard about the things and people I placed so much stock in.

What I came to see was that while much of what Kyle had said about me at the hotel was out of anger, he was right about one thing—I wasn't really, really listening to the needs of everyone around me. And Kyle wasn't the only person who was suffering because of it. From my mother to Tasha, the people closest to me were trying to reach out to me for love and help. And I was so busy with my own life and what I wanted to focus on that I wasn't able to see what they wanted—what they needed from me.

I started with my family. It was hard, but after much coaxing, I was finally able to get my mother and Grandma Lucy to attend therapy with me. While they continued to say they didn't see how it would help up until we were actually in our first session, it seemed that the act of sitting and talking in a controlled environment was exactly what they needed all along. "I've been hurting for a long time. I don't know if I'll ever get over some of the things my own mother put me through as a child . . . don't know if I'll ever be able to discuss them openly with anyone," Grandma Lucy said one day in a session. This revelation had a strong affect on my mother. For the first time she was really able to see my grandmother as a true victim—someone as hurt by the situation as she had been. She'd made excuses for Lucy in the past, but she admitted that it was out of pity, her trying to reason with what was going on. She'd never really wanted to understand Grandma Lucy. "I'll never forgive you for lying to my father," my mother admitted one day with tears in her eyes. Grandma Lucy's eyes grew sad as she fell back in her seat and recalled aloud for the first time how and why she did what she'd done. Apparently, it was just another fear that kept her from truly revealing to the world how she felt about my mother's real father. She'd loved both men—my white grandfather probably more because of his color—but never saw my mother's real father as a plausible option for marriage because he wasn't white. She shook her head and looked down at the veins lacing the insides of her palms. "I'd been taught it was all about this," she said, turning her veins to us. "All I heard throughout my life was that only a white man could give me what I needed. The lighter I got my family, the better off we would be. I hated the idea of it, but it was all I knew so I had to believe it. I loved Oscar, but it just couldn't be." Neither my mother nor I cried with Lucy that day. Instead, for the first time, we sat on either side of her and simply encircled her in an embrace. We were far from resolving the problems, but looking into Lucy's eyes and seeing my mother grow stronger made it clear that we were on the right path.

Now, getting somewhere with Kyle was a different story. He refused all of my calls and said he never wanted to see me again. One day during a surprise visit to his church, I tried to speak to him, to tell him I was changing, but he said that while he was happy I'd found some good in the situation, he was still dealing with it and that he wasn't ready to talk to me just yet.

I really couldn't blame him for his feelings. He'd been through a lot because of me. I'd known exactly how Kyle felt about me the entire time we hung out. From the flowers at the restaurant to the rescue mission in Los Angeles, I had known how much Kyle liked me. But I was willing to ignore it as long as I got what I wanted.

I didn't realize how much I really cared for Kyle until over a month after we'd stopped speaking. When I returned from Los Angeles, I began to put most of my time into my internship at the court and preparing the girls in my dance class for the pageant. One day after a long rehearsal at the settlement, I decided to treat the girls to ice cream. As all sixteen of us sat in the park licking our ice cream cones, laughing and enjoying the last bit of summer sun, I felt like a kid again. Shanika sat down on the grass next to me and smiled. "You should've invited your boyfriend," she said, giggling. At first I wondered who she was talking about, then

I remembered the day Kyle had surprised me by stopping by the center. I remembered the look on his face and how happy he'd made both Shanika and me. Then I wished Kyle was there, too. He'd probably tell the girls some long story his grandfather had told him when he was younger. I smiled back at Shanika and kissed her on the forehead. "You're right. I should've invited him," I said.

Tamia was standing in front of Kids in Motion when I pulled up. She'd recovered fully after she got out of the hospital. It was discovered that she had some swelling in her heart that was similar to her mother's illness, but with treatment she was expected to live a long life. She'd stopped taking the pills and both she and her father were in counseling.

"Hey, dance teacher," she said, peeking into the car as I tried to park.

"You're early," I replied, climbing out. I hugged Tamia and looked up to see the banner Mr. Bearden's art class had designed for the pageant hanging on the side of the building. IT'S A NEW DAY, it read in brown letters painted like tree branches. "It sure is," I thought, heading into the settlement beside Tamia.

"I just wanted to make sure I got here on time," Tamia said. "I know how you can get when it comes to the kids."

"Well, I'm just happy I have someone here to help me get these girls into their costumes." I opened the door to the studio. "Nana Rue and Grandma Lucy designed them and they're a diva mess." I pulled one of the jumpsuits out of the closet to show Tamia. "Pink fur and black satin." I grinned.

"These are adorable." Tamia took the hanger. "They'll love them."

"I'm sure they will."

"Well, what did you expect having Donatella Versace and Eartha Kitt on the costume committee?" Tamia laughed, talking about Nana Rue and Grandma Lucy. "You put them together and you know something . . . fur . . . *and* . . . satin is going to come out of it."

"You're crazy."

"But I'm right."

A few students came in and Tamia handed them their costumes.

"So did you invite him?" Tamia asked, looking at me.

" 'Him' who?"

"Don't play stupid with me." She rolled her eyes.

"If you're talking about Kyle, the answer is no," I said, zipping up one of the girls. She turned around and I put my thumb up. She looked so cute. I was happy Nana Rue and Grandma Lucy had agreed to design and pay for the costumes. Most of the girls couldn't afford them. Nana Rue had adopted the class after I took them to see her play. After the performance the girls begged to go backstage to meet the lady with the beautiful voice. When they crowded into her dressing room, showering her with praise and kisses and compliments, Nana Rue fell in love. "You are all me," she said, hugging each one of them tight. "You are all my girls." From that point on, she, along with Grandma Lucy, whom she'd recruited for the project, hung out with the girls during every class session. They claimed they thought it was good for the girls, but really I thought it was good for the grandmothers too.

"Why didn't you call him, Troy?" Tamia handed me another costume.

"Because *he* doesn't want to speak to me. How many times do I have to tell you?"

"How do you know that?"

"Okay, maybe I discovered it somewhere between the eighty some-odd phone calls of mine he's refused. No, maybe it was when he kicked me out of his hotel room in Los Angeles. No, when he refused to talk to me at the church." I waved at Tamia. "Are you reading me now? Are you reading me?"

"You give up too easily, Troy."

"What? Is this the woman who hated the Take Her Man

Plan, now talking about not giving up on something you want?" I laughed.

"I was against that, but that was because it was for a man who didn't deserve you in the first place. This one does and he's worth fighting for," Tamia said seriously. "That's what you have to ask yourself, Troy. 'What's worth fighting for?' "

"I guess you're right, Mia." I shrugged my shoulders. "But there's nothing else I can do about it. The man doesn't want me. He's made that clear."

"That's a shame." Tamia exhaled softly. "I mean, just think about it . . . all the time you spent trying to take Julian from Miata, Kyle was trying to take you from Julian. Maybe he was trying the 'Take His Girl Plan.' You guys were pretty much searching for the same thing, but one of you was looking in the wrong direction."

"I never really thought about it like that," I said, "the Take His Girl Plan."

"Well, I'm just saying, I always thought things would work out between you two."

"Me too." I shook my head.

"Well, all I have to say is don't be jealous when you see me with my date tonight." She playfully tapped me on the back.

"Date? To the fall pageant?"

"That's right, trick. I have a man who loves the theater. When I told him the fabulous Troy Dancers were performing, we had to get tickets." We both laughed.

"Sounds like a nice guy," I said. "Why haven't you told me about this mystery man?"

"Maybe I have. Maybe I haven't," she replied, handing me another costume.

The pageant turned out to be a huge success. The audience was packed, the girls looked amazing, and their dance routine went by without flaw. I'd be lying if I said I was at all surprised with how things ended up. The girls had worked so hard at their routine during the days leading up to the pageant. I never had an empty space in the studio, and with the help of a few chats with Nana Rue, even Shanika was able to move up to the front of the classroom.

As the girls walked off the stage to a standing ovation, I hugged and kissed each one of them. They looked so happy; the smiles plastered on their faces reminded me of how I'd felt after my first dance recital. By the time Shanika came skipping off the stage, I was a crying mess. I was completely overjoyed for them. They'd worked hard at something and had seen the results. That's all I wanted for them—to see what it was like to really set their minds on something and achieve their goal. As Kyle and I had discussed that day in the park, that was the best thing I could ever teach them.

"I'm so proud of you," I whispered in Shanika's ear.

After I hugged her, I turned to walk back to the studio, but I heard Ms. Bessing, the settlement's director, call the girls back on. They ran past me, storming the stage. I was a little confused, because they'd only practiced one routine for the show. Ms. Bessing asked the audience to give the girls another round of applause for their hard work. The auditorium was filled with the sound of clapping hands and I could see cameras flashing from my place backstage.

"You may not believe it, but these girls have little dance experience," Ms. Bessing said. "They come here from diverse neighborhoods throughout New York so they can have the opportunity to learn how to dance. If it wasn't for Kids in Motion, they really wouldn't have had the opportunity to stand here in front of you today." The audience began to clap again. "However, while the settlement would love to take all of the credit, without the help of one special lady, none of this would be possible," Ms. Bessing went on.

I was about to clap, but when I realized Ms. Bessing was

talking about me, my body froze. *Is she talking about me?* I thought looking around. All the other teachers backstage were smiling at me.

"Troy, can you come to the stage?" Ms. Bessing called.

Completely surprised, I nervously walked onto the stage. I smiled at the girls and looked into the audience. My parents were sitting in the front row with Nana Rue and Grandma Lucy dressed in outfits that matched the girls.

"The day this angel came to volunteer at Kids in Motion was a gift," Ms. Bessing said. "Troy is one of our most dedicated teachers and while she's busy enjoying her third year of law school, she doesn't allow these girls to miss a beat. I really don't know what we would do without her."

"Thank you," I said, smiling at Ms. Bessing.

"While I could thank Troy a million times, these little girls came up with a way to really thank their favorite teacher."

I turned to look at the girls to find them looking backstage. When I looked up, I saw Kyle walking onto the stage with a bouquet of magnolias. I put my hand on my chest for fear that my heart would leap right out of my body. Was I dreaming?

Kyle walked up to me and kissed me on the cheek. I could hear the girls giggling behind us. He handed me the flowers and we embraced. The camera flashes from the audience looked like shooting stars.

"Congratulations, Angel," he whispered in my ear.

The girls ran over and climbed all over us, showering me with kisses and "thank yous." I couldn't stop smiling and looking at Kyle standing in front of me.

"What are you doing here?" I said between hugs.

"I couldn't miss it," Kyle replied, wiping a tear from my eye.

When we finally walked off the stage, I found a crowd of parents and students waiting for me in the studio. They began to clap when Kyle and I walked in.

My parents were standing with Nana Rue and Grandma Lucy collecting costumes.

"I'm so proud," my mother said, hugging me. "You did a great job."

"We're going to celebrate at the Water Club," my father said, winking at Kyle. He kissed me on the cheek. "A little party for Troy."

"We couldn't be more proud, right, Rue B." Grandma Lucy said, coming in for a hug.

"I don't think we could." Nana Rue smiled. She embraced me and looked into my eyes. "You've got it, Troy," she said. "We've given you many material things throughout your life, but tonight you proved that you've gotten the most important thing on your own."

"What's that?" I asked.

"Compassion." She placed her hand over my heart. "You've got it in here. Working with these girls, you've shown that you care about people more than you care for yourself, and that's more important than any material possession. That's love."

"Oh, Nana Rue," I said, hugging her again.

"Well, we've got to get going if we want to keep these reservations," my father said. "Kyle, I trust that you'll bring my daughter over safely."

"Yes." Kyle smiled.

"Hey, teacher," Tamia said, turning me around, "I want you to meet my date."

"Not until after she meets my date, trick," Tasha jumped in from behind me.

"Tash!" I screamed, hugging her. While we hung out many times after the drama in L.A., she wasn't able to get out much because of the pregnancy, so I hadn't expected her to come to the pageant. She was only four months pregnant but her stomach was so swollen she looked like she was going on ten months. She was having what Nana Rue called a "big pregnancy." "What do you mean, 'date'?" I asked. "Is Lionel here, too?"

"No, I have a different escort for this evening." Tasha smiled, waving at someone behind me.

"Hi, Troy," I heard someone say. I turned to find Porsche standing next to Kyle.

"Porsche." I smiled. "I can't believe you're here." I stepped back to make sure it was really her. I looked back at Tasha. "What happened?"

"We made up," Tasha said, walking over to Porsche. "After all of that stuff in Los Angeles, we decided to leave the past behind us for the baby," she added, looking at her mother. "She comes here every weekend to help me and Lionel out and she plans on coming to stay for a while when the baby comes. So everything is great."

"And we have you and Tamia to thank for it," Porsche said. "You girls risked your friendship to get my daughter back to me, and I'll never forget it."

"Aww. You guys," I cried with joy. I hugged Tasha and Porsche and rubbed Tasha's bulging belly.

"Okay, okay, I'm next," Tamia broke in.

"What is it, Tamia?" I asked, turning back around. "Who is this date you keep talking about?"

Just then Alex from school came pushing through the crowd. I looked at Alex and then back at Tamia.

"You two?" I asked, smiling. "Together?"

"That's right." Tamia laughed. "The white boy's with me."

"Hi, Troy," Alex said. He kissed me on the cheek and shook Kyle's hand.

"But I thought you . . . you know?" I said, confused.

"Well, after Professor Banks won the case and I came back from L.A., I decided to talk to Alex about my concerns," Tamia said. "We went out for a little victory dinner and over a bottle of wine I realized how much he respected me and how ridiculous I was being. We started chatting again and . . . well . . . here we are."

"We've been dating on the 'D.L.' for a couple of weeks," Alex joked.

"Oh no, what do you know about the down low, Alex?" I said, laughing. Alex put his arm around Tamia and they looked great together. My only wish was that they would stay away from the library . . . the days I was there, anyway.

"Well, we have to get going," Tamia said, winking at Tasha. "We know you have some things to clear up here." She looked at Kyle.

"Yeah, your parents invited us to your party," Tasha said, laughing. "We got you something special, an official 3T celebration gift."

"We'll be there," Kyle said as they all walked out.

"Take it slow." Tamia looked at me. She kissed me on the cheek and walked out with Alex following right behind her.

"So I guess everyone's gone." I turned to look at Kyle. The studio was empty except for one of my students, who was walking out the door with her parents.

"Yeah, they are."

"I can't believe you're here." I pinched my arm to make sure I wasn't dreaming. *"Why* are you here, Kyle?"

"I missed you, Troy. One day I woke up and I decided I couldn't continue to ignore my feelings for you anymore. I had to see you."

"Really?"

"Well, there was that and Tasha and Tamia saying they'd join the choir at the church if I didn't at least give it a shot. Do you know how bad their voices are?"

"Yeah." I laughed. "But what about L.A.?" I asked. "Are you okay with what happened there?"

"L.A. is L.A. It happened. I can't change the past. But I can forgive. I can forgive you and move on."

"Really, Kyle? You can forgive me?" I felt so humbled by his words and the sincerity in his voice. This man standing in front of me was truly amazing.

"That's what I teach," Kyle said. "It's only fair that I practice it. I might as well start with you."

"I was hoping you'd say that." I started crying again. "I really was . . . deep in here." I pointed to my heart.

Celebrate Your Sister

It Girl No. 1, Ms. Oprah Winfrey, threw the ultimate It Girl party for her girlfriends—the Living Legends. She invited and totally spoiled all of her best gal pals who had changed the world we live in. Well, you and your gal pals may not know Oprah or be able to afford Oprah party stuff, but you can certainly celebrate your girls—and not on their birthdays or when they die. Give them their flowers now, It Girls! The truth is, if we don't celebrate ourselves, no one will. So break out the good china and have a fabulous party. Why? Because you can.

Party Tips

Pick Three Diva It Girls: Pick three different ladies to be celebrated at each party. These three ladies will be the guests of honor and will be showered with flowers, expensive gifts, and words that get at who they are and why we love them so much. Speak their names into the world and let these ladies know they count. Make sure they dress up for the occasion.

Spare No Expense: Please don't give the guest of honor bubble bath and potpourri from the dollar store. You may have to pool your money to get your girl a fur for her special day, but do it. Your time will come, too. Don't think cheap, think big and beautiful. She may not be able to afford a diamond ring and no one may be there to give it to her . . . but why should she have to wait on money and a man when she has cool friends like you?

Make the time: If you're a real It Girl, you're probably saying to yourself that you have no time to plan these parties. You do! Make the time and commit to celebrating yourself. Cook good food, wear your favorite clothes, and tell the rest of the world to wait. Trust us, it will.

Epilogue

What's Worth Fighting For?

Seven years ago, I decided what kind of man I wanted to marry. It was the fifth anniversary of my parents' second marriage to each other. My parents decided to throw a huge party at Tavern on the Green. They invited everyone they knew and requested that they all arrive dressed in white. My mother had the Tavern decorated with bouquets of assorted white flowers and candles, and she had black and white pictures of the three of us put up everywhere.

It was a beautiful evening. The Tavern looked like heaven and my parents and all their guests looked like angels. That night, one week after my eighteenth birthday, was the happiest I'd ever seen my parents. They danced and danced, kissing each other like teenagers who'd just met. Before dinner they had a short ceremony where they renewed their vows. My father surprised my mother by restoring the original engagement ring he'd bought her when she was eighteen. A single tear fell from my mother's eye when he slid the golden solitaire ring on her finger. Her face turned completely red, and while I'd never seen my mother look quite the same, I knew that she felt like the most beautiful woman in the world.

Looking at my parents—half drunk from champagne and the idea of spending the rest of their lives together—I made a vow to myself that I would find someone who loved me the same way my father loved my mother. No matter how much they fought, or how much they disagreed, he loved her for who she was—the good and the bad. And no matter what happened, as had been proven once before, he would always come back to her. That's what I wanted.

When I met Julian five years later, somehow I forgot about the look on my mother's face. I was so concerned about other things—how things looked to other people and what I could gain by being on his arm—that I couldn't even be honest with myself about how I was being treated. All that was important was the man and being with him. And for a short while in my life, I thought that was all that mattered. But then . . . along came fate in the form of a six-point plan and a man named Kyle.

While the Take Her Man Plan is far behind me now, and the drama surrounding it serves to bring me and my girls lots of laughs as we play with Tasha's new baby girl, Toni (yes, we're the 4Ts now), looking back, I realize why I had to go through what I did with Julian. While it hurt me so bad in the beginning, in the end, every tear I cried forced me to turn the mirror I was pointing at everyone else toward myself. The breakup wasn't about Miata, it wasn't about my mother's curse—hell, it wasn't even about Julian. It was about me and the changes I needed to make inside of myself to find the love I deserved. And when I finished looking at my own reflection in the mirror, there, standing beside me, was Kyle.

After Kyle and I discussed everything that had gone on between us, we finally decided to date each other. Nothing serious or heavy—Kyle needed his space to work through some things and I needed some time to focus on myself.

On our fifth "real date," I bought Kyle a bouquet of wildflowers and made him dinner at my place. Kyle looked so happy when he walked in the door. He pulled me into his arms and hugged me so tight I could hear his heart beating.

Standing there in Kyle's arms, I thought about the day I almost lost him. While I fought so hard to ignore it at first, Kyle reawakened in me the love I saw between my parents on that starry spring evening at Tavern on the Green seven years ago. It was the sweetest thing, the most indescribable feeling I felt so deep inside of me that I knew it was right. I could fall in his arms and know Kyle would be there to catch me, and if he ever needed it, I'd fight like hell to hold him up. What it was between us, as we stood in my living room slow dancing to the music in our heads, was hard and strong and more real than anything I'd ever felt. Listening to Kyle breathe, I realized that I was in love with him.

Just then, before I could open my mouth to say to the man who would later become my husband, "I love you," for the first time, Tamia's question came to my mind: What's worth fighting for? The answer came to me so quickly that I began to cry.

Like my mother's love, my friends' support, and my man's forgiving heart, the best-loved things—the things that are truly worth fighting for—are not things that you have to take from other people. They are simply the things that come to you . . . willingly.

So, in the end, I did have my man; it just wasn't the one I'd set out to get. Life is funny that way. God is funny that way. As I said in the beginning, I'm a fine, successful, educated black woman. The situation God put me in made me question and respect all of those things. I just had to find my way out.

**The Guide to Riding Off into the Sunset and Living
Happily Ever After Because You're a Fine, Successful,
Educated Black Woman and You Don't Have to Put Up
with Anyone's Crap . . .**

<u>Patience</u> 'pā-sh n(t)s*n* 1: the capacity, habit, or fact of being
patient—bearing pains or trials calmly or without complaint
(*Merriam-Webster's Dictionary*) 2: Knowing that the best
things come to those who wait (*The Real It Girl Guide by the
3Ts*)

Don't miss Grace Octavia's
HIS FIRST WIFE
Available now wherever books are sold!

Foolish

October 26, 2007

It was 5:35 in the morning. I was doing 107 on the highway, pushing the gas pedal down so far with my foot that my already-swollen toes were beginning to burn. It was dark, so dark that the only way I knew that I wasn't in bed with my eyes closed was the baby inside of me kicking nervously at my belly button and the slither of light the headlights managed to cast on the road in front of me.

I-85 South was eerily silent at this time. I knew that. I'd been in my car, making this same drive, once before. I kept wiping hot tears from my eyes so I could see out of the window. I should've been looking for police, other cars on the road, a deer, a stray dog that had managed to find its way to the highway in the dewy hours of the morning, but I couldn't. I couldn't see anything but where I was going, feel anything but what I didn't want to feel, think anything but what had gotten me out of my bed in the first place. My husband.

Jamison hadn't come home. I sat in the dining room and ate dinner by myself as I tried not to look at the clock. Tried

not to notice that the tall taper candles had melted to shapeless clumps in front me. Knowing the time would only make
me call. And calling didn't show trust. We'd talked about
trust. Jamison said I needed to trust him more. Be patient.
Understanding. All of the things we'd vowed to be on our
wedding day, he reminded me. My pregnancy had made me
emotional, he said. And I was adding things up and accusing
him of things he hadn't done, thoughts he hadn't thought.
But I was no fool. I knew what I knew.

Jamison's patterns had changed over the past few months.
And while he kept begging me to be more trusting and understanding, my self-control was growing thin. The shapeless
clumps on the table in front of me resembled my heart—
bent out of shape with hot wax in the center, ready to spill
out and burn the surface. Jamison had never stayed out this
late. And with a baby on the way? I was hot with anger. Re-
sentful. I was ready to spill out, to spin out, but I held it in.

I helped our maid, Isabella, clear the table, told her she
was excused for the night. Then I moved to the bedroom,
and while I still hadn't peeked at the clock, the credits at the
end of the recorded edition of *Ten O'Clock News* proved that
any place my husband could be . . . should be . . . was closed.
I wanted to believe I was being emotional, but that would've
been easier if I didn't know what I knew. Maybe he'd been in
an accident. Maybe he was at a hospital. Yeah . . . but maybe
he wasn't.

I laid in bed for a couple of hours; my thoughts were
swelling my mind as round as my pregnant stomach. I knew
what was going on. I knew exactly where he was. The only
question was, what was I going to do?

Then I was in my car. My white flip-flops tossed in the
passenger seat. My purse left somewhere in the house. My
son inside of my stomach, tossing and kicking. It was like a
dream, the way everything was happening. The mile mark-
ers, exit signs, trees along the sides of my car looked blurry

and almost unreal through my glazed eyes. The heat was rising. My emotions were driving me down that highway, not my mind. My mind said I was eight-and-a-half months pregnant with my first child. I didn't need the drama, the stress. I needed to be in bed.

But my emotions—my heart—were running hot like the engine in my car. I was angry and sad at the same time. Sometimes just angry though. I'd see Jamison in my mind and fill up my insides with the kind of anger that makes you shake and feel like you're about to vomit. And then, right when I was about to explode, I'd see him again in my mind, in another way, feel betrayed, and sadness would sneak in. Paralyzing sadness, so consuming that it feels like everything is dead and the only thing I can do is cry to mourn the loss. I wanted to fight someone. Get to where he was and kick in the door so he could see me. Finally see me and see what this was doing to us. To our marriage.

I didn't have an address, but I knew exactly where she lived. My friend Marcy and I followed Jamison there one night when he was supposed to be going to a fraternity function at a local hotel. But having already suspected something was going on, I called the hotel and learned that there was nothing scheduled. That night six months ago, before he left, I gave him a chance to come clean. I asked if I could go. "No one else will have their wives there; it's just frat," he said, using the same excuse he'd been using for three weeks. He slid on his jacket, kissed me on the cheek and walked out the front door. I picked up my purse and ran out the back where Marcy was waiting in a car we'd rented just for the circumstance. When Jamison finally stopped his truck, we found ourselves sitting in front of a house I knew I'd never forget. The red bricks lining the walkway, the yellow geraniums around a bush in the middle of the lawn, the outdated lace curtains in the window. It looked so small, half the size of our Tudor in Cascade where the little house might envy a backyard cabana. It was dark and seemed empty until Jamison climbed out of the bright red "near midlife crisis" truck he'd bought on his thirtieth birthday. Then, the living room light came on, my husband walked in. And through the lace I watched as he hugged her and was led farther away from me. I fell like a baby into my best friend's arms. What was I to do?

I promised myself I would never forget that house. So there was no need to look at the address. I knew every turn that had brought me there. I just couldn't figure out why.

Now, here I was nearly half a year later, dressed in a silk, vanilla nightgown at five in the morning, making the same trip, but with a different agenda. I knew why and where, and something in me said it was time to act.

I saw that red truck parked in the driveway when I turned onto the street. It looked so bold there. Like it belonged. Like nothing was a secret. *They* were the perfect family. There was no wife at home, no child on the way; our love, our love affair, was the second life he was living. *She* was his wife. I was just the woman he was sleeping with. Sad tears sat in my eyes, my anger refusing to let them roll down my cheeks. Every curse I knew was coming from my mouth as I held the steering wheel tighter and tighter the closer I got. My husband, the person I thought knew me better than any-one else in the world, had turned his back on me for another woman.

I pulled my car into the driveway behind Jamison's and turned off the ignition. The sudden silence hit me like the first touch of cold beach water on virgin feet. Without the hum of the engine, I realized I was alone. I'd gotten myself all the way there, but I didn't know what I was going to do. I knew I had to act, but what was I going to do? Burn the house down or ring the door bell and sell them cookies? And if she came to the door, what was I going to say? Ask another woman if I could see *my* husband? Curse her out? Scream? Cry? Should I hit her? I hadn't hit anyone in my life. What if Jamison answered the door? What if he was mad and told me to leave? If he said it was over?

The baby kicked again, but lightly, as if he was nudging me to go and get his father out of that house, away from that woman. Coreen Carter was her name. Marcy found it on a piece of mail she'd snatched from the mailbox when we followed Jamison. It was a simple name, but Coreen Carter couldn't be that simple. She had my husband inside of her house.

The anger let go at that thought and the sad tears began to fall again. What was I doing? What was happening with my life? I felt like I was being torn inside out. My baby was the only glue that was keeping me together. I felt so alone in that car.

I snatched my cell phone from the seat beside me and called Marcy. She picked up her phone on the first ring. She was an RN and her husband was an ER doctor, so she was a light sleeper.

"I guess little Jamison is about to make his arrival?" she assumed cheerfully, but I couldn't answer. I was sobbing now. Sadness was coming from deep inside and I was sure the only sound I could make was a scream.

"Kerry?" she called. "You okay? Where are you?"

"Here." I managed. There was no need for me to say where exactly. She knew.

"It's six in the. . . . He didn't come home?"

"No."

"Kerry, why didn't you call me? You don't need to do that right now. Not in your condition."

"I just want this to stop," I said sorrowfully.

"I understand, but right now just isn't the time. You have other things to take care of." She paused. "I know I sound crazy to you, but I just don't want anything to happen to you or the baby. You understand that, right?"

"Yes," I said, with my voice cracking. "But I'm just tired of this crap. I mean, what the hell, Marcy? Why? Why is Jamison here with this woman?"

"I don't know that. I can't answer that. Only Jamison can."

"Exactly." I felt a twist of anger wrench my gut. Again I went from feeling sorry for myself to being angry that I was there in the first place. Jamison was *my* husband and he was cheating on me and I wasn't going to just sit in a car and let it go on. I slid on my flip-flops and opened the car door.

"What are you going to do?"

"I don't know," I said. I really didn't. But, again, my emotions were driving. I was spilling out like that hot wax and before I knew it, I was charging up the walkway.

"Just don't do anything foolish," Marcy said before I hung up. Later I'd think about how crazy that sounded. How could I possibly do anything more foolish than what was already being done to me?

The little cracked doorbell seemed to ring before I even pressed it. It chimed loud and confident, like it wasn't past 6 AM and the sun hadn't already begun to rise behind me. It was quiet. The only noise I heard was my heart pounding, shaking so wildly inside of me that I couldn't stand still. I waited for another five seconds which felt like hours. My husband was on one side of the door and I was on the other. Our wedding bands and my large belly were the only signs we were connected. I looked at his truck again. It was the only piece of Jamison I could see from where I was and my heart sank a bit farther. The shine of the paint, the gloss on the wheels, it looked so happy, so free, so smug, so complete. Everything he wanted. I was tired of making this all so possible for Jamison. Making his life so comfortable, so happy. His perfect wife, carrying his perfect son. I was alone in my marriage and I was tired.

I began pounding on the door then. Ringing the bell and

then pounding some more. My fist balled up and it pounded hard like a rock threatening to burst through. Someone was inside and they were coming out. If there were children inside, a mother and father, a dog, a parrot. . . . I didn't care. They were all getting up and out of that house.

A small, light brown hand pulled back the sheet of weathered lace covering the square at the top of the door. A woman's face appeared. Her eyes were squinting with the kind of tired worry anyone would have over a knock at the door at 6 AM I'd seen those eyes before, and before she widened them enough to see who I was, my fist was banging at the glass in front of her face. I was trying to break it and if I could break it, I'd grab her face and pull her through the tiny square.

"Tell my husband to come outside," I hollered, my voice sounding much bigger than I was. She looked surprised. Like she never expected to see me or hadn't known Jamison even had a wife. I pressed my face against the window to see inside. To see if Jamison was there behind her. The flap fell back down over the little window and I heard heavy footsteps. I was beside myself. Had totally let go of whoever I was. My baby grew lighter, as if he wasn't even there, and a thunderbolt inside shocked me into action.

"Jamison!" I shouted heatedly. "Jamison, come outside!" I began banging on the door again. I couldn't believe what was happening. I knew it was her. Coreen Carter. I saw her only once before in my life. But when she came to the door that time to let Jamison in, I learned her face the way a victim does her victimizer.

She was what most men would consider beautiful. She had short, curly red hair. From the car I thought it was dyed, but up close I could tell it was her natural color. Fire engine red, like the truck, from the root. She had freckles of the same color dotted around her eyes and her skin was the color of Caribbean sand. Really, she looked nothing like me. In fact, we were complete opposites. My hair was so black and long, most of my friends called me "Pocahontas" growing up. My hair wouldn't dye and most days it wouldn't hold a curl of any kind. And if the skin of the woman in the window was the color of Caribbean sand, then mine was darker than the black sand on the beaches of Hawaii. My mother didn't like to talk about it, but my grandfather on my father's side was half Sudanese, and while he died long before I was born, my father always said the one thing he left behind was his liquorice color on my skin and my perfectly shaped, curious almond eyes.

My cell phone began ringing. I opened it, certain it was Marcy making sure I hadn't killed anyone, but it was Jamison.

"Jamison," I said, looking again in the window to find him. What was this? What was going on? I felt far from him already. Now he couldn't even come to the door?

"Kerry, go home." His voice was filled with irritation.

"What?" I asked. "Are you kidding me? Jamison, come outside." I couldn't believe what I was hearing. He sounded as if I was doing something wrong, like I was out of place.

"I don't want to do this here. It's not right," he said.

"Not right? Not right to who, Jamison? Her? I'm your wife!"

"I know that."

"No, you don't because if you did, I wouldn't be standing out here in my nightgown, eight months pregnant. Or did you forget about that?" I started banging on the door again. Thinking of my child made me furious. I wanted that door down. I'd forgotten all about where I was. People were starting to come out of their houses, but I didn't care. I wanted it to stop and Jamison being on the phone from inside the house wasn't making it any better.

"Kerry, she didn't do anything to you. Just go home and I'll be right behind you." He was whispering like a schoolboy on the phone with his girlfriend late at night.

"I'm not going home. You come out here now or I swear

I'll bust the windows in your car and set it on fire if I have to." I couldn't believe the things I was saying, but I felt every syllable of them. At that moment I was willing to do anything, and Jamison must've felt it too. He hung up the phone.

The door opened fast, like he'd been standing on the other side the whole time. Jamison stood there alone, dressed in a pair of boxers I'd bought him.

"Did you really think I was going away?" I asked. Through the corner of my eye, I could see an old lady standing in her doorway next door wearing bright pink foam rollers in her hair and a flowery nightgown. I wanted to lower my voice, but I was beyond caring about embarrassing myself. "What is this? What is this?" I started crying again, but I didn't bother to wipe my tears. I just wrapped my arms around my stomach and held tight. The baby felt heavy again, like he was feeling the weight of the moment.

"I can explain it—" He stopped mid-sentence and reached for me. "It's nothing. I'm just . . ."

I stepped away.

"Just what?"

"Look, Kerry, I think you should go. I'll put on something and then come too, but I need to get dressed."

"I'll be damned if I let you walk back into that house with that woman," I hollered. "Does she know you're married? That you have a son on the way? Why can't she come out here and face me? Don't be embarrassed. I'm here now." I tried to push my way through the doorway, but Jamison held me back.

"Let me in," I said, pushing my way in farther. "I just want to see her. I just want to see her. I want to see the woman you chose over me."

"Don't do this," he said, pulling my arms. "Don't do anything foolish."

I pulled back and looked my husband in the eyes. We'd known each other for twelve years. He was my first love. The only man I'd ever imagined marrying. He looked so naked standing there in front of me. So defenseless. He had pale, milky white skin, looked almost white sometimes in pictures, and the centers of his cheeks were beet red, the color they turned when he was sad or angry.

"Don't do what? *Anything foolish*?" I cried. "*Foolish*? You jerk. You fucking jerk."

I practically jumped into Jamison's arms and started pounding my fists into his face. He was 6'5", well over a foot taller than me, but I was towering above him then. Every bit of anger and frustration I felt grew me taller. I was swinging and screaming and hitting to make him feel the pain I felt. I was beat down and beat up by his lies and now I wanted him to feel the same thing. It didn't stop what I was feeling, but it felt good, like I was releasing something. Letting go, or at least loosening up my anger.

"*Foolish*," I screamed. "I'll show you *foolish*."

"Ma'am, stop it!" I heard an authoritative voice before I felt a hand pull at my shoulder. "Ma'am."

My body was being lifted up. I felt two hands on both of my sides.

"She's pregnant," Jamison said, reaching for me as the hands pulled me farther back. I turned to see two police officers standing beside me, while two others were holding me. Suddenly, I could see the flashing lights from their cars in the street, the flickering blues hitting small groups of people huddled in different places along the curb. There had to be at least six cars out there, and all I could think was where they'd come from and who they were there for.

"He ain't worth it," one woman said in the crowd.

I turned to look at Jamison. There were so many people there, so many people I didn't know, and I felt like adding Jamison to the list. He seemed a part of this place, farther and farther away from me than I thought.

"Do you live here, ma'am?" one of the officers asked me. She was the only woman and she was so small the blue uniform seemed to swallow her up.

"No," I said.

"That's Coreen's house," someone called from the crowd.

Then, as if the person had summoned her, Coreen Carter came shuffling out the door. Her face was streaked with tears that seemed bigger than mine. Her eyes were red and she was visibly shaken. She stepped outside and stood beside Jamison in front of the door.

Seeing the cops had brought me back to reality, but seeing Coreen stand beside my husband sent me into what I can only call an out-of-body experience. Baby and all, I twisted out of the police officers' hands and charged after her. The word "nerve" was echoing in my head and if I had my way, I wanted to cut it into her chest with my bare hands. I was filled with rage. With disbelief. My life wasn't supposed to be like this. My marriage wasn't supposed to be like this. And love wasn't supposed to feel like this. All I could do was blame her for all three.

The female cop and another tall, white cop caught me and pulled me farther down the walkway, away from Jamison and Coreen, who were standing together.

"Ma'am," the female officer said, standing in front of me. "I'm Officer Cox. What's your name?"

"Kerry . . . Kerry Taylor."

"Ms. Taylor, I can see that you're upset, but I need you to calm down, so I can talk to you and figure out what exactly is going on here." Her eyes were soft and brown like my Aunt Luchie's. The look on her face was sincere, kind, like she was the only person out there who understood what I was feeling. "Now we don't want anything to happen to your baby. You understand?"

"Yes," I said. I wiped a tear from my eye and looked over at Jamison. He was talking to two male officers, a fat white one and a black one who seemed like he was in charge. Coreen was standing beside him with her hand over her mouth.

"You don't live here?" Officer Cox asked me again.

I shook my head no.

"Were you sleeping here?"

"No," I said, looking at Jamison. He was looking back at me. Tears were in his eyes. The other officer was telling him not to come over to me.

"Is that man with you?" the other, tall officer asked me.

"He's my husband."

The weight of my words must've surprised both of them. Officer Cox stopped writing on her little pad and looked at the other officer.

"Yes," I said, confirming what they were both thinking.

"Hum," she said and looked over at Coreen. "He's here with her?"

"Yes," I said again.

"Should've told us that first," the tall cop said. "We would've given you more time on him." They both exchanged glances and a short, nervous laugh.

"I know what you're feeling. We see this all the time," Officer Cox said, writing again. "But you have to control yourself."

"And not let the cops see you hit your husband," the tall cop said.

"Cox," the officer in charge called, coming toward us as he adjusted his holster.

Jamison turned toward the house when the officer walked away, but I could tell he was crying. He punched the door so hard it sounded as if a gun had gone off.

"Ma'am, I need you to go on in the house," the white officer said to Coreen. "We'll come in and speak with you after we're done out here."

Coreen turned and looked at me quickly, her eyes still wet with confession. She went to walk into the house, reaching first for Jamison, who stepped away from her immediately.

The older officer signaled again for Cox to walk toward him.

"You just stand here, calm, and I'll be right back," she said, stepping away.

"What's going on?" I asked. I could see some trace of dread in her eyes.

"She's just talking to our captain is all," the other officer said. "Standard procedure."

"Am I in any trouble?" I watched as Officer Cox talked to the captain. Her eyes dropped and she placed her hand over her mouth just like Coreen had.

"Probably not," the officer said. "They'll probably let you go."

"Let me go?"

I looked back at Jamison.

"Baby," he tried, his voice filled with desperation.

"Sir, I'm going to need you to stay where you are," the fat officer said, putting his hand over his gun.

"Jamison?" I called. "Jamison."

"She's my wife. You can't take her." He kept coming toward us. Two other cops ran to him and held him back from either side. Suddenly, there were at least ten cops between us.

"Take me? What's going on?" I asked. I looked back to Officer Cox. She was obviously pleading now with the captain, but he kept shaking his head, and then finally she looked me right in the eye and mouthed the word "sorry."

"Just be patient, ma'am," the officer beside me said timidly. "They'll be back over in a minute."

"Can't I just speak to her before she goes?" Jamison yelled. "She's pregnant. She can't go to jail."

"Jail?" I said. The word slapped me so hard my bladder dropped and urine came flowing from between my legs, wetting the front of my nightgown. "Jamison!" I cried. "Stop them!"

The female officer came toward me, pulling handcuffs from her hip.

"Mrs. Taylor," she said, her voice deep and throaty, as if she was forcing it to be stern. "I'm going to have to place you under arrest—"

"No," I hollered. "No! I didn't do anything. I was just here to get my husband. He's my husband." I began crying again. My adrenaline was wearing thin and the thought of being arrested for the first time in my life suddenly made me feel desperate and ugly. Not who I was. Not Kerry Taylor who'd grown up privileged, on the right street, in the right part of Atlanta. Not me. Jail? I looked at Jamison, for him to do something. To stop them from taking me away. This thing wasn't for me.

"Baby," he said, still being held by the officers, "just go with them and I'll come get you. I promise."

"But I didn't do anything."

"Mrs. Taylor," Officer Cox said, "because we all saw you assault your husband, we're going to have to take you in for domestic violence."

"Domestic violence?" I couldn't trust the echoes vibrating through my ears. "But he's here with that woman cheating on me." My spine began to twitch as the baby shifted, panicking, from side to side.

"I know. But because we saw you and our captain is with us, we have to do this. If the captain wasn't with us, we could let you go, but we have to protect ourselves. You understand?" Her voice turned to reason for a second and she slid the cuffs on and began to read me my Miranda rights. The crowd, which had grown even larger, stood silent in fear and amazement.

"That ain't necessary, officer," one woman said, "She's pregnant. Just let her go."

"Yeah," other people agreed. But it was too late. My hands cuffed on top of my belly, I watched them all desperately as the officer began walking me to the car. I turned again to see Jamison still standing there, looking at me helplessly. He'd done this to us, to me. I was being sent to jail for hitting a man who had beaten my heart to a pulp.

"You'll be out quickly," the female officer said, helping me into the car. The rainbow of lights went shining again and we were off.

Don't miss Grace Octavia's
SOMETHING SHE CAN FEEL
Available in trade paperback in July, 2009
wherever books are sold!

Prologue

DOA

June 22, 2008
Ghana, West Africa

There was a click. There was a bang.

And then everything behind me went frozen. Dead.

My arms reached out toward the man falling to the ground in front of me. My heart stopped beating. The only sounds in the room were the bracelets clanking on my wrists and the thump the stranger's head made as it bounced hard against the bar room floor. I stood above him, frozen in place, and my throat felt tight and grainy. I couldn't breathe. Couldn't think of what to do next. This was the closest I'd ever been to someone so near death, and the farthest I'd ever been from home.

When it was done, when it seemed that I and everyone else in the back room was sure the thing was over, time flickered from being a still, silent thing to something real, something moving, quick and sneaky. This was no picture. No fiction. Not a part of the love poem I'd written in my notebook. It was the real thing. What in the hell was I doing there?

I gasped.

I heard the sound of a woman, who I thought was one of the waitresses, screaming, a glass hitting the floor. I could see the gun, pointed up now, in his other hand.

"He's dead. Oh-oh, my God, he's dead," I said, falling out of the bar behind Dame. The street was empty and we rushed, one behind the other, to hide behind an old van parked a ways down. "You killed him," I said.

I turned and tried to stop to look at Dame. I wanted to see his eyes, So I could know that we both knew what was going on, what had happened in just seconds.

Minutes earlier, we'd been laughing with the stranger in the red shirt and tan hat. His skin was the color and shine of oil. He hovered above our table, his teeth and eyes perfectly white and glowing in the dim light. He'd smiled wide when I told him that since we'd been in Ghana, Dame's already-shadowy skin had tanned to the color of midnight and my once-permed hair had sweated out into a moist, perfect afro. We were two lovers, mismatched and careless in the middle of a strange place, drunk from liquor that had no label and heat that made my reality a blissful haze.

"I ain't kill that fool," Dame said, tossing me back around before I could get a look at his eyes. "He was dead long before I got a hand on him."

I heard wrestling and shouting coming up the street. I craned my neck around the back of the van to see the bar emptying out. People were pointing in different directions along the dirt road and speaking a language I didn't know.

"Go," Dame said, his hand pushing hard at my back.

We hustled fast, in silence now, to the car, which seemed so far away. One of my bracelets popped and the wooden beads—red, black, and green, spelling out my name in rude, hand-painted white letters—scattered J-O-U-R-N-E-Y everywhere.

*   *   *

"Get everything. Everything," Dame said after he'd kicked in the door to our hotel room. "I'm calling Benji. We going back to Accra right now."

He paced the floor, flipping his cell phone open and closed as I sat motionless in the space I'd found in the middle of the bed. Dame was in a rage. Moving his body around heavily, deliberately like a boxer.

I didn't know what would happen next. I had to think. I needed to pray.

With my purse still on my shoulder, I looked around. Everything was the same. The same as it was when we'd left the room that morning. My sea-colored sarong was on the floor. His sneakers were next to the nightstand. Outside, the black night above the beach was awaiting our nightly walk. It was still Kumasi. But everything was different.

I closed my eyes to pray for clarity. For forgiveness. For the man's soul. For Dame's soul. For anything I could think of. Just in that one second. To try to understand. But all I could hear was *bang. Bang. Bang.*

"This shit ain't working," I heard Dame say. I opened my eyes and looked up to see him looking at the phone and then at me. "Journey," Dame called, walking to me, "What you doing? We got to go."

"I—I . . ." I wanted to say something, but I kept remembering the blood choking out of the man's stomach as he landed at my feet.

"J," Dame said softly, bending down in front of me at the foot of the bed. "We don't have time for you to get all nervous now. We got to get out of here. You saw those people. They gonna come for us."

I watched as he tried to soften his eyes to persuade me. But I could not be moved. The man I was in love with just took someone's life. Was he a man at all? Had I just been lying to myself all these weeks? Was everyone else right about Dame?

"You didn't have to do that," I said.

"Fuck!" Dame got up and turned his back.

"If you'd just let Benji come with us . . . everything would've been . . ." I got up and followed him as he rushed to the closet.

"Fine?" He looked at me as he pulled out our suitcases. "You said you wanted me to yourself."

"Yeah," I cried, "but I didn't think anything like this would happen."

"What do you think the bodyguards are for, J? You ain't with some random nigga. Everywhere I go, some fool comes up to test me," he said frustrated. He threw the bags onto the bed and then began clumsily tossing things from the floor inside of them.

"But you still didn't have to do that. You shot that man."

"He pulled out a gun. He would've killed both of us."

"It was just on the table. He didn't say he was going to use it. He just wanted your watch." I looked down at the circle of diamonds and platinum hanging heavy and oversized from his wrist. Suddenly it seemed incredibly out of place.

"So, I was supposed to give it to him and then he was just gonna let us walk out of there? It don't work like that."

"I don't know," I said. "But I know that you didn't have to let things get out of control."

"Look, I ain't no country nigga that's about to have some fool that ain't even pointed a gun at me take my shit. He took the gun out first. He should've used it first. I ain't no pussy and if you want a pussy, I believe you got one at home waiting on you."

"Don't bring him into this."

"Well, that's what you wanted, right?" Dame stopped again and looked at me, his dark eyes seemingly looking right through me. "Me to talk it out and shit? Give that motherfucker my watch and then buy him dinner? Drinks on me? Right?" He turned to me and I could see beads of sweat swelling across his tattoo-covered skin. A picture of Mary and Jesus on his stomach; a cross etched over his chest; his grandmother's name on his right arm; the entire continent of Africa across his back, the northernmost tip near his left ear and the southernmost by his rear. He was all strength. His muscles moved in consistent, solid shapes when he took a single step. Massive and strong. I once loved this. But now he seemed larger than anything I could handle. Almost dangerous. He snatched the bag from the bed and turned around, nearly hitting me with it.

"I just don't understand you."

"Understand me?" He threw the bag down angrily and hurried over to me, grabbing my arms and pushing me up against the wall. A vein shuddered in his right temple. I saw the devil in him suddenly, pulsing in erratic red threads in his eyes. He wasn't even thinking. Pressed against me, I could feel his heart thumping madly, faster than the seconds that ran by. "Don't try to fucking understand me. I told you not to." His voice was hard and distant. "I ain't that man. I ain't him. I ain't . . ." He shoved me against the wall again and pushed away from me. "Shit," he shouted, turning away and balling up his fists, punching at the air in anger. "I knew this would happen if I brought you here. You don't belong here."

"What?" Still up against the wall and afraid to move, I began crying. Now my heart was thumping and twitching in fear. I struggled to breathe. "Now I don't belong here? What about everything you said?"

"Look," he turned and came back to me, "I ain't trying to be understood. I ain't that motherfucker. I'm from the street. All I know how to do is live. Stay alive." Spit gathered at the sides of his mouth and tears glossed his eyes, but in his rage not one would fall. "I'm an animal." He swung at the wall to the right of my head and his fist went right through to the other side. He pulled his hand out of the wall and blood dripped to the floor. "I'm a fucking king. No one in the world understands me. Not supposed to."

"Oh, my God, what did you do?" I said. I tried to grab his arm, but he pushed me to the floor.

"Take the car and go," he said, his voice now void of any emotion. He reached into his pocket, pulled out the car keys and threw them at me. "Go back to Accra and get on the first plane back to Alabama. Get as far away from me as you can."

"But, Dame," I said, picking up the keys and fighting to see him through the tears in my eyes. He wasn't thinking. "They're gonna come for you."

He looked at me hard and just before a single tear fell from his right eye, calm and clear as the waves outside the door, he whispered, "Go," and walked out.

Journey . . . Just Living

June 23, 2008
Sunrise

My father lied to me. Love does hurt. In fact, sometimes, love can hurt so badly it burns your insides fast and heartless like the reddest part of a flame. Now I'd known this for a long time. I'd seen that red flame in my mother's eyes when my father didn't come home from Bible study some nights, even heard it in the cutting cries of my best friend when the love of her life hurt her and let her down again and again, so hard all she could do was weep. But I'd never felt it for myself. Never been there, out on the flame, burning and ready to die for something I'd loved with all of my living heart. I'd been safe from it all. In the incubator my life had built around me. Until that morning. The morning after Dame left me alone on the floor of a hotel room in the middle of nowhere in the world. Through the blue-black night, I'd found my way out of Kumasi and to the airport just as the sun rose in the sky. After spending every nickel I had on each of the plastic cards in my wallet to get on a plane home, I was standing outside on the tarmac of the runway waiting to board a plane back to the United States.

Flicking the ticket in my hand back and forth to create some coolness in the already-humid morning heat, I felt a sinking in my insides I'd never known. Hours ago I had everything I ever wanted. Freedom. Music. And true love. Out of my incubator, I'd convinced myself that that was all I needed from the world to survive. I'd risked everything for that. Walked away from my whole life. And now it was all gone. Just like that. I was going home. Alone. Hopeless. And feeling like a complete fool. My mother was right. I was thirty-three years old and playing with my life like I was a child.

I kept running through everything that had happened. Dame's hand on my thigh. The man sitting at our table. The watch. The gun. The bang. The fight. It wasn't real. I wanted so badly to hate Dame for everything that had gone wrong. For leaving me. But the Dame from last night wasn't the Dame I knew. Wasn't the Dame I loved. And standing there in that line, hurt from everything else in the world, my heart felt pain because I really wanted him to come chase after me. To at least apologize. Even I knew that was crazy. But it was true. Hidden in my heart, it was true. And I kept peeking over my shoulder to see if he'd appear. Lord, I prayed he'd come running. To make this all right. To make me not seem so crazy for turning my back on my life—my family, my friends, my world—for him. Foolish. But I looked and looked and he never came.

"Mother Africa will wait for you to return. Don't worry," a voice announced behind me as I looked out of the window after boarding the plane. I turned to see a slender, dark brown man, dressed in a navy blue business suit seated next to me in the aisle. He was handsome and I could tell by his accent that he was Ghanaian.

"I hope so," I said weakly and praying he would just leave me with my thoughts. I didn't feel like talking. I looked back at the gate door outside of the window.

"Oh, I see this all of the time—people crying as they lift off. Thinking this lovely place will just disappear. Just die. But no worries. Your mother is stronger than time. She has a secret and she is the only continent that can survive a living death. She'll survive forever. She'll always be here for you." He sounded eloquent and melancholy, like a poet. Through the corner of my eye I saw him ease back in his seat and put on his seatbelt as the flight attendant walked by.

"You must fly a lot then," I said.

"More than I'd like to. But it comes with the job." He extended his hand to shake mine. "Kweku Emmanuel Onyeche, attorney at law."

"Journey Cash. And I'm . . . just . . . living."

It takes sixteen hours to get to the United States from Ghana—and that doesn't include the layover. When I first got on the plane on the way over to Ghana with Dame, I wasn't even worried about the time. Others had Sudoku and laptops and DVDS and iPods, anything to keep them busy. All I had was my hand in Dame's and a smile plastered on my face. We'd laugh and joke and touch the whole way and even when we slept, we'd still be together. It seemed then that that was all that mattered.

Now I was two hours into my return flight and with only my mind to occupy me, I was feeling restless and burdened by my sadness. A baby, who'd been wailing during takeoff, probably because of the air pressure building up, had finally been calmed and the flight attendants were busy serving drinks in the aisles, so I couldn't get up to walk around. Kweku, who I could tell was a bit older than me by his graying, distinguished side burns, was reading a magazine and clearly avoiding a stack of papers he'd set on the table in from of him. I looked out of the window at the blueness surrounding the plane and thought of Dame. Of our poem.

"I am worried about what people will say," I heard Kweku say. I turned to see him still looking at his magazine, so I didn't say anything. Perhaps he was reading aloud. "I wonder what they will say if I let you return to the U.S. looking so sad, 'Journey Cash . . . just living.' "

"I stopped caring about what people had to say a long time ago," I said, looking back to the blueness.

"Point taken. But this is my homeland we're talking about here. And I can't have them thinking it was Ghana that gave you such a sad face. So I'm thinking, "Kweku, how do you get rid of this sad face to ensure the positive image of your country?' Ah! I must cheer up this pretty girl." He wagged his index finger in my face knowingly and we both laughed. "Now I could turn on my lethal charm and romance her like any true Ghanaian man would . . . but something tells me that perhaps it is not the attention of a man she needs." He tilted his head toward me for a response.

"No," I said with sadness infiltrating even this single syllable.

"So . . . then I think, perhaps it is an ear she needs."

"No, not that either."

He slid the magazine onto the pile of papers and folded his arms across his chest as we sat there in what seemed an unexpected silence. A man seated behind me began coughing and wrestled to clear his throat.

"Look," I started, "I've been through some crazy stuff and now I just want to go ho—" I couldn't finish my sentence. My voice splintered and I knew not to keep talking or I'd begin to cry.

"Easy," he said calmly. And when he moved to pat my knee, I could smell jasmine and oak. It was soft, yet masculine, a familiar scent I'd gathered in sniffs surrounding most of the well-to-do men I'd met in Ghana.

"I just—" I whispered. "I can't."

"We have a long time together. And nowhere to go. So we might as well talk. Now, I could talk about myself, but my life is all contracts and reports." He pointed to the pile. "It would bore you to death. At least it did to my last wife."

"She left you?"

"No, she died. Literally . . . was listening to one of my stories from work one day and just died."

I wanted to laugh, but the solemn look on his face was so serious. And I didn't know if he was kidding or not.

"Just fooling with you," he said finally and we both laughed. "But I am making a point. No one wants to hear about my life."

"Fine, but I don't know if I'm ready to talk about what happened."

"Well, maybe you don't have to. If you don't want to talk about what's wrong now . . . maybe start with when everything was right."

"Right . . . my life . . . when everything was right?" I exhaled and looked at him. Even in my gloom, pictures, moments came and I felt silly for even pulling them toward me. I had no clue who the man was sitting next to me. But something about him relaxed me. His confidence, the sincerity in his voice. He had the patience of my grandfather in his eyes and somehow I felt I could trust him. I had to trust somebody. I looked at the time. More than twelve hours to go. "Are you serious?" I was feeling weakened and wanting to embrace anything that would quiet my sadness. If for just a moment.

"Yes! Start wherever you like. When times were good— great." He looked off as if he was imagining my doing something fun. Dancing. Canoeing. Camping. "Before any of this thing that's troubling you even began."

"But that was a long time ago."

"If we have nothing, we have time," Kweku said, pushing back his chair to relax. "And if we run out of stuff, I guess we'll talk about . . . the contracts."

"Funny," I said, looking to the other side of the plane and

wondering where I could begin to tell my story to this stranger. "Well," I began, "and I still don't know why I'm telling you this . . . but," I took a deep breath, "if I had to start with when everything seemed good—great, I'd have to begin with my wedding."